AF251695

TOM QUINN

AND THE
OTHERWORLD

K. A. CANAZZI

First published by Dog Ear Publishing
4010 W. 86th Street, Ste H
Indianapolis, IN 46268
www.dogearpublishing.net

ISBN: 978-159858-572-8

This book is printed on acid-free paper.
This book is a work of Fiction. Places,
events, and situations in this book are
purely Fictional and any resemblance
to actual persons, living or dead,
is coincidental.

Printed in the United States of America

ILLUSRATIONS   KATHRYN DONATELLI

TO CREATIVITY'S HANDMAIDEN,

PERSEVERANCE

1

NOT SO LONG AGO

Not so very long ago, spring was blossoming into summer. A soft blue mist was settling over the evening mountains. The land was covered in a coat of bright, rich greens. Streams ran sparkling waters down through the sloping forests to the meadows below. Night-blooming flowers were just opening their petals and releasing an intoxicating scent into the twilight. It was the smell of new life, powdery, sweet, and fresh. It was the time for uncurling, undoing, unwrapping all that had been hiding, waiting to come out from under the folds of winter.

Even the dreary coal town at the end of the mountain road was feeling the effects of spring. Ordinarily, the coal dust and street dirt had a permanent grip on this place. It was everywhere. It was in your mouth when you talked and in your lungs when you breathed. It crawled up the sides of newly painted houses and into the cupboards where food was kept. The women engaged in a daily battle, washing it back from the floors and soaping it out of their clothes.

Indeed, this town was covered in a pall of greys and black. The early spring hadn't brought much promise with its storms of rain and mud. But now, tonight, as if by magic, there was an overpowering appearance of green—green leaves overhead in the scanty trees—green grass along the spattered fences—green buds everywhere, forcing their way out of scrawny twigs.

People opened their doors and windows to the breezes. Instead of hurrying their children to bed, the women let them continue to play in the yards and on the porches. The night had a marvelous floating quality to it. People just hung about outside, suspended in the moment. The men tramped home from the mines to their usual watering hole at the corner pub. Somehow, they didn't feel the same eagerness to drown their day's end in drink. A number of them had pulled a couple of tables out front and were leaning back in their chairs, swapping stories and sipping their beers.

Up in the mountains
the blue mist swirled and
descended closer to the trees,
revealing the first stars
in the sky...

2

ANN QUINN

Ann Quinn felt the change in the air. She was drawn from her vigil at the bed, drawn from her cares, to open the door and to go out upon the porch. Sitting there on the steps, she took a long breath of the sweet air and couldn't help but feel all the aching, lovely beauty of existence. All around her, she could feel the wonder of life renewing itself.

If only one could live on just these sensations alone. If one didn't have to hunger and to struggle so endlessly. Oh, if she could have things as they were in the beginning. If she could have her husband back, young and strong again, instead of as he was now— lying there so weak and fretful, dying from black coal dust smothering his lungs.

Looking back at him, she remembered how everlastingly tired she was. The scent of the flowers in the air made her hope and cry at the same time. Caught she was: caught in a terrible grind that was wearing her down. She thought of her son Tom. What could she tell him of life? Why had she brought him here? Certainly it wasn't to suffer so.

It seemed such a short time ago when she was young: when she was going to have her chance to make a home, to have a family, to make things better in spite of her poverty. Her love was strong then, and she and her husband were going to make a difference. They were simple folk. They worked hard with their hearts and their hands. But working hard had not made a bit of difference. Her husband had given his life to the mine, and it had simply crushed him under. She had worked and scrubbed and kept faith, only to sit here now and wait for her husband's final moments. What of her son Tom? What would become of him? She could feel her own strength failing with every labored breath her husband took. Without him she could go no further. What about Tom? What was to become of Tom?

Ann turned her back on the summer night and went again to her candle by the bed. As she often did, she took out her little book of prayers and opened it at random for guidance. It said, "Therefore, my beloved, be steadfast, unmovable, always excelling in the work of the Lord, because you know that in the Lord your labor is not in vain." On another page it said, "Teach me the way I should go." *Yes,* she thought, *let not our living be in vain. Show me the way I must go.*

She washed her husband's sweaty face and touched him with infinite tenderness. There was something wonderful between them, something so fulfilling and beautiful that none of life's misfortunes could ever take away. Their son had been born of it. In the midst of all this sorrow, had she managed to transfer any of this joy to her little son? His spirit was buoyant and open, but what was to become of him now? So ran Ann Quinn's thoughts as she held her husband's hand and stroked his brow all through the night.

3

SUMMER NIGHT

In the dark trees silhouetted against the turning sky, a crow called three times. An owl looked down with blazing eyes to the forest floor. Below, the cool mist was swirling now, as if it were alive. A great charge of energy was moving within it. There was a powerful surging up and coming down of air, but not the slightest disturbance amongst the leaves.

In a grassy circle surrounded by giant oaks, the mist concentrated. Tiny sparkles began to appear, rushing up and down the currents of air like sparks shooting up from a great fire—except there was no fire. If anyone had seen this, it would have struck fear and amazement into their eyes and their feet would have turned and run, for surely this was the work of the devil. But there was no one there, and this energy came not from the devil, but from life and the Light.

Indeed, there was no *Human* there, but other presences were making themselves felt. It became apparent first in the look of the trees. The great oaks that formed this forest ring appeared to step out of themselves to form a second inner ring. No, it was not the trees themselves, but somehow their essences moved forward in slow measured steps. These shadowy giants moved with solemn knowing to create a kind of protective boundary for all this electric energy.

Now, even more strangely, from the roots and earth about the trees emerged vaporous creatures that grew more solid as they became more active. Their brownish bodies were Human-like, but short and stubby. They moved, or rather bounded about, quite happily, shouting things to each other that couldn't be heard, pointing up and creating a silent racket about the sparks dancing above. Those sparks were becoming larger, and inside each of their glowing shapes a lovely winged creature could be seen unfolding as if from sleep. Faeries they were—faeries of the Light. They were not solid, but translucent, tinged with color. Some glowed in reds and oranges and left fiery trails in the air, like fireflies; others were green and violet with opalescent wings.

Some of these enchanted beings swept down amongst the grasses, where they stretched and danced, assuming a height of almost Human proportions. Nothing but pure joyful exuberance was reflected in their beautiful faces. The energy in these creatures seemed to come from the very breath of life, as all around, nature burst forth with growth and abundance. Such was the faeries' magic. What was happening appeared to be some great joyous event with no other purpose than just to be. The little brown gnomes rolled on the ground, mimicking the faeries' flights, and made great sport of trying to catch their dancing feet.

And now the trees began to stir, their leaves making a glassy bell-like sound. Descending into the energy field came a magnificent presence that caused all the faeries to surge up and around it like a magnet. An angelic form of trailing crystal mist drew all within the circle into its aura and imbued them with a shining light. The faeries flew up and showered down again and again, creating a fountain of sparking energy suspended in the air. All night long the faeries danced, sending out wavy vibrations from this whirling center. And in the morning, not a trace was left of these mysterious fireworks, but the hills had burst into flower.

LIFE AND DEATH

"Go on out," Tom's mother had said. "Go out and take a walk. I'll be all right." For days now, things had been unbearably sad in Tom's house. His father was going to leave him forever. There had been many silent comings and goings of the neighborhood women as they tried to do what they could to help his mother. They formed a hovering pattern, circling, waiting for that final moment when his father would die. What was that going to be like? When would it be all over? What was life going to be like when his father was dead? It felt like a stone wall was crumbling at the base of his being. He should wait; he should stay with his mother. But at her urging he did go out. He walked out the door, down the streets, across the fields, to the edge of the mountain forest. He began to climb up the mountain slowly, and as he did, it was like a weight was being lifted from him. He had walked into another world. The trees were full of chirping birds; the sunlight dappled down through the leaves.

Back in town, what was going on in his house? That horrible nightmare wasn't real here. It was easy to think of returning home and finding everything as it had been for all of his twelve young years. His father would be there, washing up. His mother would be calling for them both to come in to supper. Tom sat down on a rocky outcropping and looked down at the town. Even while his father had been sick, things were still sort of all right. Tom had gotten used to his being at home in bed. But now he felt frightened to the core. Something was going to happen. He could feel it— everyone could.

Tom leaned back and felt the heat of the sun-warmed rocks radiate into his back. It felt good. It felt good to breathe the fresh air. It felt good to stretch his arms and feel the clear expanse of nature instead of the cramped, stale interior of his house. It felt good to be alive. Somehow that sensation made Tom feel guilty, for his father was dying.

Tom lay still for a few more moments, trying to soak up as much strength from the rock as he could. Then he stood up and braced himself for the return. On the way back, he walked as if he had lead in his shoes. He savored every bit of the reassuring beauty that nature had to give, for ahead of him was an uncertain future. Tom could see the whole town now, just a short ways away. Any moment he would be walking down its blackened streets. *Sad,* he thought, *the town is such a dark spot upon this beautiful countryside.* Trees had been felled; land had been flattened. Shabby little houses leaned together in faint-hearted rows. *Was it like this everywhere? Or was it because they were so poor that everything looked so bleak and ugly?* Tom thought again of his mother. Now he really had been gone too long. He found himself running in a panic to meet his fate.

The door to the house was open. The neighborhood women waited silently on the porch. Inside he could hear his mother crying. It had happened. His father was dead.

5

THE MINE

The mine was a cold place. Even when the men worked up a sweat, it would turn back to a chill if they stopped for long. Something about mines made a man work with a kind of urgency. Maybe because they were so far under the earth. Maybe because everything was so concentrated down there. There was nothing to deflect one's attention, nothing but the work of extracting coal from the walls of the earth. Or maybe it was because the air was so close and so precious there that every breath, every move, had to count.

Tom's father had never wanted him to work for the mining company. It had all been planned. Tom was going to school, and when he was seventeen, he would go to the city and live with his aunt until he could find a good job. But Tom was twelve now, and though he could read and write, there was nothing he could do but work in the mine if he was going to stay with his mother. He wouldn't leave her, even though she tried to convince him it would be best if he went to live with his aunt.

The mining company was only too happy to enroll another new worker who would learn to spend his life in its service. Officially, he was too young to work, but unofficially he was given the job of hauling coal in tunnels that were too small for the mule carts. And so, one sunlit day, Tom found himself crowded onto a platform elevator, and descending into the cold damp night of the mines. He pressed his forehead against the railing and peered into the void with ever-widening eyes. The men loomed tall above him, talking, laughing, coughing, while Tom felt smaller and smaller as the darkness engulfed him.

At the bottom, the giant cage lifted its door and the men spilled out into the underworld. They were in a large central cavern where an ailing generator grunted out just enough energy to infuse a dusty string of light bulbs with flickering light. Everyone seemed to know what they were doing and where they were going. Teams of men marched into black-mouthed tunnels, and mules emerged from the jaws of others with full carts of coal. They crossed through the main cavern and returned to the surface in a long, laborious ascent.

Tom was handed over to Jacob, or "the Little Man," as the men called him. This strange little being promptly sized him up and proclaimed, "You won't last two weeks."

"That's just ten days longer than we thought you'd last," smirked one of the other men.

The Little Man didn't take too kindly to that remark and gave Tom a gruff shove, saying, "Follow me."

Tom fell in behind this child-midget-man as he walked off in the direction of the mule carts. Jacob was a perfect little caricature of a grown man, although he was younger and shorter than Tom. His walk, his gestures, the way he wore his clothes—even his gear appeared to be miniaturized for him. From his belt hung little picks and axes. He wore his miner's hat like a veteran.

"This here's this, an' this here's that," he was saying, throwing back explanatory remarks for Tom to catch as he stumbled along. At one point, he stopped short, turned to Tom, and said, "Whatever you do, if the canaries stop singing, run for your life!" Tom was about to ask what he meant, but the Little Man was off marching again, explaining something else over his shoulder.

Then Tom remembered that his dad had talked about the caged canaries hanging in the tunnels. Those delicate creatures warned of sudden death in the mines. They were the first to be killed if a pocket of poisonous gas was released by the digging. Tom was already beginning to feel oppressed by this place, and the thought of the canaries' purpose there made him want to turn and run for the elevator shaft. He took a determined breath and walked faster; after all, this was going to be his life from now on, and he'd better get used to everything in this dark prison.

He began to feel the cold dampness his father had complained about, and he noticed that the walls looked like they were sweating. Water seeped into the mine from underground streams, and there was constant danger from breakthroughs and floods. Tom remembered many a time when he and his mother had run to the mining office at the sound of the alarm. They would wait there with the other wives and children for news of injuries or an all-clear sign.

* * *

Tom's duties were simple enough, although exhausting. He was to stick with the mule carts, help load, keep the animals moving, and pick up their droppings. The Little Man was a celebrated mascot and a general to the small force of children working in the mines. Jacob was the envy of his little army. Nobody else was outfitted like him. He had a feisty dash, while the others remained a sorrowful, reluctant troop.

In the ceaseless days ahead, Tom found the only spark of spirit he felt was when he got to walk back up the grade with the mule carts to the surface, where there was fresh air and light. It was then that he fell in love with the color green. He couldn't bear to return to the mine without carrying with him some sign of life, and for him that was leaves—green leaves. He would stuff sweet-smelling leaves into his pockets and tuck them in the brim of his cap. The men were quick to dub him Leaf Boy or

Elf Boy. Tom didn't mind. It gave him a kind of joking notoriety, and any kind of distinction was better than nothing in this drab colorless life.

* * *

The folklore of faeries and elves was very much alive in the year 1917. In the countryside, tales of ghosts and forest spirits, of people disappearing overnight and returning to swear they had been captured by faeries, were well known. Although these were modern times, such beliefs lived side by side with electric lights and motorcars. Science and logic were making great strides, but nobody saw anything incongruous in keeping a healthy respect for the spirit world. Over the centuries, man has been helped or hindered by all manner of creatures from a Parallel World that a few of us are fortunate enough to perceive.

Stories began to circulate about Tom. The one that stuck was that he was not the real Tom Quinn: the real one had been captured by faeries and he was their weakling replacement. As Tom passed by, a miner would call out, "So where is the real Tom Quinn?" Tom was ready with some fantastic answer, "He's sitting at a banquet eating a fine steak, with the Queen of Faeries pouring him a drink." The men liked his imaginative alternatives to the drudgery they performed day in and day out.

As the months went on, Tom began to wish more than ever that at least one of his stories were true. That he wasn't there, that he could be somewhere else, was all he ever thought of—until he remembered the sorrows of his poor mother, and then he worked on with grim determination.

6

UNDER THE OAK TREE

Sometimes a being exists that doesn't have the slightest idea of how it got here. It just is, and that's the sum total of it. That's the kind of creature Braggs was. He didn't even know how he got to be called Braggs. As far as he knew, he had always been so, and that was enough for him. He had his own place, he knew what to do, and he did it, for centuries.

Braggs lived in the world parallel to ours—a seldom seen world. For a hundred years, he had lived at the foot of an oak tree. He took care of it; he assisted it. He could disperse himself down through to its very roots and materialize again outside its bark. He could swing on the leaves at the very top near the sky, or he could run down its limbs to the ground below as if it were a spiral staircase. He could fully materialize, looking as dense as a Human, but that took a lot of energy and there wasn't much need for it these days, so he preferred to stay in a semi-transparent form when he wasn't resting in the earth by the tree. Braggs could do a bit of shapeshifting if he wanted to, but mostly he remained about four inches tall, a stubby, gnarly-looking old man, much like the tree he lived by. He wore a brownish cap and tunic that had been in style in medieval times. He saw no reason to change, but he could conjure up any kind of clothing, feathers, or furs when he was doing one of his famous "imitations" for his friends.

There were things Braggs knew and many things he didn't, but he was full of bluster about those he did. He liked to stomp about for others of his clan and make proclamations, much like the schoolteacher he'd once seen pointing out plants in the forest. Whatever he saw that interested him, whether animals or the occasional Human passing by, he incorporated into his colorful mirror-like personality. He and his fellows could laugh for hours somersaulting through imitations of things they saw: they were all great mimics. Braggs's life was joyous and busy. He really loved his tasks, but he liked to make a big deal out of everything. He always seemed to be grumbling or exasperated. One thing he really didn't like was change. In all the places he had lived—and that hadn't been many—he hated it if he had to move.

Humans called him a gnome, brownie, or elf, or nothing at all if they couldn't perceive him. But he was Braggs, and he existed, all right. If he could have made himself heard from the Parallel World, he would have had a lot to say about it, too. Humans who do perceive this other world say that they can see these little creatures' mouths moving and hands waving about, but they can't really hear them. It doesn't come through. It is only by a kind of telepathy that Humans and those in the Ethereal World are able to communicate.

Braggs wasn't exactly what one would call a thinker, but he did have some thoughts about his tree and other occurrences in his world. His favorite time to do this thinking was in the late afternoon, when the sun shone through the leaves at the base of the tree. This year, conditions had been just right and he'd been able to cultivate a crop of mushrooms on one side of the tree among the roots. He derived great pleasure from these umbrella-like mushrooms. They didn't come up every year, so it was a great treat when they did.

One summer afternoon, he was sitting on top of a mushroom having his afternoon think when he heard a great angry thrashing and crashing in the woods. Braggs immediately evaporated into the tree. When he stuck his head out again, he saw a young Human boy tramping through the woods carrying a big dry branch, angrily beating the wind and the grass with it as he trudged toward Braggs's very tree. Braggs could see that the boy was looking about for some place to rest, and he hoped it wasn't going to be against his oak tree.

Closer and closer the boy came, with his swinging branch and his sad, angry face. Braggs jumped out of the tree half-materialized, but it was too late. Here came the boy's shabby-britched backside down against the oak roots, and down went the branch beside him, square on top of the mushrooms!

Braggs was furious, jumping all around, shaking his fists, and uttering the most horrible curses. "Look what you've done!" he shouted, and cursed again. But the boy was oblivious to him, and besides, he looked cursed already, he was so withdrawn inside his troubled self.

Braggs had to be content with shapeshifting into a gnat and insanely dive-bombing about, trying to roust the intruder. When that didn't work, he had one of his bird friends perch on a branch above and drop a real bomb on top of the boy's head. That did it. Braggs was beside himself with laughter and triumph as the boy jumped up in surprise and disgust and picked up his branch.

The boy was about to move away when he did the strangest thing. As he lifted up the branch, he realized he had knocked over the most perfect little mushroom patch. He knelt down and tried to prop up the ones that weren't damaged. He spent time replacing everything he had disturbed. Braggs was in the midst of transforming himself back from his gnat shape, but he was so amazed at what he was seeing that he just stood there, half gnat, half gnome, watching as the boy repaired his little mushroom grove.

Braggs was disturbed. To dislike something was understandable, but to dislike something and like it at the same time was just too confusing, especially if that something happened to be Human. For the rest of the afternoon, Braggs sat thinking in that same half-transformed state, looking like a bizarre carnival costume with legs.

7

HOLDING ON

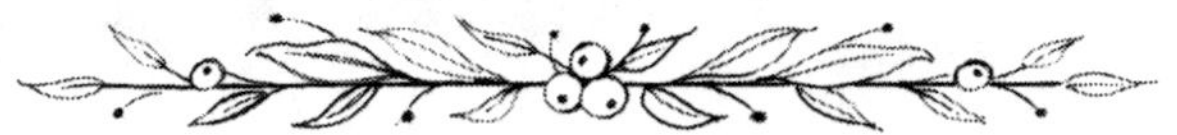

Ann Quinn tried to hold the fabric of her life together, but everything seemed to be unraveling since her husband had died. She went about now in a distracted way, never completing anything she did. She worried constantly and couldn't concentrate. Truth was, she didn't care about anything any more except her son Tom. Her dresses went without buttons and her hair was always in slight disarray. She tried to make everything seem normal, but she frightened Tom with her wandering mind. She couldn't stand to be in the house alone and was always inviting one of the neighborhood wives to come and spend time with her. Everyone felt her mental distress. She prayed to God for strength, but she felt so alone and half dead. Things were slipping away from her.

Tom tried to be everything to her: son, friend, father, protector. He went whistling to the mines every day and came back with a smile on his face, but Ann knew he was miserable. She was afraid for him all the time down in the damp tunnels.

One evening, Tom came home with his usual show of happy nonchalance. He hummed a tune as he opened the door and flung his hat on the hat rack like his father used to do. He was surprised to find the house cleaner and neater than it had been since his father died. The floors smelled of cleaning wax and the windows were shining. The table was set like it used to be, with flowers in the middle. When he went into the kitchen, there was his mother with her hair combed nicely and her apron pressed. The most wonderful meal was cooking on the stove, and bread was warming in the oven.

Tom fairly melted with happiness as he sat down for dinner. Ann served him a delicious supper, and they both ate in warm appreciative silence. Afterwards, Ann sat back and looked lovingly around her little house. When her eyes met Tom's, she said, "Son, I want to talk something over with you."

Tom froze solid as if she had just thrown a bucket of ice water at him. "What about?" he stammered, holding down a wave of anxiety.

"Well, Tom, some people are coming over tomorrow to look at the house."

Tom looked around. "Wh-wh-what do you mean?" Something big, a big bad thing, was coming, and Tom squirmed in his seat against hearing it.

"Some men from the mining company are coming over. I'm thinking of selling this house, and the mine has agreed to buy it back from us with a little extra for the improvements we've made over the years. I don't want you—"

Tom jumped up from the table and ran to his mother in disbelief. "Sell our house? What do you mean? I'm working, we're doing all right! Why are you—"

"Tom, Tommy!" Ann held him close. There were tears in her eyes as she stroked his tousled hair and rested her head on his young shoulder. "Tom," she said, straightening up and gathering herself together, "We're not doing all right, and you know it. Winter is coming, and it will get even worse for me, and especially for you, working in that cold dampness. Your father didn't want that for you. I must do something before everything slips away."

Tom struggled against her words and her grasp. "What are you talking about, slipping away? Everything is all right! I can do more—you'll see..."

"No, listen to me, Tom," Ann said with all the strength she could muster. "Here's what I want to do. It's for the best. I want to sell this house, and with the money, I want to send you to your Aunt Petra in the city."

Tom angrily started to cry. "I won't leave you!" he said desperately.

But Ann went on like she was reading from her last will and testament. "With the money from the house, I'll rent a room with the neighbor, Mrs. Kearny, and I'll help her with the children. She will take care of my food and other little necessities."

"Other necessities?" Tom wailed. "What necessities? I'll get you anything you need!"

Ann went on, "I haven't been feeling well. I need rest and some medication—nothing serious. But I would feel so relieved and would get well so much faster if I knew you were living with Aunt Petra in that nice house and going to a good school."

By this time, Tom had collapsed back into his chair. He was not listening any more. His world was crashing down around him. He just kept saying, "No, don't do this, I don't want to go."

Ann finished by saying, "Tom, I'm telling you all this because it's been on my mind. The men will come tomorrow and they will make their offer in a few days. We'll talk about this again, but I've got to go to bed now. I'm so tired. Will you clean up the dishes?"

Tom saw a ray of hope. The die wasn't cast yet. Maybe the deal would fall through. He would do something—anything—to get more money to keep his mother from selling the house. As he put the dishes away, he dreamt up all sorts of fantastic schemes to save his mother and the house. But by the time he laid his head down to sleep, he was feeling anxious and hopeless again.

8

AUNT PETRA

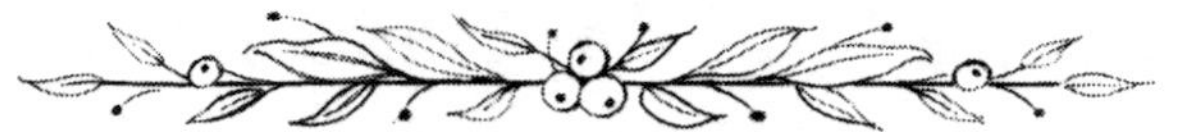

The city where Great-Aunt Petra lived had been built with money from the mining company and the surrounding farmlands. There were banks and offices and motorcar traffic that now competed with the horse-drawn carriages. This was a town in transition, marching with burgeoning confusion into the new century.

Aunt Petra lived in the old section of town, the part of town built with graciousness and planning. There, the trees formed shady canopies overhead. Streets radiated out from a circle that once was planted with beautiful rose bushes. The area was called Parkmont. No longer considered the fashionable place to live, it was becoming slightly weedy around the edges. There were other more modern affluent sections of town, but none had the same effect on a person as Parkmont. Everyone who entered it gave an unconscious sigh of relief. The great, leafy trees formed a kind of sound barrier against the noisy street racket all around. The atmosphere made one instantly relax and walk slower. Upon leaving, everyone always had the same thought: *Now, why can't the rest of the city be like this?* But soon such nostalgic notions would be swept away again in the scurry of modern city life. There was no time any more to sit on those cool verandas in Parkmont. No, what was needed were more apartment buildings and corner markets, more bars and hotels to accommodate the great, restless influx of jobless men and women looking for salvation in the city.

Aunt Petra had been born in the same foothill town as Tom; she was Tom's great-aunt on his father's side. Petra had been a sunny, bright spot in everyone's lives from the moment she was born. She had a natural joviality and saw only the best in people. She was simple-hearted and had no great expectations for herself other than to remain loving and happy.

One day a young man, an accountant, came to the coal town to do some short-term work for the mining company. He fell instantly in love with Petra's plumb freshness as she walked by him on her way down the street. Everyone in the family always considered her the lucky one, the one that got away, for she soon married the accountant and went to live in the city. Her husband adored and idolized her. He bought her pretty clothes and antiques. An accountant's salary didn't allow extravagance, but he was able to buy the house in Parkmont and live very comfortably with his little "Pet."

In the early years of their marriage, they employed a housekeeper named Mrs. Savage. She was devoted to Aunt Pet and her husband. "Good Mrs. Savage," as they called her, was especially helpful during the sudden illness of Petra's husband, and after his passing, Good Mrs. Savage moved in to look after Pet and keep up the house. Aunt Pet always referred to her companion as her guardian angel, for as the years passed and after Petra had her first stroke, she could do nothing without the help of Mrs. Savage.

* * *

Visitors were not a common occurrence anymore at the Parkmont house. When the letter came from Ann asking to send young Tom to her, Petra was delighted and positively rejuvenated by the idea. Since she was paralyzed now on her right side, she asked Mrs. Savage to write the return letter.

Mrs. Savage dutifully went to the writing desk to carry out the task. There was something almost peevish about the way she drew up the chair and took out the pen and paper from the drawer. Maybe it was the summer heat, or maybe she didn't want to take the time to answer the letter at that moment, but whatever it was that made her set her lips just so, Aunt Petra didn't notice. She was so happy, gazing out the window, thinking about what it would be like when youth came back to live with her.

9

A FAERY WHIRL

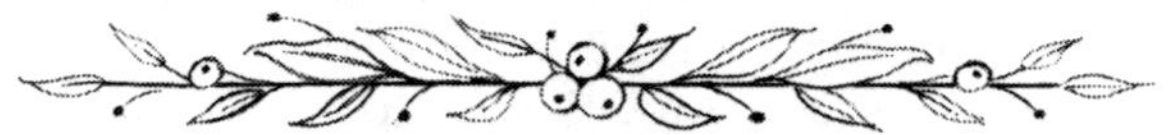

There is a saying that country people know:
"Betwixt the between,
that's where faeries can be seen."
Where water meets land, where earth opens to air, where elements cross, that's where entrances and exits to the Parallel World can be found. In the past, there have been minglings between Humans and the Faery World. The worlds were once much closer than they are now. It is said faeries liked to capture and keep young children to rejuvenate their lineage. While their world affords them many pleasures and powers, faeries are fascinated with humanity. It is the Human soul and consciousness they are drawn to, but cannot really fathom.

A faery's essence is like that of a stringed musical instrument—a harp, perhaps. They respond to the delicate vibrations in nature. They absorb vital energies and infuse them back again, amplified, into their surroundings. In nature, where faeries thrive, there is lushness and growth; where they are not, there is harshness and drought.

* * *

Something peculiar happened one afternoon in late summer when the miners were having their annual picnic. Many of the families caravanned up to a grassy spot at the forest edge. It was a beautiful place, with a bubbling brook nearby, down in a tree-shrouded gully. All the children scampered off to play in the brook, while the women set up tables and cookfires. One man sat under a tree in his T-shirt and bowler hat, playing the harmonica. Others were drinking beer or playing softball.

Sophie, the four-year old daughter of the Fenners, was told in no uncertain terms that she couldn't go down into the gully with other children. She was too young and could get hurt. Her mother told her to sit on the blanket in the shade and play with her raggedy doll.

Mrs. Fenner went off to help the other women prepare lunch while Sophie sat there and cried in protest. Her mother looked back a few times to scold her and then got caught up in all the talking and the cooking going on. Sophie gradually got tired of crying, seeing it had no effect. She picked up her doll and was about to scold it, when she heard something in the bushes nearby. It was a delightful sound. Was that her name being sung?

Sophie's little face broke into a giggly smile. She told her dolly to be good and go to sleep on the blanket. Then she got up and toddled off in the direction of the sound. She stopped at a flowering, weedy bush.

Wherever she looked, she could see little sparkling things around it. Sophie plopped down on all fours and crawled in for a closer view. Those sparkly things were actually tiny creatures flitting about. Sophie was enchanted. They were like little human butterflies to her. She could hear them laughing and singing as they flew up to her and circled her head. Nobody was afraid—neither Sophie nor the faeries. It was a beautiful meeting of two worlds. Sophie was mystified and tried to keep from grabbing at them, which was what she liked to do with every new wonderful thing she saw.

Her attention was drawn to the base of the plant, where she thought she saw something else. Sophie crawled in further until all that was left to see of her were two little sandaled feet at the bottom of the bush. There she saw a funny old man a little bigger than her hand, digging a hole with great vigor. He was making good progress with his tiny shovel, and beside him she saw a coin and a ring—a pretty little jeweled ring that Sophie suddenly wanted very much. She couldn't resist reaching for it.

The little gnome was so startled when he looked up and saw this fat, dimpled hand coming toward him that he fell over backwards on his treasures. Sophie thought this was the funniest thing she'd ever seen; the whole bush began to shake with her laughter. The gnome was most annoyed at being discovered. He shook his shovel at her and opened and closed his mouth like he was shouting, but Sophie couldn't make out what he was saying.

The gnome saw there was no putting her off, so he had to make some quick decisions. He dropped the shovel and picked up the coin, then thought better of it, dropped the coin, and picked up the ring. Then he ran lickety-split out of the bush and toward the gully.

Oh! A game, Sophie thought as she ran after him. It was all great fun as she followed him toward the gully. Once there, the gnome looked back, shook his fist, and then jumped down the incline. Sophie was just about to do the same—and break her neck in doing it—when a silvery arm reached down and caught her up.

Before she knew it, she was staring into the eyes of the most beautiful girl she had ever seen. The girl had green eyes and brilliant red hair that streamed all around her like there was a breeze blowing it. Sophie put her arms around the girl's neck and said, "Rhea." The girl smiled and held her close.

Sophie looked around and down. They were there by the gully, but Rhea wasn't standing on the ground. They were in the air by the edge, with the land sloping down below them to meet the running brook at the bottom. Sophie thought this was the best ever, and together they floated down to the water.

The faery let Sophie play by the stream for a while, watching her, fascinated by her. Sophie walked around gleefully, talking in her four-year-old prattle to the faery, who seemed to understand everything. Suddenly, the faery swept the child up in her arms and went flying over the water like the wind. Sophie squealed with delight. They came to a place in the brook's flow where the water swirled around and around before going on. Right there above it, there were others like Rhea, dancing and laughing in a whirling ring. Rhea joined in with Sophie. Sophie laughed until she began to cry. A faery's energy can take a good deal more excitement than Humans can stand.

Sophie suddenly became scared; she felt like she was coming apart. The beautiful Rhea saw this and withdrew from the ring, immediately bringing Sophie down gently on the grassy bank. Rhea calmed the child, rocking her and saying her name so sweetly. Then the faery went down to the brook and scooped up some water in a leaf for Sophie to drink. She was just about to do so when she heard her mother's frantic calling. Sophie was alarmed and started crying again.

The faery looked frightened. She stayed just long enough to see the mother running down the other side of the stream; then she vanished.

Now that was what the people could never figure out: how did Sophie get down the gully and so far down on the other side of the stream? Yet that was where they found her, sitting in the grass without a scratch or a drop of water on her. Very peculiar, and even a little creepy—that was what everybody was whispering. Especially when all they could get out of Sophie regarding her little adventure was the name "Rhea, Rhea," over and over.

10

THE RING

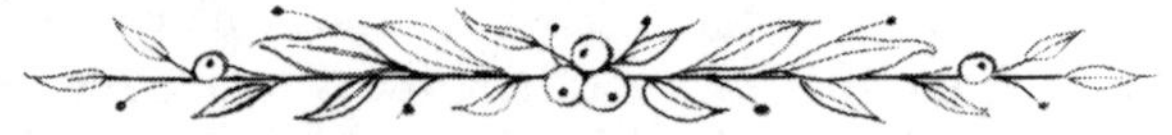

For days after the incident at the picnic, Sophie had an unusual flush to her, and she kept going to the door and calling, "Rhea." Her mother worried that someone might have tried to kidnap her down in the ravine. Mrs. Fenner asked all the children who had been playing down there that day if they had witnessed anything strange, but they all said nothing happened, and they'd never even seen Sophie by the stream. Mrs. Fenner also took Sophie to the doctor to see about the skin flush she seemed to have. After much talk and examination, it was decided Sophie was simply in the "pink" of health and had probably made up an imaginary friend, as children of that age are wont to do.

The whole matter had been happily resolved until something else unsettling occurred. Late one night, silvery light showered down upon the dark coal town. Everyone in the Fenner household was fast asleep. The three children, Sophie, Jeff, and Brian, slept in the same little room upstairs, and their parents had a room down the hall from the kitchen.

Everything was still and quiet except that there were two luminous creatures looking about in the kitchen. They were unusually curious, like people on a tour in a foreign land. They walked and floated about as if they were taking inventory of everything. They looked like very beautiful young girls, except that they were dusted all over with a green iridescent powder that gave off a soft glow. Their hair streamed about them as if blowing in the wind. Both had green eyes, but one of them had red hair; the other had brown. The red-haired one took a tiny cordial glass from a set in the cupboard and put it in a pouch that hung from her shoulder. The brown-haired faery was just about to take a little embroidered napkin out of a drawer when Sophie woke up. The two faery creatures felt her awakening and faded their emanations until they were barely visible, like ghostly wisps of air.

Sophie got out of bed and slowly went down the stairs to see if her friend was there. When the faeries realized it was Sophie and no one else, they restored themselves to their full radiance, and Sophie ran to Rhea's arms again just like the first time she'd seen her. They clearly loved each other. Rhea picked up the little child and held her for her friend to see. Rhea seemed to be asking questions, and Sophie responded by pointing here and there. Then she led the two lovely creatures down the hall to her parents' room. The door was half open, and Sophie pushed it ever so softly while they all looked in.

There were Carrie Fenner and her husband John, wrapped in each other's arms in a twist of bedclothes. The faeries could hardly contain their curiosity at this sight. They had to go in and hover about at closer range. Sophie began to giggle; her parents looked so funny, like a pair of raggedy dolls thrown on the bed. Rhea gave the little girl a warning glance, and they left the room quickly.

Back in the kitchen, Sophie watched in wonder as the faeries transformed her humble hearth into an enchanted scene. She could still see her familiar surroundings, but over that image grew an ever-brighter vision of a forest grove, and in its center, a magnificent tree with golden leaves. Shafts of light illuminated it against the dense green. Sophie was hypnotized as the faeries danced round and round.

Then, wonder of wonders, Rhea called forth the little gnome Sophie had met that day at the picnic. He didn't seem any too happy about this second meeting, either. But there he was, walking right up to the little girl with his bag of treasure over his shoulder. He put it down at her feet and looked back at Rhea; then, with a little sigh and heave of his shoulders, he opened the bag and pulled out the sparkling ring that Sophie had wanted so much. She smiled as the gnome made a bow and presented it to her. It was too big for her finger, so he put it in the pocket of her nightshirt.

At that moment, Carrie Fenner woke up. She listened, then unwound herself from her husband and the sheets to stand in the hall and listen some more. That was Sophie, all right. What was she doing out of bed and downstairs?

Carrie marched into the kitchen just in time to see her daughter going out the back door. "Wait a minute, you little rascal. Just where do you think you're going?"

Sophie was wide awake and giggling, like she was playing some secret game. Carrie tried to scold her as she carried her back to bed. "What's got into you, Sophie Fenner? Have you been sneaking some of your father's coffee at the dinner table? And how did you unlock that door? I've never seen a child so wide awake in the middle of the night." It took Carrie several minutes to calm her daughter down, but once she was back in her bed with her doll, it wasn't long before she was fast asleep again.

* * *

That incredible night became a marker in little Sophie's life. Her mother would say that was when her daughter began to have what people there called "the sight." Sophie remembered it as the most magical night in her life. She would never be parted from that ring. All the rest of her days, it was either on her finger or around her neck on a golden chain.

The first unusual thing Sophie found she could do was locate objects that were forgotten or lost (though the cordial glass from her mother's cupboard never reappeared). As she grew older, she began to sense things about people and know when something was going to happen before it would occur.

Now, in those times, when individuals displayed unusual abilities such as Sophie's, it could go either good or ill for them. These special qualities could be considered gifts from the devil, in which case the person was looked upon with fear and suspicion and literally shoved into a life of darkness by others' distrust of them. On the other hand, God himself might have blessed the person with these powers, in which case the person was revered and sought after for their clairvoyance. So it was for Sophie. As she grew older, her gentle, sweet nature drew people to her. They trusted her. They came with their questions, and she would answer with sometimes startling clarity.

All this would later become a responsibility and somewhat of a burden to her, as she would see many things about people she wished she hadn't known. But for now, as a child, she knew how to do something her brothers couldn't do. Life was full of magic, and it was all a great game.

ANTICIPATION

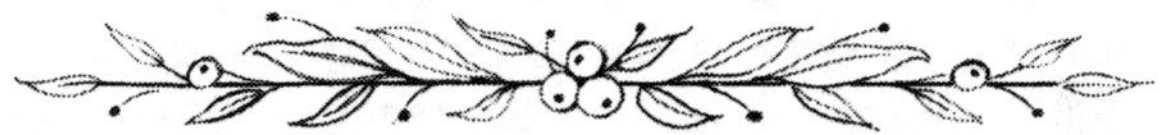

The months went by, and time sailed Ann Quinn past the turbulent waters of her grief into a time of calm—dead calm. She couldn't decide what to do about the house. Her son was making such a valiant effort at taking care of her. He pleaded with her not to sell it and send him away. She didn't want to separate from Tom, but the life they were forced to live now was taking its toll on him. Soon he would never be able to get out, to be free of the mines, and the whole story would repeat itself. He would grow older, marry some simple-hearted girl, then proceed to give his life away to the mines, just like his father. That wasn't how they'd planned it. Their son was going to do better than they had. These days, Ann could sit for hours, motionless over some work she had forgotten she was doing, her mind going back and forth, back and forth over the same black thoughts.

For Tom, time had become an effective barricade against the incomprehensible pain of the loss of his father. The passing months piled heavier, one on top of the other, and Tom felt safely buried under them. It was December, and though the mine was colder and wetter than ever, his spirits had risen a bit.

Christmas had always been a happy time. His parents were good friends with the family next door, the Paxtons, with their three children, soon to be four. They made quite a deal out of Christmas. Mrs. Paxton would cook up a storm, starting days ahead. Mr. Paxton would search for the biggest evergreen tree he could find. Sometimes they had to cut it down some to get it into the house. Years ago, Tom and his parents had been caught up in all the goings-on, and it became a tradition that they would spend Christmas Eve over at the Paxtons', decorating the tree, singing carols, and feasting on the best meal Tom would have all year. Ann Quinn would bake her two best pies, pumpkin and apple, and Sean Quinn would carve and paint little angel ornaments for the tree. Tom would do his best to entertain the three little Paxtons without getting too out of hand himself.

Tom hoped it would be the same again this year—that this one thing would be as it was before. He hoped his mother would get swept into the festivities as she used to, bustling back and forth between the houses. Tom remembered the delicious smells of pine cones, popping corn, and cinnamon. He wanted to see his mother with her eyes sparking, her sleeves rolled up, and her cheeks all flushed from the heat of the oven.

How he longed to sit at that feast of good and plenty once more, with candles and the hearth fires burning.

Many poets have written about the passage of time—how it quickens or slows according to the one who is contemplating it. But Tom could attest to its actually having stopped since he began anticipating Christmas Eve. The shortened hours of light in winter made Tom's life one long, unending night. He woke in the dark, worked in the dark, and returned home in the dark. The atmosphere in the mines had become even gloomier with the cold weather. Chills and fevers jumped like fleas from one man to the next. Cases of influenza were cutting the workforce in half; coal production was way down in the season of its highest demand. The sickness affected many, but the children were hardest hit. The Little Man's troop of stragglers was listless and pale. Anxious to keep his leadership status, he bullied and pushed them, but there wasn't much work to be gotten out of those miserable, aching bodies.

The Little Man himself wasn't doing so well, either, though he would never let on. One day at lunch break, some miners were sitting down in one of those cold, sweating tunnels. Although it was against the rules, a flask of whiskey appeared from someone's pocket, and as it was passed around, each man took a good long swig from it. When it came by the Little Man, he reached for it, only to have the flask ripped from his hand by the next miner, who said, "Oh, no ya don't. I'll not be helpin' ya turn into a nasty drunk like yer father."

The Little Man stood up in a rage. "You damn liar! Take that back!"

The miner simply looked at him and replied, "I can't. It's true."

The Little Man, clenching his fists, glared at each and every one of them, then turned and ran into the shadows.

Hours went by, and none of the children had heard any of the Little Man's sharp commands in quite a while, so Tom went out to look for him. He walked past the miners to the perimeter of light cast by the last light bulb in the working part of the tunnel. There was no sign of him. Tom lit his hat lantern and proceeded slowly into unknown territory. It was so cold and wet; water was seeping into the soles of his shoes. "Jacob," he called. Nothing. He was just about to turn back when he thought he heard a kind of whimpering from the back of a chiseled-out niche in the rock. Tom had to crouch to look inside it. There, suddenly revealed by the light of Tom's lantern, sat Jacob, his clothes all soggy and his face wrinkled with pain and tears.

"Who's that? What d'ya want?" he lashed out.

"It's me, Tom. I...I was looking for you. Our shift is almost over. Aren't you coming up?"

"All right, all right. Now get out of here."

"Okay," Tom said. "Okay. I just..."

"All right, I said! Now leave me alone."

Tom quickly backed out, leaving Jacob to gather himself together. Tom knew he was mortified at being discovered, just as having found the Little Man in such a state shocked him. He hurried back to the comfort of that last light bulb and its pale, familiar glow. For the rest of his life, he would remember that sight of poor, crumpled Jacob as the very image of despair.

12

CHRISTMAS

The wind blew in a freezing rain. Puddles in the street froze overnight, leaving chunks of dirt and stones suspended in the ice like fossils. Tom half-walked, half-skated his way down the main street of town. He was going to the company store to get his mother a Christmas present. He wanted to get something she would keep forever and ever, but what that was, he hadn't yet decided.

Once there, he realized there was nothing special about anything the store had to offer. No, he'd have to make something himself. He decided to make a Christmas angel, as his father would have done. The tools, paints, and glues were all there, just as he had left them, in the shed behind the house.

What Tom knew about carving, he'd learned mostly from watching. He had the procedure pretty well in mind. First he selected a nice cylindrical piece of wood about six inches long. Then he carved a cone shape for the bottom to the waist, then an upside-down triangle shape from the waist to the shoulders. Then he carved in further for the round head on top of the shoulders. His father had been able to carve the whole thing in one piece, including the face of the angel, but Tom would have to do with a clever paint job and plenty of glue for the wings on the back. He did all this during the night after his mother went to sleep.

* * *

Back in the mines during the day, work went on as always. The men went down and the carts came up with coal. Black coal. There was never enough to feed the fires of a growing nation. The Little Man was bossier than ever: he was at the forefront of every tunnel search, acting brash and taking dangerous risks.

Tom, for his part, became almost ridiculously cheery. He seemed to have taken on the job of lifting the spirits of the world—his world, anyway. He wanted nothing to spoil that Christmas. No pain or suffering was going to prevent him from climbing back up on the lap of happiness just one more time. He became the self appointed fool in the court of gloom. Though his motives were selfish, his antics did more good than he knew. They stopped calling him Elf Boy and renamed him St. Nick.

Finally, the angel was done, work in the mines had finished, and the holiday had arrived. To his endless joy, his mother was baking her pies and actually laughing with Mrs. Paxton as they prepared all those wondrous treats for Christmas Eve dinner. Mr. Paxton hauled home the biggest, chubbiest tree—it fairly burst out of its corner into the room. The stage was set now. The only thing left was to actually live the moments he had waited so long for.

That evening, just before they left to go next door, Tom gave his mother her present. She unwrapped the little angel and held it in her hands. "It's beautiful," she said, giving him a teary kiss. "Your father would be proud." Together they left the silence of their home and crossed over into the noisy confusion of life at the Paxtons'.

Though he had been there just hours ago, it looked somehow different, more wonderful than before. In the glow of candlelight, amongst those good people, Tom almost made it. He was almost completely happy like he used to be, except for the awareness of a dangerous sleeping dread that lay coiled in the back of his mind. There were moments when he was able to forget, and others when he felt outside of it all, like a guest from another planet. Every once in a while, he'd catch his mother looking at him with her sad knowing eyes. They decorated the tree, putting Tom's angel at the top. They sang and were merry. Tom never wanted to leave the warm protective spell that evening had cast.

But eventually it was time to go, and they had to cross the yard back to their dark house. Tom sat at the kitchen table while Ann put some dishes away; then she sat down next to him and pulled a letter from her pocket. "I thought about this all evening—whether I should give this to you now. It's a letter to you from your father." Tom's eyes widened in disbelief. "He was going to write more as you got older, then present them to you on your eighteenth birthday. This is the only one he got to write. I think you should have it now." She laid the letter on the table and left him there to read it alone.

Tom looked at his father's handwriting, and memories of him flooded up from the grave where he had buried them. It took him a while to open it up, but when he did, the letter read:

Dear Tom,

Right now you are eight years old and I have just scolded you for talking back to your mother. You are sitting at the kitchen table, writing out "I will not be disrespectful to my parents" fifty times. I'm sitting across the room watching you. I can hardly stop myself from chuckling as you sit there, twisting your hair and kicking your feet against the chair, madder than a hornet at me and the world. Seeing you as I am now has given me the idea to write something too. I'm going to write you a letter every so often and keep them till your eighteenth birthday. I think it should be quite interesting to read them then from that perspective. Tonight, as I say, you are scribbling over there as I am watching you, trying to restrain myself from saying "Forget everything" and just give you a big bear hug. But I can't, because there is something you have to learn, Son. You don't understand me now, but there are many ways of communicating with people without angering or hurting them in the process. When I said, "Watch your tongue, lad," I meant watch your words. They can be sharper than any knife you would throw at a person. Knife wounds can heal, but words flung out in a wicked temper can sink deep into the mind of the person who has heard them and fester there for a lifetime. But I'm not worried about you, Tom. You're going to be a better man than me. We see how smart and quick you are already. And you're going to have an education. I'm making plans for that. So, Tom, you little rascal sitting over there, you might not believe it now, but I love you very much.

Your father, Sean Quinn

Tom carefully folded the letter, then put his head down and cried the tears he had been holding back for seven long months.

13

ABOVE AND BELOW

Snow fell quietly in the mountains. The wind played a soulful song in the pines high above. One would think that was all to be found there—just the snow, the pines, and the wind—but that would not be true. Indeed, many things were in motion on this silent winter night. A great celebration was taking place at that very moment, though it would be hard for a Human to perceive it. One would have to know that there existed a Parallel World and one would have to know the secret of entering that dimension.

For the truth of it was, an ancient winter rite was being held, with all the elementals and spirits of nature in attendance. Straight down into the earth a person would have to go to see this faery revel. In a great cavern with walls gleaming gold and silver, a host of faery creatures was gathered. Each one outshone the next in beauty and form. A great feast was in progress, and the hall was bright as day with all the lamps and candles that were lit. There, a hundred tables were spread with sweetmeats and drinks of nectar. They played the sweetest music that was ever to be heard, and they were dancing and turning, going round so quickly and lightly that they blurred before the eye.

Now, at one end of the hall were two grand chairs that were occupied by no one. At intervals, the whole group stood up, raised their glasses in that direction, and cheered,

"To Boadag once—
To Boadag and then
To him with the raven's hair
That shall be king again!"

At the other end of the hall, a heavenly light encircled a grand cornucopia overflowing with fruits, nuts, and other delicacies. The fiery-haired Rhea was dancing there. She was clothed in a robe of flame-colored silk and wore a collar of gold and rubies round her neck. The drinking, toasting, and dancing went on for days,

> and all the while
>> in the forest above,
>>> it was silent but for the wind's song
>>>> high in the pines.

14

TEA AND BISCUITS

It takes a natural force of immense power and eons of living and dying to create a lump of coal, but it took no time at all for Man to destroy the land in search of it, once he realized coal's value. As Nature's son, he had a right to it, and he was impatient to have it all. Now, the mountain which had the unfortunate luck to contain this coal could only take so much digging, clawing, and blasting of its innards before it seemed to want to do some collapsing, crushing, and sliding of its own. It wasn't going to give up its treasure without a price. Every once in a while, it demanded a sacrifice.

Christmas had jingled its way into memories. Snow gave way to slush. The coal town resumed its coat of spattered mud and dreariness. Tom Quinn brought home a case of the sniffles and a sore throat from the mines, but while he remained strong, his mother became very ill. The cold settled in her chest. Once she started to cough, she couldn't stop—terrible, deep, hoarse coughs that left her weak and dizzy.

Though Tom insisted she stay in bed each morning, Ann could hear him clattering around in her kitchen, and she couldn't help trying to sit up and breathlessly calling out directions as to where things were and what to fix for his lunch. Tom would answer, "Oh, yes, I found it," and "That sounds good," but mostly he would simply brew up a thermos of tea and grab a tin of biscuits to eat for lunch. Just before he was ready to leave, he would stoke up the fire in the stove so it would last most of the day and make sure his mother was bundled back into bed; then out he'd go into the damp grey dawn.

Ann alternated between coughing, sleeping, and shivering. Sometimes she would get up and try to do things, but her body ached so, and she would go back to bed exhausted. Soon all she could do was wait. Wait for Tom to come home—wait for one of the neighbors to stop by—wait to take up her life again. She knew somewhere a clock was ticking, time was passing, slipping, by. In her exhaustion, a terrible guilt descended upon her, oppressing her spirit even more. She should get up. She had to get up. Her attempts to rest were futile and tormented.

One day she lay waiting. Hours went by. Nobody came. No neighbors with food or a cheerful word, and no Tom. Where was he? It was almost dark. The fire was going out. The house was becoming damp and cold again. It was strangely silent. A familiar icy sensation ran through her blood. It was fear. A death-like fear. Something was wrong. She waited, holding her breath, listening. She knew it. Something had happened. She hadn't heard the alarm siren, but she knew it just the same. Ann got dressed and walked like one possessed over to the mining office.

As she came around the corner, she could see the crowd near the door. One of her neighbors turned and saw her coming. "Why, Ann, dear, you shouldn't be out. We were coming to tell you—"

"What's wrong? What's happened?" Ann said. In the wind, her hair and the fringe of her shawl whipped about like snakes writhing around a madwoman. She listened grimly as they told her of a gas leak, an explosion, and men trapped in a rockfall. "Has anyone come up?" she asked. "What about the children?"

The women said none of the men had come up. They wouldn't leave their comrades, and they were all working to clear the rockfall to free them. Some of the children had been sent up, but Ann's son Tom wasn't among them.

Just then, a mining official came out of the office to say that there was nothing new to report, but they were sending up a medical supply truck. Everyone in the group insisted on climbing into the truck and riding up the mountain to continue their vigil there. Ann was among those in the truck, her eyes burning with the conflicting fires of her fever and her will to remain standing.

Down in the mine, there was noise and confusion. Fires and steaming waters crackled and hissed at each other. Men ran this way and that in the flickering light. Everyone was shouting and working in a desperate attempt to free the miners before they ran out of air. They were trapped in a little pocket. They were all right, just cold and wet. Finally, a small hole was punched through the rubble. Everyone cheered. It wouldn't be long now.

Reports came up top that no one was hurt and the trapped men would soon be free. Everyone relaxed and felt much relieved, except for Ann. She was still enduring some mighty conflict and didn't change her expression at all.

Down in the mine, the men had made the hole larger, almost large enough for someone to crawl through. Tom and the Little Man were there, digging and hauling away with the best of them. It looked like soon this would be just one more lucky story to talk about over drinks at the pub. The men inside the hole were becoming a little more confident and joking a bit with their rescuers; they asked if they couldn't be passed a spot of tea while they were waiting to be delivered. Tom immediately offered his thermos and box of biscuits. They tried to poke them through to the men, but it was too long a reach. Tom volunteered to crawl through, but the Little Man brushed him aside, saying, "Ah, no ya don't. I'm the only man for this job." In a flash, he took the tea and tin of biscuits and was gone into the hole. They could hear the trapped men hailing him as he popped through to the other side. Everyone cheered again.

Almost immediately, there was a terrible groan and then a roaring noise. The miners watched in disbelief as the rocks caved in over the trapped men.

It was as if the Little Man and his refreshments had been the last part of the sacrifice demanded by the mountain, for now all was quiet and still. The only sound was the generator pumping, and the only movement the eyes of the men who had been spared. Everyone stood as they had been, picks raised, arms around stones they were hauling away, just blinking, not quite comprehending.

Tom had fallen back into the rubble. He lay there, panting in the settling dust. Just a few feet away from him, two men and a boy had died. He had survived, and for the life of him he couldn't figure out why.

News of the deaths came up with the first load of bedraggled miners in the lift. A profound sorrow settled over the whole community. Ann waited before the gate of the elevator shaft, her troubled eyes scanning for her boy. She looked as if she had locked horns with the devil in a mighty struggle for the life of her son. She was ravaged, but she had won. Here was Tom coming toward her. When she finally clutched him to her breast, she sobbed, "I'm selling the house! You're leaving for the city!" It was all she had the strength to say.

15

TURMOIL

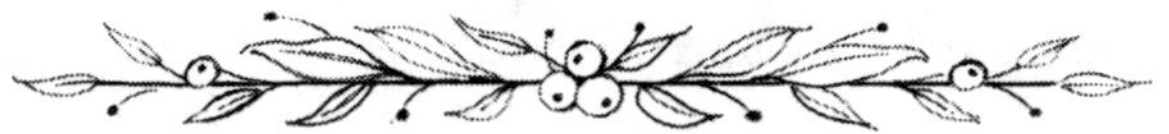

After the mining tragedy, all hell broke loose. It began to rain for days on end and many more people became sick with influenza. An angry wind swooped down the streets of the coal town. People said they'd never seen the like of it. That mighty wail brought with it a fearful omen of change. The old beliefs surfaced that a night wind like this bore a wicked host of flying creatures who liked nothing better than to snatch up hapless mortals who made the bad mistake of crossing their path. These victims were made to do horrible things for the delight of their captors, then dropped senseless to the ground, all bruised and broken.

Old Man McCormick was found unconscious by the side of the road one morning. His clothes were all torn and he looked like he had been in quite a tussle. When he came to, he said that when he was coming home late the previous night, the wind and the rain were something fierce. He had to lean forward to walk. All of a sudden, leaves and mud came up in a whirlwind. He was choked and blinded by the flying debris. Next, he thought he heard some high-pitched screams and it scared the bloody life out of him. That was all he could remember.

So, the townspeople went to church to light candles and pray, but just in case these forces might be outside the rule of the church, they also began carrying nails in their pockets and wearing one glove inside out. Everyone agreed that such old superstitious protections had no place in this modern day, but then again, these were uncertain times and one couldn't be too cautious.

* * *

It continued to storm with lightning and drama, fueling people's fears. The little ravine where Sophie had danced a faery whirl became a raging river that overflowed its banks, taking down trees and etching out chunks of hillside as it churned wildly over the rocks.

For some creatures, the coming of such a torrent was not as much a disaster as an inconvenience. Keb and Kabeb were two such beings. They had a more philosophical approach. They had had centuries of experience with such upheavals and thought them so much botheration, an interruption of what they always did. There might be some higher purpose to all this turmoil, but that was none of their concern; they were just Creek-tree creatures and their home had just been washed away. There they sat in the pouring rain, waiting for some sign to tell them where to go now. A Human could easily have mistaken them for broken tree roots; they were so much a part of the nature in which they lived. They had many crooked arms and gnarly, twisted legs that bent in all directions. Their heads joined their bodies on scrawny necks. Their faces looked more like lines in tree bark than anything else, and their straggly hair had tangled together, binding them to each other.

Keb and Kabeb had been separate many years ago, but they found they had so much in common that they grew together. Now they were literally inseparable. Their job was to hold on: hold on to the earth around the tree and the land in their keeping. They embedded themselves in the ground and held together the soil out of which the forest on this mountain grew. Theirs was a simple, slow consciousness without any sense of time.

They had held on tight to their ground as long as they could, but the storm and the rising water were too much for them. They had to let go. Now they waited, watching out of squinty eyes for what to do next. Keb and Kabeb sat wound around each other, legs entwined, their mossy heads dripping with water. They looked up and down, this way and that. There was no sign yet. Could they have been forgotten?

Everything in the Parallel World lived within a certain order, much like in the Human realm. Beings there had varying degrees of ability and intelligence. Some were like Keb and Kabeb; others were highly evolved, possessing more knowledge than any Human. All possessed an inner certainty of a higher presence that imbued them with life and would take care of them. The higher the consciousness, the less corporeal these beings became. The more they knew and the closer they came to the source of all life, the less they needed to embody anything at all. They were perceived as astral beings, as emanations of light.

Keb and Kabeb never really doubted they would receive a sign. But it was wet and cold, and it had been a long wait. They were ready to sink themselves down and entrench again in the earth.

Kabeb saw it first: a movement not too far off. A branch fell and hung suspended by a vine. It twirled and whirled in an uncanny manner, then suddenly stopped, pointing to the right, down the bank from where they were. Kabeb nudged Keb, and they both agreed it was the sign. Together they moved away in that direction...

16

RHEA'S WORLD

The sun glittered in a clear blue sky. The atmosphere felt clean and calm in the aftermath of the storm. There was much work to be done in the mountain forest after such a disturbance. The waters in the ravine had receded, and clumps of grass and bushes that had somehow hung on during the torrent were drying out and standing tall once more.

Keb and Kabeb had found their new home. They liked it much better, for they were much less isolated than before. They found they were to hold together part of an ancient faery path that had led down the ravine, through the woods, and into the meadow beyond. The whole mountain was crisscrossed with these paths, though they were imperceptible to the unaware. Those of the Otherworld knew them well.

It was on such a path that Rhea could be seen, riding a faery horse. How she rejoiced in the energy that abounded in that day! Her sensibilities were such that she absorbed the life force around her and gave off a spectacular radiation as she galloped along the path. Her red hair flamed out around her as she and her golden horse took to the air and vanished amongst the trees. She appeared once again down in the meadows and there brought her steed to a halt.

Rhea spread out a marvelous blanket in the sunny field, a multicolored quilt with braided edges and golden apples at each corner. She sat there to drink in the life about her. Everywhere, creatures of her world were busy. There was so much repairing, building, and growing to do after such a storm. Little green winged emanations hovered near the grasses, inducing them to recover and grow. Troops of faeries were going this way and that over the paths.

Rhea shone like a ruby jewel in a golden green setting. She stretched her arms and filled her being with wondrous draughts of air. As she leaned back, she caught sight of the red tips on three of her fingers and was reminded of her mysterious past.

It never ceased to intrigue her, this long-lost tale of who she was. The old people had told her that she was descended from a Human tribe that had long ago crossed over to the Parallel World. They had once lived in the far north country. They were a noble people who were excellent horsemen, had a great love of music and poetry, and were skilled in medicine and the magic arts. They had lived peaceably among other Human tribes for many centuries. Then there came a wave of barbaric peoples who wanted nothing but to pillage and conquer the Tuatha de Monayans, for that was what her ancestors were called. They sought protection in the

Parallel World. The Great Beings that presided there allowed them entry on the condition that they could never go back. The Monayans faced extinction at the hands of the invaders, so they agreed.

They were told to assemble at the edge of the forest lake. They took everything—their horses, their livestock, their treasures—and waited there, watching over the rippling water. At a certain hour, crystal boats emerged out of a dense mist that had gathered in the center of the lake. They boarded those boats and so left forever the world as Humans know it for the Parallel World, the Land of Faery.

Life went on. Her people lived as they always had. They rode their horses and built their castles. Nothing was different, yet nothing was the same. In the course of time, some of the Tuatha de Monayans began to mingle with the other folk of Faery. They lost some of their ways and took on others. In the centuries that followed, those who stayed isolated simply began to disappear.

When Rhea came into being, the only traces that revealed her once-Human blood were those three red stains on the tips of her fingers. Because of this, Rhea was heir to thoughts and emotions that were not known by those of pure Faery.

Rhea lay for a long time looking up at the sky, pondering this story, feeling alternately the tingling of life around her and a wispy sense of longing that trailed around inside her. Her eyes dreamily followed the flight of a crow circling above her. She came to her senses as it flapped noisily down to land beside her. "Yes, and what have you to say about all this?" she asked.

The crow looked around and cocked a glistening eye her way, but never said a word.

17

DOWN THE MOUNTAIN

It was nearly two months before Ann Quinn was well enough to write Aunt Petra, sell the house, and make her arrangements for living with the neighbors. Tom no longer even tried to protest. Ever since he'd seen the look on his mother's face that day of the mining tragedy, he'd known it was all over. He was going away, perhaps forever. His mother was quiet but firm about everything she did. There was no going back on any of it.

The day came for him to leave. A friend offered to take them down the mountain to the train station. They rode in a horse-drawn wagon. His mother sat up on the buckboard seat with the driver. Tom, in the back, watched everything that was familiar stream out behind him, getting smaller and smaller. His home, the forest, the mountain, all receding now behind him. By the time they reached the station, Tom was somewhere he'd never been. Never been down the mountain, never been on a train, never been to the city—all this newness was exhilarating and wrenching at the same time.

As he looked around, gathering it all in, his mother was running on, telling him again what she had said before: "Mrs. Savage will meet the train...just stay put till she finds you...be sure to give Aunt Petra the money you've got stashed in your shoe. Don't forget to tell her each month I'll send the money for your school and keep. Here's the train...it's time...eat the lunch I packed you...watch your suitcase and don't forget— don't forget I love you..."

She embraced him in tears. This was the moment of his departure. Tom could hardly collect himself, but this was a time for bravery, to make a show of courage for his mother. He kissed her and climbed the steps into the train. Soon he was watching the landscape stream out behind him again, his mother a tiny part of it, getting smaller and smaller until a curve in the tracks hid her from sight completely.

For Tom, being on that train provided an unexpected respite. The pain of parting was over, and the anxiety over what was to come had not yet set in. He felt a kind of delicious neither-here-nor-there-ness. The sun coming through the window was warm and cozy. The subtle rocking movement and the clickety-clack sound on the tracks made him so sleepy he couldn't hold his head up. He leaned against the window and fell into a deep, much-needed sleep.

The train's giant engine pulled its many cars steadily across rich farm country, over rolling hills, and through lush meadows. Horses in the fields kicked up their heels and cantered along with the train for a while, then dropped back to their grazing. The train continued on seamlessly through the landscape as the hours of the day went round to evening.

Tom woke with a start. He looked about, not comprehending. He couldn't make out which felt more unreal: where he had just been or where he was now. People around him sat dozing, reading newspapers, looking out the windows, or contemplating something far off in themselves as they stared into nowhere. A pang of hunger reminded Tom of the sandwich his mother had made. He unwrapped it like a priceless treasure and ate it as it if were magic. It came from home, his mother, and love. He felt how caringly she had put his little meal together. He relished every bite. When it was finished, he was profoundly depressed. Now he was really alone. He turned his face to the window and struggled to hide his emotion.

Tom had dozed off again when the train pulled into the city station with a blast of steam and a screeching of metal. Everyone immediately jumped into action, gathering their things, glad to be at the journey's end. Tom was jostled awake and looked with sleepy eyes out the windows. It was pitch dark except for the electric lights in the station. Tom felt the cool air coming in from the open doors. He got up quickly, took his suitcase, and climbed down out of the train into the night.

His mother's words, "Stay put," echoed in his head. He found himself smiling in spite of his uncertainty. That was good advice, he thought, since he hadn't a clue which way to go anyway. He stood there in the cold air, shifting from one foot to the other, looking about for this lady who was supposed to meet him...

A little ways away in the station café sat a grim-looking woman sipping a cup of tea. As she looked out the window, she saw the train empty out, saw people moving off the platform, saw the child standing there with his satchel, but she didn't make a move. She just sat and sipped her tea. *That must be the little blighter*, she thought. *Well, let him stand there till I finish. It was a cold ride coming and it will be a cold one going back. I've got enough on my hands taking care of that old woman. Now I've got to take in that little bugger as well. He can just wait until I finish.* Good Mrs. Savage sat back with her tea and showed no signs of finishing it any time soon.

Tom was getting cold. He'd stay put for a while longer and then he'd...then he'd what? He didn't know.

When Mrs. Savage emptied her cup, she straightened her hat, put on an incredibly radiant smile, and went out to meet the little bugger. She descended upon him like an angel of mercy, all solace and concern for his having waited so long. She took up his little case and bundled him into a taxi, insisting he sit right next to her so he could warm up.

Tom was so relieved that she had appeared, he really did think she was an angel. The taxi went through dark streets, around corners, and past buildings, big and small. He had no idea where he was. Finally, they stopped in front of a house that was set back in a very large yard. Tom could smell the grass and trees about him.

Mrs. Savage led him through a gate and up a long walk to the veranda of the house. As they climbed up the front stairs, she said, "Now when you go in, you'll have to be quiet. I'll take you right to your room. I gave your Aunt Petra her medicine and she's asleep. You'll see her in the morning."

Mrs. Savage opened a fine wooden door with an oval of etched glass in it, and there they were, in the entry of Aunt Petra's house. Tom couldn't see much in the darkened rooms about him, but the smell of flowers and mustiness swept over him. "We don't keep the lights on around here nowadays. We try to conserve as much as we can," Mrs. Savage was saying as she lit a kerosene lamp on the hall table. Still smiling that brilliant smile, she led the way up the stairs to his room.

This certainly was the biggest house Tom had ever been in. They must have passed four doors on the second floor and they still hadn't gotten to his room. Mrs. Savage finally paused and opened the door to a little room. "You'll sleep here tonight," she stated.

Just as Tom was about to enter, he was stopped by the sound of the loudest fit of snoring he'd ever heard. "Aunt Petra?" he asked hesitantly.

"No," Mrs. Savage said dryly. "No, that's Toddie, the dog. Or Toadie, as I call him. He's as old as Methuselah and then some. He sleeps with your aunt. Good night, dear. See you in the morning."

There he was, moments later, clothes off, inside a strange bed, looking with drooping eyes at his surroundings. For all its grandeur, this house had very small rooms. He felt as if he were in some sort of broom closet. A low window let in a dim, gaseous light from the street, revealing a room whose ceiling slanted to the floor against which his bed was tucked. The soft sheets convinced him, however, that he was in paradise, and Tom fell fast asleep.

NEW WORLDS

Petra Wimpleton received Tom like a savior—a young knight come to invigorate her surroundings again. There she was in her room of so many years, dusty shafts of light paling through velvet curtains, flowers drooping over a marble-topped table, and herself in a wheelchair beside it. Everything was pastel pinks, whites, and yellows. She looked like a delicately frosted pastry sitting in a faded taffeta morning gown.

"Here," she said, beckoning him nearer with her lace-covered hands. "Let me give you a hug for all your troubles. Oh, now, that's a darling dear."

The ever-present Mrs. Savage stood close by, all smiles and benevolent nods. Tom was quite taken aback at this scene of such welcoming femininity. Everything seemed to be adrift in powder, flowers, and sunlight.

"Aunt Petra, my mother thanks—" he started to say, as Petra drew him into another perfumed squeeze.

"Oh, now, now," she said, "none of that. 'Tis I who am happy to see you here. I feel better already."

The only bass note in this whole euphoric scene was the heavy breathing of Toddie—or Toadie, as he was so aptly nicknamed. He sat on his pillow, breathing faster or slower according to his own inner tempo.

"Thank you for having me." Tom stepped back, determined to continue. "I shall do my best to work hard at school and be no trouble to you."

What am I doing here? he thought. He had never really seen this person before. This was the widowed great-aunt who lived in the city. Here sat his future, as the family fable had been told to him. He was now to become what his parents had so longed for— that *something* was...and then everything became cloudy before the downy, soft, frilly presence of Aunt Petra. She giggled and chattered while Tom looked around him. She excitedly jumbled out her gladness, her concern about his circumstances, her hope for his future there. Tom forced a smile in response, but really, he felt painfully adrift for the first time in his life.

"We're going to have such a good time now that you're here," Aunt Petra went on, until Mrs. Savage leaned over her to remind her not to excite herself so. Aunt Petra drew back her enthusiasm like a petulant child, admitting as to how she might want to rest a while. In a wink Mrs. Savage took over the proceedings, and before he knew it Tom was back in his little broom closet, sitting on his bed.

Mrs. Savage leaned in at the door, saying, "Come down to breakfast whenever you're ready. Aunt Petra takes hers on a tray in her room." Then she leaned in further to say in a confidential tone, "You know, your aunt is a lot worse off than she thinks she is. God knows, I'm doing my best. She's very glad you're here, but please don't overexcite her. She's a very sick woman." She closed the door, arching her eyebrows and nodding to him in a conspiratorial way.

Tom didn't know what to make of anything. His aunt appeared quite silly, but sweet, and Mrs. Savage seemed to run hot and cold at the same time. That smile of hers was frightening.

The house had a front staircase and a back staircase. The latter wound down to the kitchen. Tom found Mrs. Savage there, preparing the morning meal. He sat at the kitchen table, where he saw a place was set for him. The "angel of mercy" had no more smiles for her tasks at hand; in fact, she appeared downright angry. She eyed him sideways as she ladled his porridge into a bowl. "Your Aunt Petra isn't as rich as you might think. This isn't Easy Street by any stretch of the means." But then she was all smiles again as she set the food in front of him. He was sure he must have mistaken what she'd just said.

After he had eaten, Mrs. Savage ushered him out the back door. "There now, go on out, have a look around, and let's not see you before lunchtime."

Tom wasn't sure whether he'd been let out or kicked out, but he walked to the front yard and swung on the gate for a while, trying to take everything in. After a time, he swung the gate closed and walked on down the block. Wide maple trees stretched over the streets, and the houses were like none he had ever seen. They had entries with columns and filigree. Ferns hung on hooks over verandas and stood in tall wrought-iron holders before the doors. Everything felt so lush and safe. He breathed in deeply the quiet of the street, so different from where he had been just the day before. He thought of his mother and hoped she was calmer now, knowing he was there and doing his best.

The city was sprawling all over itself in an attempt to keep up with its growth. Aunt Petra's neighborhood was only a small island of quiet in a sea of surrounding development. Tom quickly emerged from the shade trees into a street spilling with confusion and traffic. He was on some commercial thoroughfare at the end of nature's domain. Here the trees were chopped and pruned with little wire cages pressing around their trunks. He wandered, looking at the shops, the people, and the motorcars that sputtered down the streets. Occasionally he would see the reflection of a worn-looking boy in a window, and he was embarrassed to have to claim that being as himself. He walked for hours, and when he felt he had been gone long enough, he turned back down onto his aunt's quiet street.

Lunch at Aunt Petra's was upstairs in her bedroom. Since she was wheelchair-bound, she never came downstairs. "Oh, someday I'd like to go down and sit in the front room again," she said. "Now that you're here, Tom, I think I shall. I'm not completely incapacitated."

"Nonsense," Mrs. Savage said under her breath.

"I've had Mrs. Savage make up the guest bedroom, so you should have all the room you need," Aunt Petra continued.

"Thank you," Tom said, never thinking his accommodations were meant to be anything other than what he had been shown. Mrs. Savage gave him a satisfied smile from across the room.

"Have you met Toddie? Do say hello to Toddie. He's my only friend left from the old days when my husband was alive."

Tom looked at old Toddie, heaving away on his velvet pillow, his wall-eye rolling over at him, his mouth draped back in an extended-tongue smile. Mrs. Savage flinched in disgust.

"This afternoon I'm going to have Mrs. Savage bring me downstairs, and we can sit under the tree like I used to," said Aunt Petra. "I'm going to do that. I'm feeling much better!"

"My dear woman." Mrs. Savage smiled exasperatedly. "How do you propose to get downstairs? I certainly can't carry you."

"I can do it, I know I can."

"Nonsense," was Mrs. Savage's only comment.

Aunt Petra looked at Tom for help. "Yes, really, I can help," he offered.

"I'm not going to be responsible," Mrs. Savage snorted.

"There, you see, Tom and I are going to be such good friends. You shall help me, and I shall help you find your way. Yes, now...school's the first order of business, isn't it, Mrs. Savage? You've got to take your learning seriously, Tom. My husband certainly knew about that. Now, Mrs. Savage. What shall we do?"

"Well, the boy will have to be tested and tutored, perhaps, before he can be placed in the city schools. I would suggest employing Mr. Sidney Snyder. He has quite a scholastic background. I know him well. He has an excellent reputation."

"Oh, yes. Your friend, Mr. Sidney. Mr. Snyder. Yes, he's very smart, to be sure. I didn't know he was a tutor."

"Of course. Sidney Snyder Student Tutorial Service. I've told you about him many times."

"Yes, yes, I remember now. Well, if you think that's the right way to go...we wouldn't want the boy to get in over his head and off to a bad start, now would we? Oh, definitely not. We must first employ Mr. Sidney."

19

BETTER DAYS

In another, even older section of the city, there were several hotels that had been converted into apartment dwellings. They were inhabited mostly by those whose finances were in an extreme state of flux. One could rent them by the week or the month. These buildings had grand façades, complete with patterned stone carving and gargoyles watching out over the drain spouts. Inside, however, accommodations were decidedly cramped. Tiny rooms once designed for a bed and nightstand now were outfitted with makeshift kitchens, tables, chairs, closets, and bookshelves.

It was in one of these cluttered cubicles that Mr. Sidney Snyder stood one morning, wedged between the end of his bed and the legs of his "kitchen" table. He was brewing his morning cup of tea. Dressed as he was in his loose bathrobe and slippers, he had no trouble at all reaching with his long skinny arms from one wall to the other to set down the tea, the cup, and the sugar before his boiling pot.

When his long, angular body was all tucked into his formal shirt collars, vests, and jackets, he made quite a tidy and even elegant presentation. But when he was all undone, as he was this particular morning, he was a rather frightening, disheveled wraith.

Those first sips of hot English tea did wonders for his waking constitution, and when he added a few shots of brandy to the concoction for taste, he seemed once again ready to assume the full embodiment of his six-foot-two frame.

One hour later, after much folding and unfolding of beds, arms, legs, and chairs, Mr. Snyder extricated himself from his apartment. His clothes gave him the high-waisted, pinched look of a deacon or professor, although he was neither. In fact, Sidney Snyder wasn't much of anything but a collection of should-have-beens and would-have-beens. He was still waiting for the world to provide him with the right opportunity to "come into himself," as it were. He walked with the imperious gait of a "very busy" man down the street to a little restaurant that had the word "Bistro" on its awning. Inside, he greeted none other than the smiling Mrs. Savage.

She looked somehow different: maybe it was the touch of rouge on her cheeks or the silk pansy pinned to her lapel. In any case, she positively glowed for a moment when Mr. Snyder kissed her outstretched fingers and sat down. The little bistro chair he sat in did nothing for his elegant demeanor, however, for his knees rose up to engulf the table. Mrs. Savage seemed to take no notice as she leaned over them to smile and say, "Sidney, where have you been the last few days? I have some news for you."

"Oh, my dear, it's been simply drastic! So many things. You can't imagine. I hardly have time for anything. It's very difficult for a man like me...very difficult...."

"I know, I know." She gave a sympathetic sigh, then added sarcastically, "But if you can find some time between miseries, I think I might have something for you."

Sidney looked up from his troubles, whiffing some new possibility.

"That Wimpleton woman has seen fit to take in some ragged back-country relative of hers. I don't like it. I don't like it one bit. It complicates things intolerably. The one good thing is that he comes with money for his board and schooling. I've taken care of his board money, and I've set things up so you can be his scholastic tutor."

"Tutor!" Mr. Snyder's pomaded hair rose with his eyebrows. "Me? A tutor? Don't be absurd!"

"Well, I see. A weekly compensation for a few hours' work means nothing, does it?"

"Now, Lillian, don't start that again." Sidney seemed poised for an argument; they had been down this road before. He eyed her exasperatedly, weighing this newest of "possibilities." The idea began to take hold. Such a position wasn't entirely abhorrent. A tutor...hmm...a man of his caliber could do that sort of thing temporarily without too much damage to appearances.

Sidney relaxed back into his chair. "All right. How much and for how long?"

"Half of his monthly stipend, and just as long as I need to figure out how to get rid of him," was her answer. "Look, this urchin can read and scratch his name on a piece of paper. That's about it. Whatever you do, keep him perplexed and confounded every day for half a day. I don't want him getting any ideas of his own. My plans remain the same. Things might just take a little longer, that's all."

"My, you are an astounding woman, my savage little Lilly!" Mr. Snyder chuckled as he popped a tea cake into his mouth.

THE CROW'S NEST

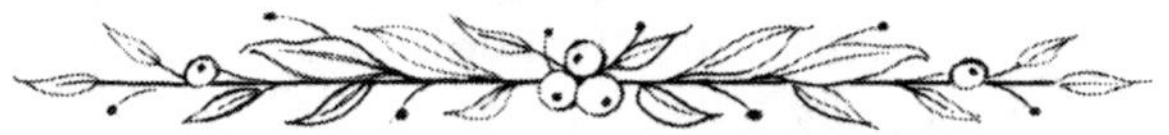

Sidney Snyder's Tutorial Service arrived first thing the next morning. Mrs. Savage opened the door to Sidney's grand bow. He was all high collars, pomade, and grins. "Good morning, Lilly." She couldn't help but smile. She *was* susceptible to his particular kind of manners and dash.

"Shh, quick now." Squashing his salutations, she ordered him to follow her and led him through to the kitchen. "Leave it to you," she huffed over her shoulder, "to come just in time for breakfast. Don't make this a habit. My part of the budget doesn't include your appetite!"

The three of them sat at the table, Mrs. Savage, Sidney, and a very quiet Tom, eating the hot griddle cakes she had just prepared. "This is your tutor, Tom," she said.

"How do you do, sir?" Tom offered politely.

"Um, ah, yes. Delighted, my boy," Sidney answered amid alternate swallows of griddle cake and coffee. "We'll have you caught up in your studies in no time, no time at all."

"That will be very helpful, sir," said Tom

Mrs. Savage reached over and patted Tom's arm. "Yes, Tom's a lovely boy and we want the best for him."

"Quite so, quite so." Mr. Snyder nodded.

"I'm going upstairs with Petra's tea and get her ready to greet you. Wait here till I call you." Then she disappeared up the stairs.

So Tom was left alone with Mr. Snyder and Mr. Snyder alone with Tom. Quite an awkward situation for both of them. "Yes, well," Sidney said as he pushed back his chair and stood up. Tom felt awed by his height and bearing. "Tell me, what grade were you in at your last school, Tom?"

"Grade?" he answered. "Well, I'm not sure. We all studied in one room and there were a lot of levels going on at once."

Sidney put his hands behind his back and took a professorial stance. He looked down at Tom and then back over to the griddle cake pan. "Hummmm," he said, sounding very grave. For the life of him, he couldn't think of what to say next. So he just said, "Hummmm," again with more emphasis. Several minutes passed in this manner until at last they heard Mrs. Savage call for them to come upstairs.

Aunt Petra appeared to have had a bad night, and she hadn't been dressed very well. Tom was alarmed. Her mind seemed fuzzy and her speech slow. "She's not feeling tip-top today," Mrs. Savage said cheerily while she helped the old lady to her breakfast table. "She has her good days and she has her bad days. She gets better once she's eaten something. Now don't stay long. This is Mr. Snyder. Petra, say hello to Tom's new tutor." Mrs. Savage was talking loudly, gesturing like she was trying to communicate with a deaf-mute. Toddie started a low growl, which Mr. Snyder took very personally.

Aunt Petra was struggling to come out of some sort of fog. She looked around confusedly, but when her eyes met young Tom's, things seemed to come together. "Tom, Tom, come give your auntie a kiss."

Tom gave her a hug and stood by anxiously while Mrs. Savage continued, "This is Mr. Snyder. He will be teaching Tom in the mornings, as we discussed, remember?"

"Yes. Good. I know. How do you do...Tom, Tom..." Aunt Petra looked up at him. "Stay with me, Tom. You are going to stay here with me, aren't you?"

"Of course, of course. I—" Tom started to say, but Mrs. Savage cut him off, abruptly pushing Petra's chair square to the table and flapping a napkin across her lap.

"Tom will be back later in the day. Right now you've got to drink your tea and finish your medicine." Mrs. Savage motioned for both of them to leave. As Tom went downstairs, he felt a sudden pang in his heart at the sight of his poor Aunt Petra looking so helpless, trapped in her wheelchair.

* * *

A new routine quickly established itself in Tom's life. He was up at seven to take out the garbage and put the dishes away from the night before. Mrs. Savage made breakfast and he did the dishes again. From eight to twelve, he had his lessons; then it was a quick lunch and visit with Aunt Petra, after which Mrs. Savage made it clear she wanted him gone until dinner and she didn't care where.

His studies with Mr. Snyder were indeed perplexing. They crisscrossed through history, bounced over math, and skipped into Latin. But mostly, these sessions became opportunities for Mr. Snyder to lecture. Somehow he always got around to his personal grievances and took great pains to explain how the politics and injustices of the world had spoiled everything for everybody, but mostly for him. When these lectures started, Tom knew he had a good half hour to drift and dream, for there was nothing to be gained by listening to them.

At such times, Tom would look out the window and think about his tree. Actually, it was Aunt Petra's tree, a stately old giant whose spreading limbs kept the whole back yard in dappled shade. In the afternoons when he was supposed to disappear, he would go for walks, then secretly return to climb the tree and lie for hours in its arms.

It was during one of those lectures, while Tom was contemplating that towering tree, that he saw a perfect spot where he could put a hidden platform. He scouted the neighborhood for just the right piece of scrap wood, and one day, when Mrs. Savage was out, he tied it to a long rope and laboriously hoisted it up the tree. He had quite a struggle making it secure, but finally there he was, standing on his platform high in the air. He then climbed up further and tied the rope around another sturdy branch. Now he could take great swings out and back from his platform, like the man on the flying trapeze. Eventually, he snuck up a blanket, and there he lay, looking up through the leaves to the sky. In those moments, he felt light and happy. He was at home in nature's house, and he hated to leave his contentment to descend every evening into the uncertainty of the world below.

One day as he was dozing up in his hideaway, he heard Mrs. Savage come running out the back door, waving an angry broom. The object of her wrath, he could see, was a large crow that had landed atop her laundry pole.

"Don't you dirty my clothes, you filthy beast!" she ranted. But the crow was determined to sit on that very pole. Whack! Whack! went her broom. The crow would fly up with an indignant squawk, then settle right back down again. It was hilarious, seeing the crow get the better of that bossy woman.

Finally the bird tired of the game and flew up into the tree. Tom drew back amongst the branches, fearing he would be seen . He heard the screen door slam, and then, to his amazement, the crow landed right on his platform. "Looking for a new crow's nest, are you?" Tom whispered. "How do you like our Mrs. Savage?" The crow flapped its wings and cocked a glistening eye his way, but didn't say a word.

21

THE CASTLE OF THE MOUNTAIN KING

Somewhere among mountain peaks, halfway between the slanting shadows and another place in time, King Mabon sat in the castle he had built in the land of Faery. He was one of the last of those who had come from the Human world, the last of the Tuatha de Monayans who had waited by the rippling shore and stepped onto those crystal ships. He alone had not blended with the faeries. Mabon remained thus a Human suspended in the realm of Faery.

Mabon's castle lay in ruins, and the king was now the oldest Human alive, yet he looked just as he had when he entered the Parallel World. His beard was gray, and his brow was furrowed; that was all. Mabon was a good king, but a contemplative, melancholy sort. As his people took up the life of the Otherworld, he withdrew more into himself. He thought about what it was to be Human and what it meant to be a creature of Faery. He thought of how these beings lived only as an expression of their essential spirit, and how no Human in all the many centuries had known how to be what he truly was. Man remained a mystery to himself—a combustible jumble of urges with a dangerous desire for power, unmatched by spiritual growth. Mabon saw Human history repeat itself with each oblivious generation.

Mabon's contemplations led him down many paths and brought him wisdom. In return, he became a kind of interpreter of Humanity for those of Faery who found its actions inexplicable and destructive. In time, the Great Beings began to appear to him: the Great Ones who guarded the centers of living force that linked the past to the future, who could provide secret openings through which the inexhaustible energies of the cosmos could pour. His communications with them made him less of a Human and more of a spirit. As a result, he was rather transparent in appearance, a somewhat ghostly form. His castle reflected his mind, for some parts of it were there and other parts of it were gone. A staircase would end nowhere; a corridor would lead into the ether; balconies hung in midair. His halls echoed with emptiness and no one came to his court anymore, save the lovely Rhea.

She lived a free impulsive life, but always came back to be near him. He could feel her energy coming toward him from a great distance. When she appeared in his court, Rhea threw everything into colorful relief again. As she passed up the stairs, it was as if she were a candle, lighting the darkness all around. When she sat beside him, the great fires would roar in the hearth. Those three drops of Human blood in her bound her to him like a daughter. She looked to Mabon when she reached the boundaries of her faery nature and the edge of her Human traces.

When Rhea returned this time, the castle was much less present than before, and King Mabon's own outline seemed to be disappearing into vapor. But the fires blazed, and they sat together once more. Rhea embraced him. "Can't you come with me?" she asked. "Can't you rest from your thoughts and restore yourself in the beauty of this world?"

"No, my little flame, it isn't as simple as that, for I know the beauty of two worlds. I also know that what is happening in one is causing the diminishment of the other. The time is coming again when something must pass between our two worlds to save them both. The boundaries separating these worlds must be crossed by a few so that the many can continue to live. This is not for me to do, but it might be for you."

"Me?" His words began to disturb her.

"Now, don't let me worry you. If such a time comes and you are asked, you will *want* to go, or you won't have to."

Rhea became frightened. The horrible story of the Women of the Wells was very familiar to her. Early in the history of mankind, relations between the two worlds were amicable and frequent. The faeries saw in Humans the shape of things to come. Humans possessed a greater capacity for creativity; their minds had greater scope; their emotions ran deep and strong. They were to be the inheritors of the earth. What Humans would do with their gifts weighed heavily on those who lived in the Parallel World. The faeries gave freely of their knowledge of magic and healing, and helped to create the abundance on earth that was there for Humans to reap.

At that time, there were many magic water wells maintained by faery nymphs. When a Human found his way to one of those fountains, the nymphs would offer him a drink from a golden chalice. They granted one wish and gave him his fill of whatever he most wanted to eat.

One black day, a king named Golgedan and his men found such a place. The nymphs came forth with the golden cup and offered its mystical contents. The men ravished them, spilled the precious water, and took the cup to melt down for its value in gold. Since that time, the two worlds had lived together in the same earthly atmosphere, but in separation and mistrust.

Rhea looked up at Mabon. "What you say is so troubling. Why can't things just stay as they are? You haven't been out in such a long time. There is so much freedom and beauty in our world. Let the Humans fight amongst themselves. I don't care."

Mabon smiled knowingly at her and then silently returned to his contemplations, looking deeper into the fire.

22

THE SILVER TRAY

In the months that followed, Tom did his best to gain knowledge from his studies and be some comfort to his aunt. It had become clear that Aunt Petra was as demanding and childish as she was lovable and endearing. It was also clear that Mrs. Savage could barely tolerate her after fifteen years of smiles and service. An eerie tension quickly grew between Tom and that unpredictable lady. She seemed always to be suspecting him of something, and he her.

Aunt Petra had not an inkling of all this, and sought to bring them closer together by having everyone eat dinner in her room each night. Mrs. Savage was quite put out by this, as she was accustomed to having her dinner alone with one of the fine bottles of wine left in the cellar by the late Mr. Wimpleton. Tom also found these dinners wearing. He wanted to be cheerful, but since the news had come of his mother's continued illness, jovial spirits were difficult to come by.

One fortunate discovery Tom made was that he could delight his aunt by describing his walks around the neighborhood. He told her about the people, the houses, the gardens, and the stores along the commercial streets. She especially loved it if he would describe some pretty thing he'd seen in a window display. His colorful ways of saying things amused her. She had great fun deciphering his puzzling words. A hat with shiny fabric and feathers that looked like eyes? "Oh, yes," she'd say nostalgically, "that would be satin with peacock feathers."

Mrs. Savage always smiled unceasingly in these moments, nodding her head and adding little "ums" and "ahs" to their conversations, all the while getting up and down, moving efficiently to bring the dinner hour to a prompt close. The one thing for which Mrs. Savage was eternally grateful in these proceedings was the dumbwaiter that Mr. Wimpleton had installed many years ago at the end of the hall.

A dumbwaiter is a kind of obsolete elevator for food. In the old days, they were installed in the houses of the wealthy so that the maids could hoist the meals up from the kitchen to the floors above without carrying everything by hand up the stairs. It worked by a series of pulleys: one rope pulled the platform up and another lowered it down again. Without that convenience, Mrs. Savage would not have been able to endure this insufferable new task.

One night, as Mrs. Savage was bustling down the hall with the empty dishes, she heard Tom say something that made her stop in her tracks. He was describing an antique shop he had seen with all this silver in the window. "It looked like a treasure trove," he said. "I've never seen anything like it. Silver candlesticks—silver goblets—silver knives, forks, and spoons."

Mrs. Savage quickly came back and took her seat, with as much interest in this story as Aunt Petra. "Well," Tom said, remembering all the things he had seen, "there was a silver tray that was really unusual. It was all leaves and vines around the edges, and the handles were like the branches of trees." Aunt Petra gasped. Mrs. Savage held her smile.

"Why," his aunt said, "that sounds exactly like the tray Mr. Wimpleton gave me."

"My goodness, that sounds like the very one," Mrs. Savage remarked with great curiosity. "Tell me, Tom, did this one have an etched pattern on the tray itself?"

"Etched pattern?" Tom wasn't sure what she meant. "I don't know. I don't think so..."

"Well, it's quite a similar description," Mrs. Savage said, rising from the table like a judge dismissing court. "But yours is very different. I remember it quite well."

"Well, still. We should get that out and use it again. I'd quite forgotten about it," said Aunt Petra.

"And so we shall. Why not?" Mrs. Savage replied, gathering up the rest of the dishes and whisking down the hall, cursing Tom under her breath.

23

AUNT PETRA'S OUTING

There must be some way to get Aunt Petra out of that stuffy house, Tom thought as he lay up in the crow's nest one lovely afternoon. *If I could get her downstairs somehow, I could roll her down the street, and I know she'd love that.* Tom worried about his aunt now as much as he did about his mother. For all the medicine she was taking, Aunt Petra didn't look well at all.

The news from home wasn't too encouraging, either, but his mother was adamant about his staying there. She never wanted him to come back to that coal town, no matter what. As soon as she was feeling better, she would come to see him. Thinking about what he would write to her in his next letter, he absentmindedly swung the rope that hung from above him out and back to the platform, out and back. Out and back. Up and down. *Wait a minute,* he suddenly thought. *Up and down. Why, of course. The dumbwaiter. It pulls things up and down. Maybe it can get Aunt Petra up and down and out of the house.*

He couldn't wait to try it himself. The next day, when Mrs. Savage had gone marketing, Tom went into the kitchen pantry where the door to the dumbwaiter was. Yes, it certainly was big enough for someone to climb into. But how much weight would it take? Tom climbed in and sat on the platform. Nothing happened. Nothing broke. *Well, now,* he thought, *I'll just see if I can haul myself up to the second floor.* And that he did with wonderful ease. The ropes and pulleys worked perfectly.

Now, just how heavy was Aunt Petra? That was his next question. He pulled himself back down to the pantry and got out to look for something heavy to add to his weight on the platform. He found that the books in the study would do perfectly. One by one, he added volumes, till finally he was satisfied when he was hauling the whole *Encyclopedia Britannica* up and down with him in the dumbwaiter. Now, whether he could actually convince his chubby little aunt to get in the dumbwaiter was another question entirely.

There was no telling Mrs. Savage about any of this. In fact, he had to hurry to get all the books out of the dumbwaiter before she returned. When she came back just as he was replacing that last volume, he pretended to be reading about zebras in the Zs. She eyed him suspiciously, plunking the grocery bags down and removing her hat. Mrs. Savage had a particular way of sticking her hat pin back in her hat that was very unnerving. "I'm glad to see you taking your studies so seriously. Now help me put away these things."

Tom had to wait till the next market day before he dared mention this to Aunt Petra. Those were the times when Mrs. Savage was gone longest from the house. He was sure Aunt Petra would be too scared and say no, but he had to try anyway.

To his surprise, Aunt Petra thought the idea was great fun. She trusted Tom completely. If he thought she could do it, she would. Anything to get outside once more. So Tom wheeled his aunt down the dark hall to the dumbwaiter on the second floor. "Oh, Tommy," his aunt said as he opened the little door. "How are you going to fold me up to get me in there?"

"You can stand for a little bit, can't you? I'll help you. Sit down backwards first and I'll push you around sideways."

"Oh, Tommy, Tommy," she puffed as she rose shaking and sat backwards on the platform.

"Wait a minute, wait a minute. Let me get the wheelchair ready for you downstairs." He hadn't thought about how he would get that down, but he didn't let her know.

"Okay, Tom. Okay. But hurry."

Tom clattered down the stairs with the wheelchair. He couldn't get it into the pantry exactly, but he got it angled in at the door. He raced back up to his waiting aunt and proceeded to pack her into the dumbwaiter. "Ready?" he panted.

"Ready, but I can't stay like this very long," she wheezed. "Oh, here we go!"

Tom pulled on the ropes and down she went, just like a load of dishes. Tom then ran down to the pantry, opened the door, and began to dislodge his aunt from the dumbwaiter. She emerged, hair and cap askew, her morning coat all twisted around. "Come on, Aunt, it's just a few steps to the chair."

"Hurry, hurry," she gasped, her chest heaving with the effort. Finally she collapsed into her wheelchair, triumphantly nodding to Tom. "Good, good." She smiled. "Now, quick, go up and get that bottle of pink pills on my table. I'll be all right, I've just got to catch my breath."

For the first time in many years, Aunt Petra was downstairs in her own home. She was so happy she had tears in her eyes as Tom rolled her through the dining room, across the entry hall, out the front door, and onto the porch. The two of them sat on the veranda, and Aunt Petra looked around like a child seeing the world for the first time. Tom leaped off the landing, and to her delight, did cartwheels across the lawn.

Hours later, Mrs. Savage unlocked the back door with her groceries and packages in hand. She stood in the kitchen and looked around. She took off her hat and plunged the pin back into its crown. "Something's different here." She quickly went up the back stairs to Aunt Petra's bedroom. The door was wide open and Petra was not there. How could that be? She walked briskly through each room on the second floor, thinking somehow Petra had wheeled herself around. Nothing. Everything was silent. She went downstairs, calling now, "Petra? Petra?"

She caught sight of the wheelchair through the curtain of the front window. She charged out onto the porch and there found Aunt Petra in her wheelchair sound asleep, with the summer breeze playing in the wisps of her disheveled hair. Across from her on the lounge lay Tom, also sound asleep.

"Well!" snorted Mrs. Savage. "What do you think you're doing?!" Tom woke with a start, and Aunt Petra grumbled to her senses. "Just what is going on here?" repeated Mrs. Savage, fully outraged.

Tom smiled in his enthusiasm. "Isn't it wonderful? I found a way to get her downstairs."

Aunt Petra looked up to her keeper for approval. "'Yes. Yes, isn't it wonderful? I'm so happy. I…"

"This is against all the doctor's wishes. I don't know how you did this, Tom. You had no right to take these matters into your own hands. I'm sure you've caused a serious setback for your aunt."

"No, no. I feel wonderful. You can't make me stay upstairs. I'm going to come outside with Tom now, any time I want, and you can't stop me!"

Mrs. Savage knew better than to pursue her attack. She switched tactics. "Of course. I just want what's best for you. Once I talk to the doctors and they say it's all right, why then, I'm sure it's all right." She paused to put on a composed smile, then asked Tom, "How *did* you get her downstairs?"

"In the dumbwaiter!" Both Tom and Petra laughed in delight.

"How creative," Mrs. Savage mused.

24

ONE FINE DAY

After that triumphant day of Aunt Petra's outing on the porch, life changed for the better on the surface of things. Tom made a wooden ramp to cover the steps at the kitchen door so he could wheel his aunt into the back yard or around front to the sidewalk.

This event even seemed to have a stimulating effect on old Toddie the dog. When he saw the wheelchair going out, he was motivated to lumber down the ramp and walk himself. They had to stop every few minutes for Toddie to catch his breath, but they were a happy trio, rolling along under the great arched trees of Aunt Petra's quiet street. Neighbors began to notice them and came out to greet her, saying how nice it was to see her out of confinement.

"Oh, yes," she'd say. "My grandnephew here has everything to do with it." Then she'd proceed to introduce Tom with such pride and affection that he was embarrassed.

While Tom was glowing in his aunt's praise, Mrs. Savage was growing angrier and more malevolent in her thoughts. She saw young Tom as an obstruction in her path. He was making her life much more complicated, not to mention all the additional work he was causing, what with all these dinners upstairs and teas outside under the tree and dressing and undressing the old woman five times a day. When she saw a little bloom begin to appear on Aunt Petra's cheeks, that was the last straw. She wasn't going to be thwarted by that little brat.

One fine day, Tom and Aunt Petra were outside under the tree waiting for lunch and Mrs. Savage was in the kitchen slamming dishes around, putting food on the silver tray which had suddenly reappeared in the household. The doorbell rang; Mrs. Savage grumbled as she wiped her hands on her apron and walked down the hall to the front door. She opened it to find the postman with a package for a Mr. Tom Quinn. She signed for it and went back to her kitchen duties.

When lunch was ready, Mrs. Savage yelled for Tom to come in and help her carry it out to the table. She held the tray and told him to take out the pitcher and glasses. As they were sitting down to eat, she said casually, "Oh, Tom, a package came for you. It's in the kitchen."

"For me?" He stood up, knocking over his chair. "I'll be right back."

"Don't be long. Everything will get cold," Mrs. Savage said, wrapping Aunt Petra's napkin around her neck.

Tom found the box. It was covered in brown paper, with a string around it and FRAGILE stamped on it in black letters. Tom suddenly became very quiet inside, for when he opened the box there was a letter and the little Christmas tree ornament he had made for his mother. The letter was from the neighbors where his mother was staying:

Dear Tom,

We have the very saddest of news to tell you. Your mother passed away this last week. I know this letter is a shocking way to find out about her death. But we are only following your mother's wishes in doing so. She was insistent up until the very last moment that you should not be sent for. "He mustn't come back, he mustn't come back," she kept repeating. My family and I loved your mother very much. We took care of her like she was our own. Her last wishes were that she be buried next to her husband quickly and with no ceremony. She wanted you to remember her as you last saw her, not consumed by the fever that eventually delivered her into our merciful God's hands. What's left of her money will be sent by check to your aunt so she can put it toward your education. This was your mother's wish.

Tom, we hope you will do as your mother wanted. Stay where you are. There is nothing for you here. Stay and make the better life for yourself that both your parents worked and hoped for.

In loving sympathy, Mary Kearny

"Tommy, Tommy, everything's cold," his aunt was calling from outside. "Mrs. Savage is quite put out..."

Tom opened the screen door and remained there with the letter in his hand.

"Tommy, Tom, what's the matter?"

Tom ran sobbing to his aunt. She held him tight, getting every bit as upset as he. She looked around, bewildered, as the child clung to her. "Mrs. Savage, what...what's happened?"

Mrs. Savage slowly rose from her seat and took the letter from Tom's hand. She sat back down while Aunt Petra looked desperately at her for help and carefully read the letter. After some moments, having gathered the full sense of what this all meant, she said calmly, "It seems the boy's mother has died."

"Oh, dear, no! Oh no. Oh, Tommy, no. That can't be. You poor dear. Oh, don't worry, we'll help, we'll take care of you. Ah, Mrs. Savage, isn't this awful?" Aunt Petra cried. "Oh, do something! We must do something!"

Mrs. Savage just sat at the other end of the table staring at her hands. Then she rose up and went to comfort Aunt Petra. "Yes, we'll definitely have to do something," she said, looking wistfully over their heads back toward the house.

25

IN THE DARK OF NIGHT

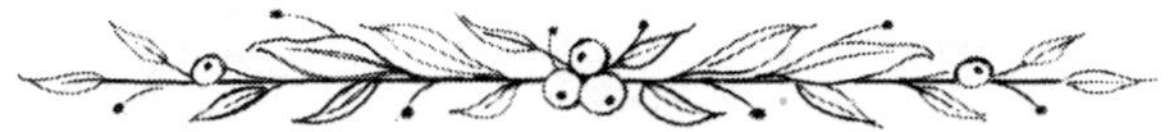

Tom felt as if he had been shot through the heart. He was in pieces, painful aching pieces. There was nowhere to go, inside or outside, to escape this pain. He just wanted to be alone. His Aunt Petra pleaded with him to stay close to her, and he tried, but he would always disappear back up into the tree. They never knew where he was. Sometimes he'd show up for his tutoring; sometimes not.

Weeks passed, and he had not taken Aunt Petra out once. She clearly was suffering for that, or so it appeared. Aunt Petra was declining. The bloom was off her cheeks, and she again took on the look of a powdered waxwork. The only one who seemed to be thriving was Mrs. Savage. She was all a-bustle with concerns and medications and ideas about what was best for everyone.

Tom lay up in the crow's nest, watching his mother's Christmas ornament swing among the leaves where he had hung it. It would be so much easier if he were the dead one and not the living. Both his parents were gone. He wanted to die as well. Anything to stop this overwhelming sense of loneliness and pain. Feelings of loss and guilt squeezed at his throat. He could neither breathe nor swallow. He resolved to be nothing, feel nothing, ever again. Many times he stayed all night in the crow's nest, sleeping, shivering, and crying.

He'd return to the kitchen in the morning, looking all stiff and aching. Mrs. Savage always had his breakfast for him, but she generally let him be. She was very busy these days. Tom noticed through his fog of grief that there was a lot of whispering going on. Mrs. Savage was always talking to Mr. Snyder, who was there all the time now, mostly in the kitchen whispering back to Mrs. Savage. They were talking about him, but he didn't care. He was tired. He just wanted to climb into the tree and go to sleep.

Those whispers even invaded his dreams, for now his dreams were full of voices talking to him from a black void. The voices whispered and spoke all at once over each other. "Is that the boy?" he'd hear a man's voice say. "My boy Tom," his mother would sigh. Other voices would say, "It's too soon." "He doesn't want to wake up." "I don't think he's the one." "Is that the boy?" "Can't tell." "What are you going to do?" "Wait." "Tommy, Tommy." "Is that the boy?" "I don't think he's going to wake up."

He would dream on, and then at some point he'd want to wake up, but he couldn't. He would want to move, but he was paralyzed and he couldn't breathe. With the utmost terror, he would struggle to consciousness, finally waking with a huge gulp of air.

One night, he awoke from one of these dreams high up in the crow's nest. He awoke out of darkness into darkness, not knowing where he was. He saw a light through the leaves. He stood up, took a step toward it, and tumbled off the platform. The tree and Tom's head made a loud cracking noise as they met on a branch below, but he managed to save himself from falling completely to the ground. The light became brighter; it was coming from a window on the second floor of the house. He saw the sheer drapes pull back, and Mrs. Savage appeared. She lifted the window and yelled sharply, "Who's out there?"

Tom blinked his eyes and held on to his branch for dear life. If he was not mistaken, that was Aunt Petra's pink dress she had on, and those were her jewels. And weren't those Mr. Snyder's long legs stretched out in the background? Mrs. Savage turned back and chastened those long legs to "Shut up and listen!" She scanned the tree with her piercing eyes. All was quiet, but there were mumbles behind her. "Shhh," she said. "I know something's there."

Just then, the crow dropped down with a screech and flew past the light. Mrs. Savage returned the report with a similar shriek and slammed down the window. She drew the curtains, adjusted her hair, and turned back to the long legs on the sofa.

"*Thank you*, Mr. Crow," Tom whispered emphatically. Then he slowly climbed down the tree and crept back to his broom closet to sleep the rest of the night, covers pulled up over his head.

26

THE AWFUL TRUTH

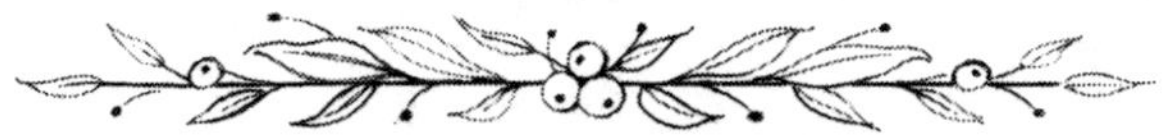

More days passed, and Tom recovered himself somewhat. He saw Aunt Petra's decline, and felt horrible for neglecting her. He tried to take her outside, but it was quite a struggle, even with Mr. Snyder helping. Aunt Petra had lost so much strength, and she would fall asleep at the drop of a hat. "Tommy, Tommy. Don't go away now," she kept saying. Even Mrs. Savage wasn't as militant with her as she used to be. There was no need; Aunt Petra was so weak.

Tom stayed by her side until he just could not stand that stuffy house any longer. Then out he'd have to go, for a walk and a climb to his crow's nest. There, he would fall asleep with those disturbing voices filling his dreams.

One afternoon, however, he woke up immediately as a voice right next to him shouted, "Tom!"

He sat up, finding himself face to face with the crow. "Yes?" he answered, looking at the bird. Tom rubbed his eyes and pushed back his hair. The crow kept looking straight at him. It raised its wings as if to fly away, then settled down again, all the while keeping its eye on Tom. Tom watched as the bird paced back and forth on the platform, then took off and landed on a windowsill of the house. He suddenly felt he must get down from the tree and go to his aunt at once.

Inside, Tom could hear Mrs. Savage's angry voice talking to Aunt Petra. "Take this, you old fool!" Then he heard a loud smack. He ran up the stairs, burst into the room, and saw Mrs. Savage standing over a whimpering Aunt Petra.

"What are you doing to her?" Tom demanded.

Mrs. Savage lashed back at him, "What am I doing? I'm doing what I've done for fifteen years! *I'm taking care of her!*" She spoke in a high-pitched, demonic tone. "Yes, *I'm giving her her medicine.* I *bathe* her, I *change* her, I *feed* her, and I *give her her medicine!*" She whirled back around to Petra. "Now take this, you silly woman!" Petra was struggling, unable to talk. Mrs. Savage pulled her head back by her hair and opened her mouth. "There!" she said as she shoved the pills down Petra's throat.

"Stop! Don't hurt her! Don't hurt her!" Tom raced over to Aunt Petra and tried to protect her. Mrs. Savage threw him against the wall with an angry shove.

"Don't you interfere with me, boy! I've had enough. I'm not hurting her. She has to take her medicine, and I'm giving it to her. It's the only way," she said, calming down a bit. "It's the only way. Your aunt knows I'm doing what's best for her. Now get on out of here."

Tom got up slowly and backed out of the room in terror. Aunt Petra was unconscious.

Tom ran to his little room and in a panic began to gather his things. What was he going to do? The woman was mad. He had to get out. He had to get Aunt Petra out. He sat there among his clothes on the bed, immobile with fear.

By dinnertime, he realized he had to act as if everything were the same. He'd have to wait till Mrs. Savage left the house long enough to get his aunt out.

Tom went down the back stairs to the kitchen, where Mrs. Savage was preparing dinner as efficiently as always. "Tom, help me cut up these potatoes and put them to boil," she said without turning around from her work.

"Yes, ma'am," he said, and set about the task.

When everything was ready, she loaded up the silver tray and put it in the dumbwaiter. "Haul it up," she said, and went upstairs to receive it on the second floor. Tom did so and then went up to his aunt's bedroom. There she was, in her chair, all neat and clean and powdered. She was awake and glad to see him. She kept looking at Mrs. Savage with the eyes of a whipped dog. "Now," Mrs. Savage said pleasantly, serving plates of food. "Did you have a nice day, Tom? How was your walk?"

Tom made an energetic attempt to describe the walk he hadn't taken. Aunt Petra smiled as Mrs. Savage fed her; she could no longer hold her own fork.

Tom endured several days of incredible tension, trying to act normal, watching his aunt like a hawk, and waiting for marketing day when Mrs. Savage would leave. Aunt Petra was having only intermittent moments of consciousness. She didn't seem to recognize Tom.

At last, Mrs. Savage secured her hat with the hat pin and readied herself for the marketing. "Your aunt is resting; she will be quite comfortable. I'll be back soon," she said, and went out the back door.

That screen door slamming was like a gunshot going off, marking the beginning of a race—a desperate race to freedom. Tom stumbled in his haste up the stairs. "Aunt Petra, Aunt Petra," he called. He tried to open her bedroom door—it was locked. "Aunt Petra," he called, but she gave no answer.

He ran outside, climbed the tree, and jumped onto the roof, then broke the window to her bedroom and climbed in. She wasn't in her chair; she was lying in bed. "Oh, no! Oh, no! Wake up! Wake up!" he cried, pulling his aunt up to a sitting position.

Aunt Petra opened her droopy lids. "Tommy?" she said in a faraway voice.

"Yes, it's me. We're getting out of here. We're going outside."

"No, Tommy, not today, I'm too weak..."

"No, you're not. I'm going to help you." He rolled the wheelchair up to the bed and pulled her chubby form into it.

"I'm sick, I feel so sick," she was saying.

"I know, I know." Tom wheeled her to the door. He was prepared to break it down, but he found he could unlock it from the inside. Aunt Petra's body sagged as he wheeled her to the dumbwaiter.

"Tommy, don't look at me, I'm going to be sick."

"No, no. Don't think that. You've got to get up. Get up and sit on the platform like you used to."

"Tommy, not any more...."

He was crying now as he tried to shove his poor aunt into the dumbwaiter like a sack of potatoes.

"Oh, oh," she moaned as he bent her legs in to close the door. *Oh God, oh God*, he prayed, racing downstairs to the pantry. He pulled and pulled on the ropes, and down came Aunt Petra. He raced upstairs and came tumbling down with the wheelchair. Back in the pantry, he pleaded with her to wake up. He couldn't pull her out of the dumbwaiter. She was grotesquely stuck in that square little space. She looked so white in that dark cabinet. Was she breathing? "Aunt Petra, Aunt Petra?"

"Oh my God, you've killed her!" thundered Mrs. Savage behind him. He turned to see her with her hat on her head and bags in hand. "You idiot, what are you doing? You've killed her!"

"No, no. I..."

Mrs. Savage dropped the bags and pushed him aside. "You don't know what you've done. Where did you think you were going? Trying to save her from Mrs. Savage? Well, now you've killed her! I'm going to call the police. I'll have you hanged for this."

Tom kept looking at Aunt Petra. "No, no! She's alive. She spoke to me!"

Mrs. Savage lunged at him, grabbing his shirt and pulling him to her. She leaned in over Aunt Petra and listened for a heartbeat. "You don't believe me? Well, look at this." She picked up Aunt Petra's arm and it fell back down with a dead slap against the wood. Mrs. Savage looked at Tom. "I'm calling the police," she said again, and dragged him down the hall to the door.

"No, no," pleaded Tom. "I didn't, I didn't. Oh, please," he begged.

Then she stopped and held him panting in her grip. She was thinking. Mrs. Savage looked deep into his soul with her wicked eyes, and the last of his resolve melted away. "I'll give you one chance. When I open this door, you better run. You better run for your life, because if I ever catch you this side of hell again, I'll have you hanged for murder!" She opened the door and flung him outside. Tom picked himself up and ran.

Mrs. Savage gave out a neat little exhale and closed the door behind her. Then she flopped down in the living room chair and let out a laugh that rang through the house.

Later that night when Mr. Snyder came to call, the house looked so different. All the windows glowed with light. He knocked, the door opened, and there was Mrs. Savage in the pink dress and jewels. "Welcome to my house," she said, smiling.

HOMELESS

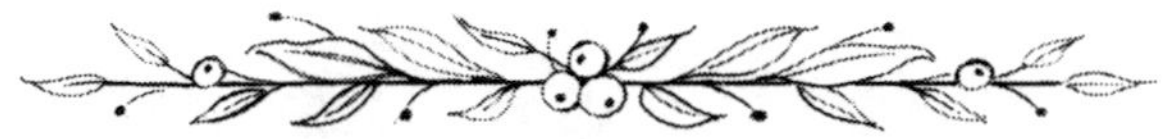

Tom ran through the streets. At every turn, he met those evil eyes of Mrs. Savage. They pursued him till he finally collapsed behind some boxes in an alley. There he slept, dead to the world, until the unearthly cries of a catfight woke him in the black of night. He crouched down and shivered till dawn.

As the sun rose, a tiny sunbeam entered the alley. The life force that ran strong within Tom's young body demanded that he get up and stand in that ray of light. He looked up between the buildings and welcomed the warmth on his face. Suddenly, he realized how hungry he was. He had to eat. So it was that his life force, with its driving instinct for survival, dragged his retreating mind back to reality. He ventured out cautiously, expecting to be apprehended at any moment.

From then on, he begged for food during the day and went back to his boxes at night. Tom kept to himself, and he soon found out that this distancing went both ways. People felt more comfortable ignoring him. They might drop a few pennies in his hand, but seldom made eye contact. They hurried away so as not to catch whatever ills had befallen him.

By day, the city was bustling. Everything whirled about him. Tom felt cast out from all that was normal and good. His nights brought on another kind of uneasiness, for he began to see that there were others like him who lived in the shadows—those who had given up the light of day. There were women who stood in doorways smoking cigarettes, and men who walked up to them, smelling of liquor. Ragpickers went through garbage. Drunks slept in the gutters and were beaten and robbed for their clothes.

One evening when Tom finally returned to his refuge in the alley,
he sank one more notch into despair, if that were possible...
The boxes had been taken...
He was homeless again....

THE FAERY RADE

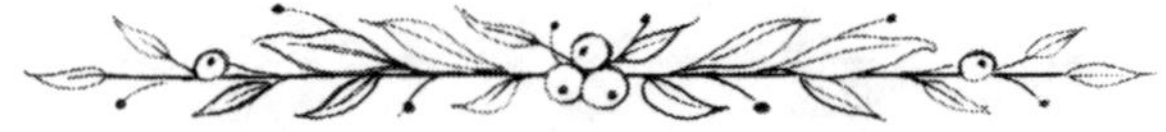

"Mabon, Mabon," Rhea called from atop a stairway in the castle that opened to the sky. She had come looking for him, but had found everything so disconnected and evaporating that she lost her way. Rhea could hear the echoes of whispers and bells. Several voices were speaking. One was Mabon's. The words sounded secret and important, but far away and muffled. "Mabon, Mabon," she called. He must have known she was coming, though, for the hearth fire was ablaze.

Rhea sat down to wait. Except for the crackling of the fire, there was an immense damp quiet in the great hall. The whispers echoed high up in the vaulted ceiling.

She grew impatient and went in search of Mabon again. Down one dark passage, she saw a light coming from under a door and opened it to find King Mabon at the window. He was surrounded by a shower of light filled with whispering voices. Mabon was looking into the light, talking, answering, agreeing with the sounds. His outline was just barely visible, so absorbed was he in the light. Rhea feared he would disappear completely. "Mabon," she called again. "Mabon, come back!" He seemed to hear her; with effort, he came back to himself and the light receded through the window.

He turned to her with ecstatic eyes and asked to be led back to the fire. Slowly, Rhea guided the old king back to the hearth, where he sat down in his antlered chair. Several moments passed in silence before Mabon finally said, "So, my little flower has brought me back to earth. How nice it is to see you. But I'm very tired. My mind has had much use tonight."

"Oh, Mabon, this is why I came—to take you with me. We are waiting for you to come. Many long to hear the old stories again and see their king once more."

"I don't see how that is possible."

"Please don't say that. We need to know our past and you are the only one left to tell the story. Besides, it is so beautiful outside. You will be enlivened, I know it."

"Oh, my dear..." He just looked at her and back again to the fire.

"The others have sent me to ask you this," Rhea went on. "They and the creatures of Faery want you to lead the Great Rade. They want to ride trooping through the country on the faery paths as we used to. Afterwards, we shall have the harvest feast. You haven't come out in such a long time—oh, please say you will. It will be good for you. It will be wonderful for everyone."

The old king looked into her young spirit all aglow and felt her love for him. "Yes, I will come." He relented.

Rhea put her head on his knee. "Oh, thank you! You'll see. I'll do everything. I shall set your colors out, and you shall carry the banner of the clan again. I'll prepare it all. Now, rest, my king, before the fire." She covered him in furs and left him fast asleep.

* * *

News flew round the realm that there was going to be an Autumn Faery Rade (for that was what these processions were called) and King Mabon was to lead it. Faeries draw their greatest joy from partaking of the beauty in nature. There is always time for revelry and fun, but this was to be an occasion of highest splendor. A sumptuous feast would be prepared; music and dancing would start with the setting sun. Along with the descendants of the Tuatha de Monayans, every sylph, deva, elf, and gnome in the region would attend. White faery horses were groomed with jewels cascading from their pale, flowing manes. Their golden livery was polished till it shone.

The day finally arrived, and the participants began to assemble. It was a magnificent autumn day. The leaves were turning scarlet and yellow, but many still held their green. The forest hills were a kaleidoscope of color. The music of trumpets, flutes, fiddles, and harps welled into a triumphant, merry tune. But all went quiet as King Mabon came before them. Many had never seen this forgotten monarch. When he mounted his horse and all saw him in his shining regalia, a great cheer went up and the procession began.

Rhea rode by his side, a velvet and crimson beauty. Then came the knights of the Faery Realm, in their green mantles fringed with gold. With them rode their ladies, dressed in scarlet silks and purple tapestries, their long sleeves billowing to the ground. Around their heads flew delicate flower sprites, emitting colors of pale yellow and pink. Elves and gnomes uttering magic words rode sprigs of rye grass that flew amongst the horses. It was again as it was before, and they all went forth on the ancient path.

Faery paths wind all over the earth. Where they cross, great power centers have emerged. Humans, not knowing why, have been drawn to build sanctuaries and places of worship in these spots. In their ignorance, Humans sometimes destroy one of these power centers, and that is cause for great sadness. It happened that on this wonderful celebratory rade, they came upon one of these desecrated places. Rhea knew of its whereabouts and made a point never to go there or think about it. When Mabon started down the path that led to it, she tried to dissuade him, but Mabon wanted to see that part of the mountain. He remembered it as having been so beautiful. Everyone tried to spare him the sight and suggested other ways to go, but no, Mabon had to see for himself. So it was that in the height of their merriment, in the glory of the afternoon, the whole party was brought up short before this sorry sight.

The procession stood silently, flags and colors waving, at the crest of a hill looking down onto what the Humans called the slag side of the mountain. It was where all the rock and debris from the mines were thrown. Nothing green could find its way through the crushing weight of all that refuse. It was a lifeless and barren place, brooded over by evil spirits that hovered amongst the rocks like flies.

Although he had seen such things before, it had been a long time since King Mabon had come face to face with such Human destruction. He was deeply affected. Through his despair, Rhea and others of the party began to realize the real horror of what they had simply put out of their minds. They were standing on the brink of a changing world they couldn't understand.

The others waited respectfully for Mabon to give the sign to turn back. When he did, they were truly relieved to forget and continue the rade. By the time they got back to the part of the forest where they were to have their autumn feast, all were merry and jubilant again.

But Mabon remembered. In his smiling eyes, tears formed, brimming with sadness.

29

APPLES AND ORANGES

The boy had walked three times past the store with the fruit stand outside. He appeared to be edging up to steal one. Wally Ripton had been watching from the second-floor window across the street for some minutes, enjoying the boy's dilemma. He motioned for his companion to come and view the drama.

"Cheng," he said, "if he steals the apple, he's ours." A burly Chinese pug of a man came and sat on the windowsill by Wally.

Outside, Tom was agonizing over his hunger and the apples that sat unattended outside the store. On his third pass, Tom stretched out his hand towards the apple. At that instant Wally flung up the window with a great clatter and shouted down, "Stop, thief!" There followed a great confusion. People stopped in alarm, looking up and down the street everywhere for the thief. The shopkeeper hurried out and saw Tom running away with the apple.

Wally smiled and pulled his head back in the window. He motioned for Cheng to go pick up his quarry, and sat down with his papers again.

Cheng quickly found Tom. Within minutes, he was being shuffled back to the scene of the crime, the apple still clutched in his hand. They ducked down an alley and went to the back of a building across the street from the grocery store.

Tom was frightened to death. He was guilty, guilty, guilty of many things, and now he had been caught. He was being dragged up some stairs; he fought with all his strength to escape, but to no avail. He found himself deposited in a small, cluttered, office-like apartment. It smelled of cigar smoke and the food that lay on a tray, precariously balanced on a pile of books. The room had a cot made up like a bed, an icebox, a safe, and lots of girly pictures bobbing about on a sea of newspapers and periodicals.

Wally unwedged his pudgy frame from behind his desk, walked to its front, and sat there, one leg up, with his arms folded across his chest. He looked as imposing as he was ever going to get. "I could have sent you to jail for this," he warned. "What's the matter with you? Where do you live?"

Tom couldn't speak, but his eyes told Wally all he needed to know. Staring at Tom with ominous concern, Wally said, "If a boy steals one thing, he might have also done some other things the law would like to know about. Cheng, this boy is not a first-timer. No, he's a seasoned criminal, he is. Don't you agree, Cheng?"

Cheng smiled and nodded.

"Now, by rights, I should turn you over to the police. Isn't that so, Cheng?"

Cheng smiled and nodded.

"But now, it just doesn't seem right to send a boy this young to prison, does it?"

Cheng shook his head and smiled.

Wally considered the situation for a few weighty moments while Tom waited motionless. "I think what I should to do in a case like this is take on the boy's rehabilitation myself. He can stay here and work for me until such time as I feel he is completely cured of his vagrant ways. I think that's the humane thing to do, don't you, Cheng?"

Another nod and smile from Cheng brought the gavel down on Tom's fate.

"Well, then. It's all settled. You certainly don't want a prison sentence to hound you all your life, do you, boy?"

"No," stammered Tom, thinking he had run into some branch of the authorities and that he had better cooperate.

"Cheng, take this boy—what's your name, son? Tom? Tom Quinn? All right, Cheng, take Tom down to Mrs. Ripton. Tell her to fix him a bowl of soup. This here's the new kitchen help she's been pestering me for."

30

OUT OF THE FRYING PAN INTO THE FIRE

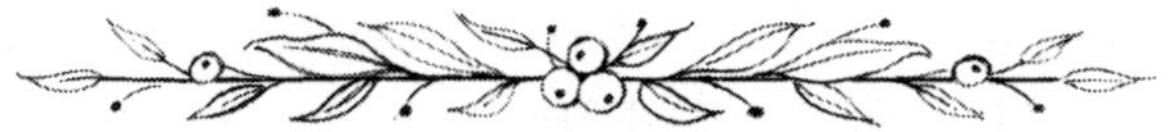

His sentence having been pronounced, Tom was quickly scuttled downstairs and marched into a large kitchen. There were things boiling, stewing, and steaming everywhere. A large black woman with mammoth hands was stirring something delicious on a fiery burner. At a table in the center stood a plump woman in a frightfully colored dressing gown, her back to him, chopping up cucumbers with speedy, decisive whacks. The top of her head bristled with pin curlers and it appeared that she had no neck, for the collar of the gown came up to her ears.

"Oh, Lor', good Lor'." The black woman looked up from her stewpot and pointed at Tom with her spoon. "What's that?"

"This... you... kitchen boy," Cheng answered, giving Tom's shoulder a shove. He swiped a couple of celery sticks and quickly disappeared back upstairs.

"Oh, Lor', Lordy, where they find you?" The black woman shook her head at the sight of poor pitiful Tom. "Um, um." She shook her head again. "Well, all I can say is, you done jumped out o' the frying pan into the fire here, boy."

"Now don't get smart, Nettie. I won't have you talking smart," the other woman said over her shoulder, chopping away. Then she suddenly whirled around to get a good look at Tom for herself.

Tom gasped and fell backwards to the floor. He had never seen such a specter in his life. The woman stood there, knife in hand, swirling in colors, with a green mask on her face. Tom put his hand up before his eyes.

The black woman roared with laughter. This was too much. She had to sit down and mop her eyes with her apron. "Oh, Lor'... oh, Lor', Lordy!"

"Nettie, Nettie, you shut up! I won't tolerate your insolence before that rag of a boy!" The masked woman looked back at him. "What's your name?" she asked, hardly moving her lips.

Tom couldn't find his voice. Nettie smiled encouragingly at him and motioned for him to come over to her. Her big hands went all over him, smoothing his hair, straightening his clothes. She smelled like sweat and sweet spices. "Now, Missus Ripton. Give the boy a chance. He's had a bad fright." She grinned, cracking up again. There was something about her laughter: it made Tom want to laugh too, though his situation didn't seem funny in the least.

Mrs. Ripton summed things up quickly. "Well, whatever his name is, put him to work. I'm tired of doing everything around here." Whereupon she piled her cucumbers into a bowl, announcing she was going to retire till supper, and promptly left them to carry on.

"Humph, that woman! She smart. She got more ways to do nothin' than the devil has ideas. I swear, the only thing she do is make me mad. Anyways, you sit here while I fixes you a big ole plate of stew. I can see that's the only thing occupying yo' mind, an' rightly so, Lord, rightly so."

Nettie watched as the boy devoured plate after plate of her thick, meaty stew. When he couldn't eat any more, he looked up with a kind of stupefied expression.

"Looks as though yo' gots to do some retiring before supper too. Go ahead. Lay down over there."

Tom made it over to a wooden bench, gratefully accepting a sack of flour as a pillow. He fell fast asleep amid the wonderful sounds and smells of that warm kitchen.

Nettie went on stirring pots and rolling dough, singing a monotonous comforting song. At one point she looked up, hearing Tom's legs running and scuffling, like a dog dreaming in its sleep. "No," he was saying. "No, I didn't, I didn't mean it."

"Oh, honey," she mused. "Um um...none of us *meant* to...but we done woun' up here anyway. Um um," she hummed. "Um um," she sang to her pots.

Outside, the day simmered down to evening. Nettie finally woke Tom, saying it was supper time, time to help her.

"This ole house is full o' people an' they's always hungry. When they set down to eat, Lordy, yo' never seen the likes of it. Go wash yo' face in that sink. There's a towel hangin' underneath."

Tom was only too glad to do as she asked. Nettie had been good to him. What was this hungry horde that was about to descend upon the dinner table?

Tom helped carry plates of bread, meat, and potatoes to another room where there was a large table surrounded by a set of mismatched chairs. The room had a haphazard feel. He'd had the same impression when he used to peer into the windows of those cluttered antique shops. Everything was a jumble of colors and styles. The long table was the only unifying force in the confusion.

The clock struck five and sure enough, the building vibrated with the sounds of doors opening, footsteps on stairs, voices in the halls. By ones and twos, the strangest assortment of people collected and took their seats around the table.

"What is it tonight, Nettie?" "Um, beef—good." "Pass the potatoes."

They all set to their dinner with vigor. There was very little conversation besides that which pertained to the consumption of the food. Nettie kept Tom busy bringing plates back and forth. When there was a moment to rest, she stood in the doorway with Tom. "Lordy," she whispered, "what a passel o' people!"

Tom looked up at Nettie and back at the table. At either end sat Mr. and Mrs. Ripton. Wally Ripton, the man who had taken Tom's rehabilitation upon himself, sat eating and smoking at the same time. His tight jacket and vest strained at the seams with each new bite of food. Mrs. Ripton, now de-masked, was made up in the cheeriest pinks and reds. Her hair sprung from the top of her head in outrageous curls. She sat daintily, devouring her meat and potatoes.

"Them's the Three Peaches," Nettie said, nodding her head toward three women busy on one side of the table. "Leastways, that's what they's called. Miz Ripton dresses 'em up like fruitcakes to dance in front of the menfolk. An' that's not all they do...them peaches is plucked!"

Tom did think the women looked a little worse for wear. Two of them wore most forlorn looks under their high arched eyebrows and ruby lips. The one in the middle, however, appeared very self-assured, almost brazen. She wore a very revealing dress whose straps kept slipping down her arms; she made no attempt to put them back up.

Next to them sat a tall man, thin but athletic. Tom saw his hands shake when he picked up his glass. "That the carpenter." Nettie motioned with her head. She sighed, wiping her hands on her apron. "He good, but he broken too. They say he used to walk on high wires and things, working in the circus. But he like to drink. One night he let his partner fall to the ground dead. Anyhow, that's how the story go, an' it were the end o' him. Now he just around here, fixin' things; that why he called the carpenter. Don't you mess with him neither. When he get drinking, he mean."

Tom saw Cheng with his broad, chunky shoulders, hunkering down over his food next to Wally. Opposite him sat the oddest creature Tom had ever seen: a dwarf. He had a big head with shaggy eyebrows and a beard. His eyes darted everywhere at once, over the food, the people, and back again, constantly sizing things up and making inscrutable calculations. Tom felt an instant dislike for him.

There were two other men there: one was very fat and soft-looking, with his long hair pulled back in a ponytail, and the other was all muscle, with tattoos popping out from under his shirtsleeves.

"Humph," Nettie said, pulling Tom back down the hall with her. "There's a whole lot of messin' around going on here. But there's one person they ain't messin' with, an' that's Nettie. An' they knows it. If'n they mess with me, I sure don't do no cookin'. An' that's the end o' that. If'n I don't do nothin', there ain't a one o' them that could scramble an egg so's you could eat it."

Nettie sat down in her kitchen and drew Tom close to her. "So now listen," she cooed, smoothing Tom's dark tangled hair. "You listen to me, my little blackbird, an' you be all right."

Tom felt those strong hands on his shoulders, and in spite of all his fears, he somehow believed her.

31

RIPTON'S THEATRICALS AND CURIOSITIES

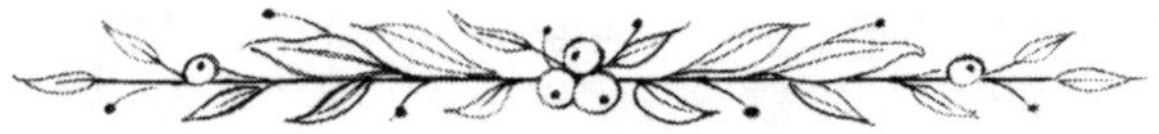

And so it was that Tom Quinn entered the employ of Wallace Ripton. He soon realized that Wally and his ragtag troop had no connection to the law. In fact, they were just as determined to avoid it as he was. Since it didn't really matter to Tom what he did or where he was anymore, he stayed on. He never thought about going back. He couldn't.

Tom had become anxious, always on guard for something awful to happen, sure that somehow everything was his fault. It was his fault that his mother had died. He should never have left her, and certainly he had killed his poor Aunt Pet. He deserved what he got. Now he kept to himself and waited miserably for his end like a prisoner on death row. When Wally Ripton met up with him, Tom had been perfect bait. Wally quickly saw his vulnerabilities and bound Tom to him with veiled threats couched in sympathy.

Wally ran a combination brothel, musical revue, and freak show called "Ripton's Theatricals and Curiosities." He gathered his "talent" from the human flotsam floating directionless at society's edges; he didn't hire his troupe so much as collect them. Though these unfortunates had to swallow regular ladles of abuse and contempt, they usually stayed for the food, the lodging, and the sense that at least they belonged somewhere. Most of the year, Wally housed his enterprise at a ramshackle emporium that he named "The Madrigal." For four weeks in the summer, however, he took his show on the road.

This had come about because of a lucky hand in a game of cards—one of many "lucky hands" of which Wally always assured himself. One night, the owner of a small traveling circus had walked into one of the poker games in the back room of the Madrigal. He walked out with nothing but the proverbial shirt on his back. Wally had won six circus wagons, one automobile, a truck, eight horses, and a small parcel of land outside the city on which to keep them—all courtesy of that unlucky man, who now also belonged to Wally.

It was at this point that he changed the name of his company from "Wally Ripton's Theatricals" to "Ripton's Theatricals and Curiosities," for he had also acquired the circus's four-horned goat and two-headed turtle, a dwarf, and a bearded fat lady who was really a man. In the summer months, Wally found he could do well by traveling the old circus route through the farm country. These trips resulted from the nostalgic tales old Ben, the previous owner, would tell of his circus days, and more especially because of the illegal liquor that could be bought from stills maintained by backwoods people living higher up in the foothills. Scoring a good batch of cheap hooch in the summer meant more profits for the Madrigal in the winter.

Wally fancied himself an impresario of sorts, and he liked things to go a certain way—his way. He had the personality of a sugarcoated knife: all chubby and rosy on the outside, but metallic and ruthless on the inside. If provoked, he could get very nasty. That is to say, his bodyguard Cheng could get nasty. Wally didn't have the body or strength to get physical with his anger. No, for that he needed an extension of himself, a strong arm to mete out justice when things got out of hand—his hands, that is.

Cheng, his burly, squat Chinese henchman, was only too happy to bash a few heads no matter what the cause. In another life, Cheng might have been a great warlord, but in this one his unfortunate soul had to reside in the body of a misfit full of anger and hate. He needed to be mighty, but instead was dull and limited. He was the son of Chinese immigrants who had worked as cheap labor on the railroads and then opened a small laundry in some obscure western town. Cheng had nothing but disdain for his parents, who had made him a permanent exile in a land where people looked down on him. Work of the kind his father did was something Cheng would never do; learning from the books of drivel that the Christian schools handed out was something else he would never do. And so he drifted, ignorant and angry, until he met up with Wally and his theatrical revue, and there Cheng stayed. His talent for head-bashing had finally found a place.

With Cheng at his side, Wally had his world pretty well in line. The one person he could not control, but could only keep at bay, was his wife Mavis. She was his match in greed, cunning, and self-absorption. Long ago they had separated their domain into two territories: his and hers. Wally brought in the business; she oversaw the bookkeeping and the household.

Mavis Ripton ran a very tight ship, except when it came to herself. She fancied herself as having been a great beauty, but now she was engaged in a continual battle with her crumbling façade. She fought back the effects of time with an arsenal of creams and pastes, and took many naps to restore her youthful splendor. The clothes Mavis wore were always too young and too flamboyant. She had a particular penchant for wearing little velvet slippers with curved heels. Those dainty shoes were never meant to support the weight she thrust onto them, and they stretched, bulged, and ran over their tiny soles in a most abject way. Knowing well that vanity was the one chink in her armor, Wally always showered Mavis with flattery to support her view of herself and keep her quiet. She was his "Little Princess," "Mighty Queen," "Cupcake," "Buttercup," "Treasure Trove," and so on, ad nauseam.

Wally, for his part, lived mostly in his office-apartment, his private lair on the second floor of the Madrigal. It was separate from the rest of the building. The only way up was by the back stairs in the alley. Only Cheng, the dwarf, and assorted female visitors were allowed access to his inner sanctum. No one knew what went on up there, except the Three Peaches, and they never spoke a word. They lived in dread of being summoned to his office, where one of them would be plied with drinks and tortured with his attentions for a few hours of an evening. Indeed, the Madrigal was Wally's world, and those that lived there knew it to be a prison, though it had no bars.

32

THE MADRIGAL

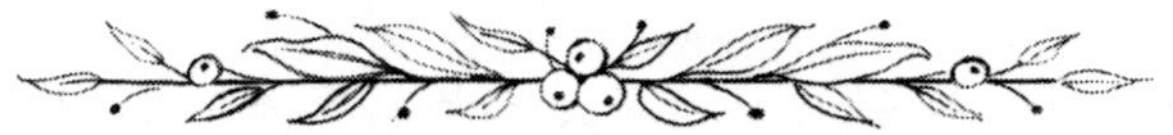

Days collected into years, and Tom was now sixteen. It wasn't because of anything Wally Ripton did that he blossomed and grew: no, it was entirely a result of Nettie's love and care. She saw him as something special—a shiny-haired blackbird, a prince among rats. She fed him, nurtured him, and shielded him as best she could from life at the Madrigal. Tom responded to this attention by growing with leaps and bounds into a handsome young man. His beauty was not lost on the Peaches, who tried to extend him their favors, but under Nettie's tutelage, Tom resisted their charms.

However, while Tom grew in stature and strength on the outside, he stayed on guard and repressed on the inside. He still felt that a great doom was about to befall him, and he dared not show his head for fear it might be cut off at any moment.

Wally knew Tom was hiding something—some great guilt. He didn't know what it was, but it cowed Tom sufficiently to keep him under his power.

Life at the Madrigal was colorful and complex. It opened around five in the afternoon and didn't close till the last drink was sold and the last card was played. The first crowd to come in were the blue-collar workers. For fifty cents, they got a pint of beer, a piece of bread, and a hearty bowl of whatever Nettie had cooked up that day. Tom served as waiter, dishwasher, pot-stirrer, and potato-peeler. This group was a relatively quiet one—mostly tired men eating their simple meals, ready to go home and flop on their rooming-house beds. There was even a separate dining room where working women of the secretarial kind could dine out in a respectable manner.

The atmosphere changed at the Madrigal after eight. Its heart beat faster: voices grew louder, men at the bar slapped each other on the back, and the little room where ladies dined turned into the little room where women drank.

Tom's job was to push the pedals of the player piano until the first show went on at nine. This was announced by the master of ceremonies, Wally Ripton. A new tune was put on the drum rollers of the piano, and a rousing dance was performed by the Three Peaches. This part of the show was Mavis Ripton's creation: she was choreographer and costume designer in one. Her girls wore what she made and did exactly as she told them. Mavis's costumes were the best part of the act. She was serious, but they were outrageous. The current ones were little red outfits with white hearts scattered all over like polka dots, topped with red satin bon-bon boxes for hats, held on with great bows tied at the top. But that wasn't all: Mavis always kept a fashion surprise for the end. In this routine, after the girls finished clattering, tapping, kicking and singing, they all bent over, bottoms up, to reveal cut-out heart panties with white edging. That surprised the audience every time. They would roar, and the girls would do an encore.

Next came the carpenter, who, when he was sober, could walk on stilts. He would enter with the dwarf, which was good for a laugh right away. Their routine involved shouting up and down at each other and getting everything mixed up because they were too far away to hear each other. It ended with the carpenter getting mad and trying to catch the dwarf while running around on the stilts.

The second show of the night went on at eleven, when the Madrigal was swilling with liquor and broad gestures. The women who drank in the little room were now slugging it down right alongside the men. At this point, fights might break out, and when they did, Cheng went into action.

Work was never done for the Peaches. When they weren't dancing, they were "entertaining" men in their rooms all through the evening. Tom kept waiting on tables and pumping the piano till the end, usually about two. Wally definitely got his money's worth out of his employees.

33

THE INNER SANCTUM

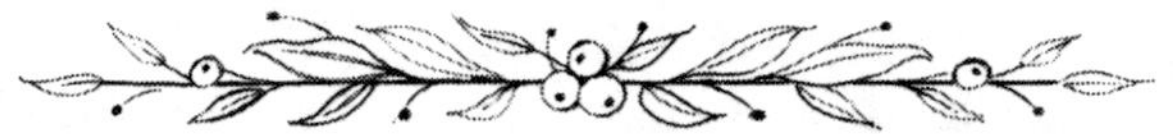

Wally Ripton was a very knowledgeable man. He read a lot. That was how he knew the meaning of the word "madrigal," while others only knew they liked the sound of it. When it came to books, magazines, and newspapers, Wally was a pack rat. His upstairs office was filled with stacks of papers he had yet to finish. He liked nothing better than to sit with his feet propped up on the desk and have a good read. Sometimes he went from there straight to sleep on his cot, never changing his clothes for days, except his shirt.

His wife liked to sleep with the windows open: that was one reason why Wally had taken up residence in his office. He liked a certain airless quality to his rooms. Fresh air had its place—outdoors. Inside, it disturbed his concentration. In certain ways, Wally was meticulous. He went to the barbershop every day for a shave and a manicure.

Wally had few friends, since he was always making sure he had the advantage over other people. After he acquired the circus and the dwarf came into his life, they had struck up a strange friendship. They were similar in their calculating ways and, they found, in their idiosyncrasies toward the opposite sex. Cheng completed Wally's inner circle of friends with his faithfulness and total lack of conscience. When those two were invited up to Wally's inner sanctum, they didn't come back down till the wee hours of the morning.

One night, Wally and the dwarf sat silently in the office with an expectant air about them. It was extremely hot and close in that room. They looked wasted and tired. They heard the sound of Cheng's footsteps on the stairs, and both looked up at the door as he opened it.

"Well," Wally said, "everything all right?"

"Yes. Done," answered Cheng.

"Good. Well, I'm going to bed," Wally said with a definite tone.

Taking their cue, the Chinese man and the dwarf left simultaneously.

Wally didn't emerge till the next afternoon. That night, he was standing in the Madrigal, cigar in hand, elbow on the bar, watching Lorna, the Peach with the loose shoulder straps. She was talking to a man sitting on a barstool at the far end.

Wally seemed all full of himself, puffed up. He was watching Lorna's bare back as it slanted this way and that while she spoke. "Lorna!" he impulsively called over the din. She answered him with a look over her shoulder, then turned again to the man.

In an instant, that pretty back became an insult—a challenge. Wally lunged forward toward the end of the bar.

Tom was stacking dishes behind the bar. He watched Wally go for Lorna and pull her around by the dress strap. "I said, come here."

"And I said I'd be there," Lorna replied.

"Oh? Well, it wasn't fast enough," Wally spit back. The man she was with started to make a move, but Cheng intervened.

Lorna glowered at Wally. "I was only doing my job."

"Your job is to come when I call you. Get it?"

Pale with humiliation, Lorna straightened her dress. "Got it," she said, trembling. Head held high, she walked through the crowd until she was outside, where she burst into tears.

Tom, watching this painful little drama, felt terrible. He quickly dried his hands and went out the back way and around to where she was.

"Lorna?" he whispered sympathetically. She turned away from him and pressed one shoulder against the wall. Wanting to do something, say something, he shoved his hands in his pockets and leaned against the wall close to her. "Lorna, I—I'm..."

"You what?" she cried, suddenly turning back to confront him.

"I'm... are you all right?"

"Am I all right?" Lorna answered incredulously. She laughed a loud miserable laugh, to the world, to herself. "You know what I don't get?" She looked at him long and hard through her dark-rimmed eyes, and Tom stepped back self-consciously. "What's keeping you here? Why don't you leave?"

He stammered a few words and glanced off down the street. *Leave?* he thought. *Leave for where?* Tom had no plans for himself. A future? What was that? He was still caught up in hiding himself from his past.

"I see," Lorna said, comprehending. She exhaled a defeated, exasperated sigh, then suddenly grasped the arm of a man walking by. "Hey, sweetie, you got a cigarette?"

"Why, uh, sure," he stammered, caught off guard. He fumbled in his pocket for his cigarettes, gave her one, then patted his coat for his lighter.

Lorna looked at Tom while the man lit her cigarette. "You go back to work," she said, all friendly-like. "I'm all right. I'm going to stay out here for a while." She cozied up to the man, who was already captivated by her.

Tom stayed long enough to watch her go into action, then disappeared down the alley, back to the kitchen and his dishes.

34

SUMMER

The carpenter was very useful—so useful that Wally put up with his periodic alcoholic binges. His name was Victor Nash. Nobody called him Victor, just Nash or "the carpenter." He was a kind man who reminded Tom somewhat of his father. Nash was good with his hands. He could repair or build anything, and it just came natural that Tom took to being his apprentice.

Before Ripton's troupe went on the road each summer, Tom and Nash were sent to "the farm" some days ahead to get the wagons and trucks in shape. Tom loved those days. It was out of the city, he was free, and there was no one around but the old circus owner and a couple of stable hands.

The first thing they did was roll out the circus wagons from the sheds where they were stored all winter. The wagons had that damp, closed-up smell, and the carpenter couldn't stand the odor. "Open them doors and windows, Tom," he would say. "Air out that mousey stink."

It was true that the birds and mice did manage to find their way in, but Tom loved the little cabin interiors. They were like gypsy wagons to him, brightly painted even on the inside. There were fold-down tables and bunk beds, little dressing alcoves, and lots of drawers. Each wagon could sleep three people—four in a crunch. Whoever had originally painted the wagons had put a lot of artistry into them: inside, there were flowers and vines painted on the paneling, and outside they were decorated in combinations of blues and reds with yellow trim. Everything was faded now, but Tom liked that about the wagons. When he went inside one of them, he felt he was stepping back in time.

The carpenter usually worked for the first five days, then jumped off the deep end into one of his benders for the last three. They'd roll him into one of the wagons and he'd sleep it off on the road.

Tom was a great help. He learned fast and was very resourceful. He also had another talent that unfortunately earned him Cheng's enmity: Tom was mechanically inclined. He could drive and work on autos like nobody else, and Cheng was extremely jealous. There was power in those engines, and he wanted to drive them, but somehow he just never got the hang of it. When he drove, everybody lurched and bounced as he gunned the motor while putting on the brakes. When Wally removed Cheng from the wheel in favor of Tom's smooth ride, Cheng never forgave Tom for the insult.

The animals had to be groomed and readied too, though the stable hands did most everything. Tom loved to run the horses out to pasture and let them roam free. There was just no prettier sight than those horses grazing in the tall flowered grass. The circus had seven ordinary horses and one Clydesdale, a giant of a horse like none Tom had ever seen. His name was Nip, because every time he was groomed, he'd reach around and nip the groomer in the pants. The stable men finally gave up and let him go rough and shaggy.

Summer was when Tom felt the best. How wonderful it was just to flop down in that meadow and disappear. Sometimes, lying on his back, he would put his arm up and wave it like a blade of grass reaching for the sky. He wondered what he would ever become in this life. He had no ambitions to gain power, accumulate wealth, or acquire possessions. It all seemed like such a vain struggle.

He was in his own prison of fear and guilt. In his resistance, his isolation from life, he'd felt like he was holding back the forces of doom. It was a matter of survival: he couldn't be hurt if he couldn't be found. But now, as a young man, his life hung upon him like a coat of chains. Sometimes, he could hardly endure the weight of it. He was living in a wasteland where his own soul remained a mystery to him. Here, lying in the field, he felt the pointless chatter of his thoughts fade and he was at peace. He felt like stretching, expanding.

Tom gathered up an armful of tall, sweet grasses and inhaled deeply. That smell, that summer perfume, wafted through his brain. Suddenly the cloistered chamber of his heart unlocked and he felt a rush of ecstasy as his inner being opened itself to the light of day.

The sun was setting when Tom roused himself to take the horses back into the barn. Tom was the only one whom Nip would let ride him without a grumble. He would lead Nip up under a tree, then ease down onto his back from a branch above. It was great, riding home on that giant, lumbering horse with the others following behind. It was no trouble getting them to go back: they all returned to the barn like homing pigeons.

Tom led the horses into the corral, where they all lined up for a long drink of water at the trough. Things were kind of quiet. Where was everybody? He heard a rustling, fluttering sound inside the barn. He pushed back the dry wooden door and peered into the cavernous, dusty interior. From up in the rafters over the stacked hay, a black crow cawed, then swooped down and out the door. Tom ducked as the crow flew over. The horses in the corral scattered nervously.

"Hey," Tom called as his eyes followed the crow's flight. Tom blinked, and the bird disappeared as if a hole had opened in the sky and swallowed it up. Tom searched the pale evening dusk for a sign of the crow, but it was gone.

"Hey," Tom called again. He needed some help getting the horses settled in for the night. "Hey!"

"Hallelujah!" was the return chorus from behind the house. *Hallelujah?* Tom thought with a sigh of resignation, for he knew the drinking had begun. He followed the Lord's praises around to the back of the farmhouse, and there they all were, smoking, drinking, and throwing sticks on the fire they were building.

"Join the cookout," the carpenter said, patting a seat on the bench beside him. His eyes had that devilish grin they got when he started to loosen up.

"Before you guys start roasting yourselves, I need some help with the horses," Tom said.

"Help is on the way." Nash jumped up and blew a trumpet charge through his fingers. The others fell in behind him in mock military fashion. Off they marched to the corral. The horses, getting a whiff of the men's altered state, became even more agitated, running in every direction. Nash kept sounding the trumpet, and the men climbed up and fell over into the corral. Tom could only shake his head at the mayhem that followed. Men ran after horses, horses ran after men, amid shouts of "Yahoo!" and "Ride 'em, cowboy!"

Tom wisely stood by the corral gate, and when one of the horses shied near it, he opened the gate like a chute and the horse ran through to the barn all by itself—gladly. So one by one, Tom got the horses stabled, till there was nothing but a pile of men left in the corral.

"Well done," Nash complimented his troops as they staggered to their feet. "What's for dinner?"

As they walked back to the farmhouse, Nash got Tom's head under his arm, knuckling him. "Tonight you're going to be initiated. Yes, sir; tonight yer drinkin' with us."

When the moon was high, they were all drunker than skunks, sitting out by the fire. Tom was laughing at something somebody said. His cheeks were red and his hair stuck up like it was drunk too. His face hurt. His sides hurt. He rolled out of the circle by the fire and rolled and rolled, laughing up to the sky, until he realized he'd just rolled over two big green leafy feet. He wavered for a moment, then looked up to see a green man, a green man all made out of leaves, standing there, hands on hips, looking down at him, laughing a deep laugh that seemed to vibrate down into the earth.

Tom lay there panting, trying to keep his balance. Even though he was flat out on his stomach, things were taking a serious twist. He rolled back to the circle of men and sat up cross-legged next to Nash, reaching for the carpenter's arm to steady himself.

Nash looked over at his handiwork and said, "Wha'sa matter, son? You gettin' the twirlies?"

Tom looked over his shoulder, then back to Nash. He couldn't speak. He just panted.

"That's right, boy. It'll pass. Jus' keep taking those deep breaths."

Tom looked over his shoulder again. Funny thing, the leaf man was still there, laughing at him. Tom blinked several times, leaning against Nash as his head spun.

"Here, eat something," Nash said. Tom pushed it away in disgust. "Well, then, drink something," Nash said, pouring him another glass.

Funny thing—now that green man was standing right in front of Tom. He took the drink out of Tom's hand, downed it himself, and gave it back to Tom. Nobody else seemed to see him: the green man just stood there, laughing. The sparks from the fire flickered all around him and through him.

Another funny thing: when Tom took a drink now, it tasted just like water, not liquor at all. He watched with fascination as this green man became an unseen member of the party. He'd walk around, sit down next to someone, listen to what they said, then shake his head, look over at Tom, and laugh. He wasn't laughing at the drunken talk; he was laughing at Tom.

As a matter of fact, he was making Tom mad, laughing at him like that. Every time he wanted to pour another glass, there was that irritating green man, taking his drink, downing it, and handing him back water. By now the men's voices by the fire were getting all mixed up with other voices—voices he used to hear in his dreams. "Is that the boy?" "Tom, Tom!" "Yes." "He doesn't want to wake up."

A wave of nausea hit Tom, and suddenly he was on a roller coaster ride, crawling on his hands and knees over to the bushes to be sick, or perhaps die; yes, that would be preferable. Tom's stomach gave out its contents in one horrible retching contraction. Afterwards, he lay there, unable to move, watching the stars circle the sky.

The leaf man leaned into his field of vision again, and behind him moved the more ghostly form of an old man. Words in a vaguely familiar language that he couldn't understand drifted through Tom's head as he stared up at constantly shifting visions. The green man's face was dissolving into leaves, and through them he was seeing a wooded glen. Over that, like a wavering mirage, a beautiful creature was emerging from water, offering him something.

Then everything shattered into a monstrous vision of war. Battle after battle was fought. Back and forth, back and forth through the wood these armies fought, till nothing was left: not a tree, not a bush, not a blade of grass. Just the earth, pounded hard and barren. There was more whispering, more voices, more questions. Finally, his sodden mind remembered the sweet-smelling field he had lain in earlier that day, and mercifully, he fell asleep to the song of a meadowlark.

35

THE NEXT DAY

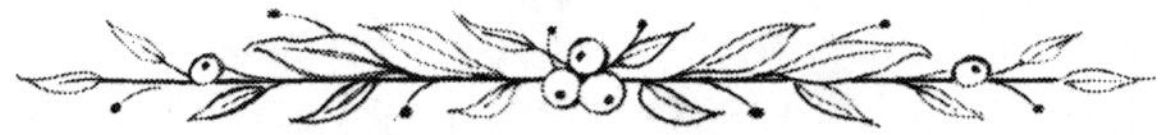

The next day came like an unwelcome guest. Tom rose to meet the morning with the utmost reluctance. He did his chores, ate an enormous breakfast, then climbed up to the hayloft to sleep the rest of the day, vowing never to drink alcohol again.

When he finally woke up, it was dark except for shafts of light coming through the dry wood planking. He opened the loft door and sat back in wonder at the most beautiful sight he'd ever seen. The sun was setting directly before him. The gently rolling countryside went on uninterrupted to the horizon, and everything was bathed in a saffron-colored glow. The clouds looked like someone had taken a broom and swept long streaks of them across the sky. They were fiery red and pink, the sun a great orange ball descending behind them. Sitting up in the loft like that, Tom felt suspended in the air, a part of it all. *How can...* he thought, *how can I find a way to live like I feel right now?*

It was then that he remembered the green man from the jumble of last night's memories. He'd looked so real, but nobody else had seen him. Tom knew he had better keep that vision to himself, lest he take the brunt of too many painful jokes at the Madrigal.

The sun finally set and the sky cooled into a twilight blue. Tom roused himself and climbed down to see what was happening on the earth below.

Most of the men had sobered up. They were sitting around the kitchen table, their faces were washed, and their hair was wet and combed back in an attempt to establish some kind of order after the chaos of the night before. The only one still airborne was the carpenter, who was fueling up for another flight. The others were quiet and sheepish-looking. Tom sat down to another enormous meal and a gallon of water, after which he finally felt right again.

Ben, the former circus owner, got up and started doing the dishes. The carpenter tried to enlist everyone in another night of revelry, but the other men waved him off, escaping outside.

"Well, Tom, how 'bout you?" the carpenter asked, that devilish grin in his eyes now overlaid with red.

"Come on, Nash, quit, will you?"

"Well, to hell with ya, that's what I say!" The carpenter stood up from the table, knocking his chair over, and staggered out the door, bottle under his arm like a walking stick.

"Good God," Tom exhaled, pushing back his lanky black hair. He knew what the next few days were going to be like. He'd been through it before, albeit in a much more innocent state. He helped old Ben with the rest of the kitchen cleanup, then went to sit for a while on the porch. He was still pretty tired and thought about going to sleep, then decided he'd go back up to the hayloft and sleep there with the doors open to the stars. What a fine idea.

Tom pulled his blanket off the bed and walked to the barn in the dark. Why hadn't he noticed it before? There were fireflies out there, hundreds of them, all dancing about to the sound of the crickets. *Funny I never noticed fireflies at the farm before; must be some new plants growing here that are attracting them*, he thought. He stood for a moment, amazed. They were dancing all about him, kind of flirting with him.

"Well, I'll be..." he whispered. *Well, I'll be goin' crazy*, he thought, shaking off that charming fantasy and moving again toward the barn.

When he opened the door, there was another sight he'd never seen before. "Welcome," the carpenter said from atop the loft. Stretching out before him was a rope that went from one side of the barn to the other, a good twenty feet up in the air. The whole scene was lit by a lantern on the floor below. Nash was just about to step out onto the rope, and step out he did.

Tom called, "God, Nash, get off of there before you kill yourself!" In a flash he knew he'd said the wrong thing.

The carpenter's tone changed from lighthearted to threatening. "Kill who? Myself, or someone else, do you mean? I used to do this for a living, you know."

"Okay, I know, I know," Tom said uneasily, not knowing quite how to handle this dark change in mood.

"Okay, what?" the carpenter snarled, stepping back and forth, balancing on the rope. "Okay, you know I did this for a living? Or okay, you know I killed somebody by letting him fall from the ropes?"

Tom answered quietly, "Nash, come on down, please."

"I was good," Nash said bitterly, now halfway out along the rope.

"I know, I know."

"No, you don't know, kid. You don't know nothing, 'cause you're afraid of everything. You're afraid of fear itself! That's how come you'll never know nothin'!" Nash cried out, knifing Tom with his words.

Tom was stricken all right—twice stricken. Once because Nash was right, and twice because he flashed on the letter his father had written him when he was eight years old, all about angry words becoming like knives and whips.

Nash was saying crazy things about himself now, about lies being better than the truth. The rope was swinging, and Nash was arching this way and that to keep his balance. Tom climbed to the side of the loft Nash was heading for. Maybe he could reach out and catch him.

The carpenter was more than halfway across when his mood changed again. He froze. He couldn't go forward and he couldn't go back. He started to look down.

Tom coaxed him. "Come on, Nash, you don't want to do that. That floor's pretty hard. You've only got a few more feet to go. Come on."

The devilish grin was completely gone from Nash's eyes, and devilish torment had replaced it. "When you've lost your nerve, you become anybody's fool," he said. "Life's not worth livin'."

"Well," Tom said, "I wouldn't know about that, 'cause as you say, I never had any nerve. So why don't you come over to this fool here and let me help you down?"

Nash had to laugh at that, caught by his own whip. He smiled. "Okay, kid. But I still can't move. Hand me that pitchfork so I can use it as a balancing bar."

"Okay." Tom extended the pitchfork toward him.

Nash reached for it and missed. He fell from the rope, but managed to catch himself by one arm. Instantly, the carpenter's mood swung back to hilarity. "Ah ey hay!" he called like Tarzan. Now he could handover-hand it to the end of the rope; he just wanted to ham it up. He swung by his knees and flipped back to his hands.

Tom swore and coaxed him till he finally made it to the edge, where Tom could haul him up. Nash was all played out now. He let Tom drag him back and make a cradle of hay bales around him so he wouldn't roll off the loft in his sleep.

"You know," he said as Tom covered him with his blanket, "I never killed nobody. Truth is, my wife couldn't stand my drinkin' and my partner had the hots for her all along. So one day they up and left together. I *said* I wanted to kill him, and the story got twisted all around. But it don't matter anyhow. Makes me sound dangerous, though, don't it? Aw, I'm really a pussycat."

"Yeah, that's right." Tom smiled, tucking him in. "You're a lean, mean pussycat." And with that, Nash passed out cold.

Tom sighed. All was quiet. He could go back to his own contemplations. He opened the loft doors and plopped down on a bed of loose hay. He felt good, somehow lighter, almost hopeful. The fireflies were still dancing for him.

36

THE NIGHTMARE

Some things are made in Heaven and some things are made in Hell. If the dwarf had come to this Earth with the blessing of Heaven, he no longer showed any signs of it. He had a dark energy. In thought, if not in deed, he matched any evil the devil might deliver. When he was angry, which was often, he dreamt of cutting people up and burning them on great fiery pyres. Cheng was stupid and aggressive, but he had a physical outlet for his anger. The dwarf was smart and hateful with no outlet for his rage. The injustices that his physical deformities had conferred upon him would have no vindication in this lifetime.

This brought about in him a strange, sensual attraction to degradation and the despoiling of things. The dwarf loved to see the good go bad, the innocent deflowered, and hopes dashed. He felt a secret satisfaction when things went badly for someone else. He would commiserate and be sympathetic, but he loved it when other people got hurt. In a twisted way, he felt empowered by their misfortunes.

The dwarf's name was Philippe La Trope. He was French Cajun, from New Orleans. He never mentioned his background, but he was educated and well-read. He and Wally had the same love of information. The politics of power was their favorite conversation topic.

Philippe's other favorite activity was to spy on people. There wasn't a room in the Madrigal that didn't have its secret peephole through which the dwarf indulged his vicarious curiosity. The rooms of the Three Peaches had several vantage points from which he could observe them unawares.

Philippe felt a special attraction to Lorna; it was something about her recklessness, her rebellion in the face of all odds. He loved it when she was nasty to him, and he went out of his way to make her angry. He baited her and she fell for it. In his twisted way, he loved her, although she abhorred him.

Lorna was a tragic being. She had a thin-lipped, sinewy attractiveness; her hair was blonde, which she made blonder with bleach. Her eyes were big, and she made them bigger with dark kohl. Lorna had been born into a downward spiral that she fought against to no avail. She was ten when her father started abusing her. Her mother never defended her or acknowledged the abuse. Instead, she called Lorna a bad girl, and a bad girl was thus what she became. By fifteen, there wasn't anything she didn't know about men, drugs, and alcohol. At sixteen, she ran away from home. She was attracted to powerful, mean men who abused her. She thought she could hold her own, but she was sadly mistaken. Her need for love conflicted with her street smarts, and she always ended up getting the stuffing kicked out of her.

It was that fight she put up, but even more, it was the knuckling under that the dwarf loved about her. He loved to see her broken over and over again; the power she gave away, he somehow picked up and was emboldened by. Many times at night he would creep into her room and watch her. After a night of heavy drinking, if he was sure she was out cold, he would sit on her bed and touch her. Her unconscious reactions to his touch amused him.

One hot summer night, just before they left to go on the road, Lorna wavered up the staircase of the Madrigal in a drunken haze, shouldered by some man or another. She was laughing as they fell against the door to her room. Once inside, she staggered to the bed where her packed suitcases lay. With a grand gesture, she threw them to the floor and flopped down, motioning for the man to join her. He did, falling on her like a stone. The dwarf was in attendance to this debacle, of course, watching through his peephole.

When the man finally left, Lorna lit a cigarette and stumbled around, cleaning herself up. It was a hot and stifling night. She opened the window wide for some air, then fell back on the bed and passed out with the lit cigarette dangling from her fingers. The dwarf silently came and sat on her bed, running his fingers along her feet to her bare calves. He watched the long ash building on the end of the cigarette, but made no move to put it out. *That'd be a good end for Lorna*, he thought, *going up in flames*. He amused himself with this and other thoughts for quite some time.

When the red-hot ash reached Lorna's fingers, she struggled awake, feeling as though a nightmarish creature were sitting on her chest. She opened her eyes and there was the misshapen form of the dwarf beside her, watching her in the dark. She gave a little strangled cry of revulsion as she recoiled under the dwarf's warning grip. "What are you doing here?" she said in a raspy whisper.

"I couldn't let you burn the house down, now could I?" he returned, picking up the cigarette and squashing it out in the ashtray beside her.

Lorna looked through bleary eyes at the cigarette and back to the dwarf. "I suppose I should thank you, but how would you have any idea what I was doing?"

"I was passing down the hall and I could smell something burning."

Lorna looked at him in disgust. "Yeah, right," she said, and crawled off the other side of the bed. She went to the mirrored washstand to put a wet towel on her face and neck. Without turning around, she said, "I know all about you, you little creep, and I know what goes on up in Wally's office with you three monsters. I should have gone to the police long ago."

"Oh, yes," said the dwarf viciously. "Yes, let's all go to the police. Let's see who runs out of crimes to tell first, you or me."

"Get out of here, you little pervert!" she cried.

"Don't say such nasty things to me. Things could go badly for you."

"Oh, yeah?" Lorna said, looking around. "How's that possible?"

"Oh, it's possible all right."

"Get out of here!" she yelled, burying her head in the towel. When she looked up in the mirror at herself, she still saw him there, watching her.

"I'm the only one who really knows you. I'm the only one who cares," he whispered.

"*Get out!*" she screamed, hurling the washbasin at him. The dwarf just missed her parting shot as he slipped out the door.

37

BETWIXT THE BETWEEN

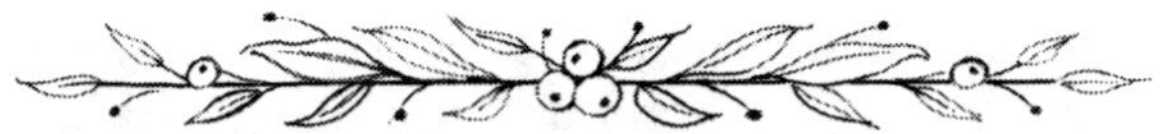

In the early days of the circus, the dwarf had a dog named Howler that he used in part of his clown act. There was nothing jolly about the dwarf, but in his wide striped pants and high hat, he *looked* funny anyway. The dog, who grew to be taller than the dwarf, would sit and howl while the dwarf leaned against him playing "Shenandoah" on the accordion.

When the circus was acquired by Wally, the dog stayed at the farm while the dwarf went to the city. This was the best thing that could ever have happened to Howler. There, he led a free, roaming life and no man called him his own. Howler was some sort of hound mix—Irish wolfhound, mostly. His coat was a grayish color, growing a little darker around his long face, and he had soulful eyes that took in everything. He was independent and intelligent. As he grew older, he acquired an air of nobility. Any man he chose to walk beside was complimented by his presence. The whole countryside was his home. Sometimes he would disappear for days.

Tom and Howler liked each other right from the start. When Tom was around, the dog stayed attentive to him alone, although he would still sit and howl for the dwarf, in deference to their former working relationship. The dwarf, however, held a deep grudge against Tom, whom he blamed for the alienation of his dog's affection.

* * *

In the summer of his seventeenth year, Tom was back at the farm with Nash. Everything was just about ready for the season's tour, and the carpenter was flexing for his ritual jump to the bottom of the liquor bottle. Tom wanted to steer clear of the whole thing for a day by taking a car trip up to Split Rock Creek. A feisty little river ran down the mountains, and at a certain point it burst into a narrow, rocky gorge that appeared to have been split by a great ax. There, the deep water twisted and turned between the rock walls before spreading out again into an unrestricted flow. Old Ben had taken Tom up there once, and he remembered it as a green and lively place.

Early in the morning, Tom and Howler took off in the car. The way Howler sat straight in the seat, head up, eyes forward, he looked like an aristocrat traveling with his chauffeur. Tom was driving along, happy as a lark. He felt so expansive and free that he felt like singing. "Oh Shenandoah, I long to see..." he started out, then looked over at Howler, who was regarding him with a most sobering gaze. "All right, all right, bad choice!" Tom laughed. "How 'bout 'She'll Be Comin' Round the Mountain'?"

And so they puttered up the road with Tom shouting, "She'll be comin' round the mountain when she comes, when she comes," while Howler, whiskers blowing, sat bolt upright, staring ahead.

When Tom finally pulled off the road to park, he concealed the car and took out a couple of spark plugs. Since this was a lonesome road seldom traveled by the law, it was better to be safe. Howler appeared to know exactly where he was going; he jumped out of the car and trotted into the woods.

Tom took a moment to stand still in the mountain wilderness. The noisy vibrations of the motorcar began to die down in his ears, and nature's sounds welled up around him. He felt the grandeur of the trees from the sound of the wind in the leaves high above him. Far off, he could hear the rush of water from Split Rock Creek. A sweet, green, damp smell filled his nostrils. He was so grateful to be alone there with no other human voice to break the intimacy he felt with the environment. He couldn't distinguish whether this feeling of calm and sensuousness was coming out of him or coming into him from his surroundings. He smiled at his own happiness.

Tom walked along, picking up a stick on the way. He went a little further, then sat down against a tree to take in all this quiet splendor. He remembered a day long ago when he'd walked through the woods with a similar stick and sat down against another tree. He was so unhappy then, he'd noticed none of nature's beauty, only his own misfortunes ahead of him. He remembered that remarkable mushroom patch and how carelessly he had laid his stick down on it. But this was a new day, and many years later. Today he seemed to see things very clearly—more than clearly. Everything had a strange, animated quality. Everything was so alive—or was it that *he* was so alive?

He looked up into one of the trees and caught sight of a small, fabulously red bird just as it gave forth the most melodic call. He was enchanted. Howler drifted back to be with him for a while. They both sat there, watching and listening in silence.

Howler took a fix on something and looked attentive. Tom followed his gaze into the trees. There for a split second, among the leaves, was the face of a green man—the very same man who had materialized out of Tom's drunken stupor last year.

Couldn't be, Tom thought. *It's just an illusion.*

Howler looked back at Tom in that moment, as if to say, "I'll be right back." He sprang up and trotted away.

"That's okay, leave me. Everybody does," Tom sighed in mock self-pity. The words came out, but they didn't sound right. Here in this setting, they sounded like words to an old habitual song that were no longer true. Just thinking them seemed to diminish his sensitivity to the beauty all around him. He stood up, shook himself, and wandered off to find Howler.

As he did so, Tom entered a most confusing passage of time. It began with a distinct feeling that he was being followed. He couldn't keep track of Howler, who was right there in front of him one minute and gone the next. Light shafts coming down through the trees were dusty with tiny airborne grains of pollen. Everything was broken up into lights and darks. He couldn't be sure of anything he was seeing. Howler went behind a tree, then appeared from behind the tree next to it. There was a gap in the continuity of Tom's sight, as if in a movie of continuous action, some of the frames had been arbitrarily cut out; the dog moved ahead in a jerky, unnatural progression. What was happening in those gaps? And what was that irritating feeling at his back that seemed to goad him on?

The two had something to do with each other. The dog was leading him, and the feeling was pushing him. Tom began to try to predict where the next gap would be from the dog's pattern of movement. He felt the urge to run and jump into the gap. He did this several times and then thought, *What am I trying to do, play hopscotch with reality?*

He called Howler to him. The dog came back and sat panting patiently, all the while looking straight ahead.

"Am I nuts?" Tom said to the dog, as if he could answer. Howler looked back at him and then ahead. He definitely intended that Tom should follow him. Howler got up and led the way again.

"Okay, all right, I'm coming."

This time, when Howler went behind a tree, Tom ran right in front where he knew the dog should come out. He jumped into the spot, and to his shock, there stood the green man, looking straight at him. "Aha!" said he.

Tom fell backwards in disbelief. The leaf man disappeared.

Then followed a most curious game of hide-and-seek between the dog, the green man, and Tom. Each time Tom discovered the man, he was congratulated with another triumphant "Aha!" from the leafy creature. Tom was beginning to think that maybe these weren't gaps in reality, but rather, a simultaneous real perception of which he was only intermittently aware. It was as if his brain were seeing one thing out of the right eye and another out of the left. If he could have fused his vision, he would have seen both views as one reality.

This was all just too fantastic to be true. Finally he let Howler go on. He would eventually get to Split Rock, but right now, he had exhausted the reaches of his perception and he wanted to stop. He had to gather his senses. Slowly, his heart calmed down, his thoughts stopped racing, and everything felt normal again. Gratefully, he sat back against a tree and dozed off. He felt wonderfully droopy and relaxed, and lulled by the buzzing of forest bees, he spiraled down into sleep.

He had just descended into that peaceful blur where deep sleep begins when he was dragged back to consciousness by Howler's incessant barking. Tom got up slowly, trying to get his bearings. By the sound of it, Howler was somewhere over by the falls.

Tom walked along, his pace quickening with the urgency of Howler's barks. As he came closer, he could see the dog on the stones above the creek, running back and forth excitedly. Something was down in the gorge. Tom climbed up the rock and looked over.

There, trapped in a deep pool surrounded by sheer rock, was a young stag. He was treading water, clattering his hooves against the rock, trying to get a foothold. The pool had an outlet on either end through which the water rushed, but the stag's antlers prevented him from swimming through the narrow openings. There, all alone, with his last bit of strength, the stag was silently fighting for his life.

Tom ran back and forth with Howler in confusion. What could he do? How could he get the animal out? He couldn't let him die. *The car*, he thought. *There's a rope in the trunk of the car*. Did he have time to run there and back before the animal drowned? He had to try. Tom went running, crashing through the woods down to the car. He yanked open the trunk, grabbed the rope, and raced back. He hadn't noticed the incline before, but he felt it now as he ran, out of breath, up to the falls. By the time he reached the rocks, his lungs were scorched and dry. He stood wobbly-legged and heaving as he peered over into the pool.

The stag was still fighting. He could get his forelegs up onto a rocky ledge, but didn't have the strength to pull himself out. Tom jumped down to where the stag was making his last effort. He was able to slip the rope around the deer's antlers. The wet rocks were strewn with slippery leaves that made the ground treacherous as he climbed back to wrap the rope around a tree. As soon as he accomplished this, he began to haul on the rope with all his strength.

The stag felt the tug on his antlers as he grappled on the rocks with his forelegs. Howler barked and Tom pulled in a mighty attempt to save the animal. Finally, the stag was able to climb up to the flat top of the rock. He lay there, muscles quivering, completely spent.

Tom eased the tension on the rope and slowly climbed down to release the knot around the stag's antlers. He carefully, quietly knelt down next to the animal. Tom was in awe; he had never been so close to such a wild thing. The stag even smelled wild, like berries and moss. His breath had a dank ripeness to it.

The stag did not take his eyes off Tom, who sat very still, waiting while they both recovered some strength. It was a magnificent moment when the animal finally got to his feet, shaking the water from his coat. He showed no fear as Tom touched him, gently slipping the rope free. Tom backed away; the stag took a few steps forward, hesitated, then bounded up the rock and in a flash disappeared.

There were no words to describe the effect that day's experience had on Tom. He had been somewhere extraordinary. He had done something extraordinary. He felt extraordinary. As he drove back, Tom thought that if there weren't any words to express his feelings, there certainly was a sound. He looked over at Howler, then put his head back and let out a big long yowl. The dog joined in, and together they howled their way home.

38

CERNOS

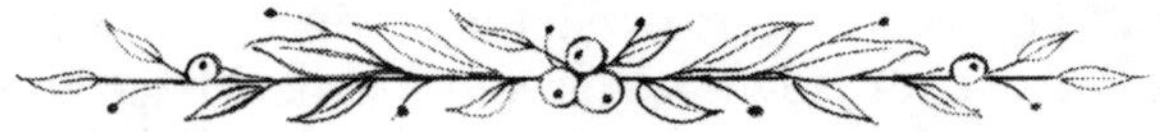

Many things were in existence before Man had enough of a brain to contemplate them. There was a time when great forests covered much of the Earth—a time when rich, dense green circled the land with the same continuity as the blue of the sky above it. The elementals and spirits of Faery had existed for many centuries when Man was just learning to stand up on his two legs. They were an integral, intelligent part of the workings of nature. Like Man, each followed its own evolution: some gathering consciousness and substance, others staying merely etheric energies.

Unlike Humans, faeries live very long lives and can change forms within those lives until finally they fade and disappear into the Light. They leave no history except what Man has been able to record of them. This has had a great effect on the kinds of forms they take, because to be seen, they must be in a form that Humans can recognize; hence, many have taken on a Human-like appearance, along with other attributes. Now one sees very little of these beings because Man has done so much damage to the faery habitat that they no longer wish to be seen. The secrets and treasures of their sphere are known only to a few.

Within the hierarchy of beings in Faery, the Green Man is a forest being of very ancient lineage. Throughout the ages, what Man has seen of him has been awe-inspiring and frightening. It is said that his footstep leaves a green print and his ivy-leaved skin looks like dragon scales. He wears horns upon his head and makes great cracking sounds that set the deer leaping through the forest. For Humans, to encounter him can be either helpful or dangerous. He would just as soon trick a man to his death as show him the mysteries of Faery; it all depends on the merit of the man.

On the day that Mabon set out to look for Rhea, Cernos (for that is the Green Man's name) was stretching his great limbs along the trunk of a fallen tree. Quite comfortable was he, face up to the warm summer sun. The leaves of his skin glowed with a green iridescence, and long trails of his ivy hair fell on the forest floor. All about him, delicate faery spirits had settled down and were gently opening and closing their wings like butterflies on a flower.

Alongside him lay Rhea, her head resting upon his shoulder, her arms a rosy garland around his neck. Birds fluttered in and out of the shadows and insects hummed a peaceful drone. They might have been lying there for hours or days; it's hard to know, for in Faery there is no such thing as time.

Above them on a branch sat a raven, its head tucked under its wing. Its movement was the first to disturb the calm. The raven looked about suddenly and flapped its wings. Cernos slowly opened one heavy-lidded eye. "Someone approaches," he sighed.

Rhea sat up and listened. "Yes, it's Mabon. I must go."

Rhea unwound herself from Cernos's resting form and slipped away into the forest. She had gone some distance when she encountered a wavering, vaporous image; it traveled straight toward her through all that was in front of it, for it had no substance. It was not Mabon himself, but a thought wave he had sent out in search of her. Rhea stepped into its path and heard without words Mabon's summons to the castle. As soon as she had understood its message, the wave evaporated.

This will be the time, she thought, *when his words, whatever they are, will change my world forever. Nothing will be the same, even if I decide not to do as he asks.*

Rhea entered the vaulted hall of the castle where the hearth fire burned. Mabon must have been staring into the white-hot flames for a long time, for when he turned to her in greeting, his eyes were ablaze.

"Ah, there is no fire in existence that can warm me as much as the sight of you, Rhea. I'm glad you came so quickly." Then he fell silent again and lost himself in thought. He seemed to be considering very carefully the next words he would say.

Rhea waited silently, spreading out lush fur pelts on the stone floor beside him. She sat with her knees drawn up to her chest and her arms wrapped around them, her red hair falling around her like a cape. The raven flew in through a window that hung in midair and settled upon Mabon's antlered chair.

After some time, Mabon began. "We are in danger, and it is the Humans who have caused it to be so. Only a few remember what was taught long ago. With their advances, now they think they know everything. They are so full of their own power, they do not even see they are in trouble. Humans will cause the death of this world, and that means we will die with them. What we know can save us all, but they won't listen. Humans have grown so vain, they think we are only a figment of their own imagination. We must find one who will cross over—one who will begin to carry back our wisdom into the souls of men. The opportunity for such a crossing is near. There is a young man...the circumstances of his life have set him adrift...his heart is in the right place, but he cannot find it...he does not know what he knows...he waits like a ripe fruit to fall from the tree but he cannot let go...so we have begun to loosen his grip a little...and this is where you come in, my lovely Rhea."

Rhea listened carefully to all of this.

"There will be a moment when the foolishness of someone he is with will bring him into our sphere. In that second, you must make up your mind whether or not to follow him into his world and bring him back to us. Those three drops of human blood running in your veins make you the chosen one. But it must be your decision. I would not force you into anything..." And there he stopped, turning his gaze back to the fire.

Rhea sat, head on her knees, her hair covering her face. She did not know how to answer.

"There is one more thing. If you decide to go, at no time may you use your powers to bring him here unaware. He must come knowing where he is going and be willing to stay."

That was all Mabon said. And Rhea could not reply. So they sat together, the raven in attendance, absorbed in their own thoughts, long into the night.

39

THE CARAVAN

Mavis disliked any disturbances in the lake of her self-absorption, and leaving each summer caused the waters to get very choppy indeed. Mavis could be very unpleasant when she had to think about things she didn't want to think about. In this case, it was packing. She always left it until the last moment, and then her ill temper set everyone else to squabbling. Explosions went off up in Wally's inner sanctum, and there were skirmishes down in Nettie's kitchen.

No one escaped Mavis's last-minute meddling with what was already going on perfectly well without her. As a consequence, there was a large collection of unhappy people standing at odds amongst the luggage on the day of departure.

Tom and one of the farm hands had driven into town with the car and truck. He had to laugh when he turned the corner to see that angry little group waiting at the curb. Wally sat, arms folded, puffing away on a Havana cigar. Mavis ran around on her tiny velvet slippers, while everyone else stood coldly looking this way and that.

Every year, things got off to a bad start, and it didn't get much better until everyone was settled down into their allotted wagons, once again separated into their own territories. There were six wagons; Mavis had her own, as did Wally. The Three Peaches had theirs. Tom, the carpenter, and Ben shared another. Then came Phil, Barnaby, and the dwarf, and Nettie had the sixth, which was the cook's wagon. Cheng slept in the truck with the farm hands when it rained, but mostly they pitched tents and slept outside.

When the caravan finally got under way, there was a big communal exhalation, and everyone looked ahead to the month in the country. There wasn't one of them who didn't enjoy it, really, once they got those wagons rolling. The girls opened the windows, leaned out, and let the sun touch their faces for the first time in a year. They let their hair fly loose and wore checked summer dresses, just like the fresh young peaches they'd once been.

They were all relieved to escape the confines of the Madrigal, but none so much as Barnaby and Phil. For that one month each summer, they could be who they really were: Barnaby and Phyllis, the couple, the lovers. All year, Barnaby was the bald, stone-faced bartender with tattoos on his arms, and Phil was the blond, ponytailed fat man with one long fingernail who dealt cards in the back room. He kept that nail long to flip the cards over at the end of a deal, but now it was summer, and he could let all his fingernails grow. He could cover his large, rounded, feminine body with a dress; he could let his hair down; he could be Phyllis at last. Barnaby loved Phyllis, and that love was as quiet and steady and strong as any two life partners could have.

It was summer, and Barnaby could smile. He could show off his tattooed body and walk arm in arm with Phyllis, as they had in the freedom of the old circus days. There was only one problem that presented itself in Phil's transformation, but this had been solved nicely years ago. He was supposed to be "Phyllis, the *Bearded* Fat Lady." So, to fulfill that requirement, he'd grown his beard once, shaved it off, and attached it to some netting with glue. Now the beard was stored carefully in a felt-lined hatbox, making its appearance for performances only.

Of the other curiosities, the two-headed turtle was still alive, but the four-horned goat had made its passage many years ago. Its horns were preserved, however, and the carpenter cleverly constructed a hidden method of attachment so they were never without an "amazing four-horned goat."

The last curiosity, the dwarf, was the only one who really hated the summer months. It was then that he would have to don those clown pants, roll around, do somersaults, and clap his hands, all of which kept him in a perfectly foul humor. He refused to bunk with Barnaby and Phyllis, much to their good fortune, and had his own tent set up next to Wally's wagon.

It took a day and a half to reach the first campsite from the farm, so they just munched on sandwiches Nettie had made in the morning. The next afternoon, they reached the site. They were to be there for four days, and now Nettie had time to prepare one of the famous outdoor dinners Tom loved so much. The troupe worked hard setting up camp. When everything was done, Tom took a walk into the evening countryside with Howler, keeping an ear tuned for Nettie's call.

Tom had a lot on his mind lately, especially after that day at Split Rock Creek. He felt more disconnected than ever from his life as he had been living it. At the same time, he felt more aware and alive. Conflicting desires, visions of the green man and pulling the stag out of the water, and the feeling of having stepped into some kind of hyper-reality kept him on edge. He was accustomed to a deadening anxiety that had traveled with him all his life. But this was a different kind of expectancy—not of doom, but of what? Hope? Change? He didn't know.

Tom and the dog walked from the grove where they were camped into a wheatfield. The land rolled out before them like a golden carpet to meet the setting sun. Their steps made a trail through the untouched grasses. Above, a raven flew a solitary path across the empty sky. In that moment, Tom felt like the first soul who had ever touched down upon this virgin country. Although he knew at his back camped the dark tangle of human lives from which he came, he felt on the brink of a new world.

Hurrying the dinner preparations, Nettie laid out last week's newspaper on a table set up by the cook wagon. She called Sudy to come and help her cut up the carrots and peel the potatoes. Sudy was the oldest of the Three Peaches at twenty-seven, but she had the mind of a twelve-year-old. Sudy was sweet and chatty; she would do whatever you asked, but would never initiate an action herself. It was almost like she was incapable of forethought. She just sat and dawdled around until somebody told her to do something else. At the moment, she was happily chattering away, chopping the carrots Nettie had given her into all different sizes.

Nettie tried to give her some direction, but gave up and went back to her preparations. She was stirring the pots and tending the cook fire when she suddenly noticed Sudy had stopped talking.

Nettie turned around and said, "What you doin', chile? Keep choppin'."

Sudy didn't say anything. She had wiped away the carrot bits from the newspaper and was slowly reading something on the page that disturbed her very much.

"What's you readin' in dat ole paper, Sudy?"

Sudy's brow wrinkled. She looked up at Nettie and said in a hushed voice, "It say here they found the body of another naked girl down by the railroad tracks."

"Oh, Sudy, don' you go readin' that ole nasty city news out here in the country. 'Sides, you knew about that all last week. Now, think about something else, honey, and concentrate on fixin' those potatoes. The water's already boilin'."

"Yes, but..."

"There ain't no buts about it. Come on now."

"Okay," Sudy sighed, covering the article back up with potato peelings, happy that someone had stopped her from going down that track and started her on another one.

When Mavis moved around in her cabin, the whole wagon shifted slightly from one side to the other. She had a way of thrusting herself from one activity to another in her haste to finish bothersome duties. She wanted this whole ordeal of setting up house over so she could resume the more pleasant task of focusing on herself. Besides, she was starving. When was that Nettie going to be ready with dinner?

Cheng and the dwarf were playing cards with the farm hands and waiting impatiently for the dinner bell. Phyllis was putting the last coat of red lacquer on her nails. Wally sat sequestered in his dark little cabin, talking with old Ben about what they could expect to earn this trip against a certain purchase he wished to make.

Tom wandered idly in the yellow field, his thoughts trying to penetrate the new world before him, when he became aware that a black bird was flying straight at him. He looked around in disbelief. Surely the bird was going to land somewhere else. But no, it had dropped down from the sky and was gliding swiftly toward him. Tom could hear the sound of the air whooshing under its wings.

He put his arm up quickly to protect himself from attack, and the bird landed on his forearm as if it were a perch. Stunned, Tom beheld the bird as it folded its wings. It was a raven, all coal-black and shiny. Something was in its beak—a large brown-red seed of some kind. The raven's claws cut sharply through the weave of his shirt, but Tom didn't move.

The bird opened its beak, dropping the seed to the ground, and gave out three startling calls. It cocked its head, then flew into the air.

Tom reached down for the seed, then looked up to watch the bird fly away, but it had disappeared. He would probably have continued searching the sky to see where it had gone if he hadn't heard Nettie's loud whistle.

As he walked back to the camp, he could see the lantern lights in the grove and the silhouettes of everyone already eating at the long table. Nothing appeared different, yet imperceptibly, everything was changing, for he was bringing something new into that which was old: the seed, and a feeling that somehow his destiny lay between this world and another.

40

SAD SARAH

That summer was one of the hottest anyone could remember. Only the evenings brought relief from the swelter. Workers toiled in the burning sun, harvesting crops. To keep cool, they wore water-soaked bandanas under their hats. When they saw those painted wagons come over the hill and roll by with the music playing and the girls blowing kisses, it sure was a sight for sore eyes. The men whistled and ballyhooed and the children ran after the caravan, scooping up the candy it left in its trail.

By sundown, everyone in the area knew the circus had come and where it was camped. Women and children came to see the amazing goat, the man on stilts, and the bearded lady. They saw these curiosities and spent their pennies on Nettie's lemonade and caramel apples. The men stayed to spend their last few dollars on gambling and drink.

The troupe had gone on this way through most of the tour, and they were now reaching the last encampment before they turned around—outside a foothill town named Pine Tree. Time had fallen asleep there some seventy-five years ago, and its inhabitants saw no reason to wake it up. They still wore homespun clothes and spoke in a dialect that was hard to understand. They were poor, closemouthed, and clannish. Strangers and novelties made them suspicious. Three families owned all the land thereabouts; everyone else rented or just squatted in shacks up in the hills. The town had a main street, a few shops, a church, a post office, and little else.

Wally picked Pine Tree because he had heard of a family there with a secret distillery that produced the finest whiskey in the county. He wanted to make a connection with them, although he had heard they were crude and unpredictable.

The family was composed of Ma Huxtable and her three sons, each one uglier than the next. Her sons were powerful, but Ma's word was law and she could smack them down hard in any contest, for she was every bit as big and burly as they. Everything that went on in that family filtered through the narrow channels of Ma's mind first.

For a long time, Ma had wanted to acquire the land to the north of hers held by the Barton family. Over the years, she had tried every which way to bully or sweet-talk Matthew Barton into selling off that land, but no deal. Then one day, Barton's wife up and died, leaving him alone with his daughter Sarah. After a couple of months, Barton walked up to the Huxtables' cabin and said right out plain that he'd sell that north quarter to Ma if she took his daughter Sarah in marriage to one of her sons.

The boys hung around the porch, scratching their heads and looking to see what their mother would say. Ma sat in her chair and rocked back and forth, considering this new turn of events. Barton's daughter Sarah was no prize, to be sure. She was a pale, stringy thing, with a weak chin and watery eyes. People called her Sad Sarah.

Ma rocked back and forth, back and forth, while her sons had veritable fits of itches and scratches. None of them wanted to get married, and nobody wanted Sarah. But in Ma's mind, things ran something like this: *Well*, she thought, *the two older boys is done for; they've been free too long. But the youngest one, Samuel—he might just be able to do it. 'Sides, it's about time this family had an heir*. And, by God and her will, she felt sure it would be a boy.

So there it was, within a few rocks of a chair: Sam was getting married, Ma would have her property, and the family would have an heir.

That was how Sarah entered the Huxtable household—as a condition to a land transfer. Ma made things plain right from the start. "Now look," she said. "Life's hard, and there ain't no use making it harder by complainin'."

Sarah only looked at Ma with her watery eyes.

"You're gonna get a husband, a roof over your head, and three squares a day. Now, the only thing I ask for all of this is that as soon as this marriage and land transfer is legal, I want you to go in there and make me a baby—and Sarah, it better be a boy."

Sam was angry and embarrassed about the whole thing. He was not in the least interested in this fishy-looking woman who was to be his wife. Sad Sarah remained silent, trapped in the house of giants. From her expressionless face, there was no telling what the frail creature was thinking, and it was impossible to know if she cared.

At first, it didn't seem like Sarah would come forth with a child, even though Ma gave up her own room to the newlyweds so they could have some privacy. Each morning, Sam and Sarah would emerge from the bedroom as distant from each other as when they went in the night before. Trouble started brewing; Ma was getting impatient, and Sam became defensive and cruel to Sarah. The other brothers started making lewd remarks, hinting that maybe they ought to give it a try. Ma wasn't far from that idea herself when finally it became apparent that Sarah was pregnant.

Tensions eased considerably. Ma got her own bed back, and she had the boys build an extra room onto the cabin. Whatever Sarah thought about this was of no matter in the Huxtable world.

As the months went by, Sarah got bigger and bigger, until she could hardly move. They would find her just sitting in the dark cabin room, looking out the window with those pale, pale eyes. When the time came for her to give birth, it was clear she was going to bring forth another giant. Ma was in attendance, watching Sarah split open like a bird having an elephant. When it was all over, Sarah lay spent, her eyes shut, head turned to the wall. But Ma was triumphant, for in her arms she held up a kicking, screaming Huxtable boy.

Mother and son weren't long in love and sympathy, for as the child grew, he was quickly alienated from Sarah's quiet, retiring ways. He saw Ma as his mother and Sarah as some kind of servant that nobody paid any attention to. Sad Sarah never quite recovered from Luther's birth. She had constant back pain and went around in a permanent state of exhaustion. Living in the house of giants had completely worn her out. Not one bit of Sarah showed up in Luther: he was turning out as crude and insensitive as the rest of the family.

* * *

Wally set up his theatricals and curiosities outside town. Pine Tree's attendance was lukewarm, and Wally was anxious to set up this meeting with the Huxtables and get on his way.

Ma Huxtable wanted nothing to do with the strangers, and it was actually Luther who brought them all down from their mountain enclave. He wanted to see the dwarf.

One day, all the Huxtables just showed up at the troupe's campsite. Phyllis ran for her beard, Nash scurried for the goat horns, and the dwarf had to be woken up from a nap to come out and greet them in his clown pants. Luther went nuts when he saw the dwarf. He shrieked and laughed. Sarah tried to calm him down, but Ma told her, "Shut up, let the boy be, he's havin' fun."

Wally tried to figure out which one he should be talking to. He finally chose the oldest, nastiest-looking brother.

"Well," he said, "it's a hot summer day—would you all like a drink?"

"Maybe," was the answer.

"Tom, take the women and the boy around to see the animals."

Ma saw that she was being dispensed with and snorted back, "Sarah, you and the boy go. Buck, Jed, Samuel, you stay with me." That instantly established who was who in the Huxtable family.

Wally switched tactics immediately. "Cheng, bring some chairs for the lady and her sons." Ma looked around, mighty suspicious. When the Chinaman brought up a chair, there was a terrible moment when it looked like she was going to draw her pistol and shoot him for his hospitality.

Tom took the boy and Sarah around in back of the wagons to see the goat and the turtle. Luther was all over the place, getting into everything, being thoroughly obnoxious. Tom thought there had to be something wrong with him; he couldn't stop shrieking and moving. As for the woman, she called herself Sarah and said the boy was her son, but he couldn't believe it. This phantom of a woman was just skin and bones. Tom saw in her eyes how mute and trapped she was. He sympathized with her tragically suffocated spirit, and he wanted to extend to her just one simple kindness, but there wasn't time; he had to rescue the boy from being bitten in the face by Nip and keep him away from the dwarf, whose next act as a clown was sure to be murder.

Wally was making progress. He had gotten to the point of asking if the Huxtables were knowledgeable in the art of making whiskey.

"Maybe," was the answer.

After much vacillating back and forth on the subject, he finally got them pinned down to a "Yes." It took just as much effort to get across that he was interested in buying some of their stock—if it was true at all that they were even interested in selling some, depending, of course, on whether they had any to sell. It tried every bit of his patience, but he finally got them to agree to a meeting the next evening. He was to go up the road to their place in the woods, and from there he would be directed further. Maybe.

"God help me, I need a drink!" Wally took off his hat and wiped the back of his neck. "Damnedest people I ever met."

Tom watched the Huxtables march off into the woods with that manic child running circles around them as they went. He wondered just how much longer such a girl could stay alive in that house of giants.

41

THE ENCOUNTER

With no more shows to do, camping in the pine woods was quite restful. The girls slept all the next day; Mavis read romance novels; everyone just kept to themselves.

That evening, Tom and Wally started up the road in the truck to find the Huxtables. What a brilliant night it was. A full moon rose into a vast sky brimming with stars. The rough noise of the truck cut a blasphemous slice through the silent landscape. Wally sat chewing his cigar, looking up the road. Tom was driving along, his head hanging out the window, gazing at the stars.

"What's that?" Wally poked Tom's arm.

"What's what?" Tom drew his head in.

"Well, pay attention. I thought I saw a lantern light."

Tom drove along carefully now. He saw something too. Soon they recognized one of the Huxtable brothers standing in the road. When they pulled up alongside him, he told them to turn right and proceed till they saw another light.

Tom turned off the main road onto what appeared to be a footpath through the pines. They bounced and rattled along in the pitch black, hoping the truck could make it back from wherever they were going.

Then they saw a most ghostly sight. It was the thin, washed-out figure of Sarah, holding up a lantern. She stood there, clutching a motheaten shawl over a white rag of a dress. Tom stopped the truck and looked down at her as she held the lantern up to her face.

She said in her vague voice, "You are to go on followin' the path until you see another light, and that'll be the place..."

While she was saying this, Tom looked straight into her eyes and she into his. He spoke untold kindnesses to her without saying a word. When she finished, he smiled and said, "Thank you, ma'am." Her eyes gave out a faint shine as she stepped back, lowering the lantern to her side.

As he went on, Tom could see the light behind him as she lingered there. Then slowly he saw it flicker back in amongst the trees and out of sight.

"This better be worth it," Wally was muttering. "If this truck gets stuck out here, I swear, I'll make those grizzly bears carry it back!"

Tom was amused. He liked to see ol' Wally out of his element, out of control for once.

Finally they came to where the two other brothers were waiting. They told Wally to come with them and Tom to wait with the truck. That was fine with Tom. He watched little Wally go off between those two giants; then he climbed up on the roof of the truck and lay out flat, staring up at the heavens.

It was another one of those moments when the crushing anxiety that kept Tom all folded up inside somehow lifted. He was free—free to wallow in his freedom with all his senses alive and present in this star-studded universe. He listened to the crickets and to the night wind softly purring in the pines. He lay on top of the truck for the longest time; then he rolled over onto his stomach and looked down into the earth's darkness. To his amazement, as it was above, so it was below. For there, all around him amongst the silhouettes of the trees, were hundreds of fireflies dancing and twinkling. How close they flew to him! How brilliant they were! How quickly their light was gone at the first sound of another human. Wally's sudden laughter caused an instant blackout.

Tom sat up and listened. It was Wally's glad-handing laugh all right, but there was a surprising little snigger in it that Tom hadn't heard before. He must have had a cup or two of that famous Huxtable brew. It wasn't long before Tom saw the two lanterns swinging toward him. There was Wally, marching back with the grizzly brothers. Apparently they had struck a pleasant chord, for they all were ol' buddies now. Tom jumped down to hear the news.

"Yessir," Wally said, his collar band sprung open and his face all a-flush. "Yessir, tol' em I'd take it all. I'm gonna be a regular." Wally made a loose attempt to put his arms up around their shoulders as a show of solidarity. "Open 'er up, Tommy, we're gonna take on some cargo."

It was a real revelation to see Wally look like such a fool. Tom stifled his laughter as he went around to open the back of the truck. When they were all loaded, Wally hung his puffy face out the window and croaked, "Okay... how d'we get out?"

The brothers said blankly, "You gotta back out."

Tom leaned over Wally from the driver's seat. "You got to be kidding."

"Nope," was the answer.

Tom sat back and started the engine. Wally took a swig from the bottle he had secured between his legs and lit up a cigar. "Drive on," he called. "Backwards ho!" He seemed to think that was terribly funny.

"Follow our lanterns," the brothers said.

Tom was thoroughly irritated as he threw the truck into reverse and craned his neck out the driver's side door so he could see the lanterns. He had to navigate by staying between the lantern he saw on his side and the lantern reflected in the passenger-side rear-view mirror. It was a slow process with Wally bouncing around, sloshing liquor all over the cab, smoking up a storm.

"Put a cork in that thing!" Tom shouted. Wally bent forward to look for the cork on the floor, but he only spilled more whisky and hit his head on the dashboard. "Okay, all right, forget it," Tom said, pushing him up into a sitting position.

Finally they made it back up to the main road. "Hallelujah," Tom said.

"You sound like Nash," Wally belched.

"Yeah, and now I know what he means."

They were going along fine, making good time returning to camp, when Wally suddenly said, "Stop the truck. I gotta get out."

"Oh, God, we're almost there," Tom sighed.

"I don' care, I gotta get out."

"Okay, okay." Tom rolled to a stop. Wally opened the door and fell out of the truck.

"You all right?"

"Yeah, yeah."

Tom waited for a while with the motor idling. Then he got impatient, shut off the engine and got out. "Wally?" he called. Not a sound. It was so quiet he could hear his own heart beat. Not a cricket, not a bird, not a branch moved. "Wally?" he called again. He blew out the headlights. He could actually see by the light of the moon. "Wally?"

Tom walked around the truck and peered into the woods where Wally must have gone. He could see there was a sharp decline off the road, and when he looked down, he thought he saw some kind of glow. "My God, the fool fell all the way down there and set himself on fire with that cigar. He had enough liquor soaked in his clothes."

Tom plunged down through the woods, tumbling and falling like Wally must have done. When he finally got to even ground, he stopped and called for Wally again. He thought he heard a groan and went in the direction of the glow. He was brought up short by the most frightening, inconceivable, breathtaking sight he'd ever seen.

There was Wally, lying crumpled up before this enormous funnel of whirling light that drew those fireflies he had been seeing up into the center of it, then showered them down like sparkling rain. Wally seemed to be on fire, but he wasn't. He was surrounded by creatures that appeared and disappeared like whips of flame. Jumping all over him were misshapen little gnomes, pinching him, twisting and pulling his hair. Wally was gibbering away pitifully, trying to protect his head from the siege.

Tom stood transfixed. A chorus of voices filled his ears, but his mind was a jumble. He couldn't understand. As he looked into the flames hovering around Wally, there suddenly materialized the most beautiful apparition. A faery creature, a young girl with red hair and green eyes, looked directly at him. Her hair and clothes floated about her in slow motion, almost like she was in water instead of flames. She turned away slowly, as if someone were calling her, then turned her gaze back to him. The chorus of voices rose up around him again, and from an indescribable cacophony of languages, he understood, "Does this Human belong to you?"

Tom looked at the spectacle enveloping him and then down at that whimpering mess at his feet. He was sorry to have to say, "Yes."

"Then take him. Tell no one what you have seen." In an instant, all the fire and magic drew up into the funnel and were gone.

Tom inhaled deeply. It was his first breath in many minutes. He sank down beside Wally's stinking body and tried to get him to pull himself together. "Now, Wally, you're all right. Come on. Stand up."

"But I...they were...did you see that?"

"See what? You're drunker than blazes, and you just fell all the way down this hill on your head. It's a wonder you're alive. By the way, did you do what you came out here to do?"

"Shut up, will ya?" Wally growled. "Help me up."

"Gladly."

"Damn them Huxtables...God, I'm soaked."

"No kidding."

Wally heaved himself up, and with Tom's help, struggled to the truck. Once in the truck and traveling back to camp, Wally sobered up somewhat. "Now, listen, you young no 'count. Not a word of this to anybody, see, or I'll make your life so difficult you'll wish you were back stealin' apples."

With that comment, Tom knew Wally was back to his vicious self again.

"An' listen, lemme out before we get to camp. Wait till I get inside; then come around, put these clothes in a sack and throw 'em out with the trash, ya hear?"

"Yep, I hear you," Tom said, and they rode all the way back with Wally gingerly holding his head in his hands like a bomb set to explode.

<h1 style="text-align:center">42</h1>

NIGHTMARES

The camp was only a dark set of shadows by the time Tom and Wally returned. The cook fire was smoking, sending up an ashy scent. Everyone was asleep; not a lamp was lit.

When he finally got to bed, Wally found he couldn't sleep. His heart was pounding. He had no memory of what happened after he fell out of the truck. He lay clutching his chest, afraid he was having a heart attack...

Tom was awake as well. The confines of his small cabin felt like a pressure cooker, it was so hot and close. Nash, snoring in the bunk above him, was sucking up what air there was left to breathe. He had to get out. He pulled his blankets off the bed and climbed down from the wagon.

There on the open ground, Tom was more comfortable. But what to do with his thoughts? Images tumbled over themselves in his brain. Outrageous, mesmerizing, frightening thoughts led him into sleep. His dreams took him back to the coal mine.

He was in that damp cavern, the walls glistening, dripping with water. The splash of droplets plunging down into pools of water echoed in his ears. "Jacob?" he was calling. "Jacob, where are you?"

Tom tried to move, but his feet were so far away. He looked down at them submerged in the water. He couldn't feel them; it was as if they belonged to someone else. Through the sound of the crashing drops, he could hear a mournful sobbing.

"Jacob...Jacob!" Tom shouted. With all his effort he turned those feet and stumbled forward toward the cry. The water rose up to his knees. He panicked as the water rushing against him pushed him back, but struggled on.

Finally he saw Jacob. He was encased in rock, smashed flat like an ancient fossil embedded in stone. Tom picked up a rock fragment and hit the wall again and again, trying to break him free. Suddenly, further down the tunnel, the water broke through the wall and roared forth. Tom ran crazily to plug the hole. He had to create enough time to get Jacob out. And so Tom was locked into a desperate battle—between the rushing water and the imprisoned boy.

He woke up hearing himself shout, "Jacob!" into an empty grey dawn. His clothes were rumpled, his blankets full of pine needles. The morning sky was low and brooding. In the distance he saw a flash of lightning. It was unbearably muggy and the mosquitoes were already biting. Tom sat blinking, looking around the sleeping camp. No one was up.

There were only the sounds of nature's first stirrings ... birds ... insects ... chopping ... branches cracking...

Branches cracking? Who would be breaking up firewood this early in the morning? He had stacked plenty of that yesterday. Tom slowly got up and went cautiously behind the wagons, afraid that one of those strange mountain people was trying to steal from them. What he saw there he couldn't believe. Little gnomes, little gnarly men, were systematically breaking up wood and placing it under the carts as if they intended to set them on fire. Others were hard at work sawing through the spokes of the wheels.

"Hey!" Tom shouted. "Hey!" The little creatures paid no attention to him. They stood about two feet high and were shabbily dressed in bits of moss and decaying leaves. Obviously, they thought Tom couldn't see them.

"Hey, I said stop that!" This time they looked around in shock. A human could see them! They dropped what they were doing and ran into the forest. One of them turned around, shouting something before he scampered away. Tom couldn't hear him, but the words "black-haired man-boy" sailed through his head in tones that sounded like a curse.

"Who's out there?" Mavis was up. Tom could see her wagon pitching about on its springs as she rolled out of bed. Doors opened, tent flaps went up, and soon everyone was standing outside looking nervously around. Tom tried to say something reassuring, but when he got a good look at them in the morning light, he could only laugh. It was as if they had been tossed upside down in a cyclone. Their hair was all tangled, and their clothes were knotted and twisted around backwards.

Everybody started talking at once, shouting and accusing each other of this nasty trick. But when Wally opened the top half of his door and leaned out, they all fell silent. He was completely oblivious to his ridiculous state. His hair stood out like a madman's, his long johns were buttoned up wrong, and his face was covered in bright little red pinch marks.

"What's going on? Stop your yapping and get everything together. We leave today; we're cuttin' the trip short." His head went back in like a cuckoo retracting into its clock as his door slammed.

At breakfast everyone was bickering. Sudy was crying. Mavis was slicing up Wally with her wicked tongue. Nettie was the only one who had escaped the hands of the mysterious prankster.

"Whatsa'matter with all a'ya? You is the sorriest buncha misfits I ever laid eyes on. Tom, you feel all right? You all pale and green at the edges. Here, drink this coffee. What happen to you las' night?"

Tom drank the coffee down, grateful for its stimulating effect. It cleared the last traces of disbelief from his mind. Those creatures were real, just as the leaf man and that whirling funnel of light at the bottom of the hill last night were real. The beautiful red-haired fire creature existed too. He had stumbled upon her world, and now he would never be able to turn back from it. It was all terrifyingly real, as if a veil had been lifted and he could now perceive another reality that had existed side by side with his all along. *Why me?* he wondered. *Why now?*

He remembered a little girl named Sophie, years ago in his hometown. Everyone said she had the second sight. She could see things. What things? These things? For the first time, he thought about going back to that dark town someday...

Mavis's sharp voice cut through Tom's thoughts, and he looked down the table at her. She was haranguing everyone about what she would do if she caught the idiot who pulled that stunt. Tom couldn't help but focus on the bodice of her dress; it kept unbuttoning itself. She would absentmindedly button it back up as she talked, but then pop-pop-pop, it came unbuttoned again. The more Tom stared, the more the form of one of those moss men materialized. He sat like a little monkey on the table, unbuttoning Mavis's bodice, loosening her corset strings, and exposing her ample bosom.

Mavis glared straight at Tom and said, "What the hell are *you* looking at?"

"Nothing, I..."

Mavis slapped the back of her neck. "Damn those mosquitoes!" She stood up. "I can't stand this one minute longer. Nettie, bring breakfast in my cabin!" As she walked away, she caught her skirt on a twig, ripping a long tear up the back.

"Humph," was Nettie's answer as she slowly stirred her coffee.

Just at that moment, Barnaby stretched his big arms over his head and yawned. "Oh, that woman, she's always got a problem—" As he leaned on the back of his chair, it broke off and he fell over onto the ground. He stood up immediately, with a menacing look. "Now, that ain't funny."

Phyllis ran over to him. "Oh, honey, don't get excited. You know what a big man you are. You just don't know your own strength, that's all."

"Yeah, well, just the same, I catch anybody foolin' with me and they'll get this...see?" He smashed his fist into his hand.

The rest of them were choking and laughing so hard that Barnaby could only turn in a rage and stomp away with Phyllis hurrying after him.

Leaving the campsite proved easier said than done. The caravan was plagued with bad luck. The truck wouldn't start. The horse harnesses fell apart. The food turned bad, and there were toads in the drinking water.

Catching one of the little moss men was impossible, but Tom found that if he disturbed the air around them, they would leave what they were doing. He began carrying a long switch, brandishing it everywhere under the wagons and overhead. He did his best to minimize the assault, but everyone regarded this behavior as foolish and suspicious.

"I'll take care of my own mosquitoes, thank you," Lorna complained as Tom protectively swatted around her shoulders.

"Sure, sure," Tom said. "I guess I'm going batty in this heat."

"I guess." Lorna looked at him sideways.

The air was hot and charged with negative energy. By the second day of this, the camp had become a trap they couldn't get out of. Late in the afternoon, Tom finally threw the switch down and gave up. He pulled a handkerchief out of his pocket to mop the sweat running down his face, and something fell onto the ground. It was the seed that the raven had dropped in the field. Tom had forgotten about it wrapped up in his pocket. He stared, fascinated again with its many colors of browns, greens, and reds. While he held the seed in his hand, wondering about it, he had the feeling that someone was looking over his shoulder. He turned to see a few of the gnomes slowly creeping near, and didn't move as more gathered around him. He had the same acute sense of being in the presence of something wild, something *other,* as when he had rescued the stag from the river.

He sat quietly, palm open, seed in hand, while like a band of swarthy monkeys, the gnomes gathered around him. After a while, one of the braver ones moved close enough to touch the seed with a crooked finger. Tom sat stock-still and let him. The little creature's expression softened. He and Tom looked into each other's eyes, and there was a moment of connection between them, being to being. Tom suddenly knew that the siege was over. The seed meant something to them, and his possession of it was cause for a cease-fire.

The moss man tentatively touched Tom's hand. It was the strangest feeling. The little fingers blended with Tom's own as if he had no body, no boundaries of skin and bone.

Then they all withdrew, just like that. The sky made a low rumble and it began to rain. Tom roused himself and sought cover in the wagon.

It rained all night, a soft continuing shower. In the morning, the sky was clear, the air fresh. The caravan rolled out of camp and was on its way.

43

HOME AGAIN

That's the last time I do this, Mavis was thinking as she puffed her way up the stairs of the Madrigal. *Let the old fool go himself next time. Every one of them wagons is fallin' apart. I never saw so much bad luck...damn fool.* She dropped her valise by the closet, opened the windows of her room, and fell back on the bed with a sigh. *Damn fool...*

Wally unlocked the door to his inner sanctum and went straight to the humidor where he kept his cigars. He had been without smokes for days, and all he could think about was this very moment when he would strike a match to one of those carefully rolled Havanas. "Hmm..." He relaxed back in his chair, feet up on the desk, and chuckled with satisfaction to himself. *That damn Huxtable liquor is so strong I can quarter-dilute it and have enough till next summer. Not bad*, he thought. *And I got it for a song...*

Philippe, the dwarf, disappeared quickly after everyone arrived and went directly to his favorite peephole to watch Lorna undress. He could forget how much he hated being himself if he could watch her walk around the room nude, unaware...

Nettie was rattling pans down in the kitchen while Tom was putting things away in the pantry. She stopped a moment to linger by the screen door that opened onto the back alley. There, the last light of day had receded, leaving a vacant gloom. She felt sad to be facing that view again. She had just come full circle, only to find another repetition ahead of her.

Tom dragged in the last of the flour sacks from the porch while Nettie poured them some coffee. Both were quiet, sipping their brew, daydreaming out the door. After a while, Tom said, "Not much of a view, huh?"

Nettie smiled and shook her head. "I was just thinkin' about havin' *this* kitchen, but settin' it down in the country somewhere else, so when I looked out that door, I could see a big garden an' apple trees beyond that. Yep, I was already puttin' fresh-baked pies on the windowsill when you reminded me I was sittin' here in the back end of this ol' flophouse." They both laughed and fell silent again.

"Tom," Nettie said quietly, "what ya goin' to do with yourself?"

"What?" he replied, suddenly self-conscious.

"I mean...what ya goin' to do with yourself in this big ol' world? You's a young man now and it's time ya started havin' some plans."

Tom exhaled a heavy sigh.

"Ya don' belong to these people, Tom. The Lord made ya for more than this. I knew right off—"

Tom said in a compressed tight voice, "I don't know where I belong...I don't know where I'm supposed to be..."

"Somethin's holdin' ya back, Tom. I never ask nobody the why of nothin', but I'm askin' you. What's holdin' ya down? Wally's got no power over ya, does he, Tom?"

Tom stood up and went to the door. He had been filled with such painful uncertainty ever since seeing that funnel of light. His emotions surged wildly, from soaring fantasy to chaotic fear. It was all he could do to keep a lid on himself and appear somewhat normal. Nettie was threatening to unmask him. "Well, I... well, I..." and his voice drifted off.

"When I first laid eyes on ya, ya were the saddest little blackbird I ever saw. I fell in love with ya just like ya was my own boy. I know you's all bottled up and I wish I knew why. Well, I just want ya to do your life right, Tom. Ya got the makins of a fine man inside ya... an' now," she said in a more humorous tone, "I wish ya'd be so fine as ta take them flour sacks and put 'em in the pantry."

Tom looked back at her, relieved that her little interrogation was over. He lifted one of the sacks and it fell open, dumping the flour on the floor.

He had gone to get a broom when Nettie shouted for him to come quickly. "T-t-Tom, does ya see that? Does ya?" Tom saw it, all right. That flour had taken on a powdery animated shape. It flew around the kitchen and went smack through the door; then whatever it was disappeared, leaving only a fine white impression on the screen, like flour on a sifter.

"My God," Nettie stammered. "Merciful Heaven, what was that?!"

Tom began sweeping the floor as fast as he could, making a good deal of flour rise into the air. Nettie covered her face with her apron. Coughing away, she shouted, "Tom! Tom! Stop it!"

"My God," Tom said, "where did that wind come from? It blew the stuff all over the place!"

"Wind! That weren't no wind, and you're not helping with that broom. What in blazes are ya doin'?"

"Of course it was the wind. What else was it?" He coughed, continuing to sweep.

"Oh, for God's sake, lemme do that. Here, hold that sack open while I sweeps up. You's a fine boy for makin' a fine mess..."

When Tom finished confusing Nettie with all his antics, she wasn't sure what she'd seen. But Tom knew: the impression left on that screen was the faint white imprint of a woodland moss man....

44

NETTIE'S BIRTHDAY

The Madrigal was in full swing again. People had really missed it during the month it had been closed. They came back in droves. Mavis raised the prices on Nettie's early-bird dinners and nobody made a comment.

Tom was busier than ever. He and Nash were rebuilding the stage, hanging up some lights, and constructing a stairway so the girls could sashay down into the audience. In all of this commotion, however, Tom saw no sign of the forest creature. He saw traces of flour in the pantry, on the stairs, on the windowsills, and in the hallway, but he never caught sight of the creature. He felt sorry for it. The little fellow was clearly lost and disoriented. Perhaps it had escaped, or died up in the rafters. Tom wondered if a being like that could die.

One day, Nettie came back from the market with a bundle of flowers among the other provisions. She took them from their newspaper wrapping and placed them in a big bowl of water. Tom watched her silently as she did this. Nettie was smiling and humming a tune, arranging the colorful bouquet. She stopped for a moment, feeling Tom's gaze. "Well," she said, "we gotta brighten things up around here...and 'sides, it's my birthday."

"Why, Nettie!" Tom rushed over to her. "I didn't know you had birthdays!" He picked her up and gave her a big kiss on the cheek.

"Now cut that out! An' don't go tellin' nobody, neither! I jus'...I jus' wanted to buy me some flowers, that's all."

"Well, all right." Tom winked, respecting her secret. "But I know where these are going, anyway. They're going right smack in the middle of the dinner table. Nobody has to know anything." And off he went to put them in the dining room.

Nettie was fussing and fuming all the way down the hall with him, but Tom insisted the flowers would be their silent celebration. The dining room was exactly the same as it had been many years ago when he saw it on his first night there: the antique table, the unmatched chairs, the scuffed wooden wainscoting halfway up the walls with the faded, embossed wallpaper falling down to meet it. Hammers, nails, and paintbrushes never made it back this far into the Madrigal. The public didn't see these rooms, so there was no point in it, according to Wally.

Tom put the flowers in the middle of the table, then drew back one of the old damask curtains, letting a band of afternoon light pour into the room. The flowers were bathed in an amber glow while everything else faded into the shadows. "There," Tom said, gazing at the dramatic setting. "Now there's a picture for you." Nettie looked uncomfortable. "Oh, come on. Your secret's safe with me." He put his arm around her and walked her back to the kitchen.

All day long, Nettie's flowers sat on the dining table, drinking in the light from the window. The Madrigal's afternoon customers swilled their whiskies and chewed on their cigars. Tom stacked glasses behind the bar, then went to help in the kitchen. As he passed down the hall, he was drawn again to the dining room by the sight of Nettie's flowers.

There they were, caught together in a glass vase, silently, joyfully beautiful. Tom sat down in the shadows as if he had just taken a seat in church. A hushed, still atmosphere pervaded the room. Compared to the life energy emitted by the flowers, everything else in the room appeared as lifeless as a sketch drawn in dust—himself included. A familiar hopelessness threatened to cloud his mind, yet the spell cast by those flowers wouldn't permit such dark thoughts. His mind sailed right past them into that golden summer wheatfield where he had seen the crow flying toward him out of the sky. He felt for the seed in his pocket, turning it round and round in his fingers.

The light on the flowers began to increase, bringing his attention back to the present. What he was seeing now was not a static arrangement, but forms shaped by undulating rhythms of color. Shades of green pulsed up the stems and out of the leaves where the color spread like a halo. The yellow of the flowers expanded and contracted like a breath. Within the petals, the flowers bore auras that extended outward from their centers. Wavy lengths of color sent tendrils far into the room before they disappeared.

Tom sat perfectly still. Suddenly, to his amazement, the little woodland moss man appeared out of the darkness at the other end of the table and timidly approached the flowers. It wasn't aware of Tom as it came closer to bathe itself in the shower of light and energy. Making throaty cooing sounds, it ran around the bouquet like a little monkey. It sat on its haunches and raised long spindly arms up to the petals, then cupped its hands around the yellow aura and scooped the golden glow into its mouth. The gnome repeated this action over and over, drawing ribbons of wavy color into itself until it appeared satisfied. Then it wrapped its arms around its body, hung its head down, and rocked to and fro.

Extraordinary, Tom thought. *The creature hadn't eaten of the flowers themselves, but only of their essence.* The little thing looked so forlorn that Tom was moved to touch it.

The creature immediately sensed his presence, but was too weak to run. It merely put its hands over its head and shivered miserably. Tom slowly got up and stepped toward the table. "Easy now, little critter. I won't hurt you, not for the world." He spoke in a whisper, knowing his words wouldn't mean anything, but his soft tone might. "How did you get yourself so far away from home? What little prank were you going to pull in that flour sack, anyway? Look what I have here..." Tom carefully took the seed out of his pocket. "Your other friends were very happy to see this...here!" Tom moved closer.

The creature cautiously peered out from under one bony elbow. Round eyes watched Tom's every move.

"Here. See what I've got." Tom quietly laid down his open hand, the seed resting in his palm. The woeful thing looked at the seed and at Tom with evident relief; then it jumped right up onto Tom's chest, flinging its arms around his neck. Tom was completely taken by surprise. It nestled up against his cheek, mouth wide open, crying piteously. This ancient, gnarly, monkey-sized man was, in fact, a baby.

Tom held it close and patted its green, mossy bottom. "There now," he said, patting its back, walking up and down. He quickly glanced into the hallway. No one was there. Tom felt ridiculous at the thought of himself performing this pantomime; he was glad no one else could see this.

Holding the strange little gnome was very peculiar. It had density but no weight, and gave off a scent something like roasted acorns. "Why, you're just a pup, aren't ya?" Tom said softly. "That's what I'll call ya—Pup. Hey, Pup, stop cryin'...I'll help ya out. Don't run away again...stick close to me, okay?" Tom went on quietly talking, watching the flowers give off their moving colors. He wondered if he would always be able to see them now, or if the perception had something to do with touching the seed. "Do you see the world like this all the time, Pup? Hey, Pup..." But there was no reaction from Pup. He was fast asleep on Tom's shoulder, making sounds like a buzzing bee.

Tom picked up the seed, took a few leaves from the bouquet, and carried Pup upstairs to his bedroom. He put Pup to bed in a half opened drawer, tucking the leaves under his head.

"Nettie," Tom said, returning to the kitchen, "I'm going to see you get a fresh bunch of flowers every week."

"Well, I'd be happy if you'd just get this food on the table before the chowhounds get down here and eat them flowers for dinner!"

Tom smiled. "Yeah, that's a definite possibility!"

45

WALLY FINDS A JEWEL

Wally strutted along the busy street with Cheng just a half-step ahead, cutting a path through the crowd. The city was growing fast. He couldn't believe how much the traffic had increased in the month that he had been gone. People milled about everywhere, going in and out of shops, crisscrossing the streets. Horse-drawn carriages picked their way precariously through the aggressive surge of automobiles. The overall feel was definitely more cosmopolitan. Wally liked it. He was feeling as expansive and prosperous as his city today. The Chinaman's protective edge seemed to say, "Make way! Make way! Important person here! Make way for Wally Ripton!"

It was when he came out of the smoke shop that he saw her. A slim ankle rising from muddy shoes, pale skin, a shapely figure, and the lost look on her face in particular. *Yum, perfect pickings,* he thought. He watched as she hesitated at the corner. Her clothes were backcountry-style, worn and faded, her belongings wrapped in a patchwork quilt tucked under her arm. She crossed the street and went around the corner. "Well, if she's lost, then I'll find her," Wally chuckled to himself. The way he figured things, if temptation crossed his path three times, then it was meant to be. He called it fate.

The girl appeared again, coming back around the same corner. "Ah, that's number two. Come to Grandma's house, the wolf is waiting..."

The morning progressed and Wally was now reclining in the barber's chair, a steaming towel covering his face. Cheng was sitting by the window, tossing pistachio nuts from his pocket into his mouth and "reading" the newspaper. His boss read the newspaper, so of course he did too, and with great concentration. Those few years at the mission school hadn't given him much skill, however, so the going was slow.

The barber sat Wally up and unwrapped his face. He was about to apply shaving cream when Wally pushed his arm away. "There, across the street." He motioned to Cheng.

The Chinaman crushed the paper in his hands as he turned to look out the window. He scanned the people walking the street, but saw nothing alarming. He turned questioningly to Wally. "Huh?"

"The girl over there." Cheng looked back. He knew his boss's tastes very well, and soon found the slim ankles, the figure, and the face with the lost, overwhelmed expression. "Keep your eye on her," Wally said as he leaned back to accept the cooling lather on his cheeks and chin.

The Chinaman walked outside by the door. Wally emerged from his shave all pink and shining. He smoothed the sides of his hair as the barber brushed his jacket. That done, he went out the door and down the street in the direction Cheng was pointing.

* * *

Pup slept for days, constantly buzzing, with his arms around the seed Tom had left with him. Tom brought green plants for Pup and placed them about the windowsills in his room and the kitchen.

He even found a small tree to plant in the back alley. As he shoveled up the dirt, he remembered how the coal miners used to call him Elf Boy because he stuck green, leafy twigs in his hat to remind himself of the life he had left above for those dark, airless tunnels below. Now, a scant five years—or was it five centuries? —later, he was planting a tree to feed an elf, a gnome, or whatever Pup was called. What's more, he didn't even think it was unusual. Perhaps he *was* becoming an elf boy.

Just like on that day at Split Rock Creek with Howler trotting along in front of him, Tom had the feeling a path was being shown to him. And then, as always, just as he thought he might see his way, memories rushed in to kill the possibility he had opened to. Again, those black-shawled women hovered on the steps the day of his father's death. Again, he saw his mother slowly unravel until she too was dead. Again, he watched helplessly as Jacob and two men were crushed under tons of stone. And above all, there was the specter of Aunt Petra, her hand falling out like a dead fish as he opened the dumbwaiter door. As he packed the earth down around the tree, he fought to bury those memories finally and forever with each pound of the shovel.

When he looked up, there was Nettie's white smile beaming from her dark face. "Oh, Tom, I love dat! I loves it! What made ya think o' dat?"

Tom couldn't help but smile back. "I'm improving the view."

"Chile, come on in here and set yo' self down while I pull them fresh, hot sticky buns outta the oven. I'm goin' to see dem trees out my kitchen door after all!"

"I hope it grows out there," Tom said to Nettie over his shoulder as he washed up.

"Oh, it'll grow. I'll see to that. It'll grow big n' tall just like you," Nettie assured him.

She had just opened the oven door when they heard Wally and Cheng coming. "I hopes he goes straight up to dat rat's nest he call da office," Nettie said. She pulled the hot buns out and set them on the stove.

Tom replied, "Nope, we're not that lucky. Here they are."

Cheng opened the screen door. "Come on in, it's okay," Wally was saying to someone hesitating behind him. Nettie and Tom glanced at each other.

"Well, now, look what I found. Someone to help you in the kitchen, Nettie." In through the door, prodded by Wally's coaxing, came a poor ragamuffin of a girl. "This here's Ruby. She says it's Ru, or Ri, or something. But I'm gonna call her Ruby 'cause she's got red hair." With that, he pulled her headscarf off and piles of red hair tumbled down over her shoulders. The girl reacted with a catlike hiss, and Wally gasped as if he had just taken the lid off a fire. For a moment nobody spoke.

Wally broke the spell by saying, "Well...I...Well, Nettie...talk to her and see what she can do. I'll tell Mavis to come an' have a look at her. I think she'll clean up bright as a penny."

Wally went up to find Mavis. Cheng tried to get out the door with one of the hot cross buns, but Nettie cracked him with her wooden spoon and flapped him out of the kitchen with her apron. She returned to the stove to give her boiling pots an aggravated stir. "Um um," she grumbled.

Tom had not taken his eyes from the girl. Except for her remarkable hair, it was hard to see anything distinct about her. A brown-green coating of dust covered her skin, clothing, everything. She looked around as if she had never seen the inside of a house. Judging by the layers of dirt on her clothes, she must have been living outside a long time. Tom wondered how she'd ever found her way to the city. There was something frightening, primitive, about her, yet delicate at the same time. Her eyes sparkled like forest fireflies. She stood uneasily, bundle held close, ready for flight.

Nettie set her stirring spoon down and put her hands on her hips. She clearly did not like this new addition to Ripton's menagerie. "Girl, where you come from? What you doin' here?" she said angrily. "The city ain't no place for the likes of you. You'll come to no good here, I can tell you that! What can you do? You tell me, what can you do 'sides pull roots up from the ground!"

"Nettie!" Tom tried to stop her tirade. "What are you getting so riled up about?"

"I seen plenty of her kind come down from the mountain and end up in the gutter. I don' want nothin' to do with it. Go back where ya came from, hear?" She picked up her spoon and gave her pots a furious turn. The girl stood silently.

Tom said softly, "Well, she's here now. What can we do?"

"Do! What can *we* do?" And Nettie was off again. "Point is, what can *she* do? Make trouble. I sees it, clear as day."

Tom continued softly, asking the girl, "Where do you come from?"

She spoke haltingly, like she was just getting used to the words. "I came from the mountain to look for someone—a relative, he is. Gone to the city, he said he was."

"Oh, Lordy," Nettie muttered, shaking her head. "And how was ya plannin' to stay alive while yer lookin'? How was ya gonna eat?"

"Oh, I don't eat," she replied, then added, "...much.... but I do get tired." She sighed, looking for a chair.

"Well, set down then." Nettie relented. Tom was relieved. That was a good sign. Mavis came down the stairs, holding both sides of the walls as she balanced on her tiny shoes. "What have we here? A country magpie?" She went directly to the icebox to remove her cold compresses and special age-defying creams. She leaned back against the door to close it, since both her hands were full, and hesitated a moment, looking the girl up and down. "That the real color of your hair?"

"Yessum," was the small reply.

"Humph. Come on." Mavis pushed off from the icebox and teetered toward the stairs. On the first step she turned. "Well, come on. Do as you're told."

Ruby didn't move. She looked at Tom and Nettie. Nettie nodded reassuringly in Mavis's direction. The girl picked up her bundle and followed Mavis up the winding staircase with a curious, bewildered look.

And Tom... Tom looked as if his destiny
                might just
                        have come
                                to meet him.

A BAD START

Pup was gone, and the seed too. As Tom searched the house, he could hear Mavis and the girls talking about Ruby. There were many comings and goings from the bathroom to the closets to the laundry and back again. What were they doing to her in there? Behind the doors, Mavis was muttering about "disinfectants, Wally and his mongrels, not worth the trouble," and on and on. But never a sound from the girl.

When Mavis came back down the winding stairs with Ruby that evening, the girl had been given a startling makeover. She was clean all right—pale-white clean. They had done some serious taming of her back-country nature, for her hair was parted in the middle and pomaded down into a knot at the back of her neck. Her eyebrows had been plucked into fine lines, and the dress she wore had all the restrictions of a straitjacket on her young, shapely figure. Ruby stood there like a wild horse that had been hobbled, her eyes cast down. All Tom could think of was poor "Sad Sarah."

At dinner, however, Mavis felt quite satisfied with her efforts, for when Ruby went around the table serving the meal, Wally glanced up at her and was visibly disappointed. "Well," he said, squinting at his wife, "she cleaned up fine... just fine."

Tom tried to smile at Ruby, but she would not look at him. Lorna gave her a sympathetic pat as she went by.

Mavis said to Wally over the confusion of arms reaching for food on the table, "I don't know where you find them, Walter, honestly, I don't. This girl is from another planet. She can hardly speak!" Wally raised his eyebrows as he ate. "She can work in the kitchen, but I'll have to train her myself. She can have her room and board, but not a cent of money until I say so." Wally nodded in assent. Mavis buttered her bread with an overburdened sigh and ate it with another.

The dwarf had his own opinion about Ruby, but he kept it to himself. Under that plain wrap of a dress was a wild loveliness just waiting to be touched. With the special instincts of one who had spent his life on the outside looking in, he also knew this girl was something other than she portrayed. Behind that appearance there was another, and behind that, there was even something else. A curl of fear went up his back, and he hated her...

With dinner at an end, Mavis carefully blotted her lips with her napkin and called, "Girl, clear the dishes."

"Her name is Ruby," Tom said with an unprecedented insistence.

Mavis stopped mid-blot to consider his tone, then decided to let it pass. "All right, then, Ruby. Clear the dishes."

* * *

"She gonna train her herself... umm umm..." Nettie mumbled, elbow-deep in dishwater. "That'll be the day. Chile, you listen to that woman 'cause you gots to, but you do what I say an' you be stayin' on here, understan'?"

"Yessum," Ruby answered, drying the dishes beside her at the sink.

"Dat all you got to say for yo'self is 'yessum?'"

"Yessum," she repeated.

"An' stop rubbin' dat plate. It was dry ten minutes ago."

"Yessum."

That night, Tom pulled back the sheets on his bed and there was Pup. "Well, where have you been? And what did you do with my seed?" Tom got into bed and Pup jumped all over him, covering him with feathery welcoming kisses. "Oh, all right, calm down. I'm glad to see you too."

Tom turned on his side and stretched his legs out. He felt something down at the bottom of the bed. "What's this, Pup?" He reached down and pulled up one of Mavis's gaudy rhinestone pins. Pup was eagerly reaching for it when Tom whispered harshly, "Did you take this? Did you do this? Bad Pup!" He got up and put the pin in his dresser drawer, then got back into bed. Pup nestled around his neck. "Bad Pup! Bad!" Tom said with a smile on his face.

Early in the morning before dawn, Tom awoke to the muffled sound of crying. He went to the hallway and listened. Filtering through snores and the creaks that an old building makes of its own accord, he could hear a mournful sobbing. He followed the sound down the hall and upstairs to the little room they had given Ruby. She was crying. Tom hesitated, barefoot, before the door, not daring to knock...

The next morning, Lorna and Mavis had a big fight at breakfast. In the ruckus, Ruby passed among them unseen, except by Tom, who noticed everything about her: her pale face, the sad eyes, her delicate hands, the way she walked...

The fight was about a man Lorna had met. He had come into the Madrigal, watched one of the shows, and taken a fancy to her. He and his friends had started coming in regular. This was fine with Wally and Mavis, because he spent good money while he was there drinking, watching the shows, and playing cards in the back room. He was a good-looking, powerful man, immaculately dressed, with steel-grey eyes—exactly the kind of man Lorna always fell for. Now she wanted to go out with him, off the premises, so to speak, where he might spend his money elsewhere. This was definitely *not* Ripton policy.

Lorna was saying she would do what she wanted, and Mavis was assuring her she would do nothing of the kind. Wally got up from the table, brushing toast crumbs from his vest. "Mavis, my sweet, shut up. I'll take care of this," he said, and left.

Lorna set her jaw and stared straight ahead at Cheng. The other two Peaches looked frightened. Mavis huffed dismissively and left the room. Those remaining at the table tried hard to convince Lorna to stop rocking the boat. Phyllis offered, "Look, honey, there are plenty of fish in the sea. Let this one go. He isn't interested in you, he's just amusing himself."

Lorna spat out a biting insult in response to this advice, then ran upstairs to her room. The dwarf sat shaking his head and chuckling to himself.

One by one, they finished their meals and went on with the day. Tom remained while Ruby cleared the dishes. He got up to help, but she hurried back to the kitchen, leaving Tom alone.

Things continued on this way for days. Tensions mounted between the girls and Wally. Tom walked around mystified and afraid to approach Ruby. Every night, he heard her crying. Every night, he went to her door, but never knocked. Every night, he would find another trinket Pup had squirreled away at the bottom of his bed.

By the seventh night of this, Tom knew if he heard her crying again he would *have* to do something. Knocking on her door might bring other early risers into the hall, so he would silently open her door and whisper, "Ruby," through the crack. She couldn't become too frightened with that.

And so it was in the early morning hours that he heard those sobs, followed their sound, and found himself with his hand upon her door. Tom felt like an intruder breaking into the privacy of her sorrows, but he had to let her know he cared...he had to see her. He opened the door. As he leaned in to whisper her name, the walls made a cracking noise—or was that someone in the hall?

He jumped back into the shadows, his heart thumping in his chest. He waited, his eyes filled with the vision of what he had just seen. She was there on the bed; she hadn't undressed. The tight sleeves of that horrible garment pulled at her arms and the skirt twisted about her lovely legs, but her feet had escaped those shoes Mavis had given her. She was lying on top of the old quilt she had carried from the mountains. It was worn and ragged on the outside, but on the inside, it was vivid with texture and color. A golden apple hung from the edge that dropped down to the floor.

Tom couldn't wait any longer. He had to go to her. He went back to open the door, but when he did, she was gone. How could that be? There was no window in that room...no way out except past him. Tom whispered "Ruby?" A candle flickered by the bed, and the quilt gave off a silvery luminescence in its light—that was all...

* * *

"Mabon! Mabon!" Rhea called in the vast hall. Birds fluttered about high up in its vaulted ceiling and a crow flew down to perch on the great antlered chair. "Mabon, Mabon," her voice echoed back to her. Angrily, she kicked the furs lying about the hearth, then sat down to watch the wood burning up in the fire with devilish eyes.

"Is that how young human girls are dressing themselves now?"

Rhea turned, surprised to find Mabon sitting beside her. "Oh, Mabon!" She burst into tears. "I want to come back. It's horrible there. They live in dark, smelling rooms... everyone is miserable. A little misshapen human crawls about at night spying on everyone through holes in the walls. The girls who work there have no freedom. The man and his wife who own the place treat everyone like dirt—"

"Yes, but what about—" Mabon tried to interject.

"That wife...that Mavis...look what she's done to me. I'll turn her into the fat toad she is..."

"Well now, don't—"

"She's made me so ugly. I'll make her pay for this. I'll push her down the stairs right off those silly shoes she wears..."

"The boy. Have you seen the boy?"

"I'm so embarrassed. I can't even look at him like this. I can't bear that horrible place." Rhea buried her head in his lap.

With a wave of his hand, Mabon restored her to her radiant glory. She looked up into his eyes, her face glistening in golden light.

"The boy...what about the young man?" Mabon asked.

Rhea sighed. "He's very shy. The way that woman has made me look, I don't think he even notices me."

"If he is the one, he will recognize you."

"Why doesn't he leave that wretched place? I don't think he'll be brave enough to do what you ask."

"I believe he might. It's just that he closed the door to his heart long ago and now he's lost. In such a state, nothing matters. Where he is and what he does mean nothing to him."

Rhea looked frustrated and not at all convinced. "There's a baby gerking there. He can see it. He calls it Pup. When I first got there, the little thing came to me and wanted to be sent home. I told him to stay close to the one who had shown him the seed."

"That's good—that's good. You see, in many ways, the young man is beginning to cross over. What's he done with the seed?"

Rhea smiled. "Pup took it and buried it in the back alley. You know how gerkings are—they hide things all over the place."

Mabon nodded, "Well, that's good too. It will grow, and when the time comes, you can use the leaves."

"You mean you still want me to go back there?"

"Of course. A little blow to your vanity shouldn't deter you from your task. I told you, things are going to get very bad in man's world, very bad indeed. Unfortunately, this is our world as well. We must have someone cross over to save us all."

Rhea looked into the fire. "Do the ones who live in the Light say this is true?"

Mabon nodded.

Rhea sighed. "All right...I'll return."

47

ONE THING LEADS TO ANOTHER

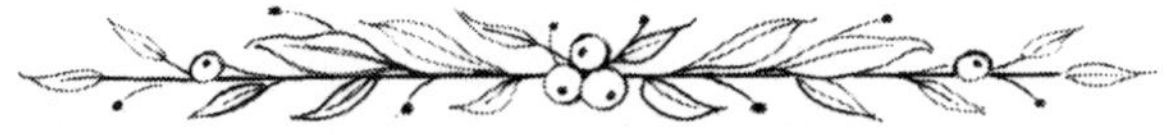

The next morning, when Ruby wasn't in the kitchen, Tom thought she was gone for good. "Where's Ruby?"

Nettie gave him a sidelong glance. "On the steps, peelin' potatoes...um um," she grumbled, watching Tom swing open the screen door and step outside.

The back alley had some sun in the morning and Ruby was sitting in a little patch of it, shoes off, doing her work. Even though her back was to him, he could tell her whole demeanor had changed. That crushed sadness was gone and a lively spirit had taken its place. Her hair was freshly washed, held to the side with a thin leather tie. Curls fell about her shoulders. The last few buttons at the back of her dress remained undone, releasing her from its tight grip.

"Mornin'," Tom said, sitting down beside her.

She looked at him with those wonderful sparkling eyes she had shown him that first day. "Mornin'," she replied.

Tom smiled. "I like your hair much better that way."

Ruby smiled back and then looked serious. "I'm not going to wear my hair the way she says." She scalped the potato in her hand as if it were Mavis's head.

Tom watched her, fascinated. There was an untouchable quality about her. Her hands and feet were very refined—not at all callused as one might expect. It was as if she had walked on air down from that mountain. He struggled to keep the conversation going. "Y'know," he said, "I bet Lorna would give you one of her dresses that would fit you better than that one. I'll ask her."

"Would you?" Ruby smiled again, and Tom fell into the spell of her smile's radiance like a diver plunging into a pool of water.

"Yes," he stammered, trying not to let her feel how much he was captivated by her.

Ruby saw his shyness and went back to her potato peeling. Tom tried to keep his eyes off her, but he could not. It was just dawning on him how really beautiful she was. The sunlight on her hair gave off a red glow all around her. For a moment, he remembered the funnel of light in the forest and the being he had seen hovering above Wally. It was then that he noticed Ruby's ears. She had small, pretty, but decidedly pointed ears.

"Ruby? You finished with them potatoes? Come on in here!" Nettie called.

Ruby flashed Tom one more radiant smile, then put her feet into the ill-fitting shoes and clumped into the kitchen.

"Ruby," Tom whispered to himself.

* * *

Lorna was flying high with excitement and confidence these days. Burt Russell had begun taking her out for drives in his car, buying her clothes, and even taking her home with him after hours. Lorna was sure it was because she had stood up to Wally and his threats, for he had stopped objecting to her going out with Burt.

This man's attention had sent all her hopes aloft again. She had a very inflated idea of her charms. But Lorna was like that. She was either depressed and cynical or overly optimistic and cocky. It was what made her so tragic. She had no in between.

He had given her a locket with a little diamond set in the middle. Her hands were shaking as she held it out for the other girls to admire. "Look," she said. "It's real gold, and that's a real diamond." She went before the mirror and one of the girls clasped it around her neck as if she were being ordained, initiated into the holy order of "The Loved One"...a state they all had lost hope of attaining. They congratulated Lorna on her good fortune and went away a little sadder within themselves.

Early one morning, Lorna climbed up the steps at the Madrigal after a night of drinking and extravagance at Burt's sumptuous apartment. There had been lots of people there, lots of pretty girls, but through it all Burt went about with his arm around Lorna. She was Burt's girl now. She was sure of it.

The dwarf sat in the dark at the bar amongst the stacked glasses and piled-up chairs readied for the morning mop-up. He drank and smoked countless cigarettes waiting for Lorna. His jealousy had turned to anger in the hours he had been there. Lorna was a fool.

She didn't even see him as she swayed up the steps to her room. The scent of her perfume trailed up after her, and the dwarf followed to spy on her as he always did. He watched her undress and slip into bed.

Lorna lay there thinking, fingering the locket on its chain around her neck. The room was dark except for the faint early morning light coming through the window. She heard the door open and sat up. "Who's there?" she whispered harshly.

"You're a fool," the dwarf whispered back.

She dropped back onto her pillow. "Oh, God, get out of here. I'm tired."

But Philippe didn't leave. He came and sat upon her bed, a thing she most detested. Lorna scrunched up in a ball. "I said, get out of here, or I'll scream."

The dwarf chuckled. "Go ahead."

Lorna gave up. "Okay, okay. Say what you want and get out of here."

"You're a fool," he repeated.

"You already said that—what else is new?"

"You think you're free to come and go as you please? 'Mr. Russell is calling on me tonight...I'm goin' out with Mr. Russell tonight,'" he squeaked in a mocking singsong voice. "Mr. Russell has bought and paid for you. Wally has sold you—get it?"

The dwarf never looked so ugly to her as he did now in that shadowy light. His hair and beard smelled like cheap wine soaking in an ashtray. She felt sick to her stomach. She pushed past him to the washbasin and heaved into the bowl.

"So what—so what?" she cried as she swung back around, leaning against the stand. "Maybe it was that way in the beginning, but it's different now. Everything's changed."

The dwarf got off the bed and came close to her, repulsing her with his touch. "Everything's changed? He's in love with you, is that it? He's in love with you just like that locket is real gold and I'm six feet tall."

He left her there, trembling now and drowning in a sea of doubt.

48

THE REVELATION

In the month Ruby had been at the Madrigal, she had blossomed into a beauty that even Mavis couldn't deny. She hated to think that Wally had been right, but this girl had something. She definitely was unusual. The dresses Lorna had given her and the way she insisted on wearing her hair all tousled and free were very appealing. Ruby did her work, kept to herself, and hardly ate a morsel. She even was able to steer clear of Wally's leering overtures. No, Mavis couldn't fault Ruby on anything. In fact, she began to think of her in a different light. If she could only dance or sing, maybe this little copper penny might add up to some real money. Mavis's theatrical wheels began to turn...

* * *

Tom found every possible cause to be around Ruby. He convinced Nettie to let him take her to the early morning markets with him. He wanted to show her around. How was she ever going to find this relative of hers if she never got a chance to look?

"You two is like two trains on the same track," Nettie told him. "You is bound to crash. If I knowed the switch to turn one a' ya off, I would. But I don't, so all I kin say is watch out. That girl ain't normal. She don't eat normal, she don't smell normal. She don't walk normal. I sends her to the pantry for something, the next minute she behind me with it—like she flew there and back. She pretty, she nice, but she give me the creeps."

Tom shivered around his room getting dressed in the frosty autumn dawn. The wholesale markets had to be shopped early, or the best meats and produce would be gone. Ruby was probably already down in the kitchen waiting, but Tom was having trouble with Pup, who wanted to go too. This was the first time the creature had ever shown any interest in leaving the confines of the house.

Quite by accident, Tom had found out how to communicate with Pup. He *thought* what he wanted to say to him—not in words, but in pictures. He had been wondering how he could get Pup to put back some of the trinkets he was always taking, and he'd pictured Pup opening the drawer to Mavis's jewelry case and slipping the rhinestone pin inside. Pup was looking at Tom, and though he didn't seem very happy about it, he got right up and did just that.

Pup was able to communicate with Tom in the same way. As Tom was hurrying to get dressed, he kept getting flashes of walking through the streets with Pup on his shoulders. "No, Pup, no," he kept saying. He wanted to be alone with Ruby and not worry about where Pup was every five minutes.

Pup was so insistent Tom could hardly think with all the pictures bombarding his brain. "Okay, okay, all right—stop—where's my other shoe?" Tom saw a picture of it under the bed. "Thanks," he said, looking over to Pup, who was just about to leap on his shoulder. "Wait a minute, wait a minute—I need my jacket. Hold your horses."

Pup was puzzled. He'd gotten a picture of himself holding on to some horses, and he didn't know what that meant.

Tom smiled. "Yeah, that's right. Think about it and let me get ready."

When Ruby saw Tom come down to the kitchen with Pup, she signaled the gerking to keep their knowledge of each other secret.

Nettie sat, disapprovingly watching Ruby pick at the breakfast she had prepared for them. Tom was quick to declare he was hungry enough for two, then whisked Ruby out the door before Nettie could grumble another "Um, um."

"Don't pay any attention to Nettie. She means well."

"I know," Ruby said, tying the wool scarf Tom had given her around her neck.

"You warm enough? It's just a couple blocks' walk to the trolley."

"Fine," she said. "I love to be outside."

They walked along in silence, each feeling the proximity of the other and the electricity that leapt between them. If only Pup would stop putting his arms around Tom's head, blurring his vision as they went along.

The market was already very busy when they got there. There were vendors for everything—fruits, vegetables, flowers, meats. Tom unfolded the wooden-handled burlap bags he'd brought with him and started filling them with the produce Nettie wanted.

Ruby and Pup loved the flower market. They both lingered in that section while Tom was buying other things. When he came back, Pup was sitting on Ruby's shoulder. Tom wondered if she knew he was there.

Tom bought Ruby some flowers and told her they just had to buy the fish and then they'd be done. As they approached that section, Ruby complained of the smell.

"Yes, it is strong," he said, "but they have very fresh fish here."

Ruby nodded, covering her nose with Tom's scarf. When she saw the fish stand with its rows upon rows of dead carcasses lying on chunks of ice, she looked visibly sick. Pup started to cry and hid his face in her hair; she instinctively reached up and patted his back. *Ruby knows Pup is there!* Tom realized. She turned away and wouldn't go any closer.

"Wait here," Tom told her, "this will only take a minute." He had the vendor wrap the fish in extra layers of paper and put it in the very bottom of his bag.

"We're finished," Tom said, putting his arm around Ruby. They didn't say a word all the way home. On the trolley, Ruby sat by the window, drinking in the air.

When they climbed up the steps of the back porch, Tom went in to put the things away, but Ruby and Pup stayed outside. Afterward, he came out to sit beside them. "What's the matter?" he asked her.

She looked at him imploringly. "Oh, take me somewhere where there are trees and leaves and green living plants. I can't stand another minute of this dead place."

Tom was silent. The only area he could think of like that was Parkmont. His dark memories were countered by his desire to please Ruby.

"All right, Ruby, I'll take you somewhere like that...and then will you tell me who you really are?"

"Yes," she said softly.

And so, with more than a little uncertainty, Tom found himself returning to a place he never intended on seeing again...

* * *

Walking down those quiet tree-lined streets, Ruby was visibly relieved. Pup leapt off her shoulder and scampered up into the trees. Tom waited for her to say something. They walked and walked till finally they were across the street from Aunt Petra's house.

"Why do you look at that house like that?" Ruby asked.

"I used to live there," Tom said hesitantly.

"What happened in that house?"

Tom looked at her in alarm. "Something awful."

They walked on, and after some moments, Ruby said, "That house still has a hold on you. It is not good."

Tom stopped and looked her straight in the eye. "Who are you? Where do you come from?"

"My name is Rhea, and I come from a world that lives beside yours." As she said that, she suddenly vanished, then reappeared further up the street. For a moment she revealed herself, and Tom saw the transparent fiery creature he had seen by that funnel of light. "Tom..." she whispered in his ear. He turned and saw her standing in front of Aunt Petra's house.

"Ruby," he called in warning.

"Yes?" she answered, beside him again.

"Don't—"

"Don't what?" she asked mischievously from a branch high above him. "I'm free—I'm free," she sang, and shaking off all the confines of human form, she danced with unbridled joy.

Tom watched from the ground amazed as she flew about, teasing him, leading him on with her astonishing acrobatics. "Wait!" he called again as she leapt and darted amongst the trees. He tried to keep up with her, but it was like following the flight of a firefly. She was there and then she wasn't. All the while, her voice was close to his ear, whispering a song in the strange poetry of an ancient speech:

"I come from the outmost stream
Of life
From the glens where the
White swans glide.
Follow me...Find me...
In the land of life everlasting.
Leave behind the world where
You are bound
Lift the veil and claim the crown."

A wind blew down the quiet street, rustling the leaves into angry motion. The air was filled with an electric energy. A strange darkness descended, as before a thunderstorm. "Ruby," he called.

Oddly, Tom thought of his mother's little Christmas angel that he'd left in the tree behind Aunt Petra's house. Was it still there, swinging from that branch where he had hung all his sorrows those long years ago? Overwhelmed with what was happening, filled with sadness, Tom felt tears run down his face. "Ruby, come back," he heard himself say.

The tumult suddenly abated. The street was calm once more. The Ruby he knew in her hand-me-down clothes was quietly walking toward him. The sudden storm had ended her wild flight. She gazed at him with questioning eyes.

Tom rushed to put his arms around her and hold her close. "Let's go, Ruby...let's go back. Where's Pup? Can you call Pup?" Ruby made a chirping sound, and in an instant Pup was with them again.

All the way home, she kept looking at Tom to see if he was all right. Ruby knew she had done something wrong. That angry wind had been her warning; she had gone too far.

* * *

That night before the crackling fire, Rhea waited for Mabon to speak.

Finally he turned to her. "You see," he continued as if she had never left, "Humans cannot change just like that. They have too many memories, too many experiences that must be filtered through before they can take the next step. You were not to reveal yourself so soon. These things take time. We have taken years with this boy. We must be sure about him."

"I'm sorry...I just..."

"You did exactly what faeries always do—just exactly what they want."

Rhea looked down at her feet. She hated being disciplined in any way. If it weren't for her growing interest in Tom, she wouldn't have cared at all about what Mabon was saying. She kept thinking about that moment when Tom had taken her into his arms. Something of her had gone out to him in a way she never felt before. Their embrace had formed a circle she didn't want to break.

"Remember the little girl Sophie? You were fascinated with her, too. Even though she was born with the ability to see into our world, it was dangerous to expose her to so much so quickly."

Rhea wanted to say something in protest, but Mabon kept on going. "Yes, I know, she turned out to be quite an adept child, but this young man, Tom, is different. He could be the one to mend the wounds that exist between our worlds. Only then can our knowledge and wisdom flow into theirs. A new human consciousness shall be created—that is what will save us all."

Mabon ended his lofty talk there, for he knew Rhea had too much faery impatience to listen to all these plans. As the Human world evolved, he knew the Otherworld would have to evolve or disappear entirely. Those three drops of Human blood in Rhea's lineage made her the one who might lead them all toward this change, though he never told her so, for the one thing faeries hate worse than discipline is responsibility.

While Ruby was lying on her quilt-covered bed thinking about Mabon's words, Tom was in his room thinking about her. She did come from another existence. She was a faery creature just like Pup. And yet he could see her, hold her, feel her—in fact, he was falling in love with her. Was he the one she had come for? What would happen to him if he followed her? Could he trust her, or was she just a wild child whose nature was governed by mere whim? These things he would have to decide for himself. There was no one to help him except perhaps this mysterious being who called herself Rhea.

He pulled up the covers, stretched his legs out in bed, and felt something. "Pup, what have you got now?"

Pup opened one eye, but didn't move from his position curled up on the pillow.

Tom reached down with an exasperated sigh. What he found, he couldn't believe. "Pup, how in this world or yours did you get this?"

There in his hand lay the weathered remains of his mother's Christmas angel.

49

THE HEART OF THE MATTER

One afternoon, amongst the cushioned hollows of a Parkmont parlor, the Alliance for Charity Relief was having a committee meeting. It had just appointed the chairladies for the next fundraiser, which was to be a masked ball in October. Accepting one of the positions as chairwoman was none other than Mrs. Savage—now known as Lillian Savage Snyder.

"I am honored," she was saying, "to do my part in assisting those less fortunate in our city. These past few years as a member of this charitable organization have been very rewarding."

The other women present smiled, nodded, and sipped their tea in approval.

"As you know, I served for so many years as nurse to Mrs. Wimpleton. When she passed, God rest her soul, I looked for other ways in which I might be of service. For Mr. Snyder and I, being members of this alliance has been our way of contributing. I shall do everything to make this year's ball a huge success."

There were more nods and signs of approval from the little group.

Lillian Savage walked home with great satisfaction that day. Things were proceeding just as she had planned. Lilly had always figured things ahead—way ahead. Her patient, plotting determination netted big rewards. Petra Wimpleton had died leaving everything to her: the house, its contents, and her bank account. Now Lillian was on a crusade to improve herself socially. She had married Mr. Snyder for this reason. He, of course, was quite agreeable to her proposal because it meant an instant upgrade in his living standards. Lillian had made it very clear, however, that the house was hers, the money was hers, and what they did with it was up to her as well. Mr. Snyder was equally content to give up the dreary considerations of money and leave the details to Lilly. Now at last he might be able to write *The Politics of Philosophy*, a great work that had been encumbering his mind for many a year.

Along her road to social respectability and power in the community, Lillian had been able to siphon more money her way in the most ingenious of manners—she stole it. Joining the women's charity league was like landing in a giant pocket that she could pick from time to time as needs be. The October Masked Ball would provide a fine opportunity to do a little creative bookkeeping.

* * *

Ever since Pup had brought home the Christmas ornament, Tom found himself unable to push away memories of Aunt Petra. At night, the evil eyes of Mrs. Savage pursued him through his dreams. There was no hiding from her; she would always find him. He would wake up in a sweat just before her eyes would devour him.

Rhea worried because he was so distraught. She called upon all that was Human within her to understand him. For the first time, she was exercising an emotional capacity that went beyond that of the pure faery.

One night, Pup appeared to her in a very excited state. Something was wrong with Tom. He wanted her to come right away. Rhea found Tom in bed asleep, gasping as if he were suffocating. She leaned close to him and let her head lightly touch his. Transforming into a vaporous, almost liquid state, she pressed her cheek to his and blended into his body.

He was having a nightmare in which he was enclosed in a tiny box suspended by ropes and pulleys, being lowered down into a dark abyss. Tom couldn't move, nor could he wake up: he was paralyzed. Rhea saw a giant pair of eyes controlling the descent of the box. She wasn't sure whether it was right to interfere with a Human's dream, but her instinct was to save him. She took hold of his hand and pulled him out of the dream back into consciousness.

Tom sat up, gasping for breath, and Rhea melted into the shadows. "Ruby?" he called. Not certain she was really there, he fell back into a fitful sleep. Rhea stroked his hair and calmed him till he was breathing easily, then waved her hand over him, relieving his memory of all that had passed.

And so Tom slept through the night in the arms of the faery.

Rhea knew these dreams had something to do with that house Tom had once lived in. She resolved to go back there and put an end to those evil eyes. As she thought about how she might do that, she also contemplated the marvel of the Human body. Lying so close to him, she was amazed at the heat emanating from his skin. In his chest pumped a heart that generated all this energy. What a shame Humans lived such a short time—and yet their lives seemed all the more poignant because they did die. Everything mattered so much more—or did it? The people in this place lived like nothing mattered at all, not even their own lives.

Rhea looked down at Tom and placed her hand over his heart, feeling the rise and fall of his chest. *But this young man,* she thought, *isn't like the others. He is kind and gentle. There is a great spirit within him. Mabon was right. He is the one we were looking for.* Tom would come with her into the Otherworld and do what needed to be done to make peace between the two realities—Mabon had thought she wasn't listening, but she was. Now, more than ever, she wanted the two worlds to meet.

She bent down and gave Tom's sleeping lips the taste of a faery kiss,
for truth be told,
she had fallen in love.

50

HEARTS AND FLOWERS

Beside the tree Tom had planted, a curious green- and red-leaved sprout appeared one day. Thinking it was a weed, Nettie nearly pulled it up, but then she decided anything that grew in that dark alley was welcome. Soon it had branches and more leaves. One day, a purple flower appeared.

"Look here, Tom," Nettie pointed out. "Where d'ya s'pose that come from?"

"Something the wind blew in," Tom joked, yet he had a strange feeling that that was where Pup had buried the seed.

When Nettie said, "Ya know, that plant kinda reminds me a'Ruby. It's all wild and colorful-like," Tom was certain that was what had become of the seed.

"Yeah, it does," he agreed. "Where is she?"

"Up with Mavis. Ya know Mavis is gonna make her dance and yammer with the other girls."

"I know. Ruby was all excited about it until she saw what she had to wear," Tom said. "Did you see those things? I mean, they are godawful—green and black stripes with skirts that roll up like window shades!"

"How does she dream up dem things she does?" Nettie let out that robust laugh he loved to hear. He remembered that hearty sound from the day he'd met her. In spite of all his miseries then, it had made him want to laugh, as it did now. Somehow, that laugh took things into its grasp and shook them into perspective. He could still hear her even after she went back to her chores in the kitchen.

Tom wished Nettie's laugh could have the same effect on the terrible nightmares that had returned to him. Rhea had touched his heart, and he could no longer ignore his feelings. There was so much pain, so much guilt, all churned up with his desire to love. Battling his demons was taking its toll. He looked tired and distracted.

Nettie worried and fussed over him, always trying to feed him, but he wasn't hungry. Something was taking the stuffing out of her Tom, and she knew it was Ruby. That girl had powers—strange kinds of powers. She never ate anything. Now she put a spell on Tom and he didn't eat anything. Nettie had always known that girl meant trouble.

* * *

Every night, Rhea went to watch over Tom in his sleep. She had been told not to interfere again with his frightening dreams, but she could soothe his thoughts once he had passed through them. Rhea was fascinated by Tom, her Tom, her Human. She lay next to him and felt his warmth, the physical density of his body. She marveled at the features of his face, his dark eyelashes and his lips that she kissed in secret each night. She longed for the time when he might wake and return her kiss.

She sat beside him and traced the line of his shoulder down to his wonderful hand with the tips of her red-stained fingers. The wonders that awaited him—if only...

Mabon had said Tom would have to step out of himself to become himself. Rhea had not known what that meant until lately. Watching him live within the confines of his own personal tortures when she could see freedom all around him had made her understand.

One night, amid his tossing and turning, he woke up and saw her sitting there.

"What are you doing here?" he whispered in surprise.

"Watching your dreams."

Tom gave out a half-laugh, half-sigh. "My dreams?" He sat up against the back of the bed, brushing his hands through his hair. "That must be pretty boring. It's the same one every night!"

He looked at her in disbelief.   "Ruby...Rhea?"

"Yes," she answered.

"Are you really here, or is this another dream?"

"I'm really here."

"Good," Tom sighed. "Don't disappear on me."

Rhea smiled, looking at him. After a while, she said hesitantly, "I have been told by the old one that there is a way to stop those dreams."

"The old one?"

"Yes, he's very old, very wise—he's almost transparent now. I don't know how much longer he will be able to be seen."

Tom looked at her, not comprehending. Rhea went on, "I have asked, and he agrees that it would be a good idea to take you back to that house you once lived in. Let the house reveal its story. That could help you."

"The house? Go back into that house? You've got to be kidding?"

Rhea went on, picking up speed and enthusiasm. "Yes. Mabon says you Humans give off heat and energy. Sometimes, when what occurs in a place is very emotionally charged, that energy lingers on long after the people are gone. Mabon, the old one, thinks what you might see there could be of great help to you. I've got it all figured out. Pup and I have been watching the woman and her husband—"

"Wait a minute...wait a minute. The woman? What woman?"

"Her name's Mrs. Snyder—she's skinny and pinched-looking, and her husband's tall, all legs and arms with shiny pasty hair on his head—"

Tom laughed with a knowing grimace. "God, she married him? What a pair they make. She got the house and everything that went with it. Damn...I can't go back."

"Tom," Rhea went on undaunted, "yes, you can. I know exactly the day when the both of them go out. Pup will stand watch to warn us just in case—"

"And just how am I going to hear what this house has to say?"

"I'll take care of that."

Tom looked down and was quiet for a long time. Then he said, "And when is this day that they are both out of the house?"

"You call the day Friday."

"That just happens to be tomorrow."

"Yes." Rhea smiled faintly.

"I'll think about it." Tom leaned his head back and closed his eyes.

"Yes, you think about it," Rhea whispered.

When Tom opened his eyes again, she was gone.

51

TALKING SHADOWS

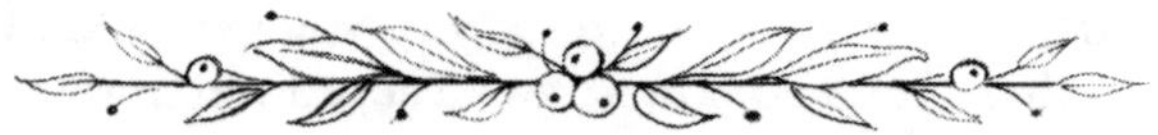

Early the next morning, Rhea was on the back steps peeling potatoes. She sat as usual, shoes off, in her little patch of sun.

Tom pushed open the screen door. "It's freezing out here." He sat down beside her, arms folded tight to his chest. "Aren't you cold?"

She turned to him with one of her blazing smiles. "I'm never cold."

"Well, I am," he grumbled. He looked terrible. He hadn't slept at all. Rhea said nothing. "What time is this 'house tour' going to take place?"

"Two o'clock."

"It takes time to get there, you know," he said irritably.

"Meet me in the kitchen when Nettie goes to rest in her room."

"Okay, all right." He got up stiffly. "Put a coat on or something," he said as he went back inside. "You'll freeze to death out there."

Ruby smiled to herself. After a while, she got up and walked barefoot over to the little wild plant. She cut the purple flower from its stem and put it in her apron pocket.

There weren't many moments of quiet during the day at the Madrigal, but around one o'clock was one of them. Nettie took a break and rested in her room off the pantry. She lay down on the bed, crossed her arms over her chest, and was asleep the moment she hit the pillow. She never moved from her dignified corpse-like position, just in case the Lord came to take her while she slept.

Rhea was in the kitchen before Tom. She prepared two cups of tea, then held the purple flower in her hands and blew on it; its petals instantly dried. She crushed the remains and stirred them into one of the cups. The liquid turned magenta. When Tom appeared, she offered him the tea.

"What's this?" he asked scowling.

"Something to keep us warm and to help you see."

With an exasperated sigh, he surrendered his resistance and downed the drink in two great gulps.

"Okay, what now?" he asked like a man who expected the next moment to be his last.

"We go! Oh, and button up your coat...it's cold outside." She winked at him.

By the time they boarded the trolley, Tom was beginning to feel strange. Pup was amusing himself by sliding up and down the poles people used to steady themselves when riding standing up.

Tom laughed out loud, and since he apparently was staring at nothing, the woman across from him looked at him as if he were an idiot. Tom cleared his throat and tightened his scarf, trying to contain himself. He felt as if he were bulging and condensing at the same time. As people got on and off the trolley, they left long trails of themselves behind like the tracks of snails. Tom slid down in his seat and squeezed Rhea's hand. "What did you put in that tea?" he whispered hoarsely.

"It's from a flower. For Humans, it's quite strong, but we like it. Mabon says it's all right for you to take it."

"Mabon? Who's Mabon?"

"The old one I told you about."

"Oh, the old one. Then he must know."

"It's better not to talk now," Rhea said. "This is our stop."

"I'm not sure I can walk."

"Try it, you'll like it."

She was right. Tom stepped down from the trolley and walked effortlessly. Rhea guided him along the tree-lined streets of Parkmont. Overhead, sunlight glittered on a forest of green branches. His senses felt so sharp he could see the molecular makeup of everything: the trees and the houses were all made up of tiny moving particles. He arrived in front of Aunt Petra's house in an ecstasy of expansion.

"Here we are," Rhea said. Her words and the sight of that house plummeted him down from the heights into a deep cavity of terror. The house loomed large and he felt himself shrinking before it. Rhea motioned for Pup to take his watch up in the trees. She opened the front gate. "Come on, we have no time to waste." Tom walked like a robot at her command. The door to the house opened at her touch.

"Don't question what you see...just watch," she told him.

As he stepped inside, the musty smell caught in his throat. He began to pant with an overwhelming sense of dread. Everything moved and swayed. He was still seeing molecular particles and he wondered what held things together. Why didn't everything just break apart and float away? Tom had the impression that he was looking through layers of mist, cloudy shifting veils, some lighter, some darker. Each had its own vague shadow play within it. At the top of the stairs, he saw a vision of a lovely young woman dressed in pink. Her laughter echoed in his head. When she appeared, the air quickly freshened.

There was an intense whooshing noise in his ears. He realized it was the rush of his own blood through his veins. Over that was the bellow-like sound of his lungs taking air in and pushing air out. He felt like he was underwater. His body swam ahead of him through the circling vapor currents.

Tom extended a shaky hand toward the banister at the end of the stairs and hung there, safely moored for the moment. Behind him he heard a muffled voice. The lady in pink picked up her skirts and came down the stairs on her tiny slippered feet. She flew right past him, through him. As he held onto the banister, Tom's eyes floated around to see a small, neatly dressed man embrace the woman with an exuberant kiss. They were speaking, but much of what they said was lost in the layers through which Tom perceived them. Only some of their words were comprehensible.

The man pulled a little box from inside his coat and held it up over the woman's head. She danced about him like a child trying to get at it. "Whom do you love, whom do you love?" Tom heard.

As the man ran into the parlor with the box held high, the woman caught up with him and they collapsed in a heap on the sofa. Tom followed unsteadily, collapsing too in the first chair he found. The couple kissed again, and the woman tousled the man's precisely combed hair. They whispered back and forth. Suddenly more serious, the man opened the box and took out a beautiful star sapphire ring. He gave it to her, saying something about "forever." Tom recognized the ring as the one Aunt Petra had always worn. Her chubby little fingers had grown fat around it, but she still had it on that last terrible day he saw her alive.

Tom felt something cold at his back. He turned and saw in the entryway two entities struggling with each other. They weren't as distinct as the man and woman, but he knew one of them to be Mrs. Savage and the other the terror-stricken image of himself as a young boy. The atmosphere became dark and disturbed. He watched himself being thrown out of the house and Mrs. Savage slamming the door behind him. He saw her walk confidently to the very chair he was now sitting in; Tom gasped helplessly as the architect of his nightmares sat down through him into the chair. In the energy that enveloped him, he could feel her malignant nature, and he heard her contemptuous laugh throughout his body. He began to scream and wave his arms in an attempt to fight off the energy settling about him.

Rhea pulled him out of the chair, and Tom breathed a giant sigh of relief as he separated from the suffocating vision. By contrast, Rhea appeared to be the most luminous and beautiful creature he had ever seen. Her hair, her garments floated about him in slow motion, radiant, magical. Then she faded from his view and he was alone with the talking shadows again.

He heard a distinct clink, clink, like a spoon against a glass or cup. The sound was coming from upstairs. Once again, his body set out to plow through the sea of molecules to climb the stairs. He felt separate from his body, as if it were a diving suit his mind wore to protect itself.

He was at the top of the stairs now, looking down the hallway. He could see the entity of Mrs. Savage standing at the narrow table outside the door to Aunt Petra's room. Tom walked in his pressurized "suit" down the hall toward her. A crying sound attracted his attention to a little room no bigger than a closet. The door was open. Inside, a forlorn boy sat on a bed looking out at him. Tom kept going. What was she doing at that table? She was mixing something into a glass of milk.

Tom tried to hurry, but his steps were leaden. Mrs. Savage picked up the glass and disappeared into Aunt Petra's room. By the time Tom got to the door, she was beside Aunt Petra, pulling her head back by her hair. He could see Aunt Petra so much more distinctly than Mrs. Savage, but there was no mistaking what was going on: Mrs. Savage was forcing Aunt Petra to drink that poisonous milk. Tom heard the window break by the bed and saw a faint impression of the little boy he knew now to be himself, climbing through the broken glass.

He saw himself rush to his aunt's bedside, where he desperately tried to wake her from her drugged and weakened state. "Not now, Tommy, not now," Aunt Petra was saying. Her unfocused eyes drifted past him to the chair by the fireplace. The boy kept trying to wake her, but Tom's eyes followed hers and saw what she was seeing. The fire was lit. The neatly dressed man was sitting in the chair. A young Petra was seated on the floor. Her head was on his lap, and he was slowly brushing her very long hair. It was clear he loved to do that for her. Petra was dreamily gazing into the fire. They were in their private world, very loving and peaceful.

Tom could see why the little boy tugging at Aunt Petra's sleeve was having so much difficulty. Who would want to rise from that pleasant drugged memory to the frightening circumstances she was really in?

Tom had by now gained sufficient control over his mental faculties to know where he must go next in this house. It was downstairs in the pantry. He turned and went to the top of the stairs, where the pink lady was about to descend again. Down alongside her he went, past the dark energy and the slamming door, through the dining room to the kitchen. There he paused, steadying himself for what he might see next.

The kitchen was totally dominated by the energy of Mrs. Savage. It was here that she cooked and concocted her plans. It was here that her anger and resentment took root. Tom felt the limits of her selfish, constricted mind bearing down on him.

He opened the back door and looked out at the giant tree that had been his home and salvation during those years. The fresh air made him feel stronger. He turned to face the shadows. As he walked toward the pantry, he could hear the sound of a great effort being made. He looked in to see Mrs. Savage and Mr. Snyder pulling Aunt Petra's body from the dumbwaiter cabinet. They were arguing, huffing and puffing, pulling and tugging. Finally, she popped out like an oversized muffin, and they fell to the floor with her weight. Mr. Snyder sat there looking annoyed while Mrs. Savage slapped Aunt Petra's face again and again.

To Tom's amazement, Aunt Petra moaned and tried to move her hand to cover her face. She wasn't dead! Together, Mrs. Savage and Mr. Snyder hoisted her up over Mr. Snyder's shoulder. With a great amount of coaxing and shoving, he carried her upstairs to the bedroom. She was alive!

In the trees in front of the house, Pup had been on duty watching for the return of Mrs. Savage. He had been attentive all the way up until he noticed a long line of ants marching single-file up the tree; then he couldn't help taking a look to see where the trail ended. He had been watching the line for some time when he suddenly remembered what he was there for. He looked down, and sure enough, there were Mrs. Savage and Mr. Snyder, opening the front gate. He sent the alarm to Rhea.

Tom was still in the pantry, leaning up against the wall, alternately laughing and crying. Rhea assumed her human form and quickly shuffled him out the kitchen door.

She leaned him up against the back of the tree and told him not to move while she returned to the house for a quick check to see if everything was in place.

Tom slid down the tree trunk and sat on the ground looking up—up into that wonderful tree whose many spreading arms leaned down to embrace him. The shadows had spoken, and he knew the truth. He felt so relaxed; his body was attached to his brain again. In fact, everything was melting into one love, one. He would have fallen into blissful sleep there if Rhea had not kept him moving.

* * *

The moment Mrs. Savage entered the house, she knew she had been intruded upon.

"What are you sniffing the air like a bloodhound for, my dear? You look most unattractive," Mr. Snyder said, heading straight for the parlor sofa.

"Don't lay about on that sofa, Sydney. That's only for company."

He got up and yawned. "Well, I'm going upstairs for a nap. These charity lunches bore me to tears."

Lillian snapped, "It's the other way round, dear. It's you who bore them with your long-winded rhetoric. I never knew there were so many words in the English language, and nobody cares if there are."

As he climbed the stairs, Sydney turned back. "I knew you were not an educated woman when I married you, but sometimes you do surprise me with your ignorance."

This was about the only level on which Sydney could put Lillian down. She walked all over him in every other respect, except when he referred to his being more educated than she. It was guaranteed to get her goat.

This time, however, Lillian didn't take the bait. She had something else on her mind. She went about the house suspiciously inspecting every-thing. All was in order, except that when she went around the kitchen and glanced into the pantry, the door to the dumbwaiter was open. How could that be?

Suddenly, as she took off her hat and stuck the hatpin into its brim, the name came to her out of nowhere. She stiffened and said, "Tom Quinn."

52

THE LABYRINTH

Tom had no idea how he got back to the Madrigal, but everything came into sharp focus when Rhea opened a little pouch and asked him to smell what was inside. In his floaty diffused state, he took a big sniff and immediately started sneezing wildly.

"What did you do that for?" Tom wheezed, giving her a hurt glance.

"It's only pepper. You need some excuse for looking so awful; now you've got it. I think you've caught a very bad cold—no one can argue with you going straight to bed."

"Bed...yes, bed." Tom trudged along. More than anything else he wanted to lie down and sleep.

Nettie took one look at him coming through the kitchen door with his arm slung around Rhea's shoulder and demanded, "What you done to my Tom?"

"Nothing, he—he said he didn't feel well all of a sudden. I think he's got a fever."

Tom tried to stop the two of them from going at it. "I'm all right...I feel all right."

"All right? There ain't nothin' all right about you. You get in bed before I take you up there and undress you myself."

Rhea went to help.

"Where you goin', girl? Ain't you done enough for one day? You go get Nash to take care a' him."

Tom kept saying "I'm okay, I'm okay," as he was shuffled upstairs. When he got to his room, he fell flat on the bed, sound asleep.

Tom's getting sick was the main topic at dinner. Mavis said that of course she had been feeling poorly for days—something was definitely going around. She felt all achy and chilled. Sudy, suggestible to anything, chimed in that she was sick too.

Before anyone else could discover some ailment, Wally said, "Wait a minute, let's not make an epidemic out of this."

Mavis interrupted peevishly, "Are you sure there isn't something wrong with *you*? You've been so disagreeable this past week...anyway, I'm not coming down to work tonight. I'm all in."

"Of course, my sweet, you must take care." Wally looked around. "But no one else feels the need to take the night off, do they? Good."

It was true: Wally had been irritable for the last few weeks. It was because he hadn't found a "little bird" to take up to his airless cage in a long time. There was a pressure building in him that only a certain kind of evening would relieve.

For a brief moment, he'd thought Ruby might be that "little bird," but she so deftly avoided him that trifling with her never seemed possible. At last, however, he had found a new quarry wandering the streets. She met all the criteria. She was always alone, she had a weak, unprotected air about her, and she crossed his path three times. That made her fair game. She could be cut from the herd with no one noticing.

These evenings started in the usual way: the girl came upstairs for a drink and a few indecent moments. But over time, events began to follow a strange route into a labyrinth of darkness. Terrible distortions of human instinct produced gratifications straight from the heart of evil.

The dwarf and Cheng played an integral part in these proceedings, for Wally preferred to watch rather than act. He would fill his "little bird" with alcohol and let her laugh and flutter about his cage until the others arrived. Then the "entertainment" got very strange.

It happened accidentally that one "little bird" got her neck twisted trying to resist such "fun." After that, these intoxicating evenings took on another dimension. Wally, the fat insignificant man, could now play God, wielding power over life and death. He never knew whether he would give the signal to end the struggle of his captive or not, but when he did, he was mesmerized by the moment of death—that moment when life took leave of its host and left behind a blank silence. All that remained of the "little bird" after that was an empty husk. Nothing to do but dispose of it, and Cheng did that.

"We are born to die," Wally philosophized. "It's just a question of when."

* * *

It was a windy, cold night. The Madrigal was crowded and noisy. People were glad to be inside the smoky, tightly packed room. The girls were dancing on the stage, counting the rhythm out to themselves as they went. Nash had finished his act with the dwarf, but he was still walking around on his stilts, which lent the scene a carnival feel.

Nettie was working in the kitchen and Rhea was washing dishes, trying to keep up with the demand for more glasses. Pup had inhaled the essences of so many half-empty mugs of beer that he was sprawled out on the counter fast asleep.

No one noticed Wally taking someone up the back stairs and into his office...

The noise from the bar could be heard up in Tom's room, but the sights and sounds of his dreams carried him elsewhere. Voices called out to him, one over the other. Images of his past unhinged from his mind and drifted away as his consciousness orbited in a vast black void. He felt calm, empty, and curiously awake. Wherever he was, his body had not followed him. He could see, hear; feel, all without the aid of a physical body. Had he died? He heard himself shout, "I am...I am alive!" The garbled voices ceased, and his own frail sounds echoed back to him.

He began to perceive that he was in the remnants of a great vaulted hall. Open sky blended with the high arches. What light there was came from the stars, and at one end of the hall, a hearth fire burned, toward which he was propelled. The hearth itself was of carved stone roiling with vines and faces made of leaves, spewing vegetation from their mouths. In a tall stag-horned chair by the fire sat an old man.

As Tom approached, the man stood up. His eyes shone as he began to speak in ecstatic verse. His words reached back into the dawn of time and raced forward with prophetic vision. The history of the Universe, the story of life from the divine spark of its beginning, was contained in those verses. As the old man recited his arcane poetry, Tom's view circled from his shining eyes, to the stars, to the fire, to those soul-bright eyes again. Although he had never heard such language before, he understood it within every cell of his being. He was awestruck by the enormity of what he was hearing.

Tom felt his consciousness whirling wheel-like through a galaxy of light, one tiny particle inextricably connected to every other moving, changing particle. That connection was alive, and within this spectacle he could hear great sweeping, stretching sounds...the song of the universe. Then, regrettably, he felt he was slipping down, losing his ability to concentrate. Like the tide receding from the shore, he was leaving this place; he couldn't hold on. *The words, I must not forget those words...the whole meaning of life is encoded within them.* He had to remember; he fought to remember. Down, down he went, into his body that lay on a bed in a darkened room. He woke up.

When he recognized his surroundings, he was relieved and saddened at the same time. He knew he had been witness to a tremendous mystery, but he could only remember some of the images and none of the words that were spoken. He had been given the gift of the universe, and he had forgotten what it was...

In the vacant hours just before dawn, Cheng went down the back stairs carrying a limp bundle in his arms.

53

TURNING POINT

Rhea was already sitting in her patch of sun when Tom came out on the back porch, warming his hands around a hot cup of coffee. He sat beside her in silence.

She glanced up from her work shelling peas. "Morning."

"Morning," he answered in a gravelly voice, not quite awake.

"How do you feel?"

Tom took a sip of coffee and thought about it. After a while, he said, "I feel like I was swallowed, chewed up, and spit back out again—don't ask me by what!"

Rhea smiled, but kept right on with her work. "Um um," she commented, just like Nettie.

Tom was silent for a while. Then, in a quiet voice full of emotion, he went on..."All this time...all this wasted time...I've lived my life like I had no right to it. In my heart, I felt I was guilty...somehow, you see..." his voice wavered, "everything was my fault, and when my aunt died, I thought I killed her. I was damned, nothing mattered to me, not anything...and now...now I'm all mixed up. Am I still dreaming? That was true, what I saw in the house yesterday, wasn't it?"

Rhea nodded.

"Then I'm not guilty...not damned?" Tom stared hard at the ground before him, feeling raw inside. "Then who am I, if I am not those horrible things? I don't know." He took a deep breath and looked up into the sunlight. "I can tell you one thing I do know. I'm going to do something about that murderous thieving Mrs. Savage, and then—and then I've got to find out. I've got to remember what that old man said."

"Old man?" Rhea questioned. "Did you see Mabon?"

"Everything that happened in the house I remember clearly, but after...after that, I don't know. I was somewhere in a great hall that had no ceiling. Starlight, firelight, it all got mixed up in the old man's eyes. He was raving all the time, saying something very important...I can't remember. But somewhere inside of me, I know what it means..." Tom drifted off, trying to remember.

"You saw Mabon," Rhea said definitely. Then, in a soft voice, she continued:

"In the beginning
there was darkness and
all the lands were sea,
no reed had sprung up,

no creature lived or breathed
out of the eternal night
there came an all-pervading light...
...That's how *he* began."

Tom turned Rhea around to face him, looking closely into her eyes. "Who is this Mabon? Do you know what he was saying?"

Rhea looked up at him. For a moment, nothing was said; they simply drew together in the kiss that had been on their minds since the day they met.

"That's all I know...only the beginning."

A lock of her hair fell forward as she bent her head, revealing a delicately pointed ear. Tom traced its outline with his fingers. "Am I the one you've come to find?" he whispered tentatively.

Rhea nodded.

"Why?" he wondered.

"Mabon will answer that. I only know I want you to be with me always. Not here in this ugly place, but in a world of such beauty you cannot imagine. If you would just—"

Nettie came to the screen door. "Come in here, gal! Quit your whisperin'."

The spell between them was broken.

"Meet me tonight on the roof after the Madrigal closes." Rhea impulsively kissed him again and hurried inside.

* * *

Mavis wanted the girls to rehearse one more time before the evening show. This was to be Ruby's debut in the chorus. She was quick on her feet, but she couldn't get the hang of her costume; she kept pulling and chafing at it like it was a harness. This irritated Mavis no end. After all, she'd spent good money on these creations. The whole number would be spoiled if Ruby didn't learn to handle the strings and pulleys in them.

The dresses were dark green with black stripes. The corseted tops had tassels hanging at their hems. By pulling a certain tassel, the girls could raise their skirts, first on one side and then the other. The effect was like a curtain going up on the girls' legs and was sure to bring hoots and howls from the audience, the loudness of which was Mavis's measure of success.

"That's it now," she coached. "Tap, turn, tap tap turn, and slide, now pull the left tassel...that's it...now kick and kick...now the right tassel..."

Ruby, Lorna, Sudy, and Mae, the third Peach, were as mismatched a set of chorus girls as could be. Ruby was long-legged, but very petite; Lorna was tall and sinewy; Sudy was thick in the middle; and Mae was built like a barn.

Lorna had star status, being the most audaciously sexy onstage, but lately she had begun drinking heavily and acting more surly and uncooperative. Her boyfriend hadn't been coming around. The gifts, the parties, the attentions had all disappeared. Lorna suffered terribly from his abrupt withdrawal. Her love toppled over into a smoldering rage. There was someone else—she knew it. All she thought about were different scenarios in which she confronted him and made him pay for his betrayal.

It was Saturday night, and the Madrigal was louder and steamier than usual. People jostled each other for a place at the bar; tables were full. Ribbons of blue smoke wound through the yellow cast from the gas lamps. When the new lights went up on the little stage, it was like a bonfire had been lit. Heads turned and people clapped when Nash came out on stilts with the dwarf riding a tiny bicycle beneath him.

The girls were next. Mavis was fussing around behind the curtain. It was Sudy she was worried about now. The girl didn't know her left hand from her right. Finally, Mavis stuck one of her big rhinestone rings on Sudy's finger, saying, "Here, see that? The hand with the ring on it goes first. Got it?" Sudy nodded in relief.

Mavis had a hidden flap cut in the curtain so she could check progress on stage. At the moment, Lorna was looking through it, searching the crowd for her lover. Nash and the dwarf continued their antics down into the audience, and Tom lit them with the follow spot. There, on the edge of the light, she saw him. He and his cronies were sitting at a table with some beautiful-looking uptown ladies.

Lorna seethed. "He's come slumming, has he? Well, I'll give them a night to remember." She pushed past Mavis and the girls in the tight quarters backstage and disappeared.

"What are you doing? Where are you going? We're on in a minute!" Mavis called after her. "Sudy, go get her."

Lorna ran up to her room. She rummaged through a drawer and pulled out a bottle of whiskey, opened it, and took a long swig of the dark sharp liquor. She slammed the bottle down on the dresser, took a look at herself in the mirror, then took another long drink from the bottle. She wiped her mouth with the back of her hand and looked around crazily for her purse. She emptied its contents onto the bed. She found what she was looking for—a knife: a sleek, discreet pearl-handled switchblade.

Sudy came in just as she had concealed it in her bodice. "Mavis says you better come—now. She's real mad, Lorna, real mad..."

"Not *half* as mad as I," Lorna said in a strange voice.

Sudy looked all puzzled and flustered.

"It's okay. I'll be right there. Sudy, go on."

She left and Lorna took another drink, then smashed her image in the mirror with the empty bottle.

When Lorna joined the other girls to go on, she was a wreck. In just five minutes, she'd gone from pretty to grotesque. Her lipstick was smeared; her eyes had sunk behind her mascara. Mavis took one look at her and was about to say something, but Lorna pushed her aside, saying, "I know, I know, I'm through," and went onstage.

The girls sang, danced, and pulled their tassels. The audience loved it. Lorna moved with abandon—her steps quicker, her kicks higher. Suddenly she broke ranks and went down into the audience. Sudy and Mae glanced at the flap in the curtain, where they could see Mavis's penciled eyebrows shoot straight up into her hair.

"What's she doing? She's not supposed to do that!"

Tom followed Lorna with the spot, thinking this was a last-minute change. Lorna danced her way over to Russell's table. She sat on his lap, mussed his hair, all the while playing to the crowd and continuing her act. Russell was not amused. His lady friends shrank from the spotlight.

Without missing a beat, Lorna slashed his face with her knife and was about to plunge it into his heart when he stood up, knocking her to the floor. The ladies screamed; friends rushed to his side. Russell stared at Lorna as Cheng pulled her away. She smiled insanely back at him. Blood made an ever-widening stain on his white collar.

The audience didn't know how to react. Was this part of the show? Tom turned the spot back to the stage. Sudy and Mae stood there wondering what to do. There was a loud tap-a-ta-tap of heels pounding a hard surface.

"Ruby! Look at Ruby!" Nash called to Tom, who swung the light around, and there was Rhea standing on the bar. All eyes were on her; her skin sparkled like pearl dust, her rich red hair fell in waves over her shoulders. She flashed a radiant smile, then twirled from one end of the bar to the other. People's mouths dropped open.

"I love to get carried away!" she sang, teasing the men who were staring goggle-eyed at her. She tap-danced over the glasses on the bar, then jumped high into the air. Tom lost her with the follow spot, she went so fast. "I love to get carried away!" she sang as she landed in Nash's arms. The crowd roared when Nash walked back to the stage on stilts with Ruby in his arms. He put her down amongst the other girls, and they bowed to thunderous applause. No one saw Russell and his lady friends leaving or Lorna being dragged off by Cheng.

Backstage, the girls clustered around Ruby, wanting to know how she twirled like that.

"Lorna—how's Lorna?" Rhea asked.

"They took her upstairs," Mavis said with disgust. "You never said you could do that kind of dancing."

"Nobody ever asked me," was her reply.

"Now don't get cheeky."

"Cheeky?"

"Yes, cheeky, just because you can make up a step or two," Mavis said peevishly, wanting to regain some control. "You're good," she had to admit.

Wally came back, beaming like he'd found a pot of gold. "That's great. 'I like to get carried away'...that's great."

While Ruby was surrounded with everyone talking at once, Tom ran through the kitchen and up the back stairs to Lorna's room. The dwarf was already there, calling to her to let him in. Tom could hear her sobbing.

"Lorna, open up. We can help you!" Tom was afraid she would try to kill herself.

"Go away. Stay out of this!" she cried from behind the door.

"Go on." Philippe pushed Tom back. "I am the only one who can do anything for her now! I know her better than any of you!" The words hissed out of his mouth like a snake ready to strike.

Tom hesitated, stopped by the authority with which he spoke. He saw for the first time that Philippe was in love with Lorna. Why hadn't he noticed that before? "Don't let her do anything foolish."

"Foolish?" The dwarf laughed. "That, my friend, she has already been."

* * *

By the time Tom came out on the roof to find Rhea, the city had grown silent. Stars, sharp-edged and brilliant, cut deep into the night. The roof was a broad flat field over which he walked in darkness. The edge of the building was barely visible. Tom could have easily walked straight off into the air.

Pup accompanied him. He was running around exhilarated by the height and openness of the roof. He darted to the edge and hung over like a squirrel showing off. Tom couldn't watch. If he fell, he fell; it probably wouldn't hurt him if he did.

Tom recognized a reddish square shape lying on the ground. It was Rhea's quilt. He walked over and sat down on it. As he did, a cloud of fireflies rose up, fluttering about him. The wind blew, rustling his hair, and the fireflies took off into the air. Tom could hear the faintest sounds of music, laughter, and bells.

"Tom." He heard his name whispered behind him. He turned to see a glowing rainbow-colored vapor descending from the sky. "Tom," the voice called from the mist.

"Rhea?" he answered.

The voice he heard was echoing and raspy, beautiful and frightening:

"Between two worlds
the Raven can fly
Between two worlds
the Raven can see

Between two worlds
the future is known
Between two worlds,
Shall be your home…"
"Ruby?" he whispered. There in the mist was the fire creature he had seen on the mountain.

Undulating, flickering, gold and scarlet, she danced toward him. Tom stood up, enticed by her movements. She hovered in the air above him, moving in and out of the shades of light. Tom watched, spellbound by the mysterious reality revealing itself to him. If only he could lift his feet and step into the mist with her. He began to feel earthbound and alone.

"Ruby!" he called again. Like fireworks, the spectacular scene exploded into sparkling particles and vanished into the night. Before him stood the Ruby that he knew: the Ruby he could touch, feel, and hold. He pulled her to him, kissing her passionately. Together they sank down upon the shimmering quilt, and Tom lost himself

    in loving the girl
          from the land
               of the golden apples.

54

PLANS

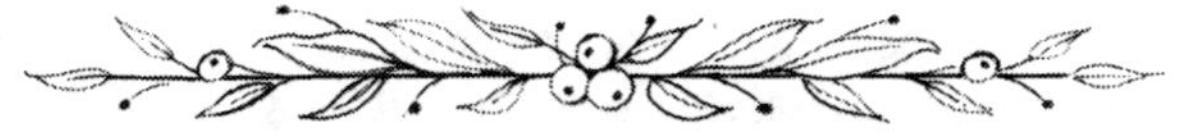

"It won't work."

"What won't work?"

"The whole thing."

"It will work if I say it will," Lillian Snyder snapped. "Every time I ask you to get involved with something really important, that's what you say."

"Well, you can't miscount money in front of people and get away with it!" Mr. Snyder unwrapped his legs from their current tangle under the table and crossed them in another. Tables and chairs were never the right proportions for his long-boned body.

"The problem with you is you haven't any nerve. I'll take all the risks; you just do what I tell you."

Sydney got up from the dining table, walked into the parlor, and draped himself over the sofa. He was most unhappy at having to be a part of one of Lillian's schemes. He had no problem sharing in the rewards of her endeavors, but helping her execute them was another matter. She was right. He was a coward, and the less he had to look that fact in the face, the better.

Lillian followed him into the parlor with two cups of tea.

"Now, look." She smiled, trying another approach. "It's really very simple. The charity is all excited about the idea of the Masque Ball and Casino Night. With six different gambling tables and the confusion of two hundred people milling about, there won't be any problem at all. Two times during the night, you go around with Mrs. Bambery, the treasurer, to pick up the proceeds from each table. Then the three of us will meet upstairs to count the money. Now, the first time, I won't be there at the appointed time, and you'll ask her to go downstairs to look for me."

"Suppose she wants me to go?" Sydney asked.

"Just say it's simply better that you stay with the money. Use your charms. She's a silly old goose."

"Then what?"

"Then you'll have five minutes to take one third of the money from each bag. You will put it in the top left drawer of the desk. The second time you go around, leave one table out of the pickup and tell Mrs. Bambery they were too busy to stop and give you the money. When you get upstairs, I'll be waiting. Again, I'll suggest you stay with the money. She and I will go down to collect the proceeds from the last table. During that time, you do the same thing and put the money in the drawer. Lock it.

Give me the key, and the next day when the committee and I go into the hall to clean things up, I will get the money."

"How do you know somebody else won't go in there?"

"The Elks Hall doesn't have another event scheduled for weeks after ours. Nobody uses that upstairs office. I've already asked for the keys to the room and desk for the committee's private use."

"The committee—suppose somebody from the committee decides to come in there when I'm taking the money?"

"Sydney. *I* am the head of the committee. Leave it to me. Now, you *must* remember to put our cut of the money in the top *left*-hand side of the desk drawer, because when you, Mrs. Bambery, and I count the rest of the money for the charity, I will show her that we are putting it in the *right*-hand side of the desk and locking it. Do you understand?"

"Right-hand, left-hand...yes...yes. It's still too risky."

"Sydney, if I could do this without you, I would, but I can't, so shut up and just do it."

Lillian especially liked this plan of hers. If the evening was as successful as she thought it would be, she could get away with a tidy little sum. There was no way to know how much money each table was making—no way of knowing the total proceeds till the end of the evening. It was the perfect setup. Nobody would find out what was going on, and if by chance they did...well, it would be Sydney who was caught, not her.

* * *

"There's going to be trouble," Wally said, puffing up the stairs to his office. The dwarf followed him, shutting the door.

"Where is she now?" Wally lit the tip of a fresh cigar and sat back in his chair.

Philippe answered, "Locked in her room."

"Why in hell did she have to do a fool thing like that for? I can't keep her now—bad for business."

Philippe leaped up onto the desk to look him square in the eye. "You can't leave her to those wolves."

"I can't?" Wally was about to get very contrary, sensing a challenge.

"No, you can't. For one thing, it would be too messy. The police would definitely get involved. I have a much better solution."

Wally waited, rolling the cigar between his fingers.

"I say we smuggle her out to the farm for a couple of months. She can go with us this summer, and we can leave her in one of those little towns along the way. Then she's on her own."

Wally smiled at the dwarf's intensity. "Philippe, this sudden concern for a fellow human is quite affecting. If I didn't know your calculating heart so well, I'd say we had some feelings showing here."

Philippe sneered. "I don't care what you think. This is the best way to handle the situation, and you know it."

Wally nodded slowly, going over to stretch out on the cot. He punched a greasy pillow up behind his head, saying, "Get Tom to drive her out in the morning."

* * *

Dawn peeked over the horizon and sent its first pink rays to edge the dark buildings. Tom and Rhea lay sleeping, wrapped in the quilt, their arms about each other. Pup snored peacefully at their feet.

When Tom awoke, he was glad to find her still there next to him. Last night hadn't been a dream. He remembered how it was when their bodies met. The touch of their skin together was shocking and rapturous: shocking because at that moment, the doors to his innermost sanctuary were flung open. The dark chamber that had been his soul's retreat and then its prison was filled with the presence of this delicate wild thing who stood beckoning at the threshold. All his senses awakened to her call, and his desire catapulted him over his fears into the arms of love.

Lying with Rhea beside him, watching the ever-brightening sky, he could feel hope and wonder pouring back into his veins from the fullness of his heart. He smiled, for he felt alive once more in a world of possibilities.

Rhea suddenly grumbled awake and sat up. "Nettie!" she said. "She's down in the kitchen looking for me." She collapsed back against Tom, trying to bury herself in the crook of his neck. "Where I come from, I never have to peel potatoes," she said reproachfully from under the covers.

Tom lifted the quilt. "What do you do?"

She replied emphatically,

"I drink from the streams
I run with the deer
I wear diamonds in my hair
But I never peel potatoes!"

Tom sat up quickly and listened with mock attention. "Ruby! Ruby!" he called like Nettie would.

Rhea abruptly tugged the quilt out from under Tom and Pup, leaving them to feel the bite of the cold morning air. Tom tried to pull the quilt away from her, but she bundled herself up and ran. Rhea squealed and laughed as he chased her all over the roof.

He finally caught up with her at the door. There she opened the quilt and enfolded him, giving him one last magical kiss
before
they went
downstairs...

55

THE NEW ONE

There was no need for Tom to drive out to the farm in the morning. When they finally broke the lock on Lorna's door, she was gone.

Lorna's empty chair at breakfast caused everyone to speak in whispers, as if they were at a wake. Wally was the only one in precipitously fine spirits.

"You know," he said, "I feel as if we are at the beginning of a new era. Lorna brought nothing but bad luck and trouble. I, for one, am glad she's gone."

"Luck, you say? She never had any. That girl had no luck at all," Nash said in her defense.

Wally fired back, "Look, to put it another way, one drunk is all I want to handle in this troupe."

Nash said no more. Wally went on with his thoughts. "Yes, that's it! A new era and a new star." He looked around. "Where is she—where's Ruby?"

"In the kitchen. Where do you think?" Mavis clucked.

"Oh no, no, no...no more kitchen for her. Spoils the hands, flushes the face...bring Ruby out here. Ruby!"

Ruby came to the door and hesitated as everyone turned to look at her.

"Come here. Sit down over there," Wally said, pointing to Lorna's chair.

Ruby didn't move.

"I said, sit down."

She timidly sat down. "I don't want to..." she began.

Wally eyeballed her. "Was that just a fluke last night, or can you do all that again?"

"Well...yes, I..."

"Great." Wally bulldozed ahead. "Mavis, if you ever had a creative idea, now's the time for one. I see her all in red, don't you? Yeah, that's it! We'll call her Ruby Red!"

Mavis nodded her head with guarded enthusiasm.

"You're a regular acrobat. What else can you do?" Wally didn't wait for an answer, and he and Mavis got into an argument over Ruby. Mavis was still a little miffed about Ruby's taking matters into her own hands. She instinctively felt Ruby's talents were a threat to her power.

Ruby alternately looked at them and down at her lap. She wanted to turn Mavis into a fat toad that instant, but restrained herself. Everyone else saw how uncomfortable she was. Clearly, she had not encouraged all this attention from Wally, and she *had* averted what could have been a terrible disaster last night.

Mae put her heavy arms around Ruby and whispered, "It's okay. We know what you tried to do. This is your chance, honey—take it."

* * *

Every day Philippe told himself he wouldn't go looking for Lorna, but every night he would scour the streets and back alleys. Wild stories circulated about what had become of her. His worst fear was that Burt Russell had found her. After weeks of searching, he finally gave up. Lorna had vanished without a trace.

56

CHARMS

Ruby's elevation from kitchen maid to dancing girl changed the attitude at the Madrigal dramatically. Her new role gave her the freedom to act with more energy and spontaneity. Everyone was affected by her charm. There was laughter and a new camaraderie between all of them. They worked on a whole new set of acts, prodded on by Ruby's high spirits. Miraculously, even Mavis became agreeable, consenting to let Ruby design her own costumes. Everyone marveled at how easily that was accomplished. It seemed Ruby had only to blink her eyes, and Mavis went along with anything she suggested.

Nash taught Phyllis how to handle the lights so Tom could learn to walk on stilts. Tom was completely embarrassed by the thought and didn't want to do it, but the day Nash finally got him up, Tom took to the height like a natural. They practiced in the back alley. First Tom and Nash worked out a silly little dance they did in unison; then Ruby climbed up on Nash's shoulders and somersaulted over to Tom.

Nettie loved to see Tom having so much fun, but she didn't like that it was all because of Ruby. That girl had powers, more than any God-fearing woman should have. Nettie was afraid that her Tom had fallen in love with the Devil.

* * *

One afternoon, Wally sat sequestered in his office, feet propped up on the desk, pants unbuttoned, completely absorbed in reading the newspaper. He happened to glance up and was shocked to see Ruby sitting on the windowsill looking in at him. How could that be? He was one story up. He struggled out of his chair and went to the window just in time to see her jump off and land weightlessly in Tom's arms.

"Very nice," he chuckled, tapping on the window. "Very clever." However, he was not at all comfortable with the fact that he could now so easily be observed. He grumbled to himself that he just didn't have enough control over Ruby. All people came equipped with strings to pull, buttons to push, but with her he couldn't find any place to sink the hooks. Tonight, that was going to change. Ruby would have to do more than dance to earn her keep. She had to start entertaining some of the clientele. Lorna, Sudy, and Mae all took men up to their rooms for a price; that was the way it was at the Madrigal.

Ruby's costume had a tight red bodice covered in feathers; her long legs glimmered in sheer tights. Her hair was clasped up with more plumes, making her look like an exotic bird of paradise.

Tom and Nash wore long black pants that covered their tall stilts, black and white full-sleeved shirts with high collars, and red bandanas under black flat-top hats with wide brims. The effect was a cross between gondolier and pirate. When they came out on stage, one carried a big white balloon and the other a large black bag over his shoulder. They set those down and began their dance. Bending their heads so only the black circles of their hat brims showed, they became anonymous giraffe-like creatures, moving with odd comical grace. Then one of them kicked the balloon up into the air. They began batting it back and forth, going down into the audience.

The rowdy crowd got noisier and people jumped up to hit at the balloon as it floated over their heads. A game ensued with Tom and Nash blowing circus whistles like referees until one of them caught the balloon again and went back on stage. Next they picked up the black bag and took it over to the bar, where they pulled the tie cord and out came Ruby as if by magic. Her appearance was startling—something never seen before, a sparkling, feathered siren from another world.

"I like to get carried away," she sang to cheers and the pounding of beer mugs. She had a sexy innocence about her, fascinating to both men and women. There was a good humor in the teasing way she danced and twirled. "I like to get carried away."

Nash and Tom joined arms and Ruby somersaulted up onto the perch they made for her. She put on an amazing acrobatic display. Just as quickly, she disappeared into the black bag again and was carried away by the whistling stiltmen.

Afterwards, to counter the surreal quality of what they had just seen, the audience was treated to a Mavis-style finale with Sudy and Mae doing their best attempt at dancing.

What a night! Everybody was happy! A man at the bar leaned over and whispered into Wally's ear. He nodded and motioned for Barney. Barney went to get Mavis, and Mavis went backstage. She reappeared with Ruby, her hair down but still in costume. Mavis brought her over to Wally and left.

Wally drew Ruby into a close conversation with the man who had whispered in his ear. Ruby looked over her shoulder, searching for Tom, but he was still backstage. Mavis went upstairs to unlock Lorna's room and then went to the balcony overlooking the crowded bar. She could see Ruby shake her red hair and push away from Wally. He grasped her waist and pulled her back, saying something to her. Whatever he said was very convincing, for Ruby let the man take her away up the stairs, the sparkle on her costume glittering in the shadows.

Some time later, Nash told Tom that he had heard Ruby went upstairs.

"Upstairs? What do you mean?"

"Barnaby said Wally put her together with some man and they went upstairs together."

"I don't believe it!"

Nash shrugged his shoulders. Tom started to make an angry bolt through the crowd. Nash caught him. "Wait a minute, wait a minute. Don't make a scene; go up the back way."

Tom pushed Nash aside, astounding him with the reply, "I'll kill him."

Never had Nash seen such violence in Tom's eyes. Whom was he going to kill? The man, or Wally?

Tom battered on the door, shouting, "Ruby! Rhea!" He stepped back. Not a sound came from within. He hesitated. Was she in trouble, or had she betrayed him? He lunged through the door, only to find himself in the most peaceful slumbering scene.

The room was dark. Rhea sat in the open window, her hands about her knees, gazing out into the night sky. The man lay on the bed, collapsed back from the sitting position he had been in when suddenly overwhelmed with sleep. Moonlight filled the room; the air smelled of fresh grass and jasmine. Tom felt his stampeding pulse calming down. He started to say something, but Rhea put her fingers to her lips, making a soft shushing sound. She looked different, not quite solid, like part of her was drifting out the window.

He watched with amazement as she re-solidified. She was so delicate, so elfin, surrounded by blue soft light. He stepped into her magic circle and kissed her faery lips. He sat beside her and she turned to lean against him, wrapping his arms around her. There it was again: that wonderful feeling Tom had when the two of them touched. He relaxed back and smiled. They sat together breathing in the fragrant air until the man on the bed snorted and snored.

Ruby looked over at him with disdain. "This was Wally's idea. I just put him to sleep."

Tom shook his head, marveling at her.

Rhea sighed. "I'll never get used to it here. When you came in, I was leaving for a little while."

Tom looked down at her and Pup, who was sitting on the sleeper's chest, riding the waves of his inhaling and exhaling while he checked for trinkets in every pocket.

Tom whispered sadly, "I don't understand any of this."

"That's why I'm still here," she replied.

"What do you mean?"

"I'm waiting for you."

"To do what?"

"Well," she said hesitantly, "to come with me, and then..."

"Yes?"

"Well, Mabon says..." She went on, reciting what she understood of the great plans Mabon had for him. Tom listened to her, thinking how very childlike she was. She spoke in a fantastic mixed-up way, but somehow he understood. "He's very old, very high up. Hardly there anymore. The beings of the Light have almost completely absorbed him into their sphere. He is the oldest pure Human alive. He never blended with the faeries. Someone must take his place. But it can only be another Human."

She glanced up at Tom, wondering if she had said too much. Then she went on anyway. "Look, see my fingers?"

Tom held her slender hand in his. He saw that three of her fingertips were stained red.

"I shall tell you something else: I'm not all faery. My ancestors were Human. These are drops of blood in my fingertips—Human blood, just like yours. My people lived far away, north across the sea. Mabon is the only one left from that time. There were many clans then. They all knew the ways of magic. But then hostile invaders came down upon them. A great battle was fought and my ancestors lost. They appealed to the King of Faery and were allowed to retreat behind the veil. For centuries they have lived there, blending with the Faery Realm. And now there are just Mabon and me."

With another great sigh, Rhea ended her tale and silently drew Tom's arms around her again. For a while Tom said nothing. They just held each other while the man on the bed puffed and chortled.

"What must I do, Rhea?" Tom finally said.

"You must tell me you love me—only me—forever."

Tom looked down at her and thought again how like a child she was. He felt so much older, so much more burdened than she. He kissed her fondly.

"Yes, only you," he whispered. "Forever."

57

THE COSTUME BALL

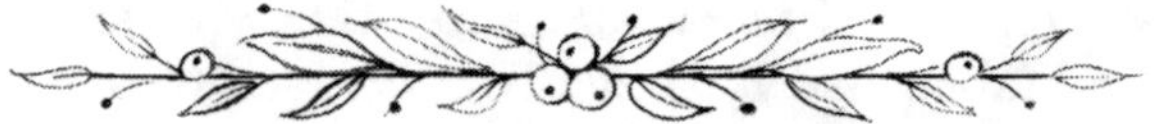

Bridgett McCarthy had a sewing shop on Alder Street. She worked out of a small storefront and lived upstairs. She'd been in business for fifteen years and never had such a high-class clientele as the two ladies standing in her modest shop right now. You could tell by the way they dressed and by the way their heads were tilted up at a slight angle, causing them to look down their noses at her.

The first lady, Mrs. Bambery, was explaining that they were attending a costume ball next month and every seamstress in town was busy making dresses for the gala affair. They were the chairladies of the event and hadn't had a moment to think about what they would wear, but now they needed a seamstress who could make their dresses in three weeks' time.

They showed her illustrations from a book of what they wanted: a Southern belle for Mrs. Bambery and Marie Antoinette for Mrs. Snyder. Bridgett looked at the costumes and saw yards of fabric, pearls, and dollar signs. Of course she could do it.

Mrs. Snyder, the thinner and more severe of the two, began saying how important this ball was. How everybody would be seeing her work. How many clients she would get from doing their dresses. This was for charity, after all, and perhaps for all this publicity she would...

Bridgett stopped her right there, knowing the next words out of that pinched mouth would be "do it for free."

"Oh, I'm sure all you say is true, but I already donate my services to the church choir; that, I'm sure, is quite enough to satisfy the Lord. As a matter of fact, since you'll be needing these dresses so soon, I'll have to be chargin' you a bit extra."

Both ladies' heads arched up higher, and they acted as if they might just tell her to forget the whole thing. But Bridgett knew she had them, for they had just admitted that every seamstress in the city was busy.

Bridgett casually looked out the window, waiting for them to decide, and saw to her horror that Mavis Ripton was coming down the street toward her store! She was wearing an impossible bright-colored hat that sat on her head like a parrot, and even worse, she had on that dreadful suit she insisted Bridgett make her with those terrible red buttons all over it.

Bridgett began to sweat—something ladies never did. If she didn't close the deal before Mavis rang the bell, all would be lost. "Well," she said, "considering it's for a good cause...it will be a lot of work, but I won't charge you any extra for the rush."

Oh, that was much better, and the ladies committed to her doing the job just as Mavis reached for the bell.

Bridgett watched apprehensively as two worlds collided in her tiny store. Mavis's bigger-than-life theatrics bounced off the ladies' reserved snobbery, and the air suddenly became very chilly indeed.

"Are you busy? Do you have a moment, Bridgett, dear?" Mavis asked, sashaying about as if she owned the place.

"Why, er, yes. Well, actually...Mrs. Bambery, Mrs. Snyder, meet Mrs. Ripton."

"Oh, if you're looking for a good seamstress, you've come to the right place. Bridgett does everything for me; simply couldn't live without her," Mavis cooed in her best uptown voice.

The two ladies were speechless. Bridgett quickly jumped in to rescue the moment. "Yes, Mrs. Bambery and Mrs. Snyder are going to a costume ball. It's coming up very soon. I know it's inconvenient, but could you stop back in a half-hour? They're in a hurry, and I have to take their measurements." She took Mavis by the arm, turned her around, and marched her right out the door.

"Well," Mavis said indignantly, "I never!" She brushed off Bridgett's hands.

"Now, Mavis, you know I always give you all the time you want. Don't get all riled up. But please do me a favor and come back in a half-hour. I've got the new fabric in, and you're going to love it."

* * *

Mavis just couldn't get over it. She was in a bad mood all day. At dinner, she sat at the table complaining to Wally as everyone else held back a smirk.

"Imagine, getting the hustle from my own seamstress! I've a mind to never go there again."

Everyone knew that wouldn't happen; Bridgett McCarthy was the only one who would produce Mavis's demented designs.

"Those two...Mrs. Bambery...Mrs. Snyder...going to a hoity-toity masquerade ball...charity, shmarity...those snobs...I'll bet their husbands are down here boozing every night with the rest of us..."

At the mention of Mrs. Snyder's name, Tom and Ruby looked at each other.

Wally replied between gulps and slurps of food, "My pet, my sweet, nobody gives my precious the bum's rush. Let me send Cheng over there."

"Oh, no. No, I'll handle it myself," Mavis said peevishly.

Tom asked casually, "What's Bridgett doin' for them that's such a big deal anyway?"

"Oh, that's really a laugh. She's making costumes. One of them wants to be a Southern belle and the other Marie Antoinette!" Mavis found this hilarious. The thought cheered her up immensely.

* * *

Tom met Ruby on the roof late that night. He paced back and forth. "This is it. This is my chance. I've got to find out more about this charity thing...If Snyder's on the committee, like Mavis says, then she's got her thieving fingers stuck all over it. All I have to do is catch her. The next question is, how do I get in there?" He thought for a moment. "I suppose I could disguise myself as a waiter and—"

"Nothing doing," Ruby said. "It's a costume party, isn't it?"

"Yes."

"Well, let me take care of it. She'll never recognize us."

"Us?"

"Yes, us. By now, you should know we're in this together."

"Okay. I guess I do." Tom smiled.

* * *

The ball was on a Saturday night. Tom waited till the last minute to tell Nash he and Ruby were going somewhere.

"What do ya mean, 'going somewhere'?" Nash asked incredulously.

"Just what I said. Make up some excuse to Wally," Tom whispered as he ran down the back stairs.

"Hey! You comin' back?" Nash shouted into the empty stairwell.

Tom's head reappeared in the doorway long enough to say, "Yes. Stop yelling." Then he was gone.

This is going to be some excuse, Nash thought, walking back to his room. He wondered what he was going to say.

* * *

Tom and Rhea rode the trolley cross-town in silence. They still didn't have any idea what they were going to do. Rhea had secretly been to the Parkmont house earlier to listen in on what Lillian and Sydney might have to say while they were getting dressed. They were definitely planning something, but what? They were talking about putting money in right drawers and left drawers. Sydney kept saying, "You can't just leave it there, someone will find it."

Pup stopped swinging on the handrails and crawled up into Rhea's lap, sensing the mood was serious.

"Here we are," Tom said. "We get off here. It's just a few blocks up."

They walked hand in hand up the dark street. Tree branches hung heavy with beads of moisture and the wet ground glistened in pools of light under the street lamps. In and out of light and shadow they walked...appearing, disappearing...seen, then unseen. Rhea stopped in the dark, pulling Tom close to her. "All right, now is the time," she whispered, kissing him. "Close your eyes and we two shall be as we were meant to be." She drew back from Tom and spoke strange words, at the end of which she said, "So be it. Open your eyes."

Tom did, and he saw they were standing in the light again. He looked down at her delicate hand on his arm and realized they had both transformed into the most resplendent of beings. Ruby wore a dress the color of roses, and her hair was all caught with diamonds.

Seeing the wonder in Tom's eyes, Rhea whispered in her peculiar wise-child way, "My world is very powerful. Someday, maybe you will know its secrets too. Come, we have a thief to catch!"

The Elks Hall had an imposing façade. Their walk up the stone steps to the entrance had a timeless quality about it. For a moment, in the mist, it appeared as if centuries had melted away, and they could have been Perceval and Blancheflor about to enter the mythical gates of Tintagel...

The evening was well under way as they arrived.

The Snyders and the Bamberys were about to leave their posts at the door when the most amazing couple appeared before them. Their clothes were no mere costumes: they clearly looked as if they had come from another time. The man wore dark green suede under a tunic of silver chain mail. His sleeves were embroidered with brown-black tree branches, and his eyes glittered behind a mask of green leaves. The girl stood beside him, one hand on his arm and the other holding up a mask of flower petals on a golden wand.

The beauty of this young man had Mrs. Bambery gushing and giggling as she walked up to greet them. "Good evening—ah, that is, welcome. Oh my, well, don't you...don't you two look beautiful? I'm **Mrs.** Bambery, and this is—"

She turned to introduce her husband, but he was already on her heels; they bumped into each other, causing her hoopskirt to flip up. She batted it down in a nervous twitter. "Being a Southern belle can be dangerous!" Mrs. Bambery giggled again at the young man, like they already had a secret together. "What did you say your name was?"

"Raven. Jack Raven," Tom heard himself saying. "And this is my companion Rose."

"Raven?" Mrs. Bambery looked puzzled, her mind going through the Rs on the guest list. Was that name on the list? She couldn't remember. "Lillian, Sydney, look who's here! The Ravens...Jack Raven and, er, his Rose." She led them over to the Snyders.

Tom took Lillian's hand. "Good evening, Mrs. Savage." He nodded.

Lillian's eyes narrowed under her powdered white wig. "It's Snyder."

"Yes, of course. Mrs. Snyder." Tom nodded again, correcting himself. Lillian's fingers felt like ice.

That's it, Tom thought. *Squirm!* He signaled Pup to jump from his shoulder onto Mrs. Snyder's. Mysteriously, her wig slipped to the side. Lillian pulled her hand away just in time to catch it before it fell off.

"I told you these things were too much bother," Sydney said as he stepped over to help steady her towering mound.

"Well, really," Lillian said, thoroughly embarrassed, looking at Tom as if he had something to do with it.

Sydney bent his long body down to introduce himself to the little jewel before him. "Rose, is it? Ah, a fresh rose from the garden indeed. I shall pluck her from your arm, sir, for a dance, if you don't mind."

"Yes," Mrs. Bambery chimed in. "Let's all go into the ballroom, shall we?"

Sydney and Rose led the way, and the Bamberys followed after. That left Tom to accompany Mrs. Savage. *How big this woman loomed in my mind all these years, and how small she really is,* he thought. He wondered what wicked little scheme she had brewing for tonight. Pup had been instructed to stay with her and send back pictures of whatever she was doing. How would they expose her? That was the question.

Who is this irksome person? Lillian thought of the young man who had taken her arm. *As handsome as he is, there is something wild about him. He doesn't belong here...he smells of chestnuts!*

Inside the ballroom, the orchestra was sawing away at a Strauss waltz. Rhea danced a few bars with Sydney and politely excused herself to return to Tom. She could see he needed to be rescued. The ladies were swarming all around him, and Lillian was now insisting he dance with her.

Rhea appeared at his side and whisked him away in the nick of time. Tom looked at the couples swirling around him. "Rhea, there's just one thing..."

"Yes?"

"I can't dance."

"Yes, you can. Just follow me. The problem is the music!" She turned to the orchestra and repeated those strange words, ending again with, "So be it."

The musicians responded as if waking from a slumber. They sat up in their chairs and played like virtuosos.

"Ah, that's better," Rhea sighed. Then she aimed a quick "so be it" to Tom's feet and said, "Now let's dance."

Before he knew it, he was twirling around the room with Rhea, his feet waltzing like a pro. Around and around they went. What had started as a humdrum charity ball suddenly turned into a magical evening. The costumed crowd milled about all through the Elks Hall, from the ballroom to the buffet, to the chairs and settees in the hallways, to the gambling room and back again.

Sydney Snyder couldn't believe how well things were going. Money was coming in from all directions: the raffle tickets, the card tables—the world was flowing forth with lovely green stuff. He was just coming downstairs after taking the prescribed cut from the first of the evening's collections.

It was so easy, he thought. *All that lovely money*. The next time, he would take an even bigger cut. Lillian was being too conservative. Sydney bobbed and bowed through the hall, smiling, nodding. He looked the perfect fop in his satin knee pants and brocade jacket. His curly white wig gave him a preposterous height. He ordered himself a drink and sat down on a couch to enjoy it.

Lillian quickly found him, and from behind the fluttering of her fan, she asked, "Well?"

He looked at her nonchalantly. "Well, what?"

"Did you do it?"

"Certainly. Piece of cake." Sydney sucked up the drink in one gulp and abruptly got up to get another.

Lillian watched him walk away from her with scornful eyes. *What a pompous ass he was!* Pup scrambled down from her shoulder and scampered after Sydney, leaving Lillian to breathe an unconscious sigh of relief.

Rhea led Tom out onto the balcony, where they could get some fresh air. Tom put his arms around her. "Are you cold?" he asked.

"No. I don't feel hot and cold like you do. It's different for me. I don't know how to explain."

"How is it you can appear and disappear? Why can I see you and other people can too, but they can't see Pup?"

"These are things that Mabon can tell you. I know that it is something like when I gave you that tea and you said everything broke up into little particles. Nothing looked solid. Well, nothing is solid as you humans think. I guess you could say we are able to break apart into the spaces between the particles and then reassemble again. This is something we can do at will. But Pup doesn't have the ability to understand this. He can't do it."

"Why can I see Pup?"

"You were given the seed—the symbol of entry into our world. Possessing that gave you special sight."

"Because of you and your curious ways, my life has changed so much for the better. Stay here with me always."

"I can't do that," she sighed. "For one thing, it takes too much energy to manifest as a human all the time. I feel too dense, like I'm encased in stone. And for another...well, your world is too dull."

"Then I shall go with you to yours."

At that, Rhea turned around and kissed him passionately. "Oh yes," she breathed, "Yes, that is what I want most of all. But it is not up to me. Such a thing hasn't happened for centuries. There are laws forbidding that...barriers to be passed."

"But didn't you say this Mabon wants me to come?"

"Yes, but it is not up to him either. There are others...there are certain conditions...but I cannot say any more now. We must wait until the time is right."

"When will that be?"

"I don't know."

Thinking out beyond that moment, they fell silent, each wondering what was going to happen to them, to their love for each other.

Upstairs in the office, Sydney was quickly dividing the money from the second collection. He felt like King Midas counting his gold. The sight of it had taken possession of him. It made him fearful to leave it in that drawer overnight. There had to be another way...

Tom and Rhea both got the image at the same time. Pup was showing them what Sydney was doing.

"So that's it," Tom said. "They are stealing the proceeds from the gambling tables. We've got to act fast. Do one of your disappearing acts and follow Sydney. I'll watch Lillian."

"So be it." She smiled and slowly evaporated, leaving her lips floating in the air like the Cheshire Cat. Tom kissed them and they too vanished.

Mrs. Bambery and all the committee ladies were so excited. The end of the evening was drawing near. Everyone agreed it was a smashing success. They couldn't wait to find out how much money they had made.

Lillian cautioned them to wait a little while longer. She would go find Sydney, and then they would all go up together after more people had left.

She wondered where that lame-brained husband of hers was. *He should be down here talking to people, making sure he's seen.* Feeling suspicious, Lillian went upstairs to the office and unlocked the door. There stood Sydney. He had found an old satchel and was madly stuffing it with the money.

"What are you doing? Are you crazy? Put that back!"

"Lillian, I'm not leaving this here overnight. I couldn't...I just can't."

Lillian started to say something, then suddenly sniffed the air. "Do you smell that?"

"What, for God's sake?"

"Rose petals. I smell roses. That girl...she smelled like roses." Lillian looked around fearfully.

"That proves it." Sydney snapped the satchel shut. "You've lost your mind. I'm handling this from now on."

"Over my dead body! Put that money back!"

Downstairs, Tom found the group of committee ladies. They all giggled when he approached. "Oh, there you are," Tom said. "Mrs. Snyder says that you should go upstairs now."

"Really? Let's go, ladies. This is too exciting," said Mrs. Bambery, and off they went in a brigade of rustling dresses.

Upstairs, Lillian was engaged in trying to bully Mr. Snyder into putting the money back. She didn't hear the office door spring ajar. Down the corridor the ladies came, chattering away.

"You fool. You simple-headed fool!" Lillian shouted. "Put that money back or you'll spoil everything."

Sydney had tucked the satchel under his arm and was backing away defensively. "Lillian, I've got it all figured out."

"*You've* got it all figured out?" Those words threw her into a rage, and she made a lunge for the satchel. The bag flew open, and money showered down like rain just as the ladies came in through the door.

Lillian was completely shocked. She just stood there holding the proverbial bag.

Sydney let go of the fistful of dollars he was clutching and stuttered, "She was...I tried to..."

At that, Mrs. Savage suddenly came to her senses and shrieked, "Oh, it's terrible! My husband was stealing! I tried to stop him!" She then promptly fainted for full theatrical effect.

The ladies blinked in disbelief as the last dollar bill floated to the floor. Then they all began shouting at once, "Call the police! I don't believe it! Call the police!"

Mrs. Bambery ran downstairs to her husband. "Help! Something terrible has happened! Call the police!"

People ran to see what the commotion was. Nobody noticed when Rhea began to appear on the stairs going down as they were going up. They even ran through parts of her as they rushed by, but Tom saw her; he was waiting for her at the bottom of the steps. Together, they walked triumphantly out of the Elks Hall and into the mist-filled night...

THE RETURN

Nettie was in the kitchen washing her pots and crying. They had run away; she knew it. Tom had left without even a word to his poor old Nettie. Nash said they'd be back, but she didn't know about that.

When Nash told Wally Tom and Ruby had to go somewhere that evening, Wally was so dumbfounded for a few moments that he couldn't comprehend. "Go somewhere? Just like that? They had to go somewhere? What are they, *nuts?* They don't have to *go* anywhere. They *have* to be right here!"

Nash shrugged his shoulders. "Don't look at me, boss. That's what Tom said." He had decided not to even try to make up an excuse. Nothing he could think of was a match for this situation.

Wally stood there puffing up like a blowfish. He was all bristles and bulges. Finally, he exploded into a tirade that sent everyone scurrying for cover. "Nobody leaves Wally Ripton like that—ever! They are out and they can just stay out!"

But as the evening wore on, he began to realize how very wrong he was in that notion. The atmosphere of the Madrigal went completely flat. People were leaving early, seeing there wasn't much going on. Wally tried to pump things up, glad-handing everyone, giving out free drinks. Nothing worked. Finally he retreated to the back room for a few rounds of poker, and even though he cheated, he still lost. It was definitely a bad night...

Nettie sat at the kitchen table staring at her knurly old hands. There was still more to do but she didn't have the heart for it. What she needed was to do some prayin', so she went to her little pantry room and returned carrying a worn black-bound missal with the faint impression of a cross on the cover. Nettie could neither read nor write, but a whole lot of God-loving energy had been pressed into that book by those big hands. In return, through the years, she had received many an uplifting inspiration. She sat head down, holding her book, letting God into her soul.

After a time, her thoughts were disturbed by the distinct feeling that there was someone out there on the back porch, although she hadn't heard a sound. At first she thought it was Tom, but then, he wouldn't be sneaking around out there in the dark like that.

"Who's there?" she called. She got up slowly and grabbed a pot off the stove, then cautiously opened the door. "Who's out there? Show yourself or I'll brain ya with this here iron pot, sure as hell!"

"Nettie?" she heard a small voice call from the shadows.

"Who is it? Come into the light so I kin see you."

A thin slight-shouldered woman with a black kerchief covering her head came forward.

"Well?" Nettie was still on guard.

"Nettie, it's Lorna."

"Lorna? Lord have mercy...is that you?"

The figure didn't answer, but began to cry.

"Well, come on in here and get out of the cold. Where have you been? We all thought you was done for." Nettie pulled her into the warm kitchen and shut the door.

Lorna stood shivering, not knowing what to do. Then she broke down into tears. "I just didn't know where to go..."

Nettie took Lorna into her arms. Lorna sobbed and sobbed. "Hush now, honey. You all right now. Nettie will take care of ya. Sit down here an' let me get some hot food into ya."

"Oh no....I..."

"Oh no, nothing. Here, give me dat ole coat and kerchief an' sit down like I tells ya."

Nettie took her things from her, and when she got a good look at Lorna's face, all she could do was sit down herself and say, "Lord have mercy...Lord have mercy..."

Seeing he was running out of glasses, Barney shouldered a heavy load of dirty ones back to the kitchen. Lorna instantly turned away. Nettie gave him the evil eye, telling him to turn around and take the glasses right back where they came from.

"But I...hey, who's that? Lorna...Lorna?"

Nettie hustled him out the door with an "Outta my kitchen" and a strong "Um, um."

"Don't you worry, honey," she said to Lorna, "you just relax and lemme get you something hot to drink."

In a desperate whisper, Lorna kept repeating, "I didn't know where to go...I didn't know where to go. He found me...he found me and left me for dead. The police came...I've been in the hospital all this time." She looked up at Nettie with haunted eyes. "I never told them nothing. Not my name...nothing. When I got out I didn't know where to go," she sobbed.

"Oh, honey, now don't cry. We gonna help ya. You comin' back here might be the best thing. Nobody would think you'd do that. Yes, Lord, I think that was the right thing to do."

Wally wandered back to the bar after giving up on poker. "What're you looking so mystified about?" he asked Barney, who was absentmindedly wiping a glass.

"You know, I just went back to the kitchen and I could a sworn I saw Lorna sitting there. But naw, couldn't be."

"Lorna? Did you say Lorna? She's back? I knew it!" He slapped the bar for emphasis. "They always come back! Well now, things are looking up!" So much for Tom and Ruby. Lorna was back. He'd throw them out like yesterday's newspaper.

Wally pushed through the kitchen door, arms wide, all smiles for the returning celebrity. "Lorn-a..."

What he saw was Nettie standing tall over a haggard little creature, her arms protectively around her. "Now wait a minute, Mister Wally..."

"Lorna?" Wally stopped dead in his tracks. She lifted her head to look at him, and all he could do was gasp. Her face looked like the hind end of a turkey, all stitched up and red from roasting. She was almost unrecognizable.

"Mister Wally, she didn't have no place to go."

Lorna crept back into Nettie's arms and cried. The air had gone out of Wally's balloon so fast he had to sit down.

"Well..." he said, pulling out his handkerchief and rubbing his eyes as if to erase what he had just seen. "Well..." was all he could say.

Tom and Ruby were walking around the back of the Madrigal to the kitchen entrance. The moisture in the air had turned into a soft rain. Impulsively he picked her up and waltzed her down the alley with Pup hanging on his shoulders. Around they went in the dark until they bumped up against the building. There they stopped, laughing and out of breath. Their clothes, no longer the fine garments they wore at the ball, stuck close to their bodies, their hair all wet and stringy.

"This was the best night of my life," Tom said, kissing Ruby so she felt it down to her little pointed toes.

"I love you, Jack Raven." She smiled.

Pup crawled between them, wanting their attention. "Yes, we love you too, Pup," Tom said tenderly. "You're my family now...my strange wonderful family."

They huddled together holding each other till Tom realized how cold he was. "I know you two don't feel it, but I'm freezing. Let's go in."

Inside the kitchen, Wally was mopping his brow, clearing his throat, trying to contain himself. Mavis had walked in, filling the room with her hysterical reaction to the sight of Lorna.

Nettie kept pleading, "You can't turn her out. We got to help her." Lorna continued her hopeless crying.

Tom and Ruby appeared in the midst of this upheaval like a ray of light, wet and bedraggled but shining with the exuberance of love.

Quickly including them in the chaos, Wally said sarcastically, "Oh, so you decided to come back too? Well, we're *all* here now, isn't that nice?"

Tom was going to say something, but Lorna stopped him. "Oh, don't look at me, Tommy," she cried, covering her face with her hands.

"She's been in the hospital all this time. That man Russell got to her," Nettie said in a low voice.

Mavis started up again, looking at Tom and Ruby. "Yes, and here comes more trouble! I'm telling you, get rid of all of them!"

"Yes, my sweet. I agree with you. But we're in a situation here...we definitely have a situation here..." Lorna turning up again was bothersome for Wally, but letting her go was not a good idea either. In her state, she could start babbling about anything, and what she could tell might hang him. He would kick Tom and Ruby out in a minute if he could think of somebody to replace them. But the fact was, the Madrigal was becoming uncommonly successful, all because of Ruby and her miraculous talents. No, he could not afford to lose them.

"What possessed you two little sweethearts to leave us high and dry this evening, anyway?" Wally questioned in sugarcoated tones.

"There was something that had to be done. That's all I can say," Tom answered, offering no more. For the first time, Tom's usually soft voice had an edge to it.

"Oh, I see." Wally smiled through his teeth. "And will you be having many more of these evenings?"

"No, not that I can foresee," Tom replied cautiously. "Anyway, last time I looked, this wasn't a prison."

"Quite so, quite so," Wally returned. "But there is such a thing as professional responsibility."

Tom laughed outright at that.

"Well, let's just say you owe me," Wally said, dropping the facade.

Tom looked him squarely in the eyes, measuring his challenge. "Not much," he answered.

"Are you gonna let him talk to you like that?" Mavis goaded.

Wally switched tactics. Now he was the poor, put-upon guardian of lost souls. God knew how much he'd done for this boy—took him off the streets, fed him, kept him all these years. "It's not been a bad life," he said.

"It's been no life," Tom said coldly.

Wally ignored that, confident he'd find another way to squelch Tom's budding independence. Turning to Lorna, he said, "Now that you're here, you can stay, but never let anyone see you—ever."

"No, I won't. Never," she swore.

Wally got up from the table, putting away his handkerchief and straightening his vest. "I'm closing things up for the night. Come along, Mavis."

"Wally," she said, haranguing him as they walked down the hallway, "are you mad, taking that girl back here?"

"Better here than out there talking her fool head off."

"Why? What's she got to say that wouldn't make it worse for herself?"

Wally knew Mavis was oblivious to many of the things he did. "You're right, my pet, you're right. But let me handle this. She can stay with us till summer; then we'll leave her off in one of the little towns we pass through on our route."

"Oh!" Mavis exclaimed, slipping her arm through his. "Now you're making sense."

* * *

The person most affected by Lorna's return was Philippe. The sight of her touched so many layers of pain inside him he could hardly bear it. Underneath the shock of seeing her so disfigured, there was anger at her for running away, not letting him help her. There was rage at Burt Russell for having done this to her. There was self-hatred at being so powerless, so unable to do what any real man would have done to avenge her. The attack on her had been an attack on him, for he had loved her. Then, finally, there was this awful feeling of revulsion which now replaced his love. Lorna had become a freak like him. He did not pity her; he cursed her for surviving and coming back to haunt him.

As for Lorna, the attack had violated her core. Her very soul had taken flight in terror and now fluttered anxiously about her on moth-like wings, homeless. Her mind and body had become a frail, spiritless apparatus, which—if shaken one more time—would fall to pieces.

Lorna was given Ruby's room. It was upstairs out of the way and had no windows. She felt safe there. She could sleep—something she hadn't been able to do in months.

One by one, as the days went by, the inhabitants of the Madrigal went up to see her. Oddly, it was Sudy who became Lorna's closest friend and protector. With her simple mind and good heart, she mothered Lorna, taking her food, helping her bathe. Her childish brain used to annoy Lorna, but now she looked forward to Sudy's little conversations about nothing. Sudy retained an innocence that belied her life of abandonment and abuse. How that could be was a mystery to Lorna, but she was grateful for her attentions and gentle goodness.

Rhea tried to make herself comfortable in Lorna's old room, but it was off the upstairs balcony overlooking the barroom and stage. It was noisy and riddled with the dwarf's peepholes. Philippe could station himself in the closet of the next room and look through a hole near Lorna's washbasin, or he could go upstairs to the attic and look down through a crack in the plaster by the ceiling fixture.

Rhea made a clean sweep of the place, covering it with charms and "so be its," sealing every crack from the dwarf's salacious, prying eyes.

Philippe was surprised to find he could no longer use his many vantage points to spy on Ruby. It was something he was most interested in doing. How was it possible that she knew about him? He began watching her even more closely. Whatever she had to hide, he made it his mission to find out.

He followed her to the roof where she met Tom at night, and saw that they were lovers. He watched her in the early morning, sitting in a little patch of sun, doing her chores. That was where he saw her doing something very curious. There was a tree growing in the alley now—Tom had planted it—but there was also a wild-looking weed growing up tall next to it. He saw her go over to the weed and pull off some leaves and a flower. She held them in her hand and blew on them. They instantly shriveled and dried up. She put them in her pocket. What was this weed? An herb? A drug? A poison?

When Ruby left, the dwarf examined the plant carefully. He sniffed it, but didn't dare taste of it. He pulled some leaves off and blew on them. Nothing changed. He decided to keep them in his room and let them dry out on their own. If he was patient, he would find out her secrets.

Rhea had drawn on the magic of the plant for Lorna. From the crushed leaves and some oils, she made a salve to put on her face. It would help the swelling and the scarring from the knife wounds. Rhea told her it was an old mountain remedy. It did help—so much so that in a couple of weeks, Lorna felt well enough to come downstairs and sit in the kitchen with Nettie. But no one else saw her, except in short glimpses. She became the ghost of the Madrigal...always in the shadows and gone the minute you looked at her.

A SALE FOR BAIL

Mavis was on her way over to Bridgett's with the morning paper under her arm. She walked with a self-righteous clip down the street, into the shop, and plopped the paper onto the counter. "Did you read it?" she announced to Bridgett, who was busy at her machine.

"Read what?"

"The morning news."

"I've got no time for such a thing," Bridgett said, whirring away at her sewing. "This has to be finished by twelve o'clock."

Mavis chuckled. "Well, I'll read it to you then. Those high-mucky-muck clients of yours. Remember them?"

"Yes, yes," Bridgett answered, trying not to be annoyed. Mavis never had gotten over that morning she had asked her to leave.

"Well, listen to this." Mavis began to read loudly over the sound of Bridgett's machine. "Society Scandal: Mr. and Mrs. Sydney Snyder were formerly charged today with grand theft and resisting police at the Ladies' Assistance League Charity Ball one week ago..."

By now, Bridgett had stopped her machine. Mavis went on, "Mrs. Snyder, the chairwoman of the event, was caught with her husband stealing the cash proceeds. They were apprehended in an upper office of the Elks Hall, where they were found stuffing the money into a satchel. Both parties claim the other was responsible for the stealing, and that the one was only trying to stop the other when the committee ladies walked into the room. It has not been determined which party is guilty, and both have been charged equally. In addition, Mrs. Snyder has been charged with striking an officer of the law. She was reported to have kicked the officer attempting to lead her away."

"Ha!" Mavis harrumphed triumphantly. "So much for your high society clients."

"Well, I'll be...I hope they won't be bringing me any trouble," Bridgett looked up, starting to worry.

"Ah, now don't bother about it. All you did was make their dresses. They can't hang you for that," Mavis said, delighting in the fact that Bridgett was upset. Then she added, to make her feel worse, "Well, it's certain you wouldn't be seeing any more clients from that end of town."

"No, I guess you're right," Bridgett answered in a humble, crestfallen voice.

* * *

The house on Parkmont was up for sale. Mrs. Snyder had given authorization to her lawyer so she could get herself out on bail. The same day the sign went up, the real estate agent had a call from a man named Mr. Biggs. An appointment was made to meet and show the house. The agent himself had never been inside. He intended to arrive early to open everything up, but no sooner had he put the key in the door when he heard a cheery "Hello!" behind him.

Startled, he turned around to see a very short egg-shaped man coming up the steps. "Mr. Cooper?"

"Yes."

"I'm Mr. Biggs. A good morning to you. Good timing, eh?"

"Well, uh, yes...you're a little early. I haven't been inside yet."

"No matter. Mrs. Biggs has her heart set on a house in Parkmont, so I want to be the first to see it."

"Yes, of course, but I usually..."

"Oh, come, come, come. Let's open the door, shall we?"

He looks just like Humpty Dumpty. I wonder what Mrs. Biggs looks like, Mr. Cooper thought as he unlocked the door. As they walked into the dark entrance hall, a distinct smell of must mixed with garbage accosted them.

"Oh, dear. Well, the house hasn't been open in weeks." Mr. Cooper smiled.

"Hmmmm." Mr. Biggs frowned.

They went into the front parlor, where only a moth-eaten rug, a chair, and an old settee remained. They paused, taking in the dilapidated state of things. Then they heard a peculiar scurrying in the walls.

Mr. Cooper cleared his throat loudly and jumped into action. He went to a window and tried to open it. He struggled, and it suddenly shot straight up so hard it knocked the glass out of the window.

"Mmmm." Mr. Biggs frowned.

The agent was thoroughly embarrassed and began apologizing for everything, including the asking price of the house. They went upstairs and found the bedrooms in disarray, with cobwebs everywhere and the curtains hanging in rags. There were holes in the walls, and in the kitchen the sinks were full of dirty dishes submerged in rusty water from a broken faucet.

"I don't know what to say," Mr. Cooper admitted, dropping all pretenses of salesmanship. "Well, I understand there is a nice back yard. I don't suppose you want to see it?"

"Yes, might as well," sighed Mr. Biggs, frowning ever more deeply.

Outside, a gigantic tree overshadowed the whole yard. Hardly any light filtered through the thick leaves.

Now Mr. Cooper sighed. "I'm sure you've seen enough? I know I have."

"Yes, yes," Mr. Biggs answered. He walked around, kicking up piles of dead leaves and thinking to himself. After a few moments he said, "Mr. Cooper, I think you'll agree that this house is in deplorable condition. I wouldn't pay full price for this. I wouldn't even pay half the price you ask."

"Oh, no, no, of course not." Mr. Cooper nodded, wondering how he was going to sell this house at any price.

"But I'll take it for one fourth that price, because I like the location."

Mr. Cooper thought for a moment. This sounded like the best offer he was ever going to get. "Mr. Biggs, I have been authorized by the bank to sell this house and its property. In view of what I have seen, I accept your offer as a fair and just price. If you will come to the bank in the morning, we will draw up the papers."

They locked up the house and shook hands on the porch. As Mr. Cooper walked away, Mr. Biggs looked back at the house, saying strangely, "As it was before, so be it now." He chuckled to himself, and with a little hop and a jump, disappeared into thin air.

* * *

"You sold it for what?" Mrs. Snyder flung herself at the prison partition, screeching like a bat.

Mr. Cooper drew back in alarm on the other side of the visitor screen. The guard pulled Lillian away and sat her down, warning that the visit would be over if she had any more outbreaks.

"Well, really, Mrs. Snyder, you should be glad I was able to sell it at all," Mr. Cooper said.

"What do you mean?"

"The house...the condition it was in..."

"That house was in perfect condition! Immaculate!"

"I daresay your idea of immaculate condition is far different than mine."

"You're holding out on me. You're trying to steal from me!"

"Wait a minute, Mrs. Snyder. You're hardly in a position to be accusing anyone of stealing. You authorized the bank to sell the house, and as their agent I was instructed to get the best price I could for it. I have done that, considering—"

"Considering you're an idiot!" Mrs. Snyder attacked the screen again in frustration.

"That's it. Visit's over," the guard proclaimed, pulling her away.

"You scoundrel! That's not even enough to pay my bail. Where's my lawyer? This man stole my house from me!"

"Yeah, yeah," the guard said, escorting her back through the inner door. "Everyone wants their lawyer."

Mr. Cooper could still hear her shouting as the door closed behind them. "Idiot! Idiot!"   He gathered his papers and made a quick exit. *Depressing place,* he thought, shrugging off the disagreeable experience. *Dreadful woman.*

60

THE MONKEY BREAD

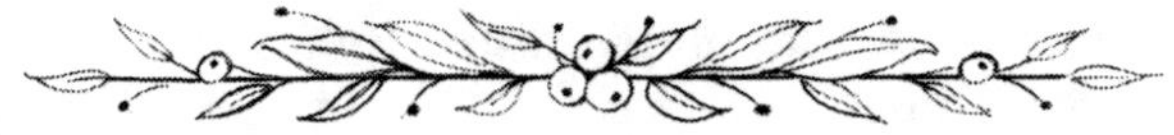

It was late at night. Tom was asleep, dreaming deeply.

He was standing before a crumbling wall. Was it for keeping something out or for keeping him in? He didn't know, but it was very old. He was tall enough to see over it. Things looked the same on both sides. He climbed on top of it, walked a little ways, and then sat down, swinging his legs over one side. He was looking over a vast silent landscape. He realized there were two setting suns: one ahead of him and one behind him in the land on the other side of the wall. His dreamer's mind was thinking about this when he heard Rhea's voice. "Tom...Tom."

"Yes?"

"No...don't move...don't wake up."

"Rhea? What is this place?"

"You're dreaming, Tom."

"I am?" It was hard to believe.

"Yes. I've come to take you with me."

"Where?" Tom turned over in his sleep. He was close to waking up.

"No, Tom. Relax. You don't need your body where we are going."

"Oh?" he answered trustingly.

"Look over your shoulder. We are going back toward the setting sun."

"What's there?"

"The Guardian of the Dead. The keeper of those that went before and whose kind live no more."

He couldn't see Rhea, but he knew she was beside him. As she spoke, he tumbled backwards into a revolving tunnel of fractured light. It was as if time was a mirror and a great hammer had shattered it into fragments. In each piece, he saw events in time undoing themselves—devolving—and in so doing, they revealed the continuum upon which they were built. Cities fell back upon the land, forests covered them only to be submerged in water, and that water turned to ice. The ice turned to green once more, then split again into molten rock. Temple ruins broke free of their jungle vines and flashed with the glory of gold once more, then were sucked back into the dense jungle, which gave way to desert sand. Tom's head was filled with the enormous scraping sounds of land plates surging against each other, pushing up mountains and collapsing whole continents as the planet sped into retrograde.

Just when he thought he could not take any more, it stopped. He was dropped into a strange prehistoric paradise of giant ferns; the only sound he heard was the call of a songbird.

Rhea was walking ahead of him. She turned and held out her hand. "We are at the end of the world; the beginning of time."

At that moment, a large golden fish glided out from between the waving ferns. Rhea took hold of its trailing fin and climbed on its back, motioning for Tom to do the same. He had no sense of his body being with him: he felt like a large pair of traveling eyes. Together they rode the golden fish as it swam slowly through this fantastic land where air was water and water, air. Animals he never knew existed grazed on tall grass. Plumed birds and giant insects flew across a blue- and rose-tinted sky. Tiny stars like diamond chips orbited through the evening dusk. Here sea, land, and air creatures all moved slowly in the same languid atmosphere.

They came to the edge of a lake. In the center, there was a tall rounded mountain. It was dotted with trees and glistening with rushing waterfalls cascading into the lake. The golden fish moved gracefully upwards toward the top of the mountain.

"We are going to see Anam," Rhea told him. "His name means 'from the beginning to the end.' He is the guardian here. Every kind of creature that has existed since time began has passed before his eyes. He knows whether they shall live and evolve or die out and rest here in oblivion. Mabon has sent us here. He says this is the first of three things you must do to gain access to our world."

"Oh," Tom said, his words coming out in slow motion while a sense of alarm raced through his slumbering mind. "What must I do?"

"You must bring him an offering—some special food."

"Food?"

"Yes. I have brought him a small drink of ambrosia. Think of something that you really loved to eat, something you didn't get very often. Only it can't be hard, because he has no more teeth. All you have to do is think of it, and it will appear."

"My mind's a blank. I can't remember anything."

"You still have some time."

At the mountaintop, they descended from the fish's back and walked toward the bright light of the sunset. They came upon a group of large rocks and went around them. There they found a small encampment. An old man sat cross-legged in front of a fire. Tom was surprised to see nestled into the rocks the remains of an old gypsy wagon, weathered and faded, not unlike the ones he traveled in. The tiny man sat with his back to the sunset, where the silhouette of a windswept pine tree marked the edge of the mountain and the beginning of the sky.

As they approached, Ruby whispered, "They say Anam's moods are ruled by his stomach. If he doesn't like your offering, he won't speak to you."

In Tom's somnambulant view, he saw Rhea and a semblance of himself sit down. He was seeing all this off to the side, separated, as if looking at a picture. The old man was so ancient he looked like a woman in his simple robe. His long gray-white hair fell in braids down his curved back. His eyes were half closed, and his incredibly wrinkled face smiled a toothless grin. Tom thought he looked like a cross between a human and a tortoise.

Rhea greeted him and set her offering before him. Anam acknowledged her by accepting her drink. Tom saw Rhea look at his semblance and ask him what he had to offer. Tom suddenly thought of the monkey bread his mother only baked at Christmas: it had a wonderful glazed crust and sweet, cheesy dough. Instantly, he saw it appear before his other self sitting beside Rhea, who picked it up and offered it to the old man.

The tortoise man mumbled something. His half-closed eyes flicked open, revealing cloudy white pupils.

Rhea said, "What is this? Anam asks."

"Monkey bread."

Rhea translated. Anam grumbled. He tore off a small piece and put it in his mouth. The seated Tom looked at Anam and smiled. Tom the dreamer became anxious when Anam remained silent, chewing. They waited for the old man to swallow. When he did, Anam gave his approval by taking another bite.

Rhea relaxed and sat more comfortably. It was a while before Anam spoke again. His eyes half opened and closed. He seemed quite indifferent to their presence. The fire crackled; the sun set further below the mountain.

Anam spoke:

"Pau glickchi chagau

man an amb gou

no og gling chi."

Rhea said, "He asks why there are two of you. You must make up your mind which one you are before he will talk to you."

The dreaming Tom looked over at himself next to Rhea. Indeed, there were two of him. He was outside himself, watching himself! Just at that moment, the seated Tom looked at the observing Tom with a candid stare. He understood then that nothing would proceed unless he changed his viewpoint.

With that realization, a dynamic change occurred. He felt his perception taking a giant leap. Suddenly he was looking out from behind the eyes of the seated Tom. A tingling sensation rushed through his body; he felt he was inhabiting a roomier, more expanded self. The fears of the dreamer vanished within this new Tom. He looked about him, infused with a sense of power.

Anam began to speak.

"He says, "Good, you have taken possession of yourself! Now he shall think of a question for you,'" Rhea translated.

Anam was silent again. Tom was restless. Too much energy was surging through him. He found himself walking to the edge of the mountain by the crooked-limbed pine. The lake spread out far below, the last of the sun submerged in an amber glow. As he looked down, he felt like a bird: he wanted to fly.

Rhea interrupted his mesmerized thoughts with a touch on his arm. "The question Anam has for you is: 'Which one thing would you take with you if you were being sent alone into an unknown world? A bag of gold that never empties, a tree that bears fruit without end, or a sword that will vanquish any foe?' When you have your answer, follow us."

Tom watched as Rhea and the ancient Anam made their way toward the gypsy wagon. He turned his gaze back out over the water and thought about the question. The sword was the obvious answer, but maybe there was some kind of trick involved. There was the possibility that this unknown land was barren and uninhabited; then a bag of gold would do no good, nor would the sword. Only the fruit tree would keep him alive.

He could make a weapon to defend himself, but he could not create a tree. As he walked to the gypsy cart, he went back and forth, trying to decide between the sword and the tree.

He climbed the steps, and upon entering, he was surprised to find he was in a dark cavern. The floor was covered in fragrant pine needles. Everywhere, ceremonial fires burned beneath ancient statues in various states of ruin scattered about the expanse.

Tom walked quietly through the shadows of what felt like a vast burial ground of the gods. Giant animal totems, winged serpents, warriors, and solemn goddesses all stood mute before their sacred fires.

A mysterious primal energy permeated the air. In the middle of the cavern, a shaft of light broke through the dark rock above and lit a pool of water with crystal blue clarity. Beside it sat Anam and Rhea. Anam was chanting softly to himself.

Tom approached them with his answer. "I choose the tree...tree...tree." Tom's voice echoed strangely as he spoke. "I wish I had a weapon...weapon...but I choose the tree...tree...tree..."

Anam stopped chanting and Rhea gave him Tom's answer. A slight smile crossed his face; his eyes flickered open and shut. Then he continued his chanting, indifferent to their presence once again.

Rhea got up and went to Tom. Smiling, her voice echoing in his ear, she said, "You have done well...well...well. He is pleased with you. Because you chose wisely, when you call...call...call...upon it, you shall have the sword...sword...as well...well...well. Now we must go...go..." She took his hand and dove into the pool, taking him with her.

An explosion of bubbles erupted from the impact of their plunge. Tom saw them rushing to the surface as he spiraled down with Rhea's long hair entwined about him. What was she doing? He couldn't breathe—he was going to die! He struggled to hold on to the air in his lungs.

Just when he was forced to breathe in the water, he woke up choking and gasping for air. It took a moment to remember where he was. He was sitting up in bed, breathing wildly, with Pup scampering back and forth staring at him, all agitated and concerned.

"Here, Pup, it's okay." Tom fell back against the pillow. Pup crawled up into the safety of his arms. Tom went to give him a comforting pat and in his hand he realized

he was gripping

a small

green

apple.

61

UNDERSTANDING

Tom wasn't the only one at the Madrigal having dreams and visions. Nash's drinking was reaching a crescendo. Twice a year he slid into the abyss: once in the summer before they rolled out the wagons and again in the winter. It was hard to know what tripped him off. Maybe this time it was the tragedy of Lorna, the holidays, or the coming new year, or maybe he just couldn't resist the lure of the bottle any longer. He would begin by becoming irritable and withdrawn. Everyone knew the signs, Tom especially. He was the one who would always bring Nash back from his sojourns in hell.

This time, Nash disappeared for two days. Tom toured around in the car searching for him. He thought Nash might be trying to make it out to the farm; he was an old circus traveler at heart and hated the confinement of the city.

Tom slowly drove out of town, looking under trees, on the sides of the road, and anywhere he might have curled up asleep. It was cold and windy. The sky threatened to let go with an icy rain. Tom drove along the country route, thinking he'd better turn around soon; Nash couldn't have gotten this far. But then, sure enough, up ahead he saw a dark figure shambling along, coattails flying in the wind. Tom drove up alongside him and yelled for him to get in the car. Nash looked at him with uncomprehending eyes and waved him off with a fury of curses.

They went on like this for some time until Tom finally gave up and followed behind while Nash trudged doggedly on. Finally, Nash was exhausted. He staggered off the road and fell down by a tree. Tom parked the car and cautiously walked up to him.

"It's freezing out here," he said casually, sitting down next to Nash.

"Get out of here!" Nash growled.

"Yeah, that's what I say."

"I ain't going nowhere."

"Well, I'm not leaving without you."

Nash waved him away with an unsteady hand and grumbled something unintelligible. He pulled a whiskey bottle out from his muddy coat and drank the last of it.

Tom waited for his mood to swing. It would be better if Nash just passed out; then he could haul him into the car without a problem. But there were no signs of that, so he waited.

After a while, Nash gave out a great sigh. "I ain't going nowhere...nowhere." He looked at Tom for the first time with recognition in his red-veined eyes. "But you're going somewhere—you're going to leave, aren't you? Funny I never thought about you goin' anywhere...I thought you were at the end of the road, just like me. But that's not true. You're just beginning. The moment that Ruby gal came, I knew it. You love her, don't you?"

"Yes," Tom answered, looking off self-consciously.

Nash sighed again. "Seeing you happy makes me sad. Isn't that terrible? You remind me of everything I've lost." He turned to Tom, all teary-eyed and blubbery. "That ain't right...I know it. I had my chance and this is what I done with it." He embraced Tom fiercely, slapping him hard on the back.

Nash let himself have a few good sobs, then pushed Tom away, swearing at himself and looking for more whiskey. "I'm out. I'm out. I gotta have some...Tommy, don't leave me here." He looked desperately around, realizing he was in the middle of nowhere without a drop of booze.

"That's what I've been trying to tell you," Tom said, seizing upon his fear of being without a drink to lure him into the car. "Let's go back to the Madrigal and I'll get all you want."

"Oh, that's right. Yes, let's go back. Help me up, Tommy. You won't leave me, will you, Tommy?"

"No, Nash. Come on, up we go."

Together they stumbled over to the car. Tom bundled him inside just before he passed out.

* * *

At last, Philippe's curiosity about the plant Ruby had picked got the better of him. He was in his room pacing about, getting angrier and angrier about things. He didn't like Ruby; he'd always been suspicious of her. Like Nettie said, she had powers. *The plant must have something to do with her,* he thought. He decided to risk it. He swallowed a few small bits of the crumbled leaves.

He didn't notice anything different right away, because he was already smoldering, ready to ignite. Tonight he'd have to ride that ridiculous tricycle to fill in for Nash, who was off on one of his benders. Tom would come out walking on stilts and he would have to ride in and out between his legs. The audience would laugh; he would laugh; but he hated their laughter. He longed to step out of himself...do something spectacular...slay them all...silence their stupid laughing mouths forever!

His thoughts went back to Ruby. He hated her lithe body that danced and bent and jumped with such supernatural ease. She was such a darling, the audience loved her, but he knew better. He knew she was a witch. *That's it—she's a witch!* His thoughts emboldened him. He would catch her; he would bring her down. Philippe felt strangely empowered.

Rhea was just coming out of her room when she was stopped in the hall by Philippe and Cheng. Something was different about their approach. Instinctively, she was on guard. Cheng was smiling—something he rarely did except when violence was at hand.

"Wait a minute, wait a minute; where are you going so fast?" Philippe cooed.

"Downstairs to get Tom," Rhea said warily.

"He's not here. He's out looking for his alcoholic friend."

Rhea started to push past them.

"No, wait. We have a question for you, Cheng and I, don't we?"

Cheng nodded, cornering her against the wall.

Rhea's flashing eyes measured the two of them. "What might that be?"

"I think you must be very special, no? You dance, you sing, the men go into your room and come out with a smile. Nobody knows what you do for them. You do something very special for Tom, no? Oh yes, I have seen you two up on the roof!"

Rhea made an attempt to move away. Suddenly Cheng grabbed her by the neck with one hand, binding her arms behind her with the other. Once she was thus imprisoned, the dwarf came in close to her body, sniffing her like a dog. "Yes, you are different. Something very mysterious."

Cheng bent over her, eager for a whiff. Rhea writhed to keep him away.

"Not so fast, Cheng. Not so fast. We are going to do this slowly, yes? Button by button."

Cheng tightened his grip around her throat in excitement. Rhea was trying to speak.

"Please, please, Cheng...you will squeeze the very life out of her, and we must save that for the very end, you know that. Yes, I think our little bird wants to sing for us. Look, she's trying to say something."

Cheng released his hand from her throat. Rhea gasped, "If you let me go, I will show you what I do for them."

"Oh, that would be very nice, very nice indeed, but we can't let you go entirely now that we have you so close to us. We will give you one hand free...yes?"

"Yes," gasped Rhea, and that was all she needed to escape. She left them paralyzed and in a trance. When she was safe downstairs in the kitchen, she released them from their frozen moment with no memory of what had occurred.

Rhea sat trembling at the table, trying to collect herself. Nettie looked over from her cooking pots. "What's wrong with you? You all right?"

"Yes," Rhea said uncertainly.

"No, you ain't," Nettie said emphatically. She sat down at the table, and looking Rhea square in the eye, asked point-blank, "Where *do* you come from?"

Rhea looked at her questioningly, but then collected herself and said what she always said when Nettie asked that question. "From the woods...on the mountains."

Nettie kept on looking hard at her. Finally, she said what she'd always thought about that answer: "I've got a notion no human has ever seen those woods."

Ruby looked back at her directly, knowing they were both going to speak the truth now. "They are there for all to see, if they wish."

Nettie nodded slowly, never taking her eyes off Rhea. "You've come to take my Tom."

"He shall go only where he desires to go."

"You're fillin' him with your fantasies."

"I offer him no illusions."

Nettie took a deep breath and sat back. What a confusing radiance this girl had. She was both good and bad alike. She continued slowly, clearly, "He's my shiny blackbird. He was starving when he came to me. I fed him. I loved him. I raised him. I protected him."

"I shall feed his soul, and where I go, he shall be a king."

Nettie continued with deadly resolve, "If you mean him harm, I shall kill you by knife or God's curse—whichever way you needs it."

Rhea returned her gaze with the same intensity. "If I do him harm, it shall be as you say."

Not another word was said between them. Nettie went back to stirring her pots and Rhea sat there, hands folded on the table.

They both were taken by surprise when Tom crashed through the kitchen door with the full weight of an unconscious Nash on his back. He let him slump to the floor, saying triumphantly, "Well, I found him."

"Lord have mercy," said Nettie.

"Is he dead?" asked Rhea.

"No, not even close. It'll take about three days to wring him out, but he'll be fine. I don't know how he can keep doing this, but he does." When Tom stopped talking, he noticed a strange tension in the air. He looked from Rhea to Nettie. "Something going on here?"

"No," Nettie answered. "We just came to a little understandin', that's all."

"Good," Tom said, still looking at the both of them "Good," he repeated, taking courage from the moment, "because I love her, you know, Nettie."

"I know, boy, I know."

"I love Nettie too," he said, looking at Rhea.

Rhea smiled. "I know."

Tom looked down at Nash, crumpled at his feet. "And I love him too." Tom laughed, realizing it seemed like he was loving everybody today.

Nettie bristled, trying not to show her emotion. "Okay, loverboy, love dat bag of bones right upstairs. Everybody outta my kitchen. I got cookin' to do."

* * *

That night, the dwarf rode his little tricycle. The laughter of the audience cut deeper into his heart, fueling his hatred.

That night, Rhea walked down a tightrope from the balcony to the floor. She was spectacular.

The audience...

held its breath...

spellbound.

62

THE DARK TRANSFORMATION

Philippe looked out his window down into the alley. Winter had bared the tree Tom planted, and the bush beside it was dry. He could see, however, that it still had green leaves close to the root. He scurried downstairs and plucked every last one of them. He had decided he liked the effect they had on him and he wanted more.

When the leaves dried out, he crushed and pounded them into a fine powder that he kept in a secret tin. Each night, he took a pinch and sniffed it. Gradually he took more and more. He wanted the effects to last longer and longer. A whole new world opened up in his head. He felt a power surge through his body that made his limbs feel like they shot out straight and tall. By day he was Philippe the dwarf, but by night he burst out of his misshapen form, born again into a prince, and darkness was his domain. He felt he was capable of anything; nothing escaped him. He was supernaturally aware. His already malicious brain sped on to incredible heights, filling with grandiose desires of power and revenge.

One night, he was out walking, feeling transformed by the powder into an omnipotent giant. The streets were deserted at that late hour. He heard something behind him and turned, but saw nothing. Again he heard it: a creeping, moaning, gravelly sound. He ducked into an alley and waited, hoping someone would appear so he could tear him apart.

Then he saw them—shapes, darker than the dark, approaching. He jumped up onto a garbage shed and showed himself, unafraid. "Come find your master!" he bellowed. "Come find your doom!"

They came all right, swooping upon him, angry and devouring. He stood in the midst of their swarming wrath, laughing, cursing these demonic wraiths into submission "So you've come from hell for me, have you? You are nothing but flies before my eyes. None is more powerful than I am. Down, I say, down! You have found me; now you are mine. You shall be my arms, legs, my armies of destruction."

He stood there exalting in himself, head back, laughing, the shadows circling obediently at his feet.

* * *

What possessed Burt Russell to come back to the Madrigal was a mystery, but there he was, watching the show, sitting with his cronies, arrogant and handsome as ever. Even the scar on his cheek was a dashing enhancement.

Backstage, everyone was whispering. Sudy was afraid and ran upstairs to Lorna. Lorna promised Sudy she would stay in her room, door locked. She waited, terrified, till finally she couldn't stand it. She had to see him, to know where he was, so her mind wouldn't dissolve with hysteria. She crept along the hallway, closer and closer to the balcony overlooking the bar. She was so thin, so frail; if she had to, she could hide within a fold of a curtain. What was she going to do? Nothing. Just watch. Just watch.

Down through the blue smoky haze, she searched the dark shapes, trying to find him. Ruby was dancing. In the spotlight, she looked like a sequined peacock, artfully dodging the hands that tried to grab her.

Ruby sang:

"Some girls are taught to be prim,

Some are very proper,

Some girls are taught to be mild,

But me, I'd rather be wild!"

She twirled and somersaulted into Tom's waiting arms. He carried her high above the crowd over to the stage.

Lorna suddenly felt someone close beside her. It was the dwarf, looking especially evil in his bright plaid pants. "Get away from me!" She recoiled into the shadows.

"You must never be afraid of me, chèrie—never. We are the same now, no?"

Lorna looked about her, frantic to escape. Philippe pulled her to him. "Listen to what I say now. You shall have your revenge. This man Russell...you will see. He will pay with his life. You wait...you'll see." He spoke in a low growl with a certainty that made her shiver.

"No, no, just leave me alone!" She fled down the hall back to the safety of her room.

True to his word, Philippe followed Burt back to the hotel where he lived in the top-floor suite. Burt strolled noisily with his friends through the spacious lobby. The two women they had in tow were trying to keep quiet, but when they reached the elevator, they burst into shrieks of laughter. The men wanted to know what the joke was, but that only made the girls laugh harder.

The night manager, Mr. Digby, looked up from his papers. Burt answered his glance with a mystified shrug and hustled the women into the elevator. In all the commotion, no one noticed a little man walking in, opening the door to the service stairwell, and disappearing.

Mr. Digby returned to the normal routine of his work, although this night would prove to be anything but normal. In fact, it would become the most disturbing night of his life. Later, when he tried to recall how it began, he could only say that after he saw Burt Russell go up in the elevator with his friends, things went from bad to worse.

First the lights flickered and dimmed. He called in the doorman, but they could find nothing wrong. Then a cold draft out of nowhere chilled the lobby till it felt like a tomb. Although Mr. Digby knew he was alone, he kept looking up from his desk, sure that someone or something was lurking behind the tall palms and high-backed chairs clustered throughout the lobby. Everything about the change in atmosphere told his instincts to get up and run, but that was absurd, his rational mind convinced him. Everything was in order.

Sometime later, two of Burt's friends came down with the ladies and left. The manager was glad to hear the foreboding silence broken by the clatter of their heels. Then all was quiet again—until that awful scream. The doorman rushed in, stuttering, "Some—somebody fell off the roof!"

Mr. Digby didn't make a move. He held onto the desk, blinking.

"I'm serious, Digby, somebody jumped off the roof. Call the police!"

By the time the ambulance and the police came, a small crowd of people in their bathrobes and pajamas had come down from their rooms to see what was happening. The doorman had taken off his coat and covered the body.

The police converged upon the manager, insisting he identify the man and tell them what room he came from. When they lifted the coat for him to see, Mr. Digby was horrified. He couldn't tell by the face, but he recognized the tie he was wearing. It was one of Burt Russell's friends.

"Get the keys and take us up to Russell's room," the police commanded.

Mr. Digby took out his handkerchief and covered his mouth. He thought he was going to be sick. All the way up in the elevator, he felt like his legs were about to collapse underneath him.

When they reached the door, he knocked. "Mr. Russell. It's the manager. Are you all right?"

There wasn't a sound from within. Dreading what might have happened, he unlocked the door and let the police go inside. He hung back in the hall, hoping they wouldn't call him. They did.

What he saw through that door surpassed his worst nightmare. The room had been destroyed. The violence that had erupted there was still palpable. The body he was made to look at appeared to have been torn apart by a pack of wild dogs. Blood was everywhere.

Mr. Digby's legs did give way then, and he asked to be taken out into the hallway. They brought him a chair and questioned him some more.

"Yes, that was Burt Russell. I can tell by the rings on his fingers. Three other men and two women went up with him to his room at about 1:30. Approximately two hours later, at 3:30, the two women and two of the men came down in the elevator and left. No, I didn't see anyone else going up or down, but there was something funny about the lights, and... well, things got very creepy from then on."

"Creepy? What do you mean?" The police wanted to know.

"It's just that I felt as if things were there and they weren't there," the manager fumbled.

"What was there?" the police asked.

"I don't know," Mr. Digby said. "Please don't ask me any more questions. I don't know."

But the police had a lot more questions to ask, questions poor Mr Digby was at pains to answer well into the hours of the next day.

* * *

"VICIOUS GANGLAND MURDERS
BURT RUSSELL, KNOWN RACKETEER AND AN
UNIDENTIFIED MAN
BRUTALLY MURDERED IN HOTEL SUITE"

When Wally read that in the morning newspaper, he took his feet off the desk and sat up in his chair. The police would be there any second. He called everyone to meet in the dining room.

"Okay, we haven't much time. Let's get our story straight, and nobody can add one sentence to it on their own—not even an adjective. Lorna, no one knows you're here, so get up in your room and stay there." Lorna nodded, trembling.

Wally continued, "Okay. this is what we say: Burt Russell used to come here with his friends. Then he stopped coming for a long time. Then he pops up out of the blue last night. He and his friends watched the show, and then they left. That's it. End of story. Nobody knows nothing else about him. Understand?"

Everyone agreed. Philippe sat there smiling strangely. Wally looked at him. "You see anything funny about that?" he asked angrily.

"No. Not a thing," Philippe replied.

"You got a better idea?"

"No, not a one."

"All right then. Sudy, if you say one more word other than what I told you, you'll end up like Lorna. As a matter of fact, Nettie, you keep her with you. Don't let her out of your sight."

"Come here, baby," Nettie called to her.

Sudy ran to her arms, crying, "I won't talk! I won't!"

"Okay. Now, everybody keep calm. We got nothing to do with this, and we're going to keep it that way."

Within hours, the police were all over the Madrigal.

63

THE CLEAN SWEEP

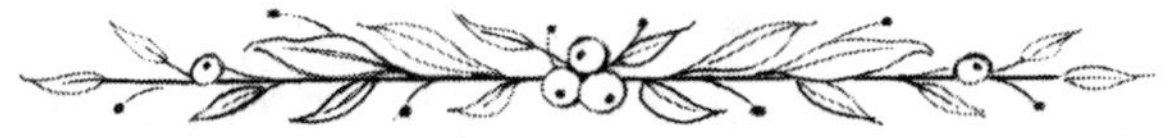

Contrary to Wally's fears, the murder and the newspaper story turned out to be great for business. Ruby became a star attraction. The surreal show with the stilt-walking and acrobatics had evenings at the Madrigal full to bursting.

But life for those who lived there was becoming strained. A dark energy had settled upon the place, and the murder investigation had everyone on edge. Mavis was constantly on Wally to get rid of Lorna. Phyllis wouldn't go upstairs without Barney; he was convinced something evil lurked about. He had no way of knowing it, but he was right.

Philippe was building his army of demons. What had once been drifting shadows, unconnected floating shreds of darkness, were now gathering power and shape through the supernatural will of the dwarf. Pup tried to alert Tom by sending him pictures of the hallway filled with black shapes, clustering around the door to Philippe's room.

Rhea knew what was happening, but she didn't know where Philippe was drawing his power from until she saw him one morning checking the plant for more leaves. While he was intent upon his task, she appeared behind him and with a wave of her hand disintegrated the bush.

Stunned, the dwarf whirled around. Their eyes locked in a wordless challenge. Philippe clenched and unclenched his fists, fighting down his desire to kill her.

"You are the worst kind of Human." Rhea's words carried such anger and disdain she could barely speak them.

"You can't stop me now. Your powers shall be mine," the dwarf said.

"You have stolen your power. It is false, and now you can't sustain it."

"I know more than you think I do, chèrie."

"You will be stopped at every turn."

"We'll see about that." Philippe tried to push her down in his fury, but Rhea was too fast for him. He let out a bellow of frustration and stormed up the steps, almost ripping the kitchen door off its hinges as he went in.

That night, Rhea met Tom up on the roof. They put the quilt over a pole and made a little tent to keep out the cold. Tom lit some candles while he told her about the images he was receiving from Pup.

Rhea cried. Tom had never seen her like this. "What have I done?

Mabon must know about it, but it isn't my fault—at least, I don't think it is."

"What are you talking about? Nothing's your fault," Tom said, trying to console her.

"The plant in the back alley came from the seed which you were given," she said.

"I know. Pup hid it there and it took root."

"Yes, well, the leaves—the leaves have magical uses."

"I know that too." Tom smiled, remembering his eye-opening trip to Aunt Petra's house.

"Yes...well...Mabon, what will he say? He's going to be so angry. You see, I guess I wasn't very careful. Philippe must have seen me picking the leaves, and somehow...I don't know how, he knew they had special powers. He stole the leaves. I don't know how many. And now his evil mind is beginning to penetrate the edges of my world." She paused, thinking, calculating how much damage had been done. "He can't get far. He can only draw negative energies to him. But grouped together, these energies can do harm, especially if they are commanded by that evil mind of his. I know he murdered Lorna's boyfriend and the other man."

Tom couldn't believe what he was hearing. Were those the dark figures Pup had been showing him gathering in the hall?

"I destroyed the plant," Rhea went on. "Philippe and I have already had a clash over it. There's nothing he can do. His powers will diminish if he can't get any more leaves. Then he will have difficulty holding those energies to himself."

Tom was silent. "If I had taken those leaves, would I have gone mad with power too?"

"Oh, Tom." Rhea looked at him with such love. "First of all, he is a thief and the worst kind of Human. You are the best kind. I would not be here if I did not believe that. The magic in the plant only magnifies what you already are. There is no desire to make you crazy. You must consent to everything with absolute clarity of mind, or you cannot help us." She sighed again. "I'm not sure how much damage has been done. Only Mabon can tell me that. I almost don't want to know..."

"Take me with you," Tom said. "I want to meet this Mabon. I'll tell him how wonderful you are. I'll tell him it wasn't your fault."

Rhea smiled and kissed him. "You can meet him only when he wants to meet you." Then she went on, "I can sweep the place clean of these energies, except the ones around his door; they are too strong. But I can fix it so they can't move, and you can help. What we need to get are new, clean brooms. Then we have to chop up garlic, vervain, and clover into a juice. We dip the brooms into the juice and sweep the halls and everywhere with them. I wish Nettie would help, and Sudy—that's a lot of sweeping."

"What's vervain?"

"An herb. I'll take care of getting that and the clover."

"Well, I can get the garlic and see about convincing Nettie to help. She's very superstitious, you know."

Rhea looked at him. "What you call superstition once came from wisdom, but you Humans have lost the meaning of it. Now you call such things stupid superstitions."

Tom took that little tongue-lashing respectfully and continued, "What I meant was, I could tell her that there are evil energies around the Madrigal coming from the association with the murders, and you know of an old mountain remedy to clean them out. Her religious beliefs are mixed up plenty with God and superstition...I mean, 'wisdom.' Sudy will do whatever Nettie says."

"Good." Rhea sank back into Tom's arms, relaxing for the first time.

Reaching into his pocket, Tom said, "Now, what I want to know is what happens when I bite into this little green apple."

Rhea replied, kissing him, "Why don't you try it and see?"

* * *

There were two distinct camps at the Madrigal, and certain kinds of information did not pass between them. On the one side, there were Wally, Mavis, Philippe, and Cheng. Everyone else was on the other.

The idea of a clean sweep took hold. Once Tom convinced Nettie, Sudy went right along. Phyllis thought something should be done to rid the building of "the creeps." Nash and Barney joined in; so did Mae.

Rhea explained that the best time to do this was on Solhaime, which was what her folk called Christmas Eve. All doors and windows had to be open so the dark energies could flee from the sweeping. They would do this in the afternoon when Mavis took her two-hour nap and Wally, the dwarf, and Cheng went up to the office. Later that night, they would secretly gather and walk the halls with candles, spreading the blessing of light into the dark.

The holidays were usually a depressing time. The Madrigal was closed and no one did much of anything but feel sorry for themselves. Now, this "sweeping" brought everyone together and gave their spirits something to rally around. Brooms were bought, and Nettie and Rhea chopped up the concoction, which remarkably didn't smell like garlic, but sweet clover. On December 24, all was quiet at the Madrigal except for those gathered in the kitchen. Rhea explained that as they swept they were to say,

"Go droth amora
Leaders of the light
God in his height
Banish the Devil
On every level."

The little group of cosmic cleaners took their brooms and went about their tasks with gusto. They swept in a line right through the bar, back into the dining room, and out through the kitchen. Then they went up the two sets of stairs to the rooms above, whispering their chant so as not to wake Mavis. Lorna's room got a special sweep. No one but Pup and Rhea could see it, but before their brooms skittered and leapt dark cobweb-like fragments; out the windows like smoke they flew.

In the hallway before the dwarf's room, many shadows collected, coiling in a dark wreath around the door. Those energies were already psychically attached to the dwarf; they wouldn't leave him. Rhea took her broom dripping with the garlic-clover juice and brushed right through them, plastering them to the wall, where they stuck like glue. She stepped back, admiring her handiwork. They would be of no use to Philippe now, except as a reminder that her power was greater than his.

At midnight, the second half of the ritual cleaning took place. Silently, each person arrived at Rhea's door. As they entered, they found the room brightly lit with candles. Rhea's quilt hung on the wall, revealing the inside, a magnificent patchwork of reds, velvet greens, and silky yellows, shimmering with silver threads. Before it was placed the most remarkable little tree—a Christmas tree decorated like none they had ever seen. It was ornamented with frosted pine cones and delicate silver stars. Each branch dripped with a glowing bronze-colored moss. At the top of the tree sat a weathered carved wooden angel.

"How can all this be?" Lorna whispered, her eyes filled with tears.

"It's magic." Tom smiled softly back.

Nettie was so amazed she couldn't even manage a "Lord have mercy."

"I wanted to do it...I mean, Ruby and I wanted to make this night memorable," Tom continued. "I never say much about my past. In the mining town I came from, life was tough for everyone, but there were a few good times, and I believe the best of them had to do with Christmas. People came together; hardships were forgotten, the women cooked and baked up a feast. I'd think about it all year long."

As Tom whispered on about his childhood memories, Nash, Mae, Sudy, Barney, and all of them fell under the spell of his nostalgic words. If they had never experienced such feelings themselves, they did now in that moment. Everyone felt wrapped up in a delicious sense of love and community.

Nash looked at Tom with Ruby standing by him and marveled at how much he had changed. He was a young man now who spoke with a quiet grace. His underlying strength was no less apparent. *That Tom...he's got character,* Nash thought to himself as he listened.

Sudy was transfixed by anything that sparkled. Since the whole room glittered and shone, this was her idea of heaven. The way Tom and

Ruby looked, so radiant amongst all the candles, they might have been a king and queen straight out of a faery tale. She wanted everything to stay like this forever.

"You see this angel on top here?" Tom said. "I carved it for my mother the last Christmas I spent with her." Then he fell silent. Everyone waited, slightly embarrassed at the intimacy of the moment.

Rhea whispered, "Bring out the rest of the surprise."

Tom brightened up again as he opened up a drawer in the little washstand by the bed. He looked over his shoulder at Nettie, saying, "Now, don't complain. I know this should be heated, but then you would have known all about it."

Nettie was about to say, "Lord have mercy!" when everyone in the room said it spontaneously for her. A fit of stifled laughter went round the room.

Tom brought out a jug of apple cider, glasses, and some curious loaves of bread. "I couldn't believe it. I found these at the market this morning. It's called monkey bread. I don't know if it will be as good, but that's what we used to have." He looked over at Rhea, giving her a wink.

When they finished the bread and cider, Rhea handed each of them a candle, repeating the chant that must be whispered as they walked through the halls:

"Go droth culhain
Fir mach bin nach
Light into dark
Opens the way.
Evil may gather
But it cannot stay."

Nettie hesitated. She still had some last doubts that she might be unwittingly siding with the devil in going along with all of this. "These words—where do they come from?"

"They are very old words, but they come from the same good place that yours do," Rhea answered.

Tom put his arm around her as she held out the candle to Nettie. No one else quite understood Nettie's conflict, since their Christian faith was either loosely held or nonexistent. To them, Ruby was just a quaint mountain girl with a lively spirit, not a questionable creature with ill-gotten powers.

Nettie looked from one to the other, searching their souls for the origin of this close bond they now shared. When she could see nothing but the reflections of pure unselfish love in their eyes, Nettie finally accepted the candle, saying, "I believe you must be right."

The procession went all around the Madrigal, and when they were through, they all went to their beds, blew out their candles, and slept like angels the rest of the night.

* * *

"Oh, it's been forever since I've been here!" Rhea flung her arms around Mabon, who was sitting in his antlered chair exactly as he had been when she last saw him. "You can't imagine how stifling it is to live with the Humans. If I didn't love Tom so much, I couldn't stand it." She got up, shook herself, and danced away, twirling about the great hall just for the pure joy of feeling free and breathing the air of her world once more. Mabon watched from his firelit chair as her red beauty enlivened everything around her. She finally came back and dropped out of breath onto the furs by the fire. Mabon smiled at her, patiently waiting.

Rhea grew more serious, knowing she must talk of important things. "You know about the little man they call Philippe?"

Mabon nodded.

Rhea sighed, lowering her voice. "I did everything I could think of to counter him once I knew he was stealing the leaves. I wasn't being careless. I..."

"I know," Mabon reassured her. "You did well. I am not angry with you." It was his turn to sigh. "This dwarf is clever and willful. He has a taste of power and is not going to let go. He knows now how to gather energy to himself and use it for his evil purposes. But this is not your fault. There is a risk in any kind of crossover interaction. We just have to be more careful in our plans...to keep ahead of him."

Rhea was immensely relieved that she was not to be held responsible for letting any more Human evil into her sphere. "Tom's going to come with me. I know it."

"I know he loves you, and that's sure. But will he cross the divide, and will those that hold sway in this world accept him? I'm not so sure."

Rhea's eyes flashed at Mabon as if he had said something traitorous. "What do you mean? Why do you doubt him? Hasn't he done everything you wanted?"

"It's not what I want," he continued, trying to calm her. "You must realize, what we are asking for is this boy's life. The steps he takes he cannot retrace."

"But what he'll have here will be a hundredfold better than what he could ever have there. Besides, he will be with me," she added petulantly.

Mabon rose from his chair and began walking away down the length of the hall. "Go back. Go back. We must let things evolve. The stars must take their turn."

Rhea looked lovingly at the fur rugs she sat on by the fire, at the great starlit hall, then blinked her eyes. In an instant, she was in her cramped room at the Madrigal. The tree was gone. The quilt lay on her bed. "I'm back," she sighed, pulling it around her. "I'm back."

64

THE NEW GAME

Wally sat in his customary pose, feet up, rocking back in his chair, reading the newspaper. The windows of his inner sanctum were shut tight against the cold. It was airless and close, just the way he liked it. Cheng sat over by the window, absentmindedly pulling pistachio nuts from one pocket, eating them, and putting the shells back into another pocket. Every once in a while, he would huff against the window and wipe it clean so he could look out before it frosted up again. It was almost the end of February, and winter hadn't yet lost its grasp. On the other side of the desk, the dwarf lounged in another chair, head back, blowing smoke rings into the choked-up air.

Wally looked over the top of his newspaper and said, "Well, there hasn't been a thing in the news about the Russell mess for over a month. We might just be clear of it."

"Umm," said the dwarf.

Wally flapped the paper down on his lap and looked over at Philippe. *What is it about him?* he thought. *He's more aggravating and insolent than ever.* He didn't like it.

The fact was, Wally was becoming a little afraid of him. Before, he'd felt like he was on top of Philippe's manipulations. He enjoyed his wicked observations and cajoling humor. But now, Philippe was playing a different kind of game, and in this one Wally was definitely not the leader. The more he looked at the little creep over there, sitting so self-possessed in *his* chair, in *his* office, the more he wanted to leap up and throttle him.

Wally hated feeling uncomfortable in his own lair, but there was no way to get rid of Philippe. He knew too much. He was as embedded in Wally's life as a tick on a dog.

As for Philippe, with each smoke ring he sent up, he was coming closer to saying something—something that began his plan to squeeze Wally out of the Madrigal.

"Umm...." he mused, sending up another puff.

Wally went back to his reading. The dwarf casually crushed out his cigarette and stood up to stretch. "You know, Monsieur Wally, I've been thinking."

"What about?"

"Well, I've been here a long time, yes?"

Wally flapped down the top half of his paper. "Yeah, and?"

"Well, I've been thinking about money, a raise..."

Cheng looked back from his gaze out the window. No one ever talked about money to Wally. Ever. They got what they got, and that was it.

Wally tried to conceal his surprise with a chuckle. "Money? What's that?" He put away his paper. "Cheng, run down and get us a couple of beers."

"Right now?" Cheng asked, not wanting to miss this showdown.

"Yeah, right now," Wally said definitely.

"Okay, okay." Cheng shuffled off.

When the door had closed, Wally took the initiative, trying to appear tough. "What is it with you lately, Philippe? Any time you don't like it here, you can leave."

"Oh, but I don't want to leave; I just want more money."

"What kind of money?"

"Oh, like one-third of the take from the Madrigal."

Wally was floored. "That's blackmail!"

"Yes, I think that's what it is."

"Well, you can take your little crooked ass and go right to hell with it."

"Ah, but if I do, you will go with me. I know so many things. Let me see...how about the way you treat your little birds? Tsk, tsk. Finding those pathetic little creatures, letting them flutter around here, then wringing their necks...tsk, tsk, what would the police say to that?"

"You were right there with me, your stumpy little mitts all over them!" Wally shouted.

"Quite so, quite so. We are together, yes? And we should stay together. But things must be more equal among friends. Yes? Maybe I should ask for half interest in the Madrigal. Yes, that's probably more fair."

"Get out! Get out of here!"

"Okay, but don't deceive yourself. I'm not leaving."

Cheng was coming up the stairs just as Philippe opened the door. "Ah, good. I'm thirsty." The dwarf plucked one of the glasses from the Chinaman's hands and left.

Wally had turned a violent, blotchy red, but he calmly took his beer and returned to his desk. Cheng went back to his post at the windowsill.

Wally was shaking. Never had anyone from inside the ranks threatened a coup like this. It was very important that nobody should see him waver. Everything had to appear completely normal until he could think of what to do.

Later that day, Wally found himself knocking at Mavis's door.

"Come in." Mavis was at her vanity and saw him in the mirror as he entered. She hesitated a moment at this unexpected visit, but then continued her powdering and coifing for the evening. "Is something wrong? Your neck is all red."

"No, no, just thought I'd come in and sit down a minute." He sat uncomfortably on the edge of the bed.

Mavis didn't turn around, but scrutinized his reflection in her mirror. "Well, I'm glad things have finally started settling down—I mean, about that murder business. Now maybe we can get on with our lives and stop having to tiptoe around."

For a moment, Wally didn't know what she was referring to. Did she know what went on up in his office? "You mean the Russell case?"

"Of course I mean the Russell case. What other murder would I be talking about?" She turned now and faced him. "I still say we should get rid of Lorna *now,* and I don't think we should go out on the road this summer. Those days are over. We've got enough business here in town."

"We've got to go out this summer for a lot of reasons. There's Lorna and some other baggage I want to get rid of."

"Humph," she snorted, turning back to the mirror. "I don't know what other baggage you are referring to, but I, for one, am not spending one more summer bouncing around in those wagons."

Wally stood up and paced back and forth. Another insurrection! That was all he needed. Mavis got the full blast of everything he couldn't say to Philippe and more.

"Now, look. You're going. This may be the last time we do, but you're going! There's too much at stake."

"What *are* you talking about?"

"I don't have to explain myself. I'm going, you're going—that's it. That's all you have to know."

"If you came in here for a fight, you're going to get it." Mavis stood up, going head to head with him.

The shouting, the insults, could be heard down in the kitchen. Nettie listened for a moment to the stomping and muffled screams. "Um, um. They been due for one o' them scenes for months. Been much too quiet around here."

* * *

The cleansing protected the halls of the Madrigal, but it didn't stop the dwarf from collecting his dark energies elsewhere. Fortunately for him, his will was as strong as his addiction to the powers of the leaves. He didn't use up what little he had. He rationed himself. If he were careful, he would have enough for three months. In that time, who knows what he could do—perhaps gather enough power to crack open Ruby's world; if not, he would at least conquer his own.

One thing was certain: he would never have to fawn and laugh for Wally again. Today he'd played his hand. He could see Wally was frightened—and why not? His new expanded self was very formidable. Cheng would see who the real boss was and follow orders—Philippe La Trope's orders.

For all his will and external control over himself, Philippe was having trouble with his mind. If he didn't concentrate, his desires and his thoughts raged and tumbled over themselves. He heard voices. He saw things. The dark energies spoke to him. He was filled with the most violent urges; his desire to kill, to rip something apart, was overpowering. During his late-night wanderings, he began catching rats and beating them with sticks just to purge himself and save himself from doing something worse.

It was true that he had power over the demons, but it was also true that the demons had secretly borne away his soul, taking it far away from humanity into regions where it could never be retrieved.

65

AN ALLIANCE IS FORMED

One Sunday afternoon, a thunderstorm rolled off the mountains, across the plains, and into the city. Tom and Rhea went up to the roof and sat together under the eaves watching the giant clouds blow in.

The drama of the mounting storm was exciting. Rhea was especially affected by the electrical currents charging the air. She sparkled with mischievous energy. They laughed and tussled with each other. She couldn't help being herself, which of course was a faery: beautiful and seductive.

She danced about in the wind with the gusts lifting and twirling her about. When loud thunderclaps shattered the air, she playfully ran for cover into Tom's arms, shrieking with delight. When the rain finally came, she wanted to drag him out to dance around in it.

"Nothing doin'," he protested. "I'll catch my death of cold."

She jumped about, letting the rain drench her. "No you won't. It's spring. This is the first rain of spring."

Tom watched her from the dry cover of the eaves, shaking his head. "It's freezing!" he shouted.

"Someday you will run in the wind and rain like me."

"Today's not the day. I'm staying right here."

She came back to him, all breathless and wet, pressing herself close to him. "Okay. Well, then, I will wait with you until you do." She tilted her face up to kiss him, her lips tasting of a curious mixture of earth and air as only a faery's could.

Mavis sat before her mirror, getting ready to do her hair up in pin curls. Her concentration was like that of a surgeon about to perform an operation. It was her most important task of the day, bestowing the look of full and youthful volume on her thinning dyed hair. She methodically curled and twisted till her whole head bristled with metal clips, then dipped a cotton ball into a dish of beer and dabbed it carefully all around. That was the secret. When she awoke from her afternoon nap, her hair would be dry and crisply curled. Finally, she applied her face crème and anti-wrinkle tape to the furrow in her brow.

A sudden thunderclap brought her to the window. She peered through the rain-splashed glass, looking like an alien from outer space draped in a Japanese housecoat.

Wally was alone, locked in his office, going over his books. He hunched over the desk protectively, as if someone were looking over his shoulder. Every once in a while, he would swivel in his chair, looking nervously around for someone.

The dwarf had put him permanently on edge. He was always there in the corner of his eye, worrying him, wearing him down. Wally began to feel the dwarf was there even when he wasn't—like now. He made another swivel in his chair. What was that in the corner? Something was watching from over there...

There was a loud clap of thunder and Wally jumped up, clasping his chest as if he had just been shot. He went to the window and saw the jagged edge of a lightning bolt slice though the sky. He was frightened. The dwarf had become a strange, eerie adversary. If Wally believed in a devil—which he didn't—it would have been the dwarf.

Wally had made a deal with Philippe and given him some money, but that was just to buy some time. He had to find a way to eliminate him. Not there—not in the city, with all the scandal already attached to the Madrigal, but during the summer, on the road. Mavis had been right, as usual. The time for bumping around in those wagons was over. This would be the last summer for Ripton's Traveling Theatricals and Curiosities, and also for the dwarf.

Wally inhaled and exhaled deeply, then straightened his vest. He didn't know how he was going to do it, but the dwarf was going to be eliminated this summer.

Lorna went down the back stairs to the kitchen, seeking some relief from her loneliness. At the bottom, she hesitated. Looking in, she saw Nettie at the table, her gnarled hands folded over her Bible. Around her, pots cooked, boiled, and baked, patiently waiting for her next touch. Lorna smiled, breathing in the delicious scents.

Before her brush with death, she'd never given Nettie much thought. Food and the fixing of it was just something you did to coat your stomach before you drank. But now she loved watching Nettie perform her everyday miracles of turning flour into bread, water into great-tasting soups, and meat tough as shoe leather into tender, juicy morsels. It was funny to think she should derive such pleasure from Nettie's kitchen after all her high-faluting dreams of love and riches.

"Come in. I know you there," Nettie said without moving.

"I don't want to bother you."

"You ain't botherin' nobody, chile. Come on in an' sit down."

Lorna pulled up a chair beside her. "Rain's coming down pretty hard. Did you hear that thunder?"

"Yes, Lord, I did." Nettie laughed, coming out of her prayer-minded thoughts. "Was you scared?"

"No. I just came down, 'cause, well, I don't know. I like it down here with you. I got nothin' to do, except keep out of everybody's way."

"You poor chile. Everybody gets their pack of troubles to carry in this world, and the Lord done give you a special heavy load. But it's all for a reason. The Lord don't do nothin' without it havin' a good reason. The greater your troubles, the greater your reward in heaven."

The old Lorna would have had a ready remark full of cynicism for Nettie's comments, but now she just looked restlessly about, saying, "Yeah, I guess."

Nettie held fast to the Good Book, reinforcing her words with a few God-confirming "Um-hums."

Lorna tried to divert the conversation from herself. "You must have read that thing backwards and forwards a hundred times by now, huh?"

Nettie took her hands from the book and smoothed her apron down upon her lap. "Read? Chile, I can't read. All them words is in my heart, but I can't read a one of them. That's my sorrow, not readin' what the Lord put down in that book." She got up to give her pots a stir.

Lorna didn't know what to say. She stared at Nettie's worn missal with the faded cross on top. Before she knew what she was doing, her hands reached out and opened its pages at random. Slowly, she read:

"Every valley shall be lifted up
And every mountain and hill
Made low;
the uneven ground shall become
level and the rough places
a plain."

Nettie came back to the table and her eyes lit up. "You could read that? It says that? There?"

"Yes." Lorna smiled.

"You know what that means? It means that the Lord's gonna make the way smooth for ya now, chile. You've had your trials and you come through. That's what it means. I know it do." Nettie gave her a great hug.

Lorna could not quite believe she had picked that passage to read.

Nettie was all excited. "Show me the place where it say that."

Lorna pointed to the words one by one. When she finished, they were silent a while. Then Lorna began timidly, "You know...if you like, I could come down here an' read to you when it's quiet, in the afternoon like this. And then maybe..."

"Maybe what, honey?"

"Maybe you could teach me how to cook?"

They both burst out laughing at the thought.

"Chile, that is the *last* thing I ever expected to come outta your mouth."

They laughed again.

"Are you serious?" Nettie asked.

"I don't know...maybe..." Lorna hid her face behind her hands, not wanting to show the scarred ugliness of her laugh.

"Well, I guess if you can take the time to read to me, I can take the time to see if you can cook. You know, I got a whole book of recipes and seasonings stored up in my head. Some of them come from my great-grandmother, and that goes back 100 years. I got nobody to leave what I know to, so it might as well be you." Nettie reached over and patted Lorna's hand. "An' something else, chile...you don't ever have to hide your face from me. I think you're more beautiful now than you ever was."

Up in the mountains, the rain passed. The last of the snow washed away with it. The late afternoon sun shone down. Out from under the dark matted covers of winter, the first green shoots of spring
found their way
to the light.

66

ETHEREAL REUNIONS

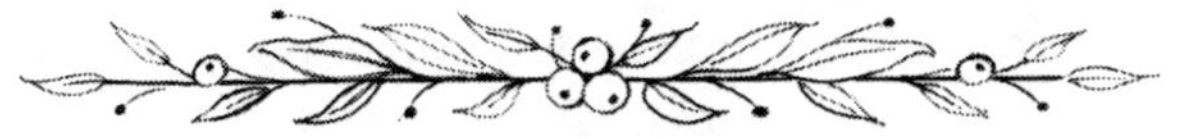

Rhea opened the window and leaned out. On the bed next to her lay one of Wally's customers.

Her instructions had been to give him the works, so she did. Rhea had flirted with him, dropping her shoulder strap provocatively, and whispered close to his grinning face, "Let's get carried away." He grabbed her tightly as she kissed him. In an instant, he fell back into a deep sleep.

Now, for a while, her time was her own. She relaxed, taking the pins from her hair and shaking it free.

Spring had finally come round to the city. She could smell green in the air, mixed with the sweet scent of baked apples. Rhea smiled as she thought of Nettie and Lorna down in the kitchen baking up a storm.

It all began when Lorna had asked Nettie to teach her to cook. Surprisingly, she had a talent for it, and baking pies was her specialty.

Lorna had filled the back porch windows and railings with her attempts at creating the perfect pie crust. She made dozens of small cupcake-sized crusts with different fillings till she was satisfied.

One afternoon, Tom was tasting the latest batch and Nettie grumbled, "Chile, this has got to stop. What we gonna do with all these here lil' pies?"

"Sell 'em," Tom suggested between bites.

Lorna's eyes lit up for the first time since she came back. "Do you think we could?"

"Sure." Tom finished one and wolfed down another. "These things are *good*. Make them just this size and call them 'Lil' Pies,'" he said, giving Nettie a mischievous pinch.

"How about 'Sweetie Pies'?" Lorna joked.

"Great! You bake them and I'll sell them. It's a cinch."

"How we gonna do this with dat ole Mavis snoopin' around?" Nettie worried.

Lorna's hopes were immediately dashed.

"Now, don't bother about her," Tom said. "Bake them at night and I'll have them gone by early morning."

The Sweetie Pie bakery was a success. Coins piled up in the pantry cookie jar, but the best part of all was that Lorna had begun to come out of her cocoon and recover some of her old feisty self.

As the delicious apple smell wafted up towards the window, Rhea looked wistfully over at the golden apples hanging from her quilt. When was she ever to return to her home, to the mountain forest she loved? She absentmindedly braided and unbraided her hair, humming a lonesome song.

Down in the alley, she heard the strike of a match. Rhea tensed and immediately drew back from the window. She was being watched.

The dwarf emerged from the shadows below as he lit a cigarette. "Oh, come, come, are we sad tonight? Summer's coming. What's going to happen when your Monsieur Tommy leaves for the farm? He will go to fix the wagons for the trip, no? You will be alone for days and days. Ah, but don't worry, I shall take good care of you. We shall have fun. Yes? Hmmm..." He sniffed the air. "Those little pies are out again tonight. Mmm, apple, my favorite." He started to walk away. "Oh, and something else. I plan to—"

Rhea shivered, quickly stepping forward to shut the window on his next words, whatever they were.

* * *

Sunday was a pleasant sky-blue day. Tom and Rhea were riding the trolley back to Parkmont. He hadn't been there since that revelatory day many months ago, but he had the great satisfaction of knowing that the Snyders were behind bars and that they no longer owned his aunt's home. Oddly enough, Rhea said she knew the new owners. Tom was mystified at this, but whenever he asked any questions, she laughed and put him off, saying he was in for some surprises.

"I don't like surprises, especially yours," he said. "They boggle the mind."

"Someone you love is waiting for you there."

Tom and Rhea walked down the tree-lined street. Pup scampered on ahead. Everything was the same, but... "Where is the house?" Tom asked, dumbfounded.

"Behind those leaves up ahead."

All around the property, tall, dense bushes had grown up, completely concealing everything. Rhea stopped before an equally tall vine-covered gate and rang a bell. A little door within the gate opened, and Rhea went in.

Tom had to stoop to get through. Once inside, he couldn't believe his eyes. He was in a wonderland with flowers and butterflies everywhere. The house was completely repaired and painted. The window glass sparkled in the sunlight.

"This is unbelievable," Tom managed to say.

"That's magic!" Rhea answered, reaching up to kiss his cheek.

The door to the house opened and four little rotund children tumbled out, followed by an only slightly larger egg-shaped man who was bubbling over with words of welcome. "This must be Tom! Solomon Biggs here. Mrs. Biggs and I are so happy you've come. We hope you like what we've done to the place. 'Course, there's lots more to do."

The little Biggs gathered around Tom, giggling and pointing, asking if he was a giant.

"Come in, come in. We've been waiting for you. Children, don't point at our guest. Go in the back yard and play."

As Tom went up the front steps, he marveled at all the changes. The cursed energy of Mrs. Savage had been lifted and life had returned to the house.

When they entered the hall, Mrs. Biggs came bustling in from the kitchen. "Oh, he's here, good, he's here."

"Shh now, mother, let's all be quiet. It's just about time." Mr. Biggs put his arm around his wife, stepping to the side of the stairs. "Tom, you and Rhea stand on the other side there—make sure the door is open. That's it."

Tom glanced at Rhea, but she motioned for him to keep silent, pointing to the top of the stairs. They all waited in the hall expectantly. Soft breezes circled about, and the curtains fluttered at the windows.

Gradually on the top step appeared the image of a young woman, Aunt Petra, in a pink dress and satin slippers. At the bottom of the steps appeared the neatly dressed young man. Tom remembered seeing this ghostly scene that repeated itself over and over. Everybody waited. Down the stairs she came, floating into the arms of her dear one who waited for her eternally—but then something miraculous happened. Instead of appearing again at the top of the stairs to repeat the cycle perpetually, she turned from the arms of her husband to face Tom. He held his breath while she hovered before him. A message passed between them as they looked at each other lovingly. She was at peace now; she could let go now.

Tears streamed down his face as she placed her hand near his heart and smiled. Then she turned, taking the arm of her beloved, and together they slowly walked through the door. In the open air, the sunlight dissolved them until they were no more.

Mr. Biggs blew his nose into his handkerchief, and Mrs. Biggs wiped her eyes. "That was a long time comin'," she said. "It's no good when Humans are caught between worlds. You set her free, Tom. She was waitin' to tell ya that...Here, Mr. Biggs, this boy needs a chair. Take him into the parlor while I get him some tea."

Just as Tom sat down, he had another jolt. Two of the little Biggs charged right through the front door and up the stairs, shouting an imaginary battle cry. Mr. Biggs went running to the landing. "What did I say? Get down here! Outside with you!" The two little soldiers went back outside, dragging their paper swords.

"I'm sorry," he said, sitting down again. "Children—they haven't got any reverence for the moment at all, you know."

Tom nodded, accepting some tea from Mrs. Biggs's tiny hands.

"I'm glad she's happy now," he said, trying to make the transition into a happier mood himself. Gradually, he brightened up, and they took him on a tour of the house.

As with the outside, the interior had an enchanted quality. Delicate vines grew in through the windows and traced their way over the ceilings. The beautiful carved wood furniture looked curiously as if it had grown that way. Paintings were hung everywhere, going up the stairs and in all the rooms—every one a landscape. These too had a mysterious beauty, which Tom remarked upon.

Mr. Biggs replied, "Oh, yes, we've had these for centuries—haven't we, mother?"

"Oh, yes, yes indeed."

When they brought Tom out into the back yard, a wonderful change awaited him there as well. The giant dark tree that dominated the land had been trimmed and aerated into a lovely, sun-filtered canopy for a garden brimming with wild flowers and roses. A path wound around the tree and back. He could see his platform and rope, still high up in its branches. The little Biggs were already there swinging from the rope. Their roly-poly bodies were extremely agile. Pup was running everywhere with them, but when he saw Tom, he jumped out of the tree and into his arms.

"Well, who's your little gerking friend?" Mr. Biggs asked.

"This little guy's name is Pup."

"Hello, Pup! He's awfully young to be away from his clan, isn't he?" Mr. Biggs looked at Rhea.

Tom reassured him, "Oh, he's doin' fine. Ain't ya, Pup?"

Pup became very shy and wouldn't look at Mr. Biggs.

"That's okay, Pup. Go back and play with the kids."

He scampered away, happy to be out from under adult scrutiny.

A table had been set for lunch. Mrs. Biggs was buzzing around it like a little bee.

"Do you want any help?" Rhea asked.

"No, no, we're all set. Solomon, call the children."

The children didn't bother to climb down the tree: to Tom's astonishment, they just dropped like balls from the branches and bounced over to the table. Mr. Biggs was perturbed by all this, telling them to sit down and stop showing off for their guest.

They ate a lunch of pumpkin soup, carrot and cucumber salad, and candied pears. It was the first time Tom had seen Rhea eat a whole meal. The atmosphere was so relaxed and familial that Tom felt at home, even though he knew these people were from the Otherworld—Rhea's world. He might blink and all this would be gone. He might even be dreaming.

The afternoon went by pleasantly. Eventually, Rhea and Mrs. Biggs took the children in for their nap and Mr. Biggs excused himself, saying he had a few things to attend to. And so, Tom found himself alone. He got up from his chair, stretched, and wandered over to the tree. He was looking straight up into its great leafy arms when a voice behind him said, "Beautiful, isn't it?"

Startled, Tom turned to see a sunlit mist descending upon him. As it enveloped him, he saw everything break apart into particles, floating molecules, all suspended in yellow light. Out of all this energy and movement, the ghostly figure of a man appeared.

Tom recognized those star-like eyes. "Mabon?"

"You have remembered me? This is good. We shall not waste time with introductions. I have come to talk to you about serious matters. You must know by now that your progress has been watched for many years. It is time you knew what the stars have proposed for you."

Together, they began slowly circling the tree. In that moment, Tom felt like he was walking around the tree that grew at the center of the universe. He was listening with his whole being.

Mabon went on, "Without fully knowing why, you have come here—drawn, I believe, by your love for Rhea."

"Yes, I love her."

"And she loves you as well. Do you know what she is?"

"What do you mean?"

"She is one of the last of a dying race."

"Dying? She's not going to die. I won't let anything happen to her."

Mabon smiled. "These are good intentions, but do you have any idea what must be done to save her and her kind? This is what I have come to talk to you about—this dying world of ours. There is such beauty, such wisdom in this realm. Mankind shall be the worse for it if it goes. To save it requires a sacrifice—the sacrifice of a Human life. If I am right, perhaps it is you who will do this."

Tom's heart began to beat very fast. "To save Rhea—to save her world, I must die?"

"In a manner of speaking, yes. You must die to this world and enter ours."

"I must die?" he repeated uncomprehendingly.

"This death I am talking about is not what you Humans understand it to be. Call it a transformation. Like the snake that sheds its skin, you will leave your narrow consciousness behind and expand in new awareness."

"What awareness?"

"Now, that is hard to put into words. That can only be revealed in the experience of it."

"Why?"

"Because learning what we know will change you, and only in changing will you then understand. Because even though our worlds are separate, we both live on the same earth plane, parallel to each other. There was a time when passage from one to the other was easy. We gave generously of what we knew. Then Humans, becoming stronger and more dangerous, chose to steal what might have been given in the spirit of cooperation. We live long and see far. Men's lives are short and they are impatient. The Humans wanted to strip our world of all its power, destroying it. But what is not understood cannot be used. We retreated and took our knowledge with us behind the veil, as it is called. Now, Humans have drifted so far from the natural laws by which we all must live that something...something must be done."

Tom felt it necessary to defend his humanity. "I am human. I do not want to steal anything, and I don't want to die."

"Not all Humans are bad, and not all in our world are good. Life is both beautiful and horrible at the same time. The best anyone can do is seek to maintain a balance, but that balance is gone between our two worlds. It is leading to destruction on both sides. The nature forces that rule my realm have seen that it is necessary to allow a Human to cross over, to be initiated into the secrets of our power. This is very complicated and will take a lifetime to understand. Somehow, we must change the Human psyche with this wisdom so that we all may survive. In time, you may go back and forth across the veil, but your home will be with us forever. If you are chosen, the crown of the realm will be yours."

"If I am chosen?" Tom asked.

"Yes. It is not at all written that this shall happen. It is your decision. It depends on your own strength, your love for Rhea, and an intuitive trust that this is your destiny."

"What must I do?"

"You must find your way to the Child of the Wells and be offered a drink from the golden goblet. If that happens, you will be accepted into our world."

"How do I do that?"

"I am not sure. Something will give you a clue, something out of the ordinary; then you must have the courage to follow it. If you don't, your life will proceed as it was before you met Rhea. Your memory will fade, and you will forget what you have seen of our world."

"Rhea...what about Rhea?"

"She will want to stay with you, but she must return. She cannot survive in the Human dimension."

"I don't know if I can do as you say." Suddenly Tom felt the weight of the world on his shoulders. He wasn't at all sure he was up to the task.

Mabon could see he was overwhelmed. "Don't worry over these decisions. They will come naturally. If you have any hesitation, don't do it. Everything will be as it is meant to be." Mabon said these last words to calm him, but Tom knew Mabon expected much more of him.

"I don't know if I can do this," he repeated, almost to himself.

"If not you, then who?" Mabon's voice trailed off with that question hanging in the air. "If not you, then who?"

When the mist cleared, Tom was alone by the tree as before. The sun shone. The flowers waved their vibrant colors in response.

Rhea walked slowly toward him. How beautiful she was. "What did he say?" she asked in a hushed tone.

"I'm not at all sure. It seems I must decide between this world and yours. There is something he wants me to do, but he can't tell me what it is or how to do it."

"You've got a lot to think about." Rhea put her arms around him as they went back into the house, where the Biggs were waiting impatiently. They were awestruck; they couldn't believe they'd had such an exalted visitation right there in their back yard! They were too polite to ask what was said, but they wanted to know everything else. What did he look like? Was he big? As tall as the tree?

"I didn't really see him so much as hear him," Tom said. He looked at Rhea for help, but all she would say was that she knew him to be very wise and very kind.

"Oh, yes, of course, true indeed," Mr. Biggs said.

"Oh true, yes, true." His wife nodded enthusiastically.

The little Biggs grouped around their parents, looking up at Tom as if he were a god.

"Yes, well," Mr. Biggs said, knowing the afternoon visit was at an end. "Children, go call Pup. I'm sure our guests will be leaving soon."

"Here, Pup! Here, Pup!" they all shouted from where they stood.

"No, no," he shooed them along. "Outside! Go outside! He's probably still in the backyard. Honestly, mother. Sometimes, your children..."

"What are you talking about? They're every bit yours too, you know," she replied, looking a little offended.

Tom jumped in, telling them again how much he loved the house and garden, trying to smooth things over.

One of the children came bouncing back, saying, "Pup's in a tree and won't come down!"

Rhea said, "He probably thinks it's a game."

They all went out to the tree and called for Pup to come down, but he wouldn't move. He just sat there, calmly blinking at them.

"What's the matter with him? He's never done this before," Tom said, worried.

"I'm not sure," Rhea said. "Maybe he doesn't want to leave. He's a gerking, you know; they're very stubborn."

"Well, maybe he does want to stay here. It's perfectly all right," Mrs. Biggs kindly offered. "It is more like his natural habitat, and he *is* awfully young."

Tom couldn't believe how sad he was that Pup would want to abandon them. He got hold of himself, however, saying, "Well, if that's the best thing for him, of course. Okay, Pup," he called up to him. "We're going now."

They said their good-byes to the Biggs family at the gate, then walked through the little door out into the street.

The late afternoon sun cast long shadows. The shade gave off a cool darkness. It felt different without Pup along: unbalanced, like a cart missing a wheel. The two of them walked along silently. When they got to the end of the block, Tom said, "Give him one more call."

Rhea whistled, a long high-pitched sound. Suddenly there he was, leaping over bushes, barreling toward them, trying to catch up.

Tom caught Pup up in his arms. "Good Pup. Good boy. Your home is with us, and don't you forget it."

Tom and Rhea laughed as Pup climbed up on Tom's shoulders and settled in for the ride. Everything felt right now. Their little family was together again.

67

SHADOW FIRES

Mavis had no idea the dwarf was putting Wally under so much pressure, but she didn't like his tone toward her lately. Their détente was breaking down, and they were squabbling all the time. This morning, she was at him again about why they had to leave next month and go on the road. "Wally, I'm telling you those days are over. We'll make more money in a week just staying put."

"Mavis, you see how business is slowing down. It always does in the summer."

"I don't understand it. The place is full every night, but we're taking in half the money. Where is it going? You're doing something and you're not telling me. I warn you, Walter Ripton, if you're trying to pull the wool over my eyes, it won't work."

She was really getting up some steam. Wally had to pull the plug somehow. "Mavis, my sweet. If you'd only read the newspaper, you'd see there was a slowdown all over. It's the economy." He knew he was on safe ground here. There wasn't a chance in hell she'd ever pick up a newspaper to read about business. She was only interested in the society section. "People are coming in, sure, but they're not buying as many drinks. I'm telling you, there's really a slowdown."

"Well," Mavis said, not so sure he wasn't right, "then, we should charge a cover if they want to stay and watch the show."

"We can't do that." *Actually, that's a brilliant idea,* Wally thought. Next season, after the dwarf was disposed of, he would do just that.

"Why not?" she huffed.

"There's a slowdown. I'm telling you, you can't charge more in an economic downturn."

Mavis looked at him square in the eye. "Walter, you're full of crap, and none of your mumbo-jumbo is gonna change that fact."

They went on like that for weeks, right up until it was time for Tom and Nash to leave for the farm. In the end, she went along with Wally's plans, her own inertia keeping her from doing anything else.

* * *

The dwarf had a new trick—starting fires. He loved reading about them in the newspapers:

Small fire started in alley between Fifth and Harper; cause unknown...

Fire erupted behind warehouse on Beaton Street; arson sus-

pected...

Fire consumed an abandoned house; started by drifters' cooking fire...

"Drifters' cooking fire. How did they come up with that one?" Philippe rolled back on his bed, kicking up his crooked legs in a fit of laughter. He was no longer welcome in Wally's inner sanctum, so he read his paper alone in his room. He liked it better that way...alone. But then, he was never really alone any more. He had his "friends." He was finding out more and more fascinating things about them all the time.

For instance, on one of his nightly walks, he lit a match for a cigarette. One of his shadow friends whispered in his ear, "It could transform into a fire."

"How?" the dwarf asked.

"Throw the match into the air," the shadow said.

Philippe cast the match away from him. The shadow flew into it and exploded into a fireball. This was wonderful! He did it again and again. But then he thought, *What fun is this?* He wanted to direct it somewhere. He pointed to a discarded box in the street. "Consume it," he shouted. The fireball shot over to the box and quickly reduced it to ashes. The dwarf jumped up and down, laughing hysterically. He was given to laughing at the strangest things these days.

Philippe was delighted with this new power. He wanted to start fires everywhere, but he had to contain himself. He knew it. This was a valuable weapon to add to his growing arsenal of magical powers. The more he could penetrate Ruby's world, the more he knew the universe would open up to him. Her day was coming; he would have her, or kill her.

* * *

The day before Tom left, he and Rhea were sitting on the roof in the sun. Tom had taken off his shirt and was lying back, letting the warm rays pour over him. Rhea wanted to take her dress off and do the same, but it didn't take much faery intelligence to know that just wasn't done in the Human world. She contented herself with taking off her shoes and pulling her skirt to her knees.

Tom was going on about how great it was at the farm and how much he loved traveling in those old circus wagons. "Wait till you meet Howler and Nip."

"Who's Nip?" She had heard about Howler, but not about Nip.

"Nip is the biggest, orneriest horse you'll ever see. He's got a mind of his own. He'll bite you right in the pants if he doesn't like you."

"Maybe he's mean because he's got such a bad name. What kind of name is 'Nip'?"

"Pretty descriptive, I'd say," Tom replied.

"Well, when I see him I'll ask him his real name, and then we'll see how he acts."

Tom looked sideways at her like she was crazy. But then, she was a faery and they had their ways. "Okay, you do that," he laughed, pulling her down on top of him. "And here's a kiss to keep you while I'm gone."

The kiss was full of tender happiness, but when it was over, Rhea's mood seemed to change. She sat up, looking sad. "Oh, why do I have to wait here for you? Can't I go with you? It's stupid, having to be apart like this. I don't care about what these people think—only you. Only you, and..." She drifted off unhappily.

Tom got up too. "If it were up to me, I'd take you with me. But you aren't needed there. I suppose to you that doesn't make any sense, but in my world—"

"Oh, you and your world! I'm tired of..." She caught herself just in time.

"Tired of me?" Tom took her back into his arms. "Tired of me, Rhea?"

She started to cry. "Oh, no, never of you, Tom. I love you. I'm only here because of you. It's just that..." She wanted to tell him that she was afraid—afraid of the dwarf. But she dared not say anything that would stop him from leaving so that she too could get out of this horrible hell-hole they called a city. "It's just that I'll be so lonely here. Hurry back to me."

"Wild horses couldn't stop me from getting back to you—not even Nip." He bent down, trying to bite her neck. Rhea wriggled away. She laughed, trying to shake off her fears of being alone in the Human world.

68

ABUSE OF POWER

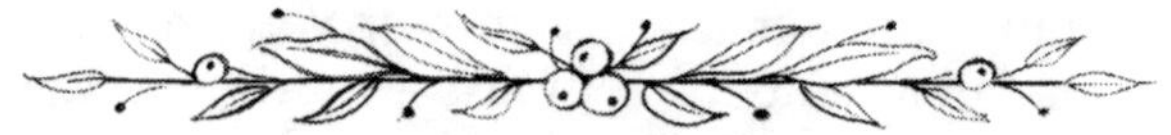

Tom and Nash rode in silence out to the farm. They both were pre-occupied—Nash with the bottles sloshing around in his suitcase and Tom with thinking about Rhea. Something was wrong. He'd known it when he left her that morning.

"Look, Nash, let's not make this a two-week bender. It's different this time. I've got to go back."

"Sure, sure, kid, I know. Ruby's waitin' for you. We'll put things in shape fast. You'll see."

"I'm serious now."

"Okay, okay."

After two hours of driving, they saw the little group of buildings that comprised the farmhouse, barn, and sheds. Shabby though they were, as Howler ran out to greet them, it felt like coming home. Ben and the two hired hands, John and Stretch, sat waiting on the porch. Stretch rocked back in his chair, his long legs propped up on the railing. There were always a good two inches between the end of his pants and the beginning of his boots: that was why they called him Stretch.

"Well, hey, you city slickers! 'Bout time you got out here. Good to see ya!"

Tom and Nash climbed down from the truck, shaking the dust from their hair and clothes.

"Come on in and have a beer," Ben welcomed them.

"You guys go ahead. I want to have a look around first," Tom told them.

"What's the matter with him?" Ben asked as they went inside.

"Oh, Tom?" Nash replied. "He's in a hurry. I'll explain once I wet my whistle."

Tom went first to the barn to check on the horses. They all looked good except Nip. He was dirtier and nastier than ever. Then he went to the sheds where the wagons were. They smelled damp and musty under their winter shrouds. A week's airing out in the sun would cure that. Howler barked and jumped around Tom as he walked along.

"Yeah, I missed you too." Tom rubbed his scruffy head. He teased him by singing a few bars of "Shenandoah," which made Howler bark even louder. Suddenly Tom stopped. "Wait a minute. Where's the goat?" He went back to the barn; sure enough, the stall was empty.

Tom hurried around to the porch where all the men were sitting back enjoying their beer. "What happened to the goat?"

Ben offered Tom a drink, which he now accepted. "Well, if you'da sat down a minute, I'da told ya. The goat died, and that's a fact."

Tom shook his head. "Great. We've got to have a goat. You still got the extra horns?"

"Well, a' course we do. Can't have no four-horned goat without 'em." Ben gummed him a smile. "Now, the fella down the way's got one, but he wants a lotta money for it. Mister Wally's not goin' to like that. I'll leave the goat-buying up to you."

"I'll have to drive down there and see what it looks like," Tom grumbled. "We're running low on 'curiosities.'"

Ben shrugged his shoulders. "Do as you like. It ain't my circus no more." He bitterly resented losing his circus to Wally, but in the end it had been the best thing. He was old and plagued with arthritis, but Wally had let him stay on to manage the farm. "It's been a hard winter out here. Real wet. I'm afraid them old wagons is got the rot."

Tom didn't want to hear any of this. Everything had to be fixed up and looking great for Rhea.

The next day, true to his word, Nash was sober and went straight to work. They pulled out the wagons, patched the roofs, oiled up the hinges, and repaired the rigging. Stretch and John groomed the horses—all except Nip, who was given a quick brush and then let out into the corral, where he stomped and thundered around on his giant hooves, shaking his wild mane. Nip was strong. He could pull one of those wagons by himself, once he consented to being harnessed. But for such a huge animal, he was very skittish: he had to wear blinders so he wouldn't be bothered by anything happening on either side of him. The other horses appeared to have calmly accepted their fate, but Nip was always chafing against the bit. He was high-strung and discontent.

On the fifth day, Nash "fell off the wagon" and got smashed. He still functioned, even while drunk, but eventually the liquor consumed him and Tom worked on alone.

* * *

Without Tom, Rhea grew remote and withdrew at every chance she could get. One night as she sat up on the roof, she let herself fall into a vague half-present form. It would be so easy to just slip away. She entertained herself by bringing forth tiny sparkling beings from the ether of her world, then shed her earthly garments and danced across the darkness with the sparkles trailing behind her.

Nothing compared to the freedom she felt in those moments—not even her love for Tom. This sense of freedom was at the core of her very nature. It grew wild within her. Nothing could tame it. Rhea twirled and twirled until she blurred into a ring of light. Finally, she came to rest, lying down upon her quilt, her skin pearlescent pink, her red hair loose and shining.

"Very pretty...very pretty." She heard the slow clap-clap of a pair of hands. "Très jolie."

She sat up, grabbing her clothes and assuming her full human form.

"Oh, don't change on my account, chèrie. I like you the way you are." The dwarf laughed at his choice of words.

Rhea pulled on her dress quickly, glaring at him. "What do you want?" She gathered up her quilt and started to leave.

"Oh no, don't go. My friends and I want to play too."

She could see the shadows gathering around him. "Nothing you can do can harm me," she said, feeling his threat.

"Oh, I wouldn't be too sure. Watch this!"

He struck a match and threw it into one of the shadows. It immediately burst into a fireball. The dwarf laughed like the maniac he had become. "Consume her!" he shouted.

The fireball went straight for Rhea. She darted to the side, and it missed her. He sent another after her; she flew up into the air, escaping it. He sent out another. "Three's the magic number, n'est-ce pas?" She countered each one, but she could not stop the relentless attack. Finally, out of anger and frustration, she escaped into the Parallel World. That was her mistake. The fireballs followed.

All was silent. The night appeared empty. The dwarf waited. Suddenly, in an explosion ripping open the air, Rhea re-entered the atmosphere, fireballs roiling around her. The dwarf was triumphant. Rhea flew at him in a rage. For a moment, they fought like hellcats in the flames.

"Enough!" Philippe shouted, and the flames turned to smoke. He sat there laughing, his face blackened, his clothes singed.

"Monster!" Rhea cried. "I shall find the way to end your wickedness."

"Oh, it's too late for that," the dwarf answered, much amused. "Yes, much too late. And what will happen to *you*, my little one, when your 'powers that be' find out you've shown me the way into your world? Yes, chèrie, the shadows can follow you now, and so I shall too. You'd better find something else to put on, chèrie; there's not much left of that dress." Philippe went downstairs taking his darkness with him.

Sobbing, Rhea picked up her quilt and held it close. What had she done? Those shadow entities had followed her...she had let them through the veil. Mabon, she wanted to see Mabon, but she was afraid to go to him for fear of bringing this plague with her.

Quietly, she slipped downstairs to her room. When she opened the door, there was Pup on the bed, staring wide-eyed at the golden mist hovering before him.

Gratefully, Rhea stepped into the aura and protection of Mabon.

"Hush now. Don't be frightened. You were very brave. He can't harm me, and he really can't harm you either. Just remember the words 'pax ol mot' and use your powers to confuse and transfix. Now wrap yourself in your quilt and rest; even a faery must do that. Sleep, child, sleep..." His words were calming, but if Mabon's face had been visible in that mist, it would have revealed much worry. Worry about mankind's terrible temptation to abuse power...worry about Tom and whether he would fulfill the promise foretold of him.

69

A TEST OF WILL

Work on the caravan was just about finished. In a few days, they would return to the city. One afternoon, Tom drove out to see the goat that was for sale and then decided to visit Split Rock Creek again. He wanted Rhea to see this place. The sweet summer air charmed him into a fantasy of the two of them walking along the stream and sunning in the rocks above. When he parked the truck, he realized it was getting a little late in the day to start the hike up the mountain, but he continued anyway. The wet winter had created a lush, dense forest. The trees and shrubs were a thick and vibrant green. Berries hung plump and ripe on their stems. Squirrels and chipmunks chattered. Birds chirped high above him. The sun poured down warm yellow light into the shadows.

Tom sat down on the rocks above the rushing water. In his mind's eye he could see so clearly that young stag fighting for his life. He remembered how they'd lain panting after he pulled the stag out of the water, exhausted from the effort. He remembered the stag's smell and his eyes that showed no fear of him. How quickly he'd climbed to his feet and leapt away into the forest, free once more. Tom wished he could see him again now, full-grown and magnificent.

He lay back on the rocks and let the last of the sun warm his face. Rhea...he longed for Rhea. If he went anywhere again, it would be with her. If he did anything in this world or another, it would be because of her.

Cooler air began to circulate, reminding him he'd better get on his way or night would overtake him. He had a long way to go, and driving that country road in the dark was not easy.

Tom bounced along in the truck, the headlamps showing him only fragments of the road ahead that sliced through a vast black void. He couldn't get lost—there was only one road—but staying on it was the problem. Suddenly, in one of the jagged beams of light, he thought he saw something white up ahead. The truck hit another pothole, and by the time he bounced back straight again, it was gone. Tom sat up in his seat, fully alert. There it was...something white. He was coming closer and it wasn't moving. Not even the gnashing sound of the truck gears disturbed it.

Tom slowed down to a crawl. He could see now it was a white hare just sitting there, frozen. He had heard about this before, but had never seen it: an animal hypnotized by the light, unable to move. Tom stopped and slowly got out of the truck. The hare didn't move even as he approached.

From the trees beside the road, he heard a low growl. Tom turned on his heels and ran back to the truck. The hare still didn't move. He reached behind the seat for a length of rusty chain that had always been there amongst other scraps of metal and broken tools. He didn't know what he was going to do: maybe scare whatever it was away and give the hare a chance.

All was silent except for the crunch of his boots in the dirt. Just as he was about to swing the chain to break the hare's trance, there was another snarl and scream as a mountain cat leapt out of the darkness and caught the hare in its mouth. Tom swung the chain, shouting, hoping the cat would drop its prey. The cougar glared boldly at him, snarling, the hare struggling in its teeth. Tom looked deep into those glowing yellow eyes. They were speaking to him, measuring him. Seconds ticked by as human and beast were locked in an uncanny stare. Then, with another growl, the cat bounded away into the woods with the hare.

Tom watched as the forest opened to receive them. It almost looked as if a curtain of darkness had parted and let them through. This was the moment: Tom knew it. This was the "something" he was to follow. He hesitated, then plunged through the curtain of darkness. Up on the road, the truck waited, its headlights dimming.

He was in a dense thicket. Tom swung the chain to break the branches and moved ahead—where, he didn't know. He went on for some time like this, then stopped, waiting. There wasn't a sound, as if the forest were holding its breath. It wasn't completely dark; he was in a strange twilight. Tom shivered, coming to his senses. What was he doing here? He told himself that he should get back to the safety of the truck, but when he saw the silhouette of the cat break through the thicket and cross a clearing, he continued on. Some force inside him wanted him to go forward, and he did.

The cat vanished into the forest on the other side. As Tom ran after it, his legs felt heavy and his feet couldn't move fast enough, as in a dream. He fell, struggling against a sinking lethargy that offered him a seductive sleep. It took all the effort he had to remember what he was doing and to keep moving.

As soon as he entered the forest on the other side of the clearing, he was snapped into alertness by the horrible acrid smell of animal dung and rotting meat. Fear entered his heart again, but there was no going back. In the eerie light, he picked his way through broken bones and fallen trees. Signs of angry, vicious destruction were everywhere.

He heard a frightening squeal. The earth shook beneath him, and out of nowhere charged a horrific wild boar. Tom fiercely swung the chain at it. The chain caught on one of its tusks, and with a twist of its mighty head, the boar ripped it out of Tom's hand. There was nothing to do but run, and spurred on by terror, Tom fled with lightning speed.

He saw a tree with one lone branch strong enough to hold his weight, and leapt for it just before the boar reached his lifting feet. He clung to the branch as he watched the boar, mad with fury, repeatedly run its head into the trunk of the tree, trying to topple it. He could only pray.

Tom prayed for the weapon that Anam had promised him—the sword that vanquished any foe. Instantly, he found he was holding the hilt of a silver sword!

The beast pounded away at the tree trunk. Tom had to find some way to distract it so he could position himself to use the sword effectively. He had only one chance. Tom took off his belt, wrapped it into a tight ball around the metal buckle, and then threw it as far away as he could. The boar turned and charged, stamping on it, ripping it apart with its tusks.

Tom lowered himself down from the tree and stood behind it. Angrier, madder than ever that it could extract no blood from the belt, the boar turned and charged with ferocious energy at Tom. Just as the boar was upon him, Tom stepped to the side and downed it like a matador with a paralyzing sword blow at the back of the neck. The boar fell at his feet, its last rank breath foaming from its mouth.

A great wail went up in the forest: mournful cries, chattering, and whispers. The words, *You have killed me, but can you save me?* echoed in his head. His own blood was rushing with triumph and adrenaline, so when he caught sight of the cat moving deeper into the forest, he quickly pulled the sword free of the boar's body and followed.

Now close, now far, the cat appeared to him. Up into the mountains he climbed after it, through tall stands of trees and past them to a rocky outcropping. The cat was looking down at him, watching with yellow eyes. Tom climbed steadily upwards. When he got to the point where he'd last seen the cat, it had disappeared. Tom turned slowly in a circle, taking in every detail of his surroundings; no cat anywhere.

One collection of shadowy rocks revealed an opening to a cave. As he moved closer, he felt cool moisture in the air coming from it. The thought of water and a sudden great thirst drew him inside. He could see in the dusky light that this wasn't a cave, but a group of giant rocks all leaning against each other, forming a round space inside that was open to the sky. From a crack in one of the rocks, water poured down and disappeared into the ground. Moss grew everywhere like a rich green carpet.

Tom knelt down and was about to cup his hands under the flow for a drink when he heard an angry snarl. He turned, sword ready, to see the cougar sitting in the shadows, the white hare at its feet. It was alive. The cat watched warily. Tom backed away till he felt the stone wall behind him. There he slowly sat down on his haunches, the sword across his knees. Cat and human stared at each other, knowing the possibility of death stood between them. Was this a time to kill or not? Tom waited.

The cold of the stone against his back began to chill him. He felt how tired he was. He tried to stretch one leg out, but the cat snarled and defensively put its paw on the hare. Tom slowly moved back to the same position. "I don't want to hurt you, but I don't want you to harm that hare either," he said aloud to it.

It's strange, he thought to himself. *The hare isn't hurt and doesn't seem afraid at all of the big cat.* Tom and the cougar waited, eyeing each other, not moving. Hours went by. Tom's body began to ache. He was so tired. The gentle sound of the water was lulling him to sleep. The cat settled down, resting its head upon its paw, never taking its eyes off Tom.

He was cold, tired, and most of all, thirsty—so thirsty now that he would give up his sword for a drink. Slowly, he lifted the sword from his knees and laid it down away from him. The cat raised its head, but did nothing. Again, he waited. Time dripped by. Tom's eyes drooped, and finally he fell asleep.

A change in the atmosphere woke him. He opened his eyes and saw neither the cougar nor the hare, but a child: a beautiful child who gave off a light like a fire, a wild child of the forest whose long palomino white hair was caught up in ivy vines and myrrh. In its delicate hands, it held a golden goblet.

Maybe this was all a dream. Tom moved slightly to see if that would dispel the vision. No—the hands that held out the goblet didn't falter. Slowly, Tom reached for the beautiful vessel and drank its contents. A wonderful warming liquid revived his body. He tried to fix the moment in his mind forever, so powerful was this experience. The glowing goblet. The sweet water taste. The wild child with those trusting expectant eyes.

Tom bent his head in thanks, and the child smiled. He gave back the goblet. The faery child said some strange words, and the cougar appeared beside it. The faery pointed to the cat, then to Tom, then to the entrance. Tom understood he was to leave. He got up, feeling transformed and energized by the waters.

When he bent down to pick up the sword, the faery frowned and pointed at it. He was to leave it there. The cougar ran out of the enclosure. Tom hesitated a moment, taking a last look at the beautiful creature and its unearthly eminence. Then he turned and slipped between the rocks into the hazy twilight.

The cougar rapidly descended the mountain, leading him back. Tom followed close behind. When they reached the road again, the cat disappeared. The acetylene headlamps had gone out, but he could see the black shape of the truck. It would be reckless to try to drive the truck without light. Tom climbed into the back, covered himself with an old tarp, and slept for the few hours left till morning.

Tom awoke to a pawing, sniffing sound. The next instant, Howler was on top of him licking his face. "You wiry-haired mongrel! Where were you when I needed you?" Tom wrestled with the dog, playfully pushing him back.

He emerged from the truck into the glory of a midsummer day. Tom looked around, feeling how wonderfully intimate and connected all life was. He felt wonderful, except for one thing—he was alone in all this beauty without Rhea. Tom hurried around to crank up the car. He had a lot to do, and it was all to get back to Rhea.

As he drove along, last night's powerful experience came back to him. *"You have killed me, but can you save me?"* Those words repeated themselves over and over. The visions of the hare, the wildcat, the boar all blended together, all became aspects of the same mystical being that was asking him, *"You have killed me, but can you save me?"*

Tom felt in his soul that he had just been through a transition so radical he could never return to his old self. It had just fallen away, like a suit of clothes grown too small. He knew he had the courage to open himself to the unknown and let whatever he found there chart his course. "Yes," Tom whispered, "whatever that means...yes."

70

PLANS

Wally was upstairs in his office getting ready to leave. Tom was due back that day. As he went around locking up, his mind chewed on the same thought he'd been having for months. How was he going to orchestrate the demise of the dwarf? Maybe Nip could "accidentally" trample him. The huge Clydesdale was just ornery enough to do it. This and other such "accidental" possibilities kept occurring to him, but he hadn't hit upon the right plan yet. No matter; Wally was confident that the opportunity would present itself.

Mavis was in the kitchen making a nuisance of herself, ordering Nettie around. "Did you pack this? Why do you want to take that?"

"Missus Mavis, how many years have I been doin' this? I knows how long we gone! I knows exactly what to take. Where is yo' bags? I don't see yo' bags down here awaitin' to go."

"Now, don't get cheeky with me, Nettie Garner. I know what has to be done."

"Good. So we both know. Now you do yours and let me do mine!" Nettie fired back at her.

Mavis huffed upstairs, threatening to fire Nettie once and for all, which of course she would never do. It was an unsaid fact: Nettie was the backbone of the Madrigal. Her tireless outpouring of energy, generating food and comforts from her kitchen, was central to life there.

"Cheeky? That woman say one more word an' I'll 'cheeky' her." Nettie tied a string around the neck of a sack, strangling it.

Up in her room, Mavis packed her bottles and creams in her cosmetics case, swearing this was absolutely the last summer for Wally's traveling circus. She would see to it. Mavis snorted peevishly, giving her bags a derisive kick with her run-over mules.

Sudy and Mae were already downstairs waiting for Tom. They were sitting at the bar, having a beer. Every once in a while, Sudy would go outside to see if she could see the truck coming. The bar was dark and dreary now that everything was closed up. The tables and chairs were stacked, the windows boarded, and what liquor they weren't taking was hidden in the stairwell behind a secret panel.

Sudy always looked forward to their long month in the country, even though her work was still the same: helping Nettie, tapping out a dance or two with Mae, and "entertaining" men at Wally's request. Still, she loved the sunshine and the freedom to walk alone in the countryside. She never went anywhere in the city. She couldn't think of where to go.

"Oh, Mae, there's the truck! Come on, Mae!" Sudy called from her lookout at the door.

Nettie was just finishing up in the kitchen when Sudy came swooning in and sat down at the table. "Oh, Nettie, you should have seen it! It was so romantic. I never seen a man kiss a girl like that before—like it's been a hundred years since he'd seen her and he was a'dyin' for her all the time..."

"Girl, what you goin' on about now?"

"It's Tom. He's here. Mae and me was the first to see him. But then there was Ruby all of a sudden, out of nowhere...and then they was kissin' and Mae and me was just standin' there...He said if he had anything to do with it, they'd never be separated again. Then they kissed an' he picked her up an' twirled her around...Tom is so handsome, don't you think?" She sighed and stopped her babbling long enough to consider. "What do you suppose he means by 'if he has anything to do with it?' Wally wouldn't try anything on them, would he?" The thought worried Sudy.

"No, chile. Wally couldn't do no harm to those two." Nettie looked happy and sad at the same time. It was hard to figure what she was thinking, and Sudy couldn't get her to say another word except for "Um um."

It took hours to pack up. Both vehicles, the truck and the passenger car, were full. Tom drove the truck with Rhea and Mae in the front, while Barney, Phyllis, Nettie, and Lorna rode in the back with all the provisions. Wally, Philippe, and Mavis went in the car with the Chinaman at the wheel, driving herky-jerky down the street after the truck.

Rhea sat next to Tom. Her quilt was folded on her lap. That was her sole possession. She smiled, looking especially radiant. Tom was telling her about all the things he had done while he was gone—omitting the tale of his extraordinary night, because of Mae. But Rhea had only to look at him to know that he had changed.

The dwarf stared at the passing countryside without seeing it. Only one thing concerned him now. How was he going to orchestrate the demise of Wally Ripton? It had to happen on this trip, and he was devising a plan. Philippe smiled, looking over at Wally and Mavis. "It's going to be a good summer, n'est-ce pas?" he shouted above the noise of the motor.

"Very good! Wonderful!" Wally laughed, nodding back to him.

Mavis mustered up a tepid smile under her windblown hat. She didn't like the dwarf—never had—and now his inflated presence was intolerable to her. Wally seemed incapable of getting rid of him. Well, they weren't coming back with Lorna or the dwarf: Mavis was also devising a plan.

* * *

They spent the night at the farm, and the next day, the caravan was on the road following the old circus route. Just as Tom had thought, Rhea loved the painted wagons and the tidy little cabins inside. She thought Nip was the biggest horse she'd ever seen, and yes, he was pretty disagreeable, but then she reminded Tom she hadn't had a chance to talk to him yet.

"I hope that talk does him some good." Tom chuckled to himself.

"You wait and see. There's a lot in a name, you know. If it isn't right, it can be very destructive to a person."

"Horses too?"

"Horses too! Dogs as well."

"Dogs?"

"Yes. I've already talked to Howler," said Rhea. "What a silly name for such an intelligent being! His real name is Hodain."

"Hodain? How do you know?"

"He told me."

"How did *he* know?"

Rhea shrugged. "He was born knowing it. That's all."

They were driving to the first campground. Tom was impatient to get to that grove of trees and start setting up camp—to get Nettie cooking that first great outdoor meal. He loved sitting outside with lanterns all around, watching the night sky bloom. He hoped the fields hadn't been plowed. He wanted to walk into them with Rhea and disappear for a while.

He remembered his last walk into those fields, when the crow swooped down and dropped the seed at his feet. That was the beginning of it all—or was it? He remembered the crow that had appeared at Aunt Petra's house. Perhaps Rhea was right: they'd been watching him all this time.

At last, the caravan pulled into the shade of the grove. To Tom's relief, nothing had changed. Everyone got out, stretched, and walked around, taking deep breaths of the sweet summer air. They all felt the quiet tranquility of the place mellowing their spirits. The horses were tethered to a rope amongst the trees, and the farm hands helped set up the long table and start the cooking fires. Mavis and Wally napped inside their wagons, waiting for dinner.

Tom and Rhea slipped away into the fields. There in the tall grass, their bodies entwined, happy to finally be alone.

"Rhea..." Tom began, wanting to tell her about what happened on the mountain.

"Wait, don't tell me. I shall see for myself." She slowly released her form into a half-vaporous state till he marveled that he was holding a glowing transparent being. He gasped as she touched her head to his, melting into him. What a strange feeling it produced: a tickling sensation, as though the layers of his mind were being ruffled like feathers. His experience of that night passed into her as if it were her own, but other images went between them as well, startling them so they pulled apart. They stared at each other in a flash of recognition as their curiosity drew them together again.

In the transference of imagery came scenes of a young girl dressed in clothing from another time, standing on the edge of a vast lake. All around her, there was chaos. People were running and carrying things hurriedly to the shore. Horses whinnied, pulling nervously at their ropes. The girl kept looking back into the forest that ringed the lake. The men in the group looked at the girl, then to the trees, but saw nothing. They went on with their rapid preparations.

What they did not see was a horse and rider hidden there. The horse was shaggy-haired and stout. Its rider, a young man, was slight but fierce-looking. Across his face was a slash of dark paint that only increased the intensity of his eyes. He looked behind him, then back to the shore. The girl remained still, fixed on him. It was clear he was the enemy, but neither made a motion to warn their tribes. Their eyes spoke of love and separation, of death and eternity. Only when she was forced by another woman did she turn her head away to look at what was coming over the water.

Out of a heavy mist, long boats covered in green moss, glittering with wet droplets hanging like crystal, floated towards them. The horses and livestock were whipped and pushed into the water as the boats came in. The girl's eyes never left the forest as she was lifted into a boat amongst her people.

Then the long ships slipped back into the mist. In a moment, all was silent except for the lap of the water at the lake's edge. The people, the horses, the boats, the girl were gone as if they had never been there...

Tom fell back into the grass. Rhea resumed her human form, laying her head on his chest. For a while, they didn't speak. Finally Rhea said, "There is much we know together that we don't know ourselves alone."

"I was there..." Tom whispered, almost to himself. "I was there." Rhea sat up, looking at him. Tom looked quizzically back at her. "Hey, it's me. I'm still the same."

"No, you're not, and I shall never be either," she said. "One thing remains the same: my love for you will never change."

Tom pulled her to him, kissing her with a passion that closed the gap of the centuries that had been lost to them...

Pup jumped from tree to tree, looking to see if any of his kind lived in the grove, but no such luck. He met only a slow–moving, bark-encrusted creature with which he could not communicate. Tom and Rhea had gone off somewhere. Rhea had told him not to come, and so he waited up in the tree, feeling lonely and sorry for himself. Down below, he could see the humans getting ready to do their eating thing again. He always found that rather distasteful, but he did like it when they left beer in their mugs for him to inhale.

After a while, he did just that and fell asleep on the table, oblivious to the commotion all around him.

71

ARDEN

The next morning, Pup was up in the trees again watching the humans eat yet another meal. He felt sorry for them having to do that all the time. He noticed they were making a lot more noise than usual. Maybe it was the country air, for everyone *did* wake up cheerful and talkative— that is, everyone except Mavis. It took hours for her face to unfold from the puffiness of sleep. She sat lumped in her chair, trying to open her eyes over a cup of hot coffee. That was why, when she saw what she saw, she couldn't believe it. "Wally...Walter! Will you look at that!"

"Well, I'll be," Wally said.

Nash called, "Tom! Tom! Come 'ere quick! Look at this!"

Tom came around one of the wagons to see Rhea walking in from the fields. Behind her was the most magnificent horse. Its mane and tail flowed straight and full, and its coat shone silver-white.

"Why, that's Nip! I can't believe it. That's Nip!"

Rhea and the great animal stopped before the long table. "He is called Arden," she proclaimed. "The speaking of his true name has restored him to his noble nature."

Rhea whispered a command. The animal bent down on one leg, and she sprang astride him.

"Look what we can do together!" She laughed, and Arden galloped around in a circle while Rhea stood on his broad back.

Wally shouted over everyone's cheers. "This is fantastic! This is great!"

"Witch! Harlot!" Philippe snarled, but nobody heard him. They all rushed into the field to have a closer look at Arden the Magnificent.

* * *

Despite the dwarf's curses, Nip's transformation appeared to be a charm. Word of the amazing horse and its beautiful rider preceded them everywhere they went. The circus drew larger and larger crowds. The only tents they had were small ones that concealed the mysteries of the bearded lady and the tattooed man until the chance to see them was paid for; to accommodate this new attraction, they drew up their wagons in a V-like formation behind a big circle of haystacks.

The show now began with Tom and Nash entering the circle from between the wagons. They walked on stilts, tossing the balloon ball back and forth into the audience. Everyone joined in, falling all over them- selves to keep the ball in the air. Next the dwarf came out, dressed in his clown regalia, pulled in a cart by Hodain. Not to be outdone by Rhea, he too had produced a new performance.

In the middle of the circle, he placed some sticks. They suddenly caught fire. As the crowd screamed in terror, the dwarf ran for a pail of water that was in the cart. Just as he was about to throw the water on the fire, it went out. The crowd laughed and clapped; then the dwarf walked away and the fire started up again. The crowd shouted, but the dwarf pretended not to understand them.

"The fire! The fire! Put out the fire!" they yelled.

"Eh? Je ne comprends pas," Philippe would say. When he finally "understood" what the crowd was screaming itself hoarse about, he ran over with the bucket of water, but the fire always went out before he got there.

After the dwarf's thrilling but creepy act came the beautiful spectacle of Rhea and the horse. Arden cantered out alone between the wagons, then started an easy slow gallop around the circle. The crowd calmed down into a hushed silence. Around and around he went while Nash and Tom walked on stilts into the middle of the ring, carrying Ruby on their shoulders. Slowly she stood up, waiting for the right moment to jump; then she somersaulted into the air and landed on the horse's back.

The audience went wild. People came with their families and stayed the day, paying to see the show twice. In between, they would picnic in the surrounding fields, wander about, have a look at the bearded lady, and buy up Nettie's cookies and candied apples.

Wally felt as if his little circus had been touched by magic...

...which was in fact...

...the truth!

72

SUNNY DAYS

Sunny days followed sunny days as the caravan moved happily along its route—or so it seemed, for little cracks and fissures began to appear in the enchanted atmosphere of the camp. Wally wasn't so taken up with his good fortune that he hadn't given some thought to the nasty business of eliminating the dwarf. Knowing Cheng's suspicious nature could dislodge his reason if properly aroused, Wally began a campaign to turn him into a weapon against the dwarf. "He keeps telling me how stupid you are, but I say that's because he doesn't know you like I do," Wally told Cheng. "Philippe is not your friend. He wants to get rid of you, but I told him, not while I'm around. You and I go back a long ways. Watch out for that little freak; he's up to something."

The troupe had come to the foothills. The mountains were just beyond. This was the last stop before their turnaround point at Pine Tree.

Just before sunset, Tom, Ruby, and Pup rode Arden to the top of one of the hills. Hodain trotted along. At that height, the big sky enveloped them. Banks of clouds tinged with orange lay in billowy mounds on the horizon.

Back in camp, the dwarf sat off by himself smoking a cigarette. When he saw the silhouettes of Tom, Ruby, and that monster horse against the glow of the setting sun, his lip curled and he spat upon the ground. After a time, he took a little box from his vest pocket and opened it. Inside were the remains of the leaves he had stolen from the magic bush. He sniffed up a pinch of the powder, inhaling strongly and savoring its potent effect. As soon as it got dark, Philippe would resume his favorite nocturnal pastime—catching fireflies. This age-old pursuit took on new meaning when one of the ever-present shades whispered in his head that these were not ordinary fireflies: no, these were energies from the Otherworld accompanying the witch on her travels. The flitting lights had begun to appear after the first few days on the road. It was a lovely, magical occurrence. Everyone thought all the lanterns hanging about at night must attract them. It was a sign of good luck.

Philippe, who never felt the need to sleep anymore, prowled for hours in pursuit of them. He sent his dark shades out before him. Like schools of fish, the fireflies darted this way and that. Sniggering away, he watched his black shadows troll the air after them. One night, lo and behold, he caught one! It flew smack-dab into his hands, fleeing from the shadows. He felt it flutter inside his cup-fisted prison. For a split second, he peeked at it, and what he saw confirmed the shadow's whisperings. A tiny creature, somewhat humanlike, flickered around desperately on battered wings.

Now that he had it, what to do with it? In one inspired moment, he opened his mouth and swallowed it. Immediately, he felt an enlivening energy spread through him. "Bien sûr! This is very good luck, yes?" Philippe chortled. His powers could be increased by these petite fireflies. The witch could no longer stop him, leaves or no leaves.

After he realized this, the dwarf went out on his silent hunt each night. These beings were difficult to catch, and no ordinary jar or sack would hold them. Only his shadows could corner them. Philippe came up with what he affectionately called his "black hole," a whirling mass of shadows that formed a funnel into which he could throw his little delicacies as he caught them. This funnel went with him on his expeditions and hid in his suitcase during the day. Philippe had to be careful not to let the witch see it—or Tom, for that matter; no telling what powers she was handing out to that gangly kid.

While she was working, Nettie had seen Tom and Ruby ride out of camp on the big horse. Now that she was done, she sat quietly, hands folded on her apron, watching the sun go down. She was feeling her aches and pains tonight. She was feeling old.

Nettie thought of her grandmother and shook her head at just how many years ago she'd been alive. Her grandmother had been a slave all her life. When the Civil War ended and slavery was abolished, Grandma still wouldn't leave the little shack where she was born, even though her children left and she was alone. Nettie's mother had tried to get her to go with them, but the old woman would have none of it. "You go on," she said, "ain't no use in me startin' over." She was tired.

The last time Nettie had seen her grandmother, she was sitting outside that shack in a dress so old the print had all but disappeared from it. Now Nettie was thinking *she* was too old. Time was running out, and there was nowhere to go.

Just as she began to entertain that thought, Lorna walked over and sat beside her.

"So, what you thinkin' about?"

"Nothin', chile, just a whole lotta nothin'." Nettie smiled and tried to recover some of her usual manner for Lorna's sake.

"Well, I been thinkin',"

"Um hum?" Nettie replied.

Lorna started out tentatively, "It's getting dark...I saw Tom an' Ruby go off ridin' ole Nip. I like to see them two together, don't you?"

Nettie nodded. "Um hum."

Lorna could see that conversation was going to go nowhere, so she went back to her original thought. "I been thinkin'..."

"You said that."

"Yeah, I know. Well, here, it's like this. What if you, me, an' Sudy were to leave? Mae can come if she wants."

"Leave? What you sayin', chile?"

"I mean—let's go somewhere an' start our own business. You know, the Sweetie Pie baking business?"

Nettie shook her head at the thought. "What am I gonna do at my age goin' off to start a new business? You crazy?" As she was speaking, she knew she sounded exactly like her grandmother, and that made her doubly irritated at Lorna's idea.

Lorna looked around her as if someone might be listening. "Well, it's—things aren't going to keep on like this. I know it. Mavis has it in for me. I got to think of something to do."

Nettie knew this was true. Her anger at herself began to melt into concern for Lorna.

"Come on," Lorna continued. "The way they treat us, if we left you could hardly say we were being disloyal."

Nettie chuckled in agreement, then got serious again. "How we can do dat? Just pick up n' leave?" There was her grandmother speaking through her again. Nettie closed her mouth with an "Um hum."

"I don't know how we gonna do it, but please think about it, will ya?"

"I don't know what to *think* about it, but I'll give it some thought, chile."

Tom and Ruby came into camp just after nightfall. Nettie looked fondly at his tall lanky shape leading in the horse. She saw him help Ruby down and saw them kiss. Her raven-haired boy was a man now. He was going to leave with that girl—she knew it—and what was she going to do then? Nettie shook her head, whispering, "The Sweetie Pie Bakery...Lord have mercy!"

Cheng stepped down from Wally's wagon. The night was now pitch dark beyond the circle of the camp's lanterns. He hesitated, deciding which way to go, then disappeared into the darkness, searching for the dwarf. Cheng walked quietly. Crickets stopped and started their songs as he passed by. As his eyes adjusted, he began to pick out shapes of trees and bushes silhouetted in the faint starlight.

A massive dark shape appeared just ahead of him. What was it? Cheng heard something. Was that laughter? Was that the dwarf laughing at him? Angry now, Cheng went ahead without caution. Darkness, blacker than black, enveloped him. Suddenly, there was the dwarf right before him, sitting in the air!

"Looking for me?"

Cheng backed up, scared stiff. *He must be sitting in a tree or something,* Cheng tried to reason. "What you do?" he blurted out in his choppy English.

"What I do? My friends, he wants to know what we are doing here!"

Cheng turned around quickly, ready for a fight. He saw no one else—just Philippe, impossibly swinging his legs, seated in the air! Cheng lunged forward, thinking he would pull him down, but was stopped by tightness in his chest. He could hardly breathe! He was being squeezed all around by suffocating darkness.

"Sssstop..." he pleaded, falling to the ground.

"Stop?" the dwarf replied in a cordial tone. "Certainly! On one condition."

Cheng looked up at him.

"Don't ever come looking for me again! You understand what I mean, Monsieur Pig Brain? My friends, give him one more hug for his boss, too. The same goes for him. Be sure and tell him that for me, yes?"

All the breath Cheng had in his lungs came out in one agonizing gasp. "Yes," he forced himself to say, and the dwarf released him.

Cheng stumbled back to camp. Ashen white, he knocked on Wally's door.

* * *

The next morning, things began to happen. A pot of water boiled over and scalded Nettie's arm. Mavis got into a fight with Wally; as he stormed up the steps to his wagon, one of them gave way and he fell backwards, twisting his ankle. All the joy of the previous weeks disappeared, leaving an uneasy tension in its place.

73

A REMINDER

Pup was excited. He could see they were going back toward his home. Wally had pulled the caravan off the road and sent Tom ahead to look for a new campsite. With their expanded show, they needed more flat ground. They would have to set up farther below Pine Tree.

Tom and Rhea bounced along in the truck, its gears whining at the effort of climbing up the incline. Hodain sat between them with his usual decorum, head up, eyes forward. Rhea had all she could do to keep Pup from jumping out the window every five seconds. She scolded him with some sharp clicking sounds. Pup looked at her, crestfallen, then looked away, his chin resting on her shoulder.

"What did you say to him?" Tom asked. "He looks as if he's going to cry."

"Among other things, I told him to sit down. We were nowhere near his home and probably wouldn't be because we were camping somewhere else. He'd have to wait till we could take him there ourselves "

"That's right, Pup. We'll take you home, just be patient."

"You're really good at that, aren't you?" Rhea laughed, patting Pup's bottom.

The landscape was uneven going up to Pine Tree. There were patches of forest, there were clearings that were too hilly, and there were flat spaces with too many rocks and brush. Finally, they found a nice meadow with only a slight slope at one end. Backlit by the sun, the brush shone like silver as Hodain dashed through it.

"There's plenty of space here," Tom said.

"Some trees will have to be cut down to get the wagons in," Rhea replied.

"Only a couple. The brush will have to go, of course, but that will come right back after the next rain."

"I suppose." Rhea was distracted by a whooshing sound. "Do you hear that?"

They turned to see a crow flying low across the land towards them. Tom instinctively put his arm up for it to land. The large bird wrapped its talons around Tom's wrist and folded in its wings.

"I've seen you before!" Tom greeted it.

The bird's hard bright eyes took them in as if someone else were seeing through them. "Mabon," Rhea whispered.

In another moment, the bird was in the air again, flying slowly away.

Rhea turned to Tom, wanting to hide herself within the circle of his arms. "The time is coming when I must leave you!"

"Rhea..." Tom kissed her, trying to chase the words from her lips. As if they were drowning, they sank to the ground, locked in an embrace. Here in this place, he could feel how they were being pulled apart. In their separation, he could see death. Was it he who was going to die? He wished for another drink from that goblet to reinforce his courage. Holding Rhea, Tom tried to imagine what his next step would be.

"I'm afraid too," Rhea said, reading his thoughts. "Nothing is for certain, is it? Strange...in your world I have learned two things: love and fear. It's not that they don't exist in my realm; it's just that here I feel their intensity so strongly, I can hardly bear it. Love of you and fear of—" Rhea stopped.

"Of what?" Tom asked.

"The dwarf. I thought his powers would fade, but they haven't. Ever since that night I..."

"What night? Something happened while I was away. I knew it."

"I said nothing to you because I didn't want anything to stop us from leaving," Rhea said. "One night I was up on the roof, and he found me there. He began to play this wicked game of hurling his shadows at me. They turned into fireballs and pursued me everywhere. I was desperate; I crossed the barrier into my world. That was a horrible mistake, because they followed me. I returned instantly, but I fear it's too late; they know how to enter now, and they will find a way to bring Philippe with them."

"And I was thinking he was getting angrier because he was *losing* his powers," Tom said. "That trick with the fire was going to be the last of his flashy shows."

"We have to find out what's sustaining him. His power is artificial. It was not granted to him."

Hodain trotted back to them, reminding them they had to leave. "We have to get the others. Don't worry—we'll find out what he's up to," Tom said. "Call Pup."

Rhea walked away toward the trees, calling for the gerking. She waited a few minutes, then returned. They both knew that this time Pup really might have run away.

"Let's go. We'll be back here in a couple of hours. He'll turn up." Tom tried to sound sure of himself. They walked back to the truck in troubled silence.

The caravan pulled into the meadow at around four o'clock—time enough to clear the brush and position the wagons before dark. Everyone was dog-tired and retreated to their wagons directly after dinner. Mavis, however, hauled herself up into Wally's wagon to have some words with him.

"So?" she demanded.

"Now, Mavis, don't start with me."

"Well, if you can't take care of that little monster, I can. What are you going to do? You act like you're afraid of him."

"No, not exactly, but he's—"

"He's off his rocker, that's what he is! He walks around like he's Napoleon or something. What's the matter? Why can't you get rid of that little freak? Does he have some power over you? I've never seen you act so paralyzed around someone."

"Mavis, relax. It's under control. Don't pester me about the details; you don't have to know. You'll see. I'm not afraid of him, you'll see."

Mavis left, not reassured at all. She felt like their world was slipping out of control, and her husband was indeed afraid.

That night, Phyllis clung close to Barney and whispered in the dark, "Something's going to happen. I feel like that line in Shakespeare—you know, 'something wicked this way comes'?"

"No, I don't know, and you're always having some kind of premonition or another. Stop being so dramatic!" Barney said.

"I hate it when you say that."

"Go to sleep. You're just tired. Everything will look better in the morning."

Philippe didn't have a plan exactly, except that the universe had given him an inch and he was determined to take a mile. Revenge and the accumulation of power came first. Where he would go from there was a question that didn't worry him. Let the moment dictate his next move; the plan would reveal itself. He was no longer a victim of circumstance: he was its master. Had he not taken down that preening gangster, Burt Russell? Didn't his guts spill across the floor just like the butchered chicken that he was? How he screamed for mercy! Philippe had loved every minute of it. He had gone there for Lorna, but he had killed to avenge himself. He would kill and kill again—all the men who had tortured him with their sneers, their insults. Now it was Wally's turn. Philippe would be repaid for all his years of flattering that man's ego and having to do his dirty work. He would see Wally strung up by his own perverted little mind. How Philippe was going to love seeing him all sweaty and exposed, hanging by the end of a rope...and then—then, it would be Ruby's turn.

74

BLACK CLOUDS

Nothing was done the next day about announcing their arrival in Pine Tree. It was hot, and Wally's ankle was throbbing. The troupe spent a desultory afternoon swatting flies and sweating.

At dinner, nobody said much of anything. Even Mavis was quiet. When the dwarf sat down, Cheng got up with his plate and left the table. Philippe couldn't resist a slight smile. Nash had started drinking again; his eyes showed up kind of pinkish in the lantern light. Tom and Rhea worried about Pup. Rhea knew he was somewhere near. Troubling dark images invaded her mind, and she was sure Pup was sending them.

After a few bites of her food, Lorna went back to her cabin, grateful to have some time alone before Mae and Sudy turned in. One by one, everybody departed till there were only Tom, Rhea, and the dwarf left to stare at each other. Philippe finally tired of their challenging looks, and with a derisive snort, he left them for the company of his shadows.

Later that night, when the camp was deep in sonorous sleep, Tom ventured out to find Pup or the dwarf—whichever came first. As he left, Rhea spoke these words:
"Down from the mountain
Out of the ore
Sword of Anam
Serve my love
As you did before."
Tom walked quietly. Outside the camp the night felt empty. A strange smothering darkness sucked the life out of the air. Not knowing which way to go, he hesitated. There were no crickets; there were no stars; the atmosphere felt like that of a tomb. Suddenly, out of nowhere, a band of fireflies descended upon him. They flitted and circled hysterically, almost as if they wanted his protection, but then, unable to communicate, they rushed on into the blackness.

Tom went in the direction from which the fireflies had come. It wasn't long before he thought he heard something. From what he could make out, it sounded like a nursery rhyme:
"Fee fi fo fum
I'll eat them all
One by one."
A lantern light appeared among the shadows. Tom ducked behind a tree. The dwarf passed by, swinging a lamp in one hand and dragging something dark with the other. He stopped, as if he sensed Tom's

presence, then growled and sniffed the air for a scent. How like an animal he had become: ugly, like the savage boar Tom had killed. Tom remembered the sight of that enraged beast ramming its head over and over into the tree from which he hung. He thought of the magnificent sword that had magically come to his aid. Instantly, it appeared in his hand, as it had then.

Philippe stared straight at Tom, but continued on as if he hadn't seen him. "Fee fi," he sang. "Fo fum," he hummed, grotesquely mimicking the nursery rhyme. His lantern light revealed a fallen tree trunk, on which he seated himself with a sigh. "Come out, come out, wherever you are! I know you're there," he called.

The dwarf waited a moment, and then, with another sigh, began rummaging around in his black shadow bag. He pulled out a lovely yellow firefly being and held it up high, watching it struggle. He opened his mouth wide and then let it slide down his throat like a spaghetti strand; a couple of swallows and it was gone.

Tom stepped out before him.

"Well, well, what have we here?" Philippe exclaimed. "Young King Arthur and his sword Excalibur? A present from that witch, sans doute. My friends, welcome him! Give him a nice big hug!"

Tom instantly felt a crushing force squeezing his body. He tried to lift the sword, but his arm remained pinned to his side.

"What do you come here for?" the dwarf went on. "It looks like to do me harm, yes? But what have I done to you? Nothing! Ah, but it is not for you that you come, is it? That little witch has sent you, eh? I tell you, you are under her spell, mon petit garçon. Have you no will of your own, mon fils? I pity you. Oh, but you have never been so brave, mon petit! Coming out in the night, all by yourself, to fight the dragon!" At this thought, Philippe exploded into laughter.

All this time, Tom had been struggling to breathe. He was going to die if he couldn't free himself in a few moments. He was losing consciousness. Tom concentrated all his energy on the muscles in his arm, praying that the sword would act for him and he would hold on—and so it did. The sword rose up, trailing a shower of sparks high over his head, and Tom held on. His shadowy coffin split open and fresh air rushed into his lungs, replenishing his strength.

Philippe was immensely displeased and no longer laughing. Tom said not a word, but brought the sword down hard into the dirt at the dwarf's feet. The blade shone like a lightning bolt; sparks of color shot out from it, blinding the dwarf with a fearful brightness. Everything was illuminated and not a shadow remained, except the ones the dwarf was clutching that hid his captives. Philippe tried to protect his swirling "black hole," but Tom raised the sword again and the shadows broke apart, scattering everywhere. Dozens of fireflies flew up into the air. On the ground, one wretched little gerking sat with blinking eyes, wondering what had happened to him.

Philippe covered his eyes and let out a sound straight from the hounds of Hell. "You...white trash! You think you're a man now because that witch is kissing your—"

"Shut up! No more about Rhea!" Tom roared, wanting to kill him. He swung the sword again. Philippe jumped to the side as the blade came crashing down, searing his shoulder.

"Oh, so it's Rhea now, is it? Not Ruby? More secrets fall my way. Keep in mind, beggar boy, you can't stop me and that devil's harlot can't either. I'm a force—a force of nature!" he shouted triumphantly.

"You are human! Your powers are the babblings of an idiot!" Tom replied.

"You'll see, beggar boy!" Philippe tried to kick little Pup, who was still sitting bewildered. The gerking jumped onto Tom's shoulder and clung to his neck.

"But enough for tonight, eh?" The dwarf brushed off his clothes, his anger replaced by a sudden boredom with it all. "Tant pis! You shall live another day. Ah well." He picked up his lantern and headed back toward camp.

Tom sat down on the tree trunk, still holding Pup. "It's okay, little guy. It's all over for now. Stop that shivering; Rhea's waiting for you, but first you've got to promise me not to wander off again, you understand?" Pup looked at Tom with big teary eyes and responded with another desperate clasp around his neck. "Okay, okay."

Tom felt the air clear around him as the last sparks from the sword died down and the sword itself disappeared from his side. As he walked back to camp, the fireflies returned to light his way.

75

DARK AND LIGHT

Old Ben hobbled over to Tom. "Wally says you an' Ruby are ta get dressed up in yer outfits and go on into Pine Tree with him an' Cheng."

"What? Just us—nobody else?"

"Yeah, he's all in a flap about meetin' up with those Huxtables. He wants to talk to ya."

The door to Wally's wagon was open, and Tom could see him sitting in a chair with his foot propped up on the bunk bed.

"Come in, come in," Wally puffed impatiently. "I want you to take Ruby and the big horse with me and Cheng into Pine Tree. I've lost time here with this damn foot and the heat. I don't want to make a big parade with everyone; just you on your stilts and Ruby on that horse will be enough. I want you ready in an hour so I can find those damn Huxtables early and do our business in daylight. I dropped a nice chunk of change on them last summer; they shouldn't mind adjusting their store hours for me. I'm not bumping down that road in the pitch of night again."

"You're the boss, boss." Tom turned to conceal his smile as he thought of Wally with his collar sprung, his face all drunk and red, walking between those hulking Huxtable brothers.

Wally's drive down the main street of each country town on their route was a bizarre and somewhat pitiful reflection of the great circus parades of the time. Like the "big boys," he did it as way of advertising and creating excitement in the community. Today, the citizens of Pine Tree looked out their shop windows or turned their heads as they walked along to see a beat-up automobile driven by a Chinaman as if it were a bronco; hanging on to the running board was a chubby man in an explosively tight suit, shouting through a bullhorn. Behind them was a stilt-walker in long striped pants, billowy shirt and black broad-brimmed hat, and behind him—now, there was something really worth their attention. A giant horse carried on its back a beautiful young girl in a red velvet costume that matched the vibrant color of her long hair. She was seated on a multi-colored quilt with a golden apple at each corner. When she stood up, opening her arms and turning round and round, they were mesmerized. Something about her lifted any reservations they might have had about such goings-on, and they followed her like the Pied Piper around the block.

"Come one, come all, this weekend, that's right, two days only, to see Wally Ripton's Magical Theatricals and Curiosities!" Wally announced through his megaphone. "It's bigger, it's better, in a new location...only a short ride to that pretty little meadow just below town! Saturday, first show at noon, second one at four o'clock. Tell your friends...bring the family!"

They carried on like this through the few dusty streets of Pine Tree, then turned down the road where the most houses could be seen. When Wally felt his "advertising campaign" had reached its saturation point, he ordered Cheng to stop the car and sprawled out on the back seat, throwing the bullhorn to the floor.

"Cheng, break out that bottle in the glove compartment," Wally ordered hoarsely. "Damn, I'm parched."

Tom bent down on his stilts and leaned in the window. "What's next?"

"What's next is, Cheng and me are going back and see if I can't scare up the Huxtables. You and Ruby return to camp. Take it nice and slow, wave, and keep up the hoopla."

"I don't know how many more people we'll see out here," Tom said. "They're all squatting up in those hills."

"Don't give me any of your lip! Just do it."

"Okay. Let me get the water out of the trunk." Tom glanced at Rhea, smiling as he went around the back of the car.

Cheng fired up the motor and lurched the gears into drive. As the car drove away, Arden blew a disdainful snort through his nostrils, as if to say, "Good riddance." Pup, who now went everywhere with them, peeked out from the folds of Rhea's quilt. He climbed up on Arden's head to stretch and have a good scratch.

Although the afternoon was still as hot as it had been moments ago, a sweet freshness returned to the atmosphere. They were alone, free for a few hours at least.

"Sit up here with me and take your stilts off," Rhea said.

"I'll wait awhile till we find a good spot to sit down in some shade. 'Sides, I like it up here; better view, good breeze." Tom gave her a little peck on the cheek and walked ahead of Arden, loosely holding the horse's reins. A painter could hardly have chosen a more fantastic image than the look of those three proceeding along that country road. Rhea hummed a soft lazy tune, letting herself rock gently with the rhythm of the horse's step.

They went on peacefully for a time until Rhea suddenly said, "I'm hot. I can't stand this costume one more minute. I'm going to change. How's this?"

"What? Wait! Hold on a minute!" Tom turned around and there she was, beautiful and naked except for the cover of her wild red hair. "Now, don't do that! This is Bible country. People don't take kindly to that kind of—of exposure!"

"Alright, I'll put my shoes on," Rhea answered mischievously.

"No, no. Here, take my shirt." Tom nervously pulled off his shirt. The taste of freedom had sent Rhea into one of her minxy unpredictable moods. The "cat" was out and wanted to play.

"Catch me!" Rhea jumped down from the horse. Tom made a grab for her, but she slipped between his legs and ran for the trees not far from the road.

"Come back here! Put this damn thing on!" Tom stumbled after her, waving the shirt. Arden thundered ahead of him, whinnying, sensing the spirit of play.

Rhea climbed onto a tree branch and curved herself around it, waiting seductively like Eve for Adam. But "Adam" never made it to the tree: he lost his balance and fell face-first to the ground, the stilts still strapped to his legs.

"Tom! Tom, are you all right?" Rhea was at his side instantly. Pup looked with wide eyes over Arden's ears.

"Get me out of these!" Tom grumbled angrily. "Here, roll up my pants. Ouch, don't twist my legs. Ow, damn it, ow."

"What do you want me to do?" Rhea asked sheepishly.

"Unbuckle the stilt straps and then *put on this shirt!*"

"You don't have to shout. I'm right here."

"Ah," Tom sighed once his legs were free. He wasn't really hurt—just hot, bruised, and ornery. When he stood up, his pant legs fell in puddles of fabric around his ankles.

"Oh, Tom, you—your..." Rhea laughed. "Oh my! You shrank! It must be the heat!"

Tom's pants were yards too long for him without his stilts. The more he fumbled, the more Rhea laughed. He knew he looked pretty ridiculous, and he couldn't stay mad. Soon he was smiling and then laughing along with her. "I forgot to get my other pants out of the car," he said.

"You want your shirt back?" Rhea asked, teasing again.

"No! Just help me do something with these."

"Here...stand still...that's good." She tucked up the fabric into his belt, picked up his hat, and put it back on his head. "I like you better *this* way." Rhea brushed her lips along his bare skin. "Let's stay here awhile."

Tom watched as the quilt flew off Arden's back and settled down under the trees. Pulling him down with her, she whispered mischievously, "Don't worry. Nobody will see us." She lay down on the quilt, the shirt draping in silky folds along her body, and said in rhyme,

> "Plain as day
>> hide away,
>>> so be it."

Tom sat down beside her. "And what's that supposed to mean?"

"It means that for a while we won't be seen." As Rhea said that, blackberry brambles appeared all around them. "Mmm...berries!" She jumped up and reached for his hat. Using it as a bowl, she gathered handfuls of the juicy fruit. "Here, open up," she said, offering to pop some into his mouth.

"Wait a minute! Are those berries, or are they—"

"Just berries!" Rhea smiled, pouncing on him like a cat. She tickled and teased him till he opened his mouth in protest, whereupon she threw in a couple of berries and sealed his lips shut with a kiss.

"Mmm...more," Tom responded, rolling over with her in his arms. "And I'd like the shirt back now." He smiled as his hands loosened the buttons and slipped inside to find her body. She felt so cool and smooth, yet as he touched her, he felt an energy under him like waves in water. If he pressed too hard, he might pass right through her or she might engulf him like an ocean. Being with her was like that: she always brought him to the edge of some abyss. In a mixture of love, fear, and longing, he tumbled into it again.

Shadows from the leaves above them flickered over their rhythmic bodies, weaving their shapes into the patchwork of the quilt. All that was separate became part of one kaleidoscope of color and light; then that light burst into a million particles to reform again in their minds as another reality. They found themselves standing high on a jagged cliff. The last rays of a silver sun went down like steaming arrows into a grey cold sea. Where was this place? They held each other, feeling a sense of panic. They were out of breath, as if they had been running. From what? There was no escape. They could only turn and go back into the dark forest from which they must have come.

The sound of the sea gave way to silence amongst the trees. They walked on, dreading what they would be shown, for something or someone had ripped them from their lovers' dream and led them here.

The echo of water dripping into water became apparent—a hollow sound that chilled their souls. In the dim light, they could see a clearing with a fountain in the center shaped like a chalice. Water slowly dripped into its reflecting pool. On the barren ground all around lay dark shapes, which they soon recognized as birds—hundreds of them, all dead. One sickly blackbird hopped weakly around the rim of the fountain, trying to skim water from a cancerous overgrowth of algae that filled the bowl and oozed down its sides.

Rhea began to sob, "Where are we? Mabon? Are you here?" Only the slow drip of the rotting water answered them. Tom watched Rhea move closer to the fountain. She appeared to be losing color, becoming fainter.

"Wait, Rhea, come away from there," Tom called, trying to comprehend this grim scene.

"I have never felt hopeless before, but I do here. It's too late. Everything is dying! Mabon, where are you? Tom, I—I'm cold..." Rhea began to tremble. "I'm never cold. So cold, Tom..."

Tom rushed to her, catching her just as she collapsed. Her face, hair, and eyes were still growing paler; she looked like a creature that lived deep in the earth or at the bottom of the sea, where no light ever penetrated. "It's all right. I'll get us out of here. It will be daylight soon. You need the sun...you need light." His desperate voice echoed in the darkness surrounding him.

At that moment, the blackbird on the fountain flew up on its scrawny wings, screeching and cawing. *"Only one way...one way,"* Tom thought he heard it say before it disappeared into the shadowed forest.

Tom lifted Rhea in his arms and ran in a frenzy, anywhere, away from there. He crashed though the trees, stumbling, falling, holding Rhea up so he wouldn't crush her. He was so tired, so spent, but he couldn't stop. Rhea was dying, disintegrating—he was clinging to a ghost. "Don't leave me...don't leave me!" he cried hoarsely.

On he went, running blindly. Then, miraculously, just as night turned into day, he staggered out of the forest and found himself in a golden wheatfield. He lay down on the soft ground, cradling Rhea. The sky was a clear blue, and soft scented air wafted around them. "Rhea, we made it! I said we would. Can you feel the warmth? You'll be all right now. Feel the sun?" He saw the color coming back to her face. An incredible sense of relief swept over him, and he let himself fall asleep at last.

For a while, Tom floated in blissful peace; then, gradually, the sound of a horse whinnying and the vibration of heavy footsteps awakened him. A giant pair of hooves and the hem of a red velvet shirt greeted his opening eyes.

Tom sat up, confused. Rhea and Arden were watching him. He put his hand up to hers and pulled her down to him, drinking in the vision of her brilliant beauty: the fiery red hair, those green eyes, the luminescent skin, and the flashing white light of the sequins on her velvet bodice. "You are so beautiful. I have never seen you look so—"

Rhea kissed him. "I let you sleep...it's so pleasant here. But it's late. I'm sure they're wondering where we are now. Let's get back."

"Wait a minute, wait a minute—I was dreaming something. It felt so real...what was it? Horrible, it was horrible..."

"If I had known that, I would have woken you, but you looked so peaceful, I just thought...Well, come on, let's not spoil our beautiful day. It was just a dream." Rhea messed his hair playfully, trying to shake him out of it.

The truth was, she knew exactly what he was talking about. She couldn't understand why Mabon had sent them there—why she had to feel the terror of life draining from her very essence. Was that place going to be the future if...what? She felt tricked, angry, like a pawn in a scheme she should never have consented to, but she dared not mention this to Tom. Let him remember what he would or what he was supposed to of that nightmare. She only knew she loved him more than Mabon, more than his world or any other.

Strange, but it was now that she could put into words what before she had only intuited. Their love, Tom and Rhea's, existed out of time. It was a spark or a ray of an expanding, loving, all-knowing light, like that into which she had seen Mabon step, and from which she could see it was hard to come back. Even if they both died, their love would manifest again somehow. It would endure any obstacle, past or future: of that she was sure.

They both rode the horse into camp, letting Arden find his way. Rhea tried teasing him, but nothing changed Tom's dark internal mood. She was angry that all the fun had gone out of their stolen moment together.

Back in camp, they were separated completely. Wally was furious that they had taken so long to return. He had contacted the Huxtables, and they would only agree to meet him at night. Tom had to drive Wally and Cheng all the way into the mountains again to pick up the bootleg liquor. Tomorrow and Sunday, they would perform; Monday, they would be on the return route to the city.

A LEAP OF FAITH

Early Saturday morning, a damp mist clung to the ground as Cheng, Nash, Tom, and the others dragged hay bales into position for the first show. The shadows returned. This time Tom could see them, always on the edge of his vision, disappearing when he looked directly at them.

Nettie carried her Bible in her apron pocket. Even though the mist had now lifted and the sun was shining on a picture-perfect day, she felt worried.

Tom was putting on his stilts when he saw the dwarf pull Sudy aside and whisper something to her. She burst into tears and ran away. Tom caught her in his arms. "What did he say to you?"

"Oh, horrible things, Tom!" She trembled. "Why would he say such horrible things to me?"

"Go and stay in the wagon with Lorna."

Tom walked toward Philippe, calling his name. He was putting the pail of water in the cart and he ignored Tom.

"I'm talking to you," Tom threatened, taking hold of his coat.

"Don't touch me, you witchmonger."

Tom picked up the dwarf and slammed him against one of the wagons. "What did you say to Sudy?"

"Nothing she hasn't heard before."

"Leave her alone. Leave Ruby alone. Limit your stunts to the circus ring, or you will regret it."

"No, monsieur, *you* will regret this."

"I don't think so," Tom answered in disgust, letting the dwarf slide back to the ground. As he walked away, he realized he had picked the little man up as if he were a toothpick.

For the first performance of the day, most of the residents of Pine Tree turned out, including those who lived in remote parts of the mountains. Tom saw the Huxtable family again with their out-of-control child, but not his frail mother. He feared the worst for her.

Dozens of raggedy-dressed children ran in and out of the haystacks, waiting for the show. Some of the more adventurous ones tried to get behind the wagons to watch them getting ready, but Cheng and the farmhands were quick to shoo them out. One little girl in a dirty white pinafore hid under one of the wagons and held her breath as she watched the dwarf pull up the suspenders of his clown pants. He knew she was there. "Hello, little pretty."

The girl froze.

"Oh, yes, I see you there. Don't be afraid. I won't tell. Look, let's have a secret, yes? You come back after I have finished, and I will give you all the candy you can eat. How 'bout that, ma petite?"

The little girl's blue eyes opened wide. She had never seen anything like the dwarf before. She didn't know whether to smile or cry.

"Now, don't be frightened. You like candy, don't you?"

The little girl nodded, as if in a trance. There was something hypnotic and convincing in the dwarf's voice.

"Then you'll come to see me, won't you?"

The little girl nodded.

"Now, off with you. Go look at the big men with long legs out there."

The girl ran away, her white-blonde curls flying.

These simple country people were still amazed at the tattooed man and bearded lady, even though they had seen them last year and the year before. They clapped for the stilt-walkers and screamed at the mysterious forces the dwarf commanded, though they were suspicious. There was a fine line between the magician's magic and the Devil's work for these folks.

When Rhea jumped onto the back of the giant circling horse, their mouths dropped open in awe. Tom watched Rhea go around while taking slow giraffe-like steps on his stilts. Out of the corner of his eye, he happened to see a little girl in a white pinafore slip between the wagons. Tom and Nash caught Rhea as she jumped from the horse to their shoulders, and when Tom looked again, the dwarf was giving the little girl some candy.

Their performance was difficult and needed all of Tom's attention. The next time he could look around, he saw the dwarf talking to Wally. Tom searched the crowd for the little girl, but didn't see her.

Wally strained back and forth nervously on his makeshift cane. This was a big crowd, and there was so much to do; he didn't have time for that conniving thief and his demands.

Philippe began poking his stubby finger at him. "What's that?" Wally sat down exasperatedly on a hay bale and leaned in closer.

"There is something in your cabin you need to see," the dwarf said.

Wally tried to brush him off. "Later. It can wait!"

"Non, monsieur, I think not."

"Listen, I'll tell you when I…" The words trailed off from Wally's lips when he saw the look in Philippe's eye. He got up and hobbled after the dwarf.

Wally was anxious as he stepped up into his wagon, thinking Philippe was coming in after him. Instead, the door slammed shut and locked itself. The air in the cabin was filled with a thick cobweb-like substance. He could hardly breathe.

Confused, Wally tried to open the door. This cobweb stuff was clutching at his throat. He could hear the dwarf outside laughing. He stumbled over to the bed, and that was when he saw her.

"Oh, no—God, no!"

The little girl in the pinafore lay on the bed unconscious, her dress all pulled apart. In the dim light, her skin and hair appeared pure white. Wally thought she was dead. Then he noticed something else. Fire! Through the cabin floorboards licked yellow tongues of fire!

"Help! Help!" He raged at the dwarf, realizing how he had been framed. Even if he escaped, the people would kill him, thinking he had done this to the girl. "Help!"

Wally broke a window with his elbow, but that did him no good. The air rushed in and the fire leaped higher. Wally pulled the blanket out from under the girl, frantically trying to beat out the fire, but to no avail. Suddenly, he heard a battering sound on the side of the wagon. He fell back on the bed with the child as two giant hooves came crashing through the wall. It was Arden, with Rhea on his back.

"Wally, are you in there?" Tom crawled through the broken boards to save him. Black cobwebbed fingers immediately wrapped around his neck, trying to choke him.

Tom began helping Wally, but then he saw the girl.

"It wasn't me! I didn't do it! It was Philippe—it was Philippe!"

Tom pushed Wally aside to gather up the girl. On her neck, tiny purple bruises were beginning to show.

By now, everyone was in a panic. Fires had started up all over. Men, women, and children ran everywhere.

The dwarf was screaming with laughter. "That's it. That's it. Run...run, run, run! There's nothing you can do!"

Tom crawled out of the wagon with the girl, handing her up to Rhea. Then he went for the dwarf. "Come here, you scum!"

The dwarf turned vicious. "You think I don't know? You and your witch...her powers will be mine! And you—you will die! You hear me? Die!"

Wally was just beginning to crawl out of the wagon as Tom pushed the dwarf on top of him.

"Put the fires out or you'll both burn in hell!"

The dwarf screamed in rage. "Follow him, my shadows! Kill him!"

Wally wrestled with the dwarf. They both fell out of the wagon, snarling and fighting. Cheng jumped on top of them. He pulled Wally free and rolled him over and over, raising up clouds of dust, trying to put out the flames on Wally's clothes.

Tom rushed back to Rhea to see about the little girl. The sight of the child in her arms reminded him of the faery who had offered him the drink from the golden goblet.

The dark forces loosed by the dwarf infected the crowd, making them suddenly see evil where there was none. "Look! They're taking the child!" someone cried. "She's a witch! Stop the witch!"

"No, we found her! She's hurt!" Tom yelled as the crowd rushed at them with murder in their eyes. "Rhea, go on, get out of here! I'll follow."

"No! I won't leave you."

"Go on!" He slapped Arden's flank hard. The horse thundered off towards the hills with Rhea and the child.

Hodain stayed at Tom's side, growling savagely and holding the people at bay.

"Listen! Listen to me!" Tom tried to calm them.

"Get him! He's the Devil's servant!" There was nothing to do but flee. Tom ran with superhuman speed, hoping to get to Rhea before the crowd tore her apart. Tom ran till his lungs were scorched and his chest hurt. He looked back and saw they were still after him, charged with the fury of righteousness.

At the edge of the forest, he could see Rhea waiting for him. "Go on! Go on!" Tom shouted.

She turned the horse, disappearing amongst the trees. Hodain ran after her and Tom followed with his pursuers close behind. He dare not call out to her. He ran breathlessly, deep into the forest.

Hodain led him toward a light. As Tom came closer, he realized it was that same mysterious whirling funnel he had seen before. Hodain barked and barked, then leapt into the heart of it, exploding into a burst of sparkling particles. Tom knew he must do the same. It was time—time for him to leap into the unknown. Whether he lived or died as a consequence didn't matter. This was where Ruby had gone.

He leapt into the whirling mass, knowing this was not the end but the beginning.

By the time the mob reached the spot where Tom had been, there was nothing: nothing but the birds singing in the trees.

* * *

The circus was imprisoned, surrounded by a mob toting guns and clubs. There had been a lot of damage to the circus, and a little girl had been kidnapped. The townspeople were waiting for word of her before they decided what to do. If she was found, they'd run the foreigners down the mountain with a few kicks and bumps to spur them on their way. If she wasn't found—well, that was another story.

The camp tried to salvage what they could from the wagons and figure out what had just happened to them. Wally had burns on his arms and legs. He was in pretty bad shape, half-delirious, howling in pain and shouting his wrath at the dwarf. Mavis had been pummeled and kicked by the angry crowd and was confused with shock, so the new leadership fell, oddly enough, to Nettie and Lorna, with Sudy as their messenger. It was to Nettie that the farmhands brought the strongbox of money they found in the ashes of Wally's wagon. It was Lorna who took on Wally's care, and Lorna who managed to band everyone together again out of total disarray.

Luckily, Nash had pulled the car and truck back from the burning wagons, so they still had those. The cookwagon had been far from the flames as well, so they had supplies. What had happened to the dwarf, nobody knew for sure: some said they saw him roll under the wagons, others thought they saw him escaping though the crowd. No one knew what had gone on between Wally and Philippe or how that little girl got in the wagon, but they all wanted to talk about what happened to Tom and Rhea and why they had vanished with the girl.

Nettie made it clear that she knew Tom had done nothing wrong and that somehow things would come out right. That was a reassuring thought, but most of them were certain they were in for a nasty dose of mountain justice no matter what.

Search parties combed the forest, looking for any trace of the girl. It was a tense few days, but then, mysteriously, she was found in perfect condition—apple-cheeked, eyes sparkling, pinafore clean and white. The townspeople released the exhausted troupe then, and Nettie knew for sure that Tom was gone from her forever.

* * *

The little girl had nothing but happy memories of the circus. But where had she been? The townspeople wanted to know. "Oh, it was wonderful," she told them. She had been with the faeries. There was a big celebration with lots of candles and food like she had never tasted before. A beautiful young man and woman who looked just like the circus people walked down a carpet that shone like gold. An old man was waiting for them, and he placed a crown on the man's head with so many jewels she couldn't count. Then they sat in chairs with animal horns and ivy leaves on them. There was lovely music, and all sorts of strange glittery beings danced and sang a song about a king with raven hair.

That was all she could remember, for she had gotten so tired that she fell asleep. Everyone listened with relief to the child's tale, but of course,

nobody

believed

her...

ABOUT THE AUTHOR

Kim Canazzi was born in upstate New York into a creative family. Her fascination with art and fantasy began at an early age. She had no trouble believing that another world full of beauty and magic existed side by side with her reality.

This world disappeared as Kim grew and and struggled through adolescence. Later in reading the works of Carl Jung, Joseph Cambell and Marie Von Franz, she came to understand the transformative power in the archetypical nature of fairytales.

Kim attended Parsons School of Design and worked in the fashion industry in New York before moving to Los Angeles where she became interested in photography. She has been a professional event and celebrity photographer for twenty-five years. Her personal photography is rich and colorful reflecting the mythical spirit of the Otherworld. Her photography may be viewed at wildrosegalleries.com . For more about the author and her books go to canazzibooks.com .